THE *H*EART OF
A *C*OWBOY

COLORADO
COWBOYS
2

THE $\mathcal{H}$EART OF A $\mathcal{C}$OWBOY

JODY HEDLUND

BETHANYHOUSE
a division of Baker Publishing Group
Minneapolis, Minnesota

© 2021 by Jody Hedlund

Published by Bethany House Publishers
11400 Hampshire Avenue South
Bloomington, Minnesota 55438
www.bethanyhouse.com

Bethany House Publishers is a division of
Baker Publishing Group, Grand Rapids, Michigan

Printed in the United States of America

Library of Congress Cataloging-in-Publication Data
Names: Hedlund, Jody, author.
Title: The heart of a cowboy / Jody Hedlund.
Description: Minneapolis, Minnesota : Bethany House Publishers, a division of
    Baker Publisher Group, [2021] | Series: Colorado cowboys ; 2
Identifiers: LCCN 2021028775 | ISBN 9780764236402 (paperback) | ISBN
    9780764239380 (Casebound, Print on Demand) | ISBN 9781493433841 (ebook)
Classification: LCC PS3608.E333 H428 2021 | DDC 813/.6—dc23
LC record available at https://lccn.loc.gov/2021028775

Scripture quotations are from the King James Version of the Bible.

Cover design by Kirk DouPonce, DogEared Design

Author represented by Natasha Kern Literary Agency

Baker Publishing Group publications use paper produced from sustainable forestry practices and post-consumer waste whenever possible.

21 22 23 24 25 26 27   7 6 5 4 3 2 1

Wherefore, if God so clothe the grass of the field, which to day is, and to morrow is cast into the oven, shall he not much more clothe you, O ye of little faith?
Matthew 6:30

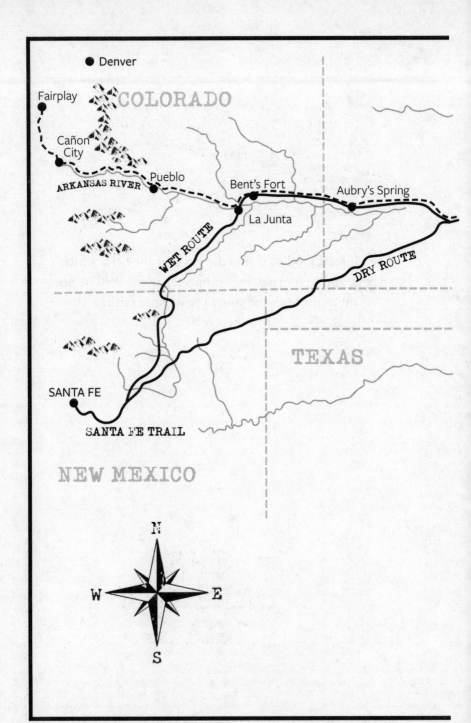

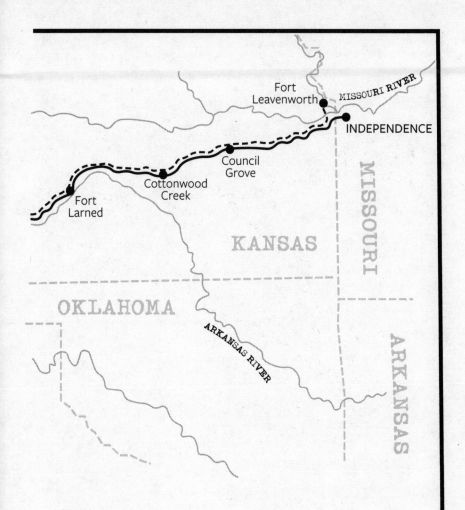

THE
SANTA FE
TRAIL

CHAPTER 1

COUNCIL GROVE, KANSAS
MAY 1863

She was going to drown.

The Neosho River wrapped its cold fingers around Linnea Newberry and pulled her down. Frantically she fought the raging current. But muddy water rushed against her face, filling her mouth and nose, making it impossible to breathe.

Above the roaring water, shouts and calls trailed after her. Her grandfather's anxious voice was the loudest of them all.

She tried to kick and propel herself toward the riverbank, but her heavy muslin skirt, combined with her petticoat and bloomers underneath, tangled around her legs and trapped her like manacles.

For a second the water tossed her high, giving her a glimpse of the back of the covered wagon where she'd perched moments ago. She'd been in the process of analyzing the southern cattail *Typha domingensis* she'd plucked from a swampy pond that morning. In the next instant, the wheels rolled over a stone in the riverbed, and the jarring threw her overboard.

Now the Neosho, swift and swollen with spring rains, dragged her low. Choking for breath, she clawed at the air, at the water, at anything to keep from going under. As she passed a fallen cottonwood dangling above the surface, she reached for it and her fingers connected with a rough branch.

God, help me. Fear and panic mingled in her chest.

"Hold on tight!" shouted a rider, directing a sorrel horse her way. The river pounded against the steed's flank, threatening to sweep both man and beast away. But somehow the horse plunged toward her, defying the river's greedy grasp.

Her wet hand slipped down the branch. Her fingers ached in her desperate attempt to hold on. With her hair drenched, muddy water dribbled into her eyes, down her nose, and over her lips. And a splash from the approaching horse hit her in the face.

Blinking hard, she spluttered.

The rider lunged for her, his gloved hands wrapping around her forearm.

She grabbed on to his stirrup, and as he began to tug her out of the water, she clutched at his saddle to aid in her upward climb. He lifted her with surprising strength, towing her up until he had her by both arms. Then with a final haul, he hoisted her into the saddle in front of him.

She coughed and swiped at the water still trickling down her face. Before she could speak or even glimpse her rescuer, he was angling his horse toward the western bank. Linnea held her breath and clung to the pommel, praying the creature would stay steady upon its feet and wouldn't be knocked downriver, taking them with it.

The rushing water drowned out all other sounds except the labored breathing of the man behind her. His arms were tense on either side of her, the reins wrapped around his hands. He hunkered low, leaning into her. The muscles in his chest rippled with his effort at controlling and directing his steed.

When the horse began to climb upward into shallower water, Linnea allowed herself to breathe again. *Thank you, heavenly Father, for saving my life.*

She'd known the journey west would be fraught with difficulties and danger. In all the preparations for their botanical expedition, her grandfather had read tale after tale of death and injury that befell so many who attempted the overland crossing. He cautioned her regarding the perils and warned her against going.

Nevertheless, she hadn't expected to face death after only ten days on the Santa Fe Trail.

The horse stumbled on loose stones and thick silt. The movement jarred Linnea, tilting her to one side. Her rescuer was boxing her in, keeping her from sliding off. Even so, she grasped his arm.

At the same time, the rider patted his horse's mane and neck, as though to encourage it. The horse steadied itself and continued plodding uphill.

The sloping dirt embankment gave way to the rolling bluestem hills with cordgrass in the low, wet areas comprised of buttonbush, eastern grama grass, and common ironweed. Burr oak, black walnut, hackberry, green ash, and cottonwood trees converged along the banks, providing shade to groups of travelers who'd already made the crossing.

"Flynn!" called a girl hopping up and down at the top of the embankment under the shady branches of a sprawling cottonwood thick with new foliage. "Howdy-doody! You did it! You saved her!"

A gangly young man of about sixteen years slid down the dirt and gravel toward them. He reached for the horse's muzzle. "Mighty fine job, Flynn. Couldn't have done much better myself."

The man behind Linnea—apparently named Flynn— gave a final nudge of his heels to the horse's flanks. The creature crested the bank, revealing the river bottoms where dozens upon dozens of cattle grazed on the grama grass, some in the shade of the deciduous hardwoods, others sunning themselves and swishing their tails against the flies.

Two other young men stood on the bank watching, having abandoned their nearby blazing campfire and an iron skillet still sizzling with frying fish.

"You sure got in there fast, Flynn." The girl bounded toward them, her dark hair hanging in unruly waves about her dirt-smudged face, her brown eyes shining with admiration. Although slender, her body showed the first signs of developing into a woman, especially because her calico dress was much too tight and short—as if she'd long outgrown it. If Linnea had to take a guess, she put the girl at twelve or thirteen years old.

"Grab a blanket to warm her," Flynn said to the girl.

She shifted her attention, staring openly at Linnea. Only as Linnea tried to formulate a smile did she realize how badly her teeth were chattering and her body shaking. After the initial shock of falling into the river, she'd been so fo-

12

cused on surviving that she hadn't paid attention to how cold she was.

But now she was aware of the numbness of her fingers and toes. Her clothing stuck to her body like an icy layer of morning frost. Frigid water ran down her arms and legs.

"Go on, Ivy." The rider spoke again, this time more sharply. "And Dylan, you stoke the fire."

The girl gave a quick nod, then scampered away. And the young man hurried off to do Flynn's bidding as well.

Were they his children? If so, where was his wife? Linnea could see no evidence of other women around his camp.

"Hang on." The man's voice rumbled near her ear. He shifted, and the warm pressure of his body and arms moved away from her, leaving her exposed to the midmorning air.

It had been warm enough when they'd started out at dawn. It had been warm enough when she'd explored the marshland around a pond they'd passed. And it had been plenty warm when they'd been in the long line of wagons waiting to make the river crossing.

But at present, a chill settled deep inside, and she hugged herself for warmth.

Flynn slid from the horse. Once standing, he peered up at her, giving her a glimpse of his face for the first time. Though he wore the brim of his felt hat low, there was no hiding the handsome features—lean cheeks tapering into a muscular jaw, a firm mouth, and a well-defined chin. A layer of dark facial scruff lent him a shadowed, almost wounded appeal. If that wasn't enough, his eyes were a bright green-blue, the color of bluegrass.

Since he'd taken charge of the children, she expected someone older, a middle-aged father. But this man, though he was well-built and filled out to the fullest, couldn't be many years past her own twenty-one.

He was scrutinizing her with the same carefulness, his brows rising as if she surprised him every bit as much as he did her. She was a mess and guessed she looked worse than a wet cat. In her flailing, her hair had come loose from its chignon and hung in tangled curly masses over her shoulders and halfway down to her waist. Even wet, the bright red was as noticeable as always.

She craned her neck to see upriver. Amidst the long caravan crossing at the river's shallowest place, she spotted their team of oxen straining to pull their wagon up the gradual incline, following the other scientists in the expedition who were riding their horses. Her grandfather sat on the wagon bench next to Clay, his manservant, and waved both arms at her.

Starting from New York City, their six-member team had traveled for weeks, first by train and then by steamboat, before they reached Fort Leavenworth in March. They'd initially planned to traverse the Santa Fe Trail starting from Independence, Missouri, but with border ruffians stirring up strife, they'd had to change their plans to avoid some of the danger.

What would Grandfather say now that she'd almost drowned? Would he force her to return home?

"Ma'am?" Her rescuer was still staring up at her. "You alright?"

She forced her lips into a smile but still couldn't control the chattering of her teeth. "Yes. Thank you."

"Let's get you warmed up." His gloved hands closed about her waist, and he lifted her down.

14

As her feet touched the ground, her legs buckled.

"Whoa now." Flynn didn't release her.

"I think I'm just a little cold and worn out." She tried to make her muscles obey a silent command to work, but she collapsed again, this time grabbing fistfuls of Flynn's vest to keep herself from falling.

In an instant, he swooped her up into his arms and started toward the fire Dylan was feeding with handfuls of brush and twigs. She ought to protest a strange man carrying her so boldly, especially because he walked with a limp, clearly suffering himself. But his determined stride—along with the fact that he'd just rescued her from the brink of death—told her this man had the makings of a hero and she had nothing to fear from him.

Ivy was hanging halfway out the back of a covered wagon, her too-short skirt revealing bare feet that were black on the bottom. She hopped down, a quilt in her arms, and sped toward Linnea and Flynn.

"Found this real nice quilt Ma made." The girl held it out, but Flynn didn't stop until he reached the fire.

He gently lowered Linnea to a log that had been smoothed and shaped, likely by all the previous travelers who'd rested there after crossing the river. Then he took the quilt from Ivy and draped it about Linnea's shoulders.

"There you are." He straightened, his brows furrowed. "That oughta do it. You'll be warm in no time now."

She held her hands out toward the flames, letting the warmth bathe her. "Oh, yes. I'm already feeling better."

Ivy plopped down on the log next to Linnea. "You're real lucky Flynn got you when he did."

"I agree." Linnea smiled up at Flynn again. He towered

above her as though he wanted to help her further but wasn't sure what to do. "I owe you my life. I don't know how I can ever thank you."

"No thanks needed, ma'am—"

"Linnea. Please call me Linnea."

He hesitated, probably unaccustomed to such informality and boldness from a woman. Most men were. Most were also unaccustomed to her bloomers, her college education, and her scientific work as a botanist. Usually once she explained that her mother was a leader of the fledgling suffragist movement, they began to make sense of her unconventional ways. In actuality, her mother and older sister were much more liberal than Linnea was, at times proposing wild ideologies that made her blush.

"Li-*nay*-uh?" Ivy tucked the blanket more securely over Linnea's legs. "That's sure a strange name."

Flynn shot the girl a glare. "Ivy, mind your manners."

Linnea chuckled. "Please, don't worry. My name is unusual, and I'm quite familiar with having to explain it."

Dylan paused in adding brush to the fire. "Mighty pretty if I do say so myself. Just like you."

"Dy-lan." Flynn ground out the word.

The youth shared a family resemblance to Flynn and was on track to turn into a man just as handsome—if not more so—than his brother. He ignored Flynn's rebuke and winked at Linnea with a carefree grin.

"My grandfather is named Linnus, and so was my father." She glanced in the direction of her traveling companions. Her grandfather was in the process of descending from the wagon now parked a short distance out of the way of other travelers. She needed to be as warm and normal as possible

16

when he reached her, so she could prove to him that her tumble into the river was nothing to worry about.

She bent in closer to the flames and rubbed her hands together. "My grandfather and father both were hoping for a boy to carry on the family name. But upon my birth as a girl, they decided the only thing to be done was call me Linnea."

Ivy cocked her head. "They didn't want to wait for a boy to come along next?"

"My mother would have been content with only one child—my older sister. But since my father wanted a son, she conceded to having two children."

"Well, that's sure strange. Didn't know a woman could control babies coming along."

Dylan snorted.

"Hush up, Ivy." Flynn tipped the brim of his hat lower and poked at the fire, sending sparks into the air.

"What?" Ivy's eyes rounded with innocence. "I always figured babies had a way of coming whether a woman wanted another or not. Leastways that's the way it was with Ma."

Flynn pressed his lips together and shook his head. The subject of having babies was clearly one he didn't feel comfortable discussing so publicly. However, Linnea was used to her mother's frank conversations regarding reproduction, babies, and birthing. In fact, there weren't many topics her mother considered vulgar. And although Linnea was perfectly at ease discussing methods of preventing conception, she wasn't in the practice of doing so with people she'd just met, particularly with a young girl Ivy's age.

"My ma just kept popping out the babies." Apparently,

Ivy had no qualms about continuing the discussion. "She had four boys, then me. After my pa died and she married Rusty, she kept having stillbirths until the last one killed her."

"Ivy! That's enough." Flynn's tone turned harsh. "Hush your mouth before I give you a whupping."

Ivy jumped to her feet and flounced her hair over her shoulders. "Twelve-year-olds don't get whuppin's no more."

Flynn faced off with the girl, their gazes locked, their hands fisted, their expressions taut. This obviously wasn't their first conflict. In fact, they were like lit powder kegs about to explode.

Linnea pushed up from the log and stepped between the two. "I don't know about you, but I could sure use a cup of hot coffee to warm up. That is, if you have extra to spare." A coffeepot sat beside the pan of fish in the grass next to the fire.

Flynn held Ivy's gaze a moment longer, then shifted it to Linnea. The crinkles at the corners of his eyes spoke of worry more than anger. She guessed he was one of the older brothers Ivy had spoken about, trying to take care of his younger siblings now that his parents were gone.

Linnea could imagine how difficult it was to parent a sibling, much less a girl like Ivy on the cusp of womanhood.

"Of course we have coffee to spare." Dylan was already reaching for the pot. He sloshed the container as though judging how much was left, and then he picked up a discarded tin mug from the grass, tipped out the black sludge, and poured from the pot.

The mixture going into the mug looked thick enough to be mud and thankfully tapered to a trickle before it reached halfway. He handed her the cup. "Here you go, darlin'."

She tried not to think about the mouths that had already touched the mug, or the decidedly cold tin against her hands. Before she lost courage, she lifted the cup, took a mouthful, and swallowed—all in one motion.

It was just as cold and bitter and awful as she'd anticipated, but she suppressed a shudder. "Thank you. You're so very kind."

Dylan's grin spread. "If you're hungry, we got some fish all fried up too. Caught it myself."

She didn't dare glance at the pan lest this time her shudder broke loose. "I appreciate the offer, but I'll start with the coffee for now."

The group they were traveling with consisted of a dozen wagons and usually stopped later in the morning for a break. That's when they ate their first meal of the day since at dawn they were too busy packing up and readying to leave. She'd heard most caravans followed that pattern and often rested for a couple of hours at midday to avoid exerting themselves during the hottest part of the day, allowing the livestock a chance to graze.

Even now, their caravan was due for a break. As the final wagon rolled up the bank, she guessed their guide would lead the group to a spot of shade in the river valley somewhere close by. Nonetheless, her grandfather was winding past the other camps and drawing near.

"Grandfather." She waved as enthusiastically as she could muster. "I'm just fine."

Attired in a crisp morning coat, bow tie, and his tall stovepipe hat, he had a distinguished air about him. His monocle hung from a chain attached to his vest and swung like a pendulum with each of his long strides. His hair—once a bright

THE HEART OF A COWBOY

crimson like hers—was now a soft reddish blond, slowly turning gray.

"Linnea!" A deep frown creased his face. "Are you alright?"

"Just a little wet." She straightened her shoulders, thankful she'd stopped shaking from the cold even if her feet were still numb.

Unfortunately she'd inherited her father's distractibility, often getting too focused on one thing to pay attention to what was going on around her. Grandfather worried she'd suffer an accident and meet her end the same way her father had.

It didn't help that Grandfather also considered her more fragile simply because she was a woman. At five foot five inches, she had her mother's thin, delicate features, making her appear dainty even though she was strong and robust— something she'd mentioned continually when she pleaded her case for taking part in the expedition. Even so, since Linnea was the first woman to be part of an exploratory trip like this, Grandfather assumed she wouldn't have the same stamina and strength as the men.

By now she hoped she was beginning to prove that her contribution to the expedition was valuable enough to outweigh the risks, especially because she was working harder than all the other scientists to catalog the flora on their journey.

Grandfather drew her into an embrace. He held her tightly, long enough that she could feel the quavering in his limbs. "I was so distressed."

She couldn't tell him she'd been distressed too. She needed to remain strong. Such was the curse of a woman, having to project an image of strength she didn't always feel. But she'd learned the hard way that showing weakness only made men question her abilities even more.

When Grandfather pulled back, he fitted his monocle into his eye socket, took hold of both her arms, and scrutinized her as he did his plant specimens.

She laughed and tugged away. "You needn't worry, Grandfather. I'm not a flower petal. I won't wilt."

"I know that, dear. But you could have drowned—"

"I didn't. And I'm perfectly fine."

Her grandfather studied her a moment longer, then sighed before holding out a hand toward Flynn. "Young man, thank you for saving my granddaughter. I cannot begin to express my gratitude."

Flynn shook his hand. "No thanks necessary, sir."

Linnea hadn't been properly introduced to these people herself, but that didn't mean she couldn't make introductions. "Grandfather, this is Flynn . . ." Except she didn't know his last name.

At her pause, he spoke. "McQuaid. The name's Flynn McQuaid."

Grandfather tilted his head and examined Flynn through his monocle. "Pleased to make your acquaintance, Mr. McQuaid. I'm Dr. Howell. And you've met my granddaughter, Mrs. Asa Newberry."

Ivy, who had been staring at Linnea during the entire reunion with her grandfather, released a low whistle. "Holy Saint Peter. You're awfully young to be married."

Flynn's shoulders stiffened at Ivy's bold statement. Before he could rebuke the precocious girl, Linnea waved off the comment. "I'm twenty-one years old. So I'm not terribly young, am I?"

"Where's your husband?" Ivy glanced around. "Why didn't he rescue you? Reckon as sweet as you are, he woulda jumped in right after you."

A strange heaviness settled on her chest. "I imagine he would have jumped in after me if he'd been along. But he's not here . . . because he's dead."

CHAPTER 2

Flynn's ready rebuke for Ivy got lost in an onslaught of questions. He hadn't expected Linnea to be married. How had she lost her husband? Perhaps during one of the recent bloody battles of the war? Maybe at Fredericksburg in December? Or the fight at Stone's River?

He prayed to the Lord Almighty that Brody hadn't been in either battle. After reading the newspaper accounts, Flynn had nightmares for nigh to a week. Even if Brody's name hadn't appeared on any of the casualty lists, Flynn hadn't been able to dislodge the image of his younger brother lying somewhere on a battlefield alone, suffering torments worse than those found in hell.

A shadow flashed across Linnea's pale face, and he had no doubt all this talk was rousing a whole passel of sad feelings for her.

"Did he die in the war?" Ivy's question popped out before Flynn could tell her to run off and mind her own business.

Even if he agreed with Ivy that Linnea looked mighty

young to be hitched, he'd learned enough manners from Ma to know better than to pry into someone's private life.

Trouble was, Ivy hadn't had the same kind of womanly training, not since Ma married Rusty. When Ma hadn't been laid up being pregnant or recovering from a failed birthing, she'd been too tired and worried to pay Ivy much attention. Mostly, Ivy's training had fallen squarely on his shoulders, and he was about as good at parenting Ivy as a hen was at mothering a porcupine.

"Come on now, Ivy." He tried to keep his voice calm, but lately she'd been more belligerent and harder for him to handle. "Stop prying into the lady's affairs."

"I ain't prying." She tilted up her chin, and her eyes flashed with defiance. "Just asking a question. Nothin' wrong with that, is there?"

"No, of course not." Linnea was quick to intervene, her gaze darting back and forth between them. He reckoned their tension was as easy to spot as a painted wagon. "My husband wasn't fighting in the war, as he was—well, he was a bit older—"

"Forty-nine wasn't that old," Dr. Howell interjected as he tucked the single eyepiece dangling from a chain back into his vest pocket.

She ducked her head, as though embarrassed to admit the age of her husband. "He died of pneumonia in Fort Leavenworth at the end of March."

"I'm sorry." The words weren't nearly adequate but still needed saying. For so recent a widow, she wasn't wearing the customary black clothing. But he guessed maybe she hadn't brought any along for the journey, probably hadn't expected to grieve the loss of her husband.

Shadows fell over her face again. Her fingers tightened against the colorful patterns of Ma's quilt as she brought the covering closer. "We were married less than two months."

Dr. Howell shook his head, his brow pinching together at the bridge of his nose. "Indeed, it was such a tragedy to lose so brilliant a scholar and friend. We'd only been in Fort Leavenworth a week, purchasing supplies and making final arrangements, when Asa contracted the ailment. None of us expected him to go so quickly."

Ivy sidled next to Linnea and reached for her hand.

Flynn opened his mouth to order Ivy to stop pestering the woman, but before he could speak, Linnea fitted her hand within Ivy's and squeezed it. His irritation fled and a strange sense of sorrow fell into its place—sorrow for all they'd lost: Brody, their parents, their home, the farm.

They were stuck without any other option but to accept his older brother's offer to move to Colorado. Wyatt had started a ranch in the spring of '62 shortly after President Lincoln's Homestead Act was signed. Now that Wyatt had land and a place of his own, he'd invited them to live there.

With Rusty kicking them off the farm that had been in the McQuaid family for generations, Flynn hadn't known what else to do but accept Wyatt's offer. Flynn had hoped the prospect of a new life out West would entice Brody enough to forgo joining the war efforts. At the very least, Flynn had intended to be out of Pennsylvania and on their way to the ranch before Brody carried through with enlisting in the Union army.

But none of Flynn's hoping had panned out. Of course, even if it had, there was still the possibility that eventually Colorado Territory would require eligible men to enlist. But for now it would be a safer place than anywhere else for Dylan, who blustered about joining the war too.

"I'm real sorry about your loss, Linnea." Ivy's dirty face took on uncharacteristic empathy. "But you're real pretty, and you'll get married again quicker than a wink and a whistle."

"I don't know about that—"

"Sure you will. You just wait and see. In fact, why don't you marry Flynn? He could use a wife, and I could sure use a womanly touch. Leastways that's what Flynn's always telling me."

"Thunderation, Ivy." He crossed his arms to keep from strangling the girl. "You don't know what you're talking about."

"Sure do." She cast a glance toward their cowhands, who'd gone back to resting in the shade and keeping an eye on the cattle. "Heard Nash tell Jericho and Dylan you're wound up as tight as a tick on a calf's rear. Said you need a woman in a bad way."

"It's true." Dylan grinned as he poked at the fire with a stick.

"Nash has no idea what he's talking about."

"Reckon he's calling it like it is." Dylan's reply contained teasing charm that never failed to defuse a tense moment. He turned his winsome smile onto Linnea again. "Ma'am, if Flynn ain't gotta mind to marry you, then I'll step right in. You just say the word—"

"Never you mind." Flynn felt a growl forming. "You and Ivy go catch more fish, and we'll have 'em for supper tonight."

Ivy opened her mouth, likely to protest, but Linnea cut her off. "Maybe you can show me how to fish. I've always thought it would be fun to learn."

Ivy's eyes took on a glimmer. "I'm real good at fishing."

"Very well. Then you can teach me everything you know."

"First thing is catching grasshoppers for bait. You ain't afraid of bugs like most womenfolk, are you?"

"No, sweetheart. I think you'll find I'm not like most women." Linnea cut Flynn a glance, one assuring him he didn't need to worry, that she wasn't bothered by the comments, and that she'd see to Ivy.

Breathing out a tense breath, he nodded his thanks. She handed him her untouched mug of coffee and then allowed Ivy to tug her away. As they wandered off in search of grasshoppers, Dr. Howell watched his granddaughter, the pinch between his brows deepening. "I need to send her home. She's a good scientist, but I'm just too worried about her surviving the trip."

Ivy and Linnea had moved into a patch of bright sunlight. Linnea repositioned the quilt around her still-dripping garments. She needed to go get changed into dry clothing. That's what she needed. But at least in the sunshine, she'd warm up real fast.

"I allowed her to come because of Asa." Dr. Howell's tone was low and confiding. "He was quite smitten with her."

Flynn could see why. Even in her bedraggled state, she was the prettiest woman he'd ever laid eyes on. In fact, a man would have to be blind not to notice her flawless features. Her long, curly hair was a stunning red. Her brown eyes were soft and doe-like. And her smile had the power to make a man forget his name.

"And now," Dr. Howell continued, "after this incident, I'm reminded all over again why I shouldn't have brought her on the expedition."

Expedition? Rather than prying into business that wasn't his, Flynn took a swig of the coffee Linnea had handed him. The brew flowed over his tongue as cold and bitter as river water. He supposed that's what he got for leaving the coffee making up to Ivy. She couldn't cook for the life of her, not even a decent pot of coffee.

The almighty truth was that Ivy did need a womanly touch in a bad way. But that didn't mean he planned on getting married. No matter what his cowhands thought, he didn't need a woman. He was getting along just fine without one and had been since he'd put an end to his relationship with Helen last summer.

Sure, there were still times he couldn't get away from his longings to have and to hold a woman. He wasn't a saint. But whenever his hankerings pestered him too badly, he only needed to think of the day his ma died after giving birth to another stillborn baby.

He'd been at her bedside, holding her hand, when she'd taken her last breath. And he vowed then and there he'd never do to a woman what Rusty had done to Ma—get a woman pregnant and put her through the horrors of child-birth. Didn't matter that women had been giving birth to babies since the creation of the world and living to tell about it. He wasn't gonna do it, and the only surefire way to keep his vow was to stay as far away from women as possible.

Dr. Howell resituated his tall black hat. "If only Asa were here. He was a good man, and he promised to watch over Linnea. Now without him, I fear I'm a poor substitute."

"You can't blame yourself, sir. Reckon she would have fallen from the wagon even if her husband had been alive." Flynn had been watering his horse at the river's edge when she tumbled out. He happened to see the whole thing from where he'd been standing. And he hadn't wasted a single second in waiting to see if she could fend for herself, especially after crossing only an hour earlier and knowing the current was swift. He hopped up on Rimrock and plunged in after her.

"She'll be devastated if I send her back East."

"You need to do what you think is best."

Dr. Howell watched as his granddaughter bent next to Ivy in the tallgrass, held herself motionless, and then an instant later cupped a grasshopper in her hand. She smiled her delight, which made her features all the prettier.

"I don't know what is best, Mr. McQuaid. She's an intelligent woman and one of the most capable botanists I know. Since my son's passing, she is my pride and joy—but so scatterbrained just like him—and I can't bear the thought of losing her too."

Flynn's attention trailed after Linnea and Ivy as they made their way to the riverbank.

"She has her heart set on being a member of this groundbreaking expedition and helping discover and catalog the plant life."

So they were scientists who studied plants. Obviously highly educated. Probably rich.

"No sense putting your granddaughter's life at risk."

"That's my thought exactly."

Ivy picked up one of the discarded fishing poles and demonstrated how to slide a grasshopper onto the hook.

"From what I hear," Flynn added, "the dangers of the trail are bound to get worse."

"After everything I've read and heard, that's what I'm afraid of. Hundreds die from all manner of diseases and accidents every year on the way to the west."

Linnea bent to retrieve the other pole. With both hands full, the blanket fell away, pooling at her feet. As she straightened, her gown and strange frilly white pantaloons stuck to her skin, outlining her lovely figure and leaving little to the imagination.

Flynn swallowed hard and tore his gaze away. Holy horses. He didn't need to be looking on a woman, stirring up all his longings and making things harder on himself. Although he was sorely tempted to take another peek, he shifted his entire body so he found himself facing Nash and Jericho Bliss.

From where they stood guard over the cattle, they had a clear view of Linnea and had stopped their jawing to stare openly at her. Dylan paused in brushing Rimrock and was watching Linnea with rounded eyes. No doubt so was every other man within a hundred-mile radius.

Except Dr. Howell, who was rubbing at his clean-shaven chin and studying the fire, oblivious to his granddaughter's womanly appeal.

Flynn tamped down a strange sense of irritation.

"I love my granddaughter dearly. But she's quite the handful for an old man like me."

Dr. Howell wasn't all that old. If Flynn had to guess, he'd put the man at sixty-five.

"Truthfully," Dr. Howell continued, "she's a handful for anyone of any age. She's full of so much energy and zest for life that sometimes she doesn't think of the consequences of what she's doing until it's too late."

"Then I reckon the best thing is for you to find a group

heading back to Fort Leavenworth and to send her packing with them."

Dr. Howell stared at the fire. The rushing water of the river and the rustling wind in the leaves overhead filled the silence. Finally, he sighed. "Young man, you're probably right. I know Linnea won't like my decision, but what else can I do?"

"Other than hire someone to stand guard over her day and night, there ain't much you can do." Of course, Dr. Howell could consider Ivy's suggestion that Linnea get married again. No doubt she'd have plenty of willing suitors if she but put the word out that she needed a husband.

His brows lifting, Dr. Howell's attention snapped to Flynn. "You wouldn't consider such a thing, would you?"

Flynn fell back a step. "Marry her? No, sir. I couldn't." Not even if someone hog-tied him and dragged him to the altar.

Dr. Howell opened his mouth to respond but stalled.

Too late, Flynn realized his blunder. Dr. Howell hadn't made a single mention of marriage, wouldn't make such a suggestion to a man he'd just met. "Of course, you ain't lookin' to marry her off so soon after she lost her husband. She's still grieving. And I ain't sayin' I'm interested, 'cause it didn't even cross my mind. Or at least not in the way you're thinking. . . ."

Flynn blew out a tense breath and palmed the back of his neck. He needed to shut his mouth and stop making a blamed fool of himself.

Dr. Howell's eyes crinkled at the corners with the beginning of a smile. "Don't worry. She has this effect on most men. In fact, she had half a dozen propositions of marriage when Asa came along and fell head over heels for her at a party her mother hosted last autumn. Even though he was busy preparing for our western expedition, he made time to pursue her, and within weeks proposed marriage."

The shade of the tree branches and even the dampness of Flynn's clothing couldn't take away the heat of his embarrassment. He drew in a breath of the cool air laced with the wood smoke from the campfire.

Dr. Howell's mirth faded. "She could have had her choice from among New York City's most eligible bachelors, but she decided upon Asa."

A sad silence fell between them. Flynn kicked at a lump of flattened grass. He had to say something to ease the man's sorrow. "Asa must've been a good man if your granddaughter picked him out of everyone else."

Dr. Howell waved his hand in dismissal. "She chose him because he supported her work in botany, just like her father had always done. Of course, it helped that Asa invited her to come along on the trip . . . as his wife. When I opposed the idea, Asa was the one who stood up for her. She also won the support of her mother, who is much too liberal in her views for what women should be allowed to do."

Flynn's gaze slid to Linnea as if it had a will and a mind of its own. She'd thrown out her fishing line and had her back facing them. Even so, she was still a stunning picture, standing at the river's edge, her hair unbound and blowing in the wind.

"I have considered suggesting she marry Dr. Greely, another scientist on our expedition." Dr. Howell peered in the direction of the crossing, searching among the wagons and riders milling on the upper embankment. "He's the only single man among the group. He's quite enamored with Linnea, but I don't think he's firm or strong enough to handle her. Even if he was, I doubt she'd consider getting married again."

"Because she's so distraught over losing her husband?" Flynn guessed he was behaving as rudely as Ivy with all his prying, but he couldn't seem to stop himself from finding out more about the fascinating young woman he'd pulled from the river.

Dr. Howell shook his head. "To be sure, she cared for Asa. But, no, they weren't married long enough to develop the kind of bond that brings true grief."

Flynn shifted the weight off his weak leg, determined not to ask anything more about Linnea. She wasn't his business. After they started out of the Neosho River valley, they'd part ways, and he'd likely never see her again.

"So, young man, what do you think? You seem like a fine and decent fellow. And after saving her life the way you did, I have the feeling you're an excellent candidate for standing guard over her for the duration of the trip." Dr. Howell gave him a winsome smile, one much like his granddaughter's, and Flynn guessed not many were able to say *no* to the older gentleman.

He didn't have any intention of guarding Dr. Howell's granddaughter, but how could he politely refuse? He took a swig of the cold coffee to buy himself a few more seconds.

"Of course, I'd make it well worth your effort. How does a hundred dollars sound?"

Flynn choked and then spit out the coffee into the grass. A hundred dollars? After using up every last cent of his savings to pay for their train and steamboat fare to get to Missouri, as well as all the supplies they needed for the next long months of journeying to Wyatt's ranch, Flynn was broke.

How could he turn down a hundred dollars? But at the same time, how could he take such an offer? Sure as the crow flies, he couldn't accept payment for doing good deeds he'd willingly offer for free.

He opened his mouth to protest, but Dr. Howell spoke first. "Two hundred dollars."

Flynn couldn't keep his jaw from dropping.

"I'm a very wealthy man, Mr. McQuaid, so you needn't worry on that score. I'll pay you half now and half after you deliver her safely to the journey's end."

"Ain't headed all the way down to Santa Fe. Fact is, I'll be branching off onto the mountain route and heading into Colorado."

"Then that's perfect. We're on our way to Colorado as well. We're planning to work our way through the Plains and up the Front Range to Denver, where we'll stay for the winter before we head up into the Rocky Mountains next spring."

Flynn scrambled to find another excuse to turn down the lucrative deal. "I'm driving a herd of Shorthorns, sir. With close to two hundred head, we're gonna move at a pace slower than the usual caravans to allow for extra grazing time."

"That's fine too. We actually would appreciate going slower and having more opportunity to explore and document the flora along the way. As long as we reach Denver before winter sets in, I think we'd all be happier to take our time."

"Gotta be well up into the high country before the first

heavy snows make traveling treacherous." Once they reached Pueblo, they'd take a northwesterly route, a gradual climb in elevation through mostly level mountain valleys. At least, that's what Tom Gordon, the Missouri Shorthorn breeder, claimed when he'd sent them on their way with the herd.

Yep, the plan was to get to Wyatt's long before they risked winter-like weather. But they couldn't push the cattle too hard. Tom had warned them that if they didn't have any major delays, the journey west could still take upward of five or six months and would be rough on the cattle even at the slow pace. The steers would grow weary, footsore, and thin. There was the very real possibility some might die along the way—or even be stolen.

But Flynn was determined to do the best he could to deliver the herd on time and as healthy as possible. Especially because from the way Tom talked, Wyatt had sunk a fortune into the beeves and needed every last head to make a go at his ranching. If Flynn made any mistakes, Wyatt would end up in big debt to his business partner without the means to finance another venture.

While Flynn didn't have the same experience Wyatt had in driving livestock, he knew all there was to know about cattle, having raised plenty on the farm. With help from Nash and Jericho, they hadn't encountered any trouble moving the herd and finding grass for grazing over the past couple of weeks. He'd been praying mighty hard their spell of luck would hold out.

With all that was at stake, he didn't need distractions from what he'd set out to do. "Your offer is tempting, sir. But I've got enough responsibility with lookin' after my family and gettin' this herd of cattle up into South Park."

The older man focused on Linnea again. She was pulling in her line weighted down with a wriggling trout. Her delighted laughter mingled with Ivy's words of praise. "She'll be heartbroken if I send her back, Mr. McQuaid." His voice was low and solemn. "Now that she's been working so hard to contribute to the research manual, I just don't know if I can do that to her. And yet, after nearly losing her today, I don't know how I can let her go on without someone watching over her and keeping her safe."

Flynn sloshed the last of the coffee around the bottom of the mug. The swirling reflected the turmoil in his gut. Two hundred dollars was appealing. Mighty appealing. Especially because he planned to stake a claim through the Homestead Act the same way Wyatt had. With that kind of money, he'd have enough to start building a home and making improvements to the land the way the Act required. It also meant he wouldn't have to rely on Wyatt, which was the last thing he wanted to do.

He exhaled a tight breath. "If I was to accept your offer, what exactly do you have in mind?"

Dr. Howell straightened, and his eyes brightened. "Surely keeping an eye on my granddaughter doesn't have to take away from your regular duties. All you need to do is make a point to travel near her, accompany her when she explores, and make sure she doesn't wander off too far or get into trouble."

All he needed to do? "Sounds to me as if you want someone to stick to her every waking moment."

"Not every moment. Of course, that would be impossible. But when you're not with her, you could keep her in your line of vision, couldn't you?"

Linnea was easing the hook out of the fish gills. Her pretty eyes rounded wide with wonder and innocence, and she nibbled her bottom lip.

From the little he knew about her, she seemed kind and sweet and easygoing. Surely she wouldn't be too much trouble.

Truthfully, as they made their way farther along the trail into Indian territory, it would help to have a few more men as part of their group. He'd heard that the larger the party, the less trouble the Indians made, especially with a show of men carrying weapons.

"Alright." He stuck out his hand. "I'll do it."

"Excellent." Dr. Howell reached out and shook with a firm grasp. "Then it's a deal."

Flynn glanced at Nash and Jericho still gawking at Linnea. He had to give them fair warning of the new arrangement.

As Flynn started to pull away, Dr. Howell held on tighter, his brow furrowing. "Young man, one more thing." He leaned in and lowered his voice. "I think it's best if we keep this between the two of us. I don't want Linnea to learn about our arrangement."

Unease rattled through Flynn, and he hesitated to respond.

"She's—well, she's sensitive to my more traditional perspective on the roles between men and women. Because her mother is progressive, I'm afraid Linnea has picked up on some of those views."

Flynn didn't have the slightest idea what Dr. Howell was referring to. But he didn't feel good about keeping anything from Linnea. If they didn't tell her he planned to look after her, she'd surely get suspicious when he started following her all over God's green earth. Either that or she'd think he was smitten with her and couldn't stay away.

He shook his head and pulled from Dr. Howell's grip. Nope, the only way he'd agree to guarding her was in telling her the truth. "She needs to know—"

"Fine. Fine." Dr. Howell waved a hand impatiently. "I'll give her some kind of explanation—but let's not mention I'm paying you."

Flynn hesitated again.

Dr. Howell's attention drifted to the thrill filling his granddaughter's face as she examined the fish she'd caught. It chose that moment to wiggle its fin and fall right out of her hands to the ground, where it flipped in the grass.

She hopped back and pressed her hands to her chest, her laughter filling the air.

Dr. Howell's expression softened.

Ivy laughed too. Gone was the belligerence that made an appearance all too often. Instead, she was carefree— even happy—in a way she hadn't been in months. Flynn missed that Ivy, the one he could tease and tussle, the one who surprised him with spiders and lizards, the one who loved and looked up to him. He was getting a glimpse of the old Ivy here and now. And he didn't want her to go away again.

But the truth was, she needed more than he could give her. Maybe with Linnea's presence and influence, Ivy would be better.

Dr. Howell watched Linnea a moment longer, then turned to Flynn. "Please, Mr. McQuaid?"

Flynn took off his hat and combed back his hair, letting the breeze cool his itchy head. "Don't feel right about hiding anything from your granddaughter, sir. But I'll go along with whatever you think is best."

"Thank you, young man." Dr. Howell's eyes lit with relief. "You won't regret this. I promise."

Flynn hoped the gentleman was right but suspected he was completely wrong.

CHAPTER

3

"I've made a change of plans," Grandfather said from where he stood across the campfire, his expression grave and his tone serious.

Linnea paused in picking a bone out of the tender bite of trout in her mouth, the fish suddenly losing flavor.

She'd known this moment was coming from the instant she'd fallen into the river. But over the past hour of learning how to fish with Ivy and then frying up their catch, she'd hoped Grandfather would forget everything that had happened, and that they could continue on the journey with no more mention of her near drowning.

She spit out the bone and swallowed the fish, and at the same time she placed her tin plate in the grass beside the campfire, her appetite gone. A sourness roiled around her stomach at the unfairness of being a woman, but she had to remain strong, especially since Ivy sat beside her.

The girl was impressionable and needed a good example of what it looked like to stand up for oneself, especially as a female trying to make her way in a world that was too quick to judge a woman as weak and incapable.

"Please don't make me go back, Grandfather. I promise I won't have any more accidents."

Grandfather gingerly ate a bite of the fish she'd dished up for him. "You promised me no more issues yesterday when you lagged behind and got lost."

From beside his horse where he was loading his revolver, Flynn halted, his brow lifting beneath the brim of his hat.

"Go back where?" Ivy paused in scraping her plate clean with her fingers.

Her grandfather started to reply, but Linnea beat him to it. "My grandfather would like me to return to New York City."

"Now, Linnea, you know I don't *want* that. But I could never forgive myself if something happened to you out here."

At the tiredness that flitted over his face, she repressed another ready retort. No doubt he was thinking of her father's deadly accident, when he'd been trapped out in the Adirondack Mountains doing research on wildflowers and had been caught in a late-spring snowstorm.

She regretted causing Grandfather undue strain. He'd been planning and looking forward to the trip for several years. And he'd been specifically chosen to be the leader out of the others vying for the position, which was a great honor since now he'd have his name attached to the manual they intended to complete by the end of their trip.

This was likely his only chance to do something like this, and she didn't want him to worry about her the whole time. Maybe she ought to give in to his wishes to return.

"I can help keep track of Linnea." Ivy licked the grease from her fingers.

Linnea could only smile at the girl's offer. From what Linnea had surmised thus far, Ivy needed more supervision than she did.

"Thank you, young lady." Grandfather smiled too. "Fortunately, I've made arrangements to ride along with your group. With the way Mr. McQuaid was so quick to rescue Linnea, I decided we might be safer under his supervision."

"Really?" Ivy paused in swiping the last drop from her plate, glancing from Grandfather to Flynn, her expression filling with hope.

Flynn resumed working, checking each chamber of his revolver as though his life depended on it.

"Really." Grandfather didn't meet Linnea's gaze but focused on his fish, picking at a bone.

"So you're not sending me back?"

"Not as long as you promise to do everything Mr. McQuaid requests, since he'll be our leader now."

"I promise." She'd promise to lasso the moon if it meant she could stay on the expedition. So far she'd loved every minute of exploring, cataloging, drawing, and preserving specimens. She couldn't imagine anywhere else she'd rather be than on this trip doing the work she loved.

"Yippee!" Ivy jumped up and down. "I told Flynn we oughta be riding with someone else so we ain't so lonesome, but he said most people don't wanna travel with a bunch of slow cattle."

Linnea listened only halfway to the rest of Grandfather's conversation with Ivy and instead examined Flynn more carefully. She had a view of his profile. And though he was focused on his gun, his body radiated tension, and the muscles in his jaw flexed.

He certainly didn't seem thrilled with the new traveling arrangements. Was he reluctant to have them ride along?

As though sensing her scrutiny, he shot a glance her way, one confirming that he wasn't thrilled in the least.

She dropped her attention to her plate. She was too relieved Grandfather was letting her continue with the expedition to call into question his methods or call attention to Flynn's displeasure. If Flynn didn't want to travel with their group, he should have told Grandfather no. It wasn't her fault he hadn't and was saddled with them.

Even so, from now on, she had to do better so neither her grandfather nor Flynn would have any cause for concern.

An hour later, they were on their way. Linnea walked beside their wagon, which trailed a short distance behind the wagon Dylan was driving. Ivy fell into step next to her, conversing nonstop, clearly starved for a woman's company.

Flynn rode alongside the cattle a short distance away from the wagons. One of the other drovers guided the herd opposite him while a third worked the swing position at the rear of the long line.

Ivy had explained that driving the cattle was fairly simple, that a few natural leaders within the herd took their places at the front and the rest of the cattle fell into line behind them. Mostly the herd walked single file rather than in a group, which made them stretch out quite a distance.

The trail out of the Neosho River valley led them to a level area of treeless prairie that spread out endlessly in all directions, meeting the vast sky on the horizon. Grandfather and the other scientists had mounted their horses and ridden ahead, having heard from a group passing east that buffalo had been spotted. They were eager to get their first glimpse of the enormous creatures they'd heard so much about.

Linnea, on the other hand, was content to stroll through the grass, reveling in the *Andropogon gerardii*, also called big bluestem or turkey-foot. For so early in the season, the culm was thin and yet erect and solid and round. The blades were a half-inch wide, bluish, and rough above while smooth below.

She'd already pressed and dried a specimen earlier in the week. Though the bluestem wasn't yet flowering and wouldn't until late June or July, she could already see the growth in just a week and wanted to measure the difference. She'd love to see it later in the summer at the pinnacle of growth, sometimes reaching as high as seven feet.

"The Shorthorns like the tallgrass." Ivy chewed on the stem, twisting it around with her tongue. "Tom Gordon told us to make sure to let the cattle graze on it aplenty if we want to keep them from losing too much weight during the journey."

"That's because *Andropogon gerardii* is full of protein, especially in the spring and summer before the chemical composition changes and the nutritious quality decreases."

Ivy halted so abruptly that Linnea tripped in her effort to stop. At the sight of Ivy's wide eyes, Linnea peered around, looking for whatever had startled the girl. "What is it, sweetheart?"

At times, Linnea couldn't help but feel as if she were walking through heaven to be in the midst of so many unique species of grasses, some that had never before been identified and catalogued. But she was equally fascinated by the flowers, insects, arachnids, and small mammals she happened upon too. Although their expedition was focused solely on developing a book on the flora, she was keeping a journal of everything that fascinated her. "What did you see? I'm sure I'd love to examine it too."

Ivy spit out the long piece of grass. "Just ain't never heard a woman talk with so many big and fancy words."

Linnea frowned, trying to remember the last thing she'd spoken to Ivy. Before she could work it out, Flynn reined his horse beside them. "Something wrong?" He tipped up the brim of his hat, revealing his brows furrowed above serious eyes.

The sky above was a pristine blue, dotted with a few fluffy clouds. The wind blew mildly, just enough to rustle the grass. And the early afternoon temperature was perfect without being too cold or too hot. They couldn't have asked for better travel weather even if they'd tried.

Nevertheless, Linnea felt strangely chilled under Flynn's scrutiny. She wasn't sure what she'd done wrong, but ever since leaving the Neosho River valley, she'd had the distinct feeling he didn't like her. Maybe she was only imagining his aloofness.

Whatever the case, she wasn't in his good graces. "Nothing is wrong, Mr. McQuaid. At least nothing of which I'm aware. Ivy? How about you? Is anything amiss?"

One of the girl's brows quirked. "Amiss?"

"Yes, you stopped so suddenly, I thought perhaps you spotted something."

"Nope, I ain't spotted nothing but the same old grass."

"Old grass? Oh no, sweetheart. This grass isn't old. It's actually in the early stages of growth without inflorescences or spikelets."

Ivy met Flynn's gaze, both of her brows raised. "See what I mean?"

Flynn's lips shifted into a slight smile. "Yep. Sure do." The smile, however small, softened the hard lines of his face. Atop his horse, he had a powerful aura that exuded strength. She could see why Grandfather had wanted to ride with him.

Now he and Ivy regarded her as though she was some strange new specimen of woman they'd never seen before.

"What?" She patted her coif, her discarded bonnet hanging down her back. She'd refashioned her tangled, damp hair before they'd set out. Of course, she hadn't minded wearing her hair down. In fact, she rather wished women like her weren't so socially bound toward particular hairstyles and had more freedom to let their hair hang loose if they so desired. But only young girls had that option.

Ivy studied Linnea's hair and then her face with open admiration. "You said you weren't like most women, and I guess you weren't jesting."

Linnea smiled. "I warned you, didn't I? Are you tired of me already?"

"Don't rightly see how anyone could ever get tired of you. Not with how pretty and smart and sweet you are. Ain't that right, Flynn?"

Flynn's full gaze landed upon Linnea and swept over her, making a slow trail from the flyaway strands of her hair, over her face, to her neck, down her body, all the way to her feet. Something about this handsome man's scrutiny made strange tingles race over her skin.

She wasn't sure why. She'd had plenty of men pay her attention over the past few years since she officially entered society. She even had plenty of men look her over from her head to her toes.

But none like this rugged cowboy. Not even Asa.

Asa had adored her. Perhaps too much. Especially since she hadn't felt anything for him beyond friendship. Asa had claimed her feelings for him would eventually grow.

But during their last few weeks together before his death, her affection hadn't increased. Instead, she'd felt stifled from his attention and compliments. She didn't like to admit to herself she'd even begun to dread his touch. His kisses and even the intimacy they'd shared during the rare nights of privacy had always felt perfunctory, like something she must endure.

One of her mother's blush-worthy discussions had involved the marriage bed and how loving should be mutual, that God intended for both man and woman to enjoy the intimacy. After hearing her mother's views, Linnea had entered her own marriage with an open mind. But no matter how hard she tried, she hadn't been able to fabricate the same pleasure Asa seemed to find.

After never experiencing a physical response with Asa, how was it possible this man she barely knew could elicit one? Even as he drew his gaze back up her body, the warmth in her stomach spread, much like an inkblot seeping deeper and wider into paper.

When his gaze connected again with hers, he didn't hide his frank appreciation. Something within the depths of his green-blue eyes said he saw her as a beautiful and desirable woman. And for a reason she couldn't explain, the warm ink inside spilled and spread its tendrils further through her middle.

"I can see you think Linnea's real pretty." Ivy's voice broke into the lengthening silence. "You can't deny it so don't even try."

"I won't." Flynn's voice was low.

Linnea focused on the strands of various grasses she held. But she didn't see them, only saw his green-blue eyes.

"But it don't matter how pretty *Mrs. Newberry* is." Flynn's tone turned matter-of-fact. "She's a widow, and she's grieving the loss of her husband."

Widow. Grieving. The words seemed to reach out and slap Linnea hard across her cheeks. Mortification welled up so swiftly, she felt the sudden need to bury her face in her hands to hide her shame.

Asa had been in the grave for less than two months. How could she allow herself to dwell on even the slightest attraction to Flynn? Doing so was not only wanton, it was disloyal to Asa. He'd been a good man and a good husband. Most of all, he'd been the first to recognize the contributions she could make to the expedition.

He deserved to have her grieve for him properly and not cast him aside the first time a man turned her head.

"You're correct." She couldn't meet his gaze. "I am grieving. Asa was a wonderful man, and I won't ever forget him."

Even though she just had, she vowed she wouldn't again. And as Flynn directed his horse away and rode back to the herd, she refused to let her gaze follow him.

CHAPTER
4

He'd been a donkey to Linnea. Watching her from the corner of his eye, Flynn leaned against the wagon bed and sopped the last bite of hard cracker in the grease from the roasted rabbit Dylan had shot and dressed. The boy was a natural sharpshooter and, after they'd stopped for the evening had easily rounded up several hares.

Linnea sat with her grandfather and the three other scientists in their group, listening raptly to their description of the herd of bison they'd come across that afternoon. Ivy and Dylan had joined them around the campfire, now blazing from the dried buffalo chips Ivy had collected. The two joined in the conversation, especially Dylan, flirting with Linnea every chance he had. At sixteen, the boy couldn't pass up the opportunity to chase after any female that gave him half a second's worth of attention.

Nearby, another large caravan had made camp for the night, circling their wagons together to provide a corral for the livestock. His herd rested a short distance away outside the fold—too big to contain—with Nash and Jericho taking the first watch. At least, this early in the spring, they didn't have to worry about the grass being overgrazed. Tom Gordon had warned that later in the summer, they'd have a harder time finding grass for the cattle, especially on land adjacent to the trail.

A couple of the cows were nearing birthing time. And one had a lame foot. But for now, their main worry at night was theft and stampedes.

Of course, with Diamond Springs only half a day's journey to the west, all the other travelers were talking about the attack there a few weeks ago. A captain of the Confederate army and his band of renegades raided the small settlement. They killed one man, wounded a woman, burned the stage station, and plundered the rest of the village. No one knew where these guerilla soldiers—and other ruffians like them—were hiding. And everyone feared more aggression.

Linnea's laughter wafted toward him, followed by Ivy's. All day and now all evening, Ivy had trailed the beautiful woman like a pup eager for a pat on the head. Linnea had happily given Ivy every bit of attention she craved. Although Linnea had been quieter and more reserved after he'd been harsh with her, she continued to shower Ivy with kindness.

The last bite of cracker stuck in his throat. He hadn't needed to be such a donkey, and he wished he could take back his comments about her being a grieving widow. He'd been angry—mainly at himself for finding her so attractive and for being stuck in a position where he was forced to keep on looking at her and feeding his attraction.

He shouldn't have accepted Dr. Howell's offer, no matter how good it was. He was swindling the man, especially because watching over Linnea hadn't been any more difficult than keeping an eye on Ivy. No doubt Dr. Howell had exaggerated his granddaughter's knack for danger, had probably wanted a nursemaid so he could run off and explore with the other scientists without feeling guilty for leaving the young woman behind.

No matter. Flynn shouldn't have lashed out at her. She hadn't done anything wrong in staring at him so curiously. Even if her eyes had flared with an appreciation that had lit a match inside him, she hadn't done anything to deserve his tongue-lashing. Dr. Howell had already told him she hadn't been married long enough to develop a bond with her husband. Besides, grieving widows got remarried all the time, sometimes quickly out of necessity, just like his ma had done.

Flynn's attention shifted first to Dr. Johnson and Dr. Parker, then to Dr. Greely, who'd positioned himself next to Linnea. The firelight reflected off his spectacles and the few strands of silver in his hair and beard. His pipe glowed orange as he took a puff. Old enough to be her father, he was a hefty man with a boisterous laugh and a loud voice. Like most other travelers who'd purchased gear in the shops in frontier towns, he wore thick woolen pants reinforced with buckskin where the legs came into contact with the saddle. His shirt was a blue flannel, his socks woolen, and his knee-length boots were wide enough to tuck his pants into them.

Flynn had only spoken with him briefly when they'd set up camp, and he'd been pleasant enough. Having lost his wife two years ago, the want of a woman dripped from Dr. Greely as readily as the dew that covered the tallgrass every morning and soaked their trousers and shoes. Even now, he leaned closer to Linnea as he relayed a description of a bison calf.

She hadn't encouraged him in any way. But she hadn't needed to. Just being herself was enough. It surefire had been enough to draw him in. Even now, he couldn't stop thinking about her.

"Thunderation," he whispered, pushing away from the wagon and wiping his plate and knife clean in the grass. Enough was enough. He wasn't interested in having a woman, not now or ever.

He grabbed the bucket containing a mixture of tallow, tar, and rosin, and set to work greasing the axles and checking each of the wheels by firelight. He made short work of securing a loose tie on the canvas, then moved on to Dr. Howell's wagon, making the same inspections.

Before sunset, clouds had been gathering to the west. The dampness of the air hinted at rain to come, and he had the feeling they'd get a shower or two during the night. So far, they'd had very few wet days or nights. But this early in the spring, they were bound to have rain, some even heavy.

"Thank you, Mr. McQuaid." Clay, the hired hand for Dr. Howell's party, stood above Flynn as he slid out from underneath the wagon. Clean-shaven with slicked-back hair, the young man was apparently one of Dr. Howell's household staff who'd come along to tend to the older gentleman.

From what Flynn had patched together, Dr. Howell came from a family of old money. One of the other scientists had made a comment about Dr. Howell having a lord in England as a relative. Whatever his history, it was mighty clear he was highborn and wasn't aiming to be without his servant even on this trip.

In addition to waiting on Dr. Howell hand and foot, Clay was apparently responsible for setting up camp, starting the fire, and cooking a decent meal. Although he seemed close to Flynn's twenty-two years of age, the manservant lacked the basic know-how for trail life.

Flynn tugged on the canvas, making sure it was pulled taut. "Everything's ready for the morning. Figured we'd pull out at five. Think you can hitch the oxen and be ready to go by then?"

Clay glanced toward the campfire and the scientists. "Dr. Howell prefers to have time to shave and have his morning tea before starting."

Flynn suppressed an irritated sigh. "You can tell Dr. Howell and everyone else, they'll have to wait for shaving and tea 'til we take our midday break."

Clay started to protest, but Flynn spun on his heels and stalked away, wishing once again he hadn't agreed to partner with Dr. Howell's expedition. They were outfitted with the highest quality of provisions and the best horses money could buy. The almighty truth was he couldn't relate to such men and had little patience for them.

He spread out a tarpaulin underneath his wagon and began piling the saddles underneath, where they would hopefully stay dry.

"Mr. McQuaid?"

At Dr. Howell's call, Flynn braced himself for opposition to his orders. He straightened and faced the group still lounging around the campfire, most in oak-framed camp chairs covered in canvas, the expensive kind that collapsed and were easily stored in a wagon. All eyes turned to him, except Linnea's. She focused instead on the open notebook on her lap, sketching another plant.

Dr. Howell nodded at his manservant, hovering over him.

"Clay has explained to me that you expect to leave at five o'clock."

"That's right."

"Is so early an hour truly necessary?"

"We need to drive the cattle in the cooler part of the morning."

The scientists began talking at once, proposing various options. Flynn crossed his arms. This wasn't a leisure trip for him. He was on a mission to get every single one of the cattle to Wyatt. And if these men didn't like the schedule that was best for the livestock, then they'd just have to part ways.

"Please, everyone!" Linnea jumped up so abruptly her notebook fell into the grass close to the fire. Ivy lurched for it, grabbing it up before it could burst into flames. Dr. Greely, apparently the ultimate gentleman, was on his feet in the next instant, lending Linnea a steadying hand.

She offered Dr. Greely a grateful smile, then turned her attention to the others as amiably as always. "Please, let us do our best to accommodate Mr. McQuaid and his companions. As they have so graciously allowed us to accompany them, the least we can do is follow their schedule."

Her grandfather and the other scientists had risen now too. "You are quite right, young lady. Quite right."

"Thank you, Grandfather."

"Young man"—Dr. Howell addressed Flynn—"you can count on us. We shall be ready at five o'clock sharp."

Though the others grumbled, no one voiced any further objections. Before he turned to go, Flynn caught Linnea watching him. As earlier, the merest touch of her gaze sent a shot of heat into his veins, a shot he didn't want but that pulsed through him anyway.

In spite of his reaction, he nodded and hoped she could read his gratefulness for standing behind his decision.

She nodded in return, then dropped her attention to the fire.

Inwardly he sighed. She was a sweet woman and wasn't at fault for stirring up attraction between them, likely didn't even realize she was doing so. Whatever he was feeling was his issue and his alone. He had to apologize to her. In fact, he reckoned he wouldn't be able to rest until he did.

Rivulets of rain ran down the inside of the canvas and dripped into the wagon bed. Linnea had already covered the chest containing their research with her waterproof coverlet. She draped a tarpaulin over the press where several species of grass were drying. And she also placed her most recent discoveries back into her vasculum. The cylindrical botanical box would hopefully keep the plants dry and safe.

Though she could hardly see in the darkness of the night, she'd done the best she could to salvage their research since she'd awoken a short while ago to find the rain pounding hard against the canvas and leaking inside.

Now she needed to go out and insist that Grandfather and the others join her inside the wagon. The dear man would resist imposing on her privacy, but she was fully dressed. And inside, though it would be crowded and dripping with rainwater, was much drier than underneath, where the men had taken to spreading out their bedrolls when it rained. That worked with a gentle sprinkle, but with the strength of this storm, she could only imagine how wet they were.

She loosened the drawstring of the back canvas and poked

her head through, only to feel the heavy splatter against her face. She shivered at the cold and drew her waterproof coat tighter, securing the hood in place. By the time she climbed out and her feet touched the ground, her skirt and shoes were already weighted down with rainwater.

The ground was saturated, and her feet sank into the grass and mud. As she trudged around the wagon, she was surprised to find tarpaulins extended from the wagon outward, forming a tent of sorts.

She poked her head underneath the waterproof covering, but she couldn't see anything clearly. "Grandfather?"

"Linnea?" His voice rumbled nearby with sleepiness. "What are you doing out in the rain?"

"I came to check on you and invite you and the others to take refuge inside the wagon. I didn't expect to find that you had fashioned a tent."

"Before the rain came in earnest, Flynn helped us rig up the tarpaulin."

Flynn had done that for the men? Even after they'd given him a hard time about leaving so early? "Are you staying dry enough?"

"It's not perfect, but certainly much better than if we'd had nothing at all." The tap of rain against the canvas nearly drowned out his voice and the snoring of one of the other men.

"You're all welcome to come into the wagon."

"Thank you, young lady. You're so sensitive and kind to offer. But I imagine we're staying as dry here as we would in the wagon."

Linnea guessed it was true. They'd likely stay drier if they didn't venture outside the way she had. "Very well. But if you become too wet, don't hesitate to climb up and join me."

"We shall be fine. But thank you for offering." He stifled a yawn. "Now, you must return to the wagon and stay there, my dear."

She stood and jumped at a movement a short distance away. She strained to see through the darkness and rain, catching a glimpse of a creature passing through the circle of wagons. Was that one of their horses wandering off? Had the rain spooked the animal?

She'd heard the tales of livestock growing frightened during storms, running off, and causing delays while search parties tracked the missing creatures. Certainly Flynn would be disappointed if the loss of a horse hindered their departure.

From among the endless amount of information Ivy had shared yesterday, Linnea learned the cattle didn't belong to Flynn, that their older brother, Wyatt, had taken out a loan to purchase the herd for his new ranch up in South Park, and that Flynn was under a great deal of stress to deliver the livestock without losing any.

With a burst of determination, Linnea started in the direction of the wayward animal. If she took action now, she could prevent the mishap and save Flynn trouble.

As the rain hit her face and trickled beneath her coat, her footsteps faltered. Maybe she ought to wait. The deluge seemed to have no intention of letting up, and the night was black, almost suffocating.

Yet Flynn and the other cowboys had to work in this weather. If they could keep watch over their cattle in it for hours on end, she could surely manage a few minutes to track down the horse or oxen or whichever animal had left the fold.

Ducking her head against the onslaught, she made her way in the direction the animal had wandered. Her feet sloshed with each step, and the drenched earth sucked at her shoes as though to warn her to stay.

She wouldn't need to go far, especially if she hurried and caught up with the creature before it had a chance to run off.

Picking up her pace, she passed through the wagons and strained to see. Ahead, she glimpsed the moving outline of a horse, its picket dangling in front of it, likely having pulled it loose from the muddy ground.

She raced after it, only to have it dart farther ahead. "Come on, now," she crooned, hoping the horse could hear her above the rainstorm. If only she'd thought to bring along an apple or carrot to tempt it closer.

A few feet from the creature, she halted and held out her hand. The horse bent its head into the grass as though to graze. She tiptoed closer, brushing first its flank and then skimming her hand toward its head and the picket. As she reached for the dangling cord, the horse lifted its muzzle, sniffed the air, and darted away.

She picked up her wet skirt and chased after it. Several more times, she crept close enough to almost capture the creature, only to have it move out of range. She finally blew out a frustrated breath and halted. She could no longer see the horse and didn't know which direction it had gone.

With a final glance around, she spun and retreated the way she'd come. The rain continued to splatter hard against her coat and hood, and her toes squished inside her shoes, her thick woolen socks wet and cold.

Disappointment churned inside. Her efforts had amounted to naught. Now they would be delayed until well after the break of dawn in searching for the lost horse, and Flynn would be frustrated.

Though he'd kept to himself the previous evening after they set up camp, he stayed busy tending the horses, servicing the wagons, and repairing one of the oxen yokes that had cracked. She'd wanted to ask Ivy what had caused Flynn's limping gait, was surprised the girl hadn't yet told her since she was so forthcoming with private information.

Ivy had told her all about her family, that the McQuaids came from southwestern Pennsylvania and that their farm had been stolen from them by their stepfather. Her oldest brother had invited them to come live with him, but long-standing animosity existed between Flynn and Wyatt. Flynn hadn't wanted to move West but had agreed to it in order to keep Brody and Dylan from joining the war efforts, only to have Brody run off anyway.

Linnea pressed onward through the rain, shivering underneath her coat. The night air was colder than she'd realized. And the distance she'd traveled away from camp was farther than she'd realized too.

Had she really gone so far?

She stopped and searched the landscape, only able to see a few feet ahead of her. The grass was bent under the weight of the rain, the same as it had been since she'd started. She wished for daylight and to be able to examine the wet grass. She always found plant resiliency fascinating. A leaf could wilt so thoroughly, almost to the point of dying, but then with a little watering, the central vacuole could regain its turgor pressure and restore firmness and shape.

Though the darkness prevented her from studying the *Andropogon gerardii*, she fingered one, the waxy, grooved stem that was bent but not broken. One of her favorite Scripture verses came to mind: *"Wherefore, if God so clothe the grass* of the field, which to day is, and to morrow is cast into the oven, shall he not much more clothe you, O ye of little faith?"

Whenever she considered God's exquisite design of something so small as a blade of grass or the petal of a flower, she was always able to put her own life into better perspective. If He cared so much about the plants and their challenges to grow and remain strong, then surely He cared even more about the challenges and struggles she faced as a woman—at least that's what she tried to remember when her grandfather and the other scientists didn't take her as seriously as they did each other.

She whispered another prayer of gratefulness that Grandfather had allowed her to continue on the expedition. His tenuous support of her ambitions had slipped with every passing day, and she needed to regain his confidence, not lose it even more.

She straightened and peered through the rain. Surely the wagons were only a couple paces ahead. She simply needed to trust her instincts to take her in the right direction.

Pushing onward, she wiped the droplets from her face, straining harder to make out her surroundings. She strode first in one direction, then changed course, guessing she'd somehow veered the wrong way. She stopped several more times, hoping to glimpse the camp or even Flynn's cattle. But every time, she saw only more of the same barren landscape.

Finally, panic began to break through her confidence. Shaking from the cold, she hugged her arms across her chest. She could no longer avoid the truth.

She was lost.

CHAPTER
5

"Linnea's gone."

Ivy's call slammed into Flynn with the power of a two-thousand-pound bull charging at full speed. He reined in his horse with a jerk so hard, the momentum nearly bucked him from the saddle.

At predawn, the rain had finally stopped, and he could make out Ivy standing at the rear of Dr. Howell's wagon. Several lanterns were lit, and the drenched camp was alive, the scientists frantically attempting to saddle their horses.

His blood, already sluggish from the past hours of doing guard duty, slowed even more. "Linnea's gone? Where?"

Ivy jogged toward him, her expression a mask of worry. "Nobody knows. One of the horses is gone too."

Reining in behind him, Dylan gave a soft whistle. They'd taken over for Nash and Jericho and hadn't noticed anything wrong when they'd left the camp. As far as Flynn had been able to tell, everyone had been asleep—at least resting as best they could through the downpour.

"There you are!" Dr. Howell rushed toward him, breathless and harried, his top hat askew, bow tie off center, and vest unbuttoned. "Have you seen her?"

"Haven't seen a thing." Flynn's muscles tightened, and he glanced over the prairie starting to lighten with the coming of the day.

Dr. Howell pressed a hand to his chest as though to stave off pain there. "This is terrible. Just terrible."

Last thing they needed was Dr. Howell getting worked up enough to have a heart attack. "Ivy, you go on and take Dr. Howell and get a fire started so he can have some tea."

She opened her mouth—likely to demand joining the search—when Dr. Howell swayed. She grabbed hold of his arm. "Come on, now. Let's get you that tea."

"No, young lady. I do thank you for the offer, but I need to search for Linnea." Even as he spoke, he leaned in to Ivy.

"Now, don't you go worrying none." She started leading him away. "Flynn's gonna find her in no time. He could find a shadow in the shade if you asked him to."

"Please, Mr. McQuaid." Dr. Howell paused to peer up at Flynn. The desperation in the gentleman's eyes yanked on Flynn's heart. "Please find her."

"Ivy's right. You ain't got nothin' to worry about." He prayed to the Lord Almighty he was telling the truth, that neither Indians nor Confederate Irregulars had gotten a hold of her.

With a few instructions to the other men—namely to keep their guns loaded, stay in pairs, and hightail it away from any Indians—he started out. Dylan had wanted to search with him, but he'd paired the boy with Dr. Greely.

Flynn didn't need anyone. He was just fine by himself. And

though Dr. Howell hadn't condemned him, a heavy burden settled on him anyway, and he needed to bear it alone. The older man had hired him to keep his granddaughter safe, and less than twenty-four hours later, the young woman was already in life-threatening danger, if not dead.

Leading his horse, Flynn held a lantern above the earth, searching the grass and the mud beneath for any signs of her or the horse she'd ridden. It was strange she hadn't taken the time to untie the horse from its picket and had instead taken the stake and cord with her—unless the horse had broken free, and she'd decided to chase after it.

If the horse had gotten loose, which direction would it have gone? He studied the dark landscape. A small creek was but a quarter mile to the east. They'd watered the livestock there the previous evening but moved on from it before making camp because the mosquitoes had been swarming and biting something fierce. Had the horse caught the scent of the creek and thought to return to it?

Flynn changed his course toward the east. A short while later, his scrutiny of the ground paid off with the discovery of a horse print filled with rainwater. Not far from that, he found a shoe indentation—a slender sole, a woman's size.

He brushed aside more grass and found another human print as well as one belonging to a horse. With the care he'd cultivated while hunting the wooded hills of southwestern Pennsylvania as a boy, he moved forward, tracking her first one way and then another. He lost her for a short while but then picked up her trail again, reversing itself.

He reckoned she'd grown weary of trying to catch the horse—either that, or realized she'd wandered too long—and had decided to return to camp. Except that with the new direction her prints were heading, she'd gone the wrong way—north instead of west.

Straightening, he attempted to study the northerly landscape through the early morning, praying she hadn't wandered too far and happened upon a Comanche camp or one of their hunting parties. Several other travelers had warned of their presence and the need to stay away. He whispered a prayer for her protection, even as chill crept through him that had nothing to do with the cold morning.

A foggy mist had settled in the low places, making the search even more difficult. He hoped the other men had enough sense not to get lost themselves and make matters worse. Maybe he should have cautioned them to wait on heading out until full daylight.

He tried to push himself faster, a new urgency prodding him. But tracking was a meticulous process, and sometimes when her footprints disappeared, he was left trying to guess where she'd gone next.

Finally her prints shortened in spacing, which meant she'd slowed down. He was getting closer. He could feel it.

He lifted the lantern, but all he could see was fog. "Linnea?"

Silence met him.

"Linnea?" he called louder.

Another heartbeat passed until a faint voice responded. "Flynn?"

Weakness hit his knees. It was her. "Yep. I'm here. Where are you?"

"Over here."

He still couldn't see anything through the haze, even with his light shining down. He bent again and followed her prints. If he could keep her talking, he'd also be able to follow the sound of her voice. "You alright?"

"I'm relieved you're here."

Three steps later, he nearly tripped over her huddled on the ground, hugging her knees, her cloak wrapped around her. As he held the lantern above her, she lifted her head to reveal a pale face, blue lips, and chattering teeth. Underneath her hood, her hair hung in wet strands, and the portion he could see of her bodice was soaked too.

As far as he could tell, she was as wet from the rain as she'd been when she'd fallen out of the wagon into the river. He set the lantern down, shrugged out of his poncho, and then began to unbutton his flannel shirt.

"What are—you doing?" She could hardly get her question out past her shaking.

His fingers flew over the buttons. "First thing we gotta do is get you warmed up."

He shed his shirt, which he'd kept dry underneath his heavy gutta-percha poncho. "Can you take off your coat?"

She attempted to move, but her hands shook too hard.

Gently, he moved her hand out of the way and unfastened the clasp at the top of her cloak. The garment was well made and had the same gum-rubber coating as his poncho, but somehow the rain had gotten underneath, so the inside layer of soft cotton was saturated, as were her undergarments.

He peeled the cloak away and dropped it onto the grass. "I want you to put on my shirt, but it ain't gonna do you any good if we don't—well, if we don't—" He was too embarrassed to tell her she needed to partially undress.

"Take off my bodice? That's a good idea." She lifted her

hand again and fumbled at the buttons. "I'm sorry to trouble you. But my hands are too stiff from cold. . . ."

He hesitated. The act of helping her get out of her clothes seemed too intimate and too bold. But the longer he waited, the colder she got, and the more chances she'd get real sick real fast.

He touched the button. It was dainty and covered in velvet, not something a man like him should be anywhere near. But what choice did he have? Before he lost all nerve, he flipped it open and worked his way down the front, trying not to accidentally graze her but to keep his fingers only on the buttons themselves.

When he finished, she released a shaky laugh. "I probably shouldn't ask how you came to be so proficient at undoing a woman's bodice, should I?"

Heat spread up his neck faster than flames flying through sun-dried hay. "Reckon I wouldn't know."

"I'm sorry." Her response was breathless. "I was only jesting and didn't mean to call into question your character. You strike me as fine and upstanding."

While her chest rose and fell, he was all too conscious—the same as yesterday when she'd been wet—of what a beautiful woman she was. He might be fine and upstanding, but he was just a man.

As he helped her strip her arms from the sleeves, he forced himself to look beyond her shoulders in the misty distance. As the bodice peeled away, he caught a glimpse of her lacy chemise. He lifted his gaze heavenward and swallowed hard. Then, without glancing down again, he tossed his shirt around her, quickly followed by his poncho.

She hugged his clothing closer, the color beginning to return to her cheeks. "Thank you, Flynn. I'm already ten times warmer than I was just a moment ago."

So was he. He cleared his throat but couldn't find words to respond.

"I loathe myself for making you cold now." Her gaze darted to his chest, then to his shoulders. Though his long-sleeved undershirt covered his upper body, he felt barren anyway.

"I'm just fine." In fact, from the heat thrumming through his veins, he was more than fine. "Don't be worrying about me. Let's just hurry you on back to camp."

"I hope you know the way because, as you can tell, I sure don't."

"Yep. I'll get us back." He took hold of her arm and assisted her to her feet. She was still shaking, and he didn't release his grip for fear she'd collapse.

Holding the ball of wet garments she'd shed, she tried to steady herself but wobbled, her legs buckling beneath her.

Without wasting another moment, he swept her up into his arms, which was easy because she weighed less than a baby bird just out of its nest. She released a startled exclamation but then easily settled against him.

"I'm sorry for wandering off and causing you so much trouble." With lips quivering and strands of hair plastered to her cheeks, she searched his face as though seeking forgiveness there. "When I saw the horse running off, I thought I could chase it down and bring it back."

"Figured that's what you'd done."

"I just wanted to help since I knew how important leaving early was to you." Her long lashes framed innocent eyes, eyes that begged him to understand. "Please don't be mad."

"I ain't mad."

"Are you sure? Not even a little?"

"Nope. Not even a little." The relief at finding her left little room for any other emotion.

"Thank you, Flynn—"

"But you gotta promise from here on out, you won't go off by yourself, not for any reason."

"I promise. In fact, I solemnly promise I won't step an inch outside of camp unless I'm with someone else."

Flynn had a notion to make her promise she wouldn't go anywhere without *him*, but he reckoned that was taking his job a mite too far.

She smiled up at him sweetly. "I'll promise you, if you'll promise me one thing."

A warning went off inside him.

"All I want you to do is promise you won't tell Grandfather how cold and wet and lost I was. I don't want to unnecessarily worry him."

He bit back his of exasperation. What was it with the two of them needing to hide things from each other?

"The truth is—" she bit her bottom lip—"if he knows how far I wandered off, this time he really will send me back East."

Was this the kind of foolish wandering Linnea had already done on the trip, leaving Dr. Howell desperate enough to hire a stranger to look after her?

"I realize I'm putting you in an awkward situation. But please, please let me talk to him and explain what happened." Her lashes fell and fanned out against her pale cheeks before she lifted them again.

How could he say no to her when she batted her eyes like

that? How could any man in his right mind deny her whatever she wanted? Apparently her grandfather couldn't any
more than the rest of them.

He blew out a breath. "Alright."

Her smile widened. "Thank you."

He shook his head and approached the horse. "Hang on,
now. We'll ride together so we don't waste any more time."

Once she was up in the saddle, he hesitated to climb up
behind her. When he'd agreed to guard her, he never bar-
gained on having to guard his heart.

Weary and cold, Linnea let herself lean in to Flynn as
they rode. More than anything, she was weak with relief.
She'd been wet and miserable, trying not to worry too much,
knowing she'd have to wait for the mist to lift before she'd
be able to take stock of her surroundings and attempt to find
her way back to camp.

She'd never expected to hear Flynn's voice calling to her.
But from the moment she had, she'd all but fallen in love
with him. Well, not truly. But she admired him more now
than ever, which only made his dislike of her all the harder
to withstand.

For a man who didn't like her, Flynn had been more than
kind and considerate. Not only had he braved the cold and
fog to come after her, but he shed his dry garments to warm
her, treated her with respect though she'd been unclothed,
and placed her upon his steed as if she were a porcelain
teacup.

His chest and arms surrounded her and radiated into her
body, lending her even more warmth. "Flynn?"

"Hmmm?"

"I hope you won't be mad at me for yesterday either—when I wasn't grieving for my husband properly."

He stiffened in the saddle behind her.

"I really do want to honor my husband's memory as best I can."

He was silent, and the thudding of the horse's hooves against the wet earth echoed eerily in the fog, as if they were the only two on the entire prairie. With only a lantern to guide them, she wasn't sure how he could find his way, but somehow he seemed to know where he was going.

"Listen." The low timber of his voice rumbled in her ear, and his breath tickled her cheek. "I'm the one needing to apologize. What I said wasn't necessary, wasn't even nice."

Her retort fell away, replaced by wonder that this man had humbled himself enough to make amends. Not that he'd needed to. Nevertheless, she'd take it and hold on to it as an offering of friendship.

"I behaved like a donkey. And I'm sorry."

With the solid pressure of his chest against her back and his arms boxing her in, she pictured his long fingers on her buttons, skimming down her bodice. Her breathing quickened, just as it had before.

She sat forward slightly, needing some distance from the powerful tug that somehow existed with Flynn. "You didn't behave like a donkey. I need to be more careful in how I conduct myself, and I shall surely try as hard as I can to remain discreet and chaste in all my interactions."

They had a long journey ahead with possibly weeks, if not months, together. She had to start today and take great care that she didn't lead this man on in any way. "Besides, I've been told by friends I'm too bold, though I don't mean to be. I suppose I have naturally absorbed some of my mother's views that women shouldn't have to be so reticent."

"Don't matter how pretty a woman is—" His voice cracked, and he cleared his throat. "And it don't matter how much a fella might have a hankering for her. Fact is, a man's got a responsibility to control himself. Plain and simple."

Hankering? "So does that mean you have a hankering for me, Flynn McQuaid?" She shouldn't tease him. Hadn't she just chastised herself to be careful? Even so, she couldn't let his comment pass by.

He shifted in the saddle. "Nope. I'm not planning on hankering for a woman now or ever."

Something in his tone told her he was serious. Even so, she kept the mood light. "Very well. Since you have no plans on *hankering* for me, then perhaps we can settle on friendship. Surely you cannot find fault in developing a friendship, can you?"

He was silent and stiff for a dozen paces before he gave a curt nod. "Suppose friendship won't hurt."

"Not with me, it won't."

When he didn't respond, she had the feeling he didn't quite believe her. She'd just have to show him he had nothing to worry about and that she could be a good friend—maybe even the best he'd ever had.

CHAPTER

6

"Flynn told me he has no interest in developing a relationship with a woman." Linnea sat back on her heels along the bank of Cottonwood Creek where she and Ivy were attempting to do laundry. Her attention swung to Flynn on the edge of their campsite, where he stood beside one of the horses, replacing a worn shoe. His shirt stretched tight as he worked on the horseshoe, outlining his broad back and shoulders.

"Does that mean he's still pining away for the woman he left behind?" Linnea asked. "Maybe still in love with her?"

Ivy swirled a blouse in the swift-moving water. "Naw. He's got his sights set on you now."

"We're just friends, Ivy." Linnea attempted to douse the pleasure Ivy's declaration brought. Over the past week of traveling with the McQuaids, Linnea had done her best to treat Flynn like a friend just as she said she would.

She made a point of walking alongside him for a few miles of traveling each day when he gave his horse a break from riding. While she'd gotten to know him a little bit, he wasn't overly talkative, and she gleaned most of her information about Flynn and the McQuaid family from Ivy.

Like now, as they laundered their clothing while waiting for Clay's call for supper, Ivy had started talking about Flynn's former love interest again, telling Linnea about the time Helen had come over to do Flynn's laundry.

"Helen sure did have her heart set on having Flynn." Ivy swatted at a pesky biting fly. At times the insects were incessant in their biting, causing all sorts of misery for everyone. "I reckon from the moment Helen was born, she decided she'd marry Flynn."

Linnea finished wringing the water from her chemise and draped it over the horsetail, where it would hopefully dry by morning when they broke camp. Several other women from another caravan were in the process of doing the same chore a short distance away.

The river crossing a couple hours ago had been dangerous and difficult, especially getting all the cattle across. With the day nearly spent, Flynn made the decision to make camp for the evening. Dylan and Ivy and Jericho had caught fish for their supper, and now the scent of the frying fish wafted toward them, making Linnea's stomach grumble.

She tried to ignore the hunger pangs that had been gaining in intensity with each passing day—from all the physical activity and fresh air, no doubt. "If Helen was so intent on marrying him, then why didn't they go through with it?"

"He was aiming to propose, leastways I heard him talking to Ma about it once. But then after Ma died, I reckon he was too torn up."

"That would make sense, although I'm not sure why that would cause him to cancel his nuptials altogether."

"Helen was still trying mighty hard to get him to marry her right up until the day we left."

"Maybe he'll invite her west once he's settled."

Ivy grinned. "Not if he marries you first."

"You're silly." Linnea ducked her head to avoid the inevitable pull to stare at Flynn and admire the fine specimen of manhood he made.

"No matter what he says, he ain't gonna be able to hold off gettin' married for too long, not after the way I saw him smooching Helen in the haymow last summer."

A strange curiosity piqued Linnea. What would it be like to kiss Flynn?

As quickly as the question came, shame followed just as rapidly. How could she even think about such a thing? It was entirely disloyal to Asa.

She plunged a pair of socks into the water and scrubbed them with a bar of Castile soap, the acrid scent of lye rising into the air and making her nostrils itch.

"He was kissing Helen like there was no tomorrow." Ivy giggled.

With Flynn's adamant statement about not being interested in having a woman, Linnea was surprised he'd been so involved with Helen. Had she broken his heart?

"He was mortified I saw him." Ivy twisted the wet garment in the water, playing with it more than cleaning it. "Later, when he came to talk to me, I never saw a face as red as his. Told me he'd behaved badly and didn't want me carrying on with any boys the way he'd been carrying on with Helen."

"I agree with Flynn. *Carrying on*, as you say, truly is meant for the bounds of marriage." As soon as the words were out, somehow they sounded glib, even insignificant, for explaining the importance of honoring the marriage bed.

Ivy shrugged, shifting her attention to the herd resting in the shade of the cottonwoods, where Dylan and Jericho were picking burs off the cattle that had wandered into the spiny cocklebur, *Xanthium spinosum*, after the crossing.

At sixteen, Dylan was turning into a fine-looking young man with Flynn's light brown hair and greenish blue eyes. His long, spindly legs and ankles poked out from frayed hems on his trousers. Like Ivy, he often went barefoot—likely to avoid his boots that were worn away at his big toes.

Linnea had learned Jericho was also sixteen and was traveling with Nash, his older brother, to the gold mines of Colorado. The brothers had signed on to help drive the cattle in exchange for transport west.

As far as Linnea could tell, Nash worked hard and got along well enough with Flynn. With the way Nash kept his eye on Jericho, Linnea sensed he was as much a father to Jericho as Flynn was to his siblings.

Whatever the case, Jericho seemed to have an easy friendship with Dylan and Ivy. He was mature and responsible and every bit as handsome as Dylan. Once in a while, Linnea noticed Ivy blushing around the hired cowhand, and sensed the girl was starting to grow up.

She reached up and gently stroked Ivy's tangled hair. "If you'd like, I can teach you how to style your hair."

Ivy tore her attention away from Jericho.

"You have such thick, dark hair. It could use some taming." Not that she wanted Ivy to start attracting the attention of Jericho or any other man. No doubt, she would be able to do that all on her own in a few years. She had beautiful features and would turn into a very pretty woman.

Even so, Ivy could use a little guidance. Especially since it hadn't taken Linnea long to realize the girl was a tomboy through and through. She supposed living in a household of four brothers was bound to influence a girl into acting more like a man.

Ivy raised dripping fingers to her hair and tugged on a strand. "Sometimes I wish I could just cut it all off and wear it short. But then other times . . ." She glanced again at Jericho, then sighed.

"I don't mind showing you a trick or two I've learned over the years at keeping my hair from being too bothersome."

Ivy hesitated. "I've seen the way the men look at you, like you're some kind of goddess."

Linnea chuckled and finished scrubbing her socks. "Our goal in taking care of our hair and bodies isn't so we can impress men. We do it because we want to fulfill the potential God gave us."

"I could never be like you."

"And you don't have to be. You just have to be the truest form of you."

Although Linnea had sometimes lamented her mother's nontraditional parenting style, she was grateful her mother had always encouraged her to be comfortable and confident in who she was. At least she'd had a mother, unlike Ivy, who had no one she could turn to for womanly advice or conversation.

Ivy sat up on her knees. "Okay."

"Okay?"

"You can help me with my hair."

Linnea squeezed Ivy's arm. "I promise you'll like it."

One of Ivy's eyebrows quirked up.

Linnea stood and wiped her hands on her skirt. "I'll go get my lavender soap, and we'll start by washing it."

"Wash it? Do we have to?"

"Yes." Linnea started back toward the camp through the long, rough horsetail, her skirt swishing against the dark green hollow stems. The tiny ridges along the length contained rough silica that gave the plant its name and rasped almost musically.

As she broke through the swampy stems and started toward their wagons, shouts and the galloping of horses startled her. She stepped back in time to watch a white-tailed deer leap from out of nowhere and bound past her.

The creature was large with antlers, giving it a magnificent, ageless quality. It moved with such speed and grace simultaneously that she could only stare at it in wonder, even as her grandfather and the other scientists charged past her on their mounts, chasing the deer with unfettered excitement, their revolvers smoking.

Flynn moved away from the horse he was attending and started after Grandfather and the others, scowling and waving his arms at them to stop. One of the men shot again, but thankfully, the deer was too far ahead and out of range of the bullet.

Yes, they would benefit from having the meat, but she was too softhearted when it came to killing animals. She hated to see any of God's creatures come to harm, and she held her breath, hoping the beautiful deer would be safe this time.

At a heavy rumble in the ground behind her, along with the bleating and snorting of cattle, she glanced over her shoulder. The herd was on the move and picking up speed. Had Grandfather and the other men spooked the cattle with their shouting and shooting?

Her gaze shifted to the swath of land that lay in the path of the herd, a path that led directly toward the wooden plant presses she'd left out, along with the crate containing the plants they'd catalogued so far. She'd placed them in a sunny spot, wanting to make sure everything was dry. They couldn't risk damp specimens growing mold and ruining their presses as well as contaminating other important research.

Her heart began to thud an urgent beat. After the past few weeks of meticulous work, she couldn't let the cattle trample everything. The Smithsonian was counting on them to include a chapter in the field guide regarding the flora of the western prairie. This research was vital to the compilation of the book.

Did she have time to try to save at least the crate?

With a glance, she measured the distance of the oncoming herd. She might have a chance.

Darting forward, she picked up her skirt and raced toward the crate, keeping one eye on the steers and one on her destination. She could do it. She had to.

"No, Linnea!" Flynn's shout rose above her thudding heart. But she ignored him and forced herself to go faster. She nearly fell to her knees as she reached the research. Heaving for breath, she grabbed the open container. Did she have enough time to rescue anything else?

The ground rumbled. The cattle were picking up speed and racing her way. A new sense of urgency rammed through her. She'd heard of stampedes, but she'd never seen one. And now not only was she seeing one, she was about to experience one much too personally.

Sucking in a breath, she charged back the way she'd come, needing to get clear of their pathway, but having only seconds to do so. At the same time she scrambled for her life, Flynn was running toward her and the cattle, his revolver outstretched.

His expression was hard, rigid with determination. He pointed his gun toward the lead steers and shot, the bang echoing above the thundering hooves. One bullet whizzed over the closest steers and another hit the ground near their hooves. The blasts were apparently enough to frighten the lead cattle, turning the direction of the stampede, so that as Linnea reached Flynn, only their scent barreled into her and nothing else.

Flynn backed into her, holding his arms out and shielding her body with his. Already Dylan, Jericho, and Nash had mounted their horses and were chasing after the cattle and forcing them to circle back around, hopefully keeping them from scattering too far.

As soon as the last of the steers bolted past, Flynn spun and grasped both her upper arms. His expression radiated concern. "You alright?"

She nodded, too shaken to make her voice work.

He took her in, his grip biting. "You sure?"

She swallowed hard, pushing down the swell of her emotion. "You go. You need to help stop the cattle from getting away."

He hesitated, as though afraid to leave her alone.

"I'll be fine. Save the cattle."

With a curt nod, he hurried off toward his horse, his limping gait hardly slowing him. She could only watch him with a growing sense of frustration at herself. This was the third time Flynn had rescued her from possible death. What if she'd been wrong to finagle her way into joining the expedition? Were Grandfather's concerns justified?

The doubts stayed with her all through dinner and afterward. As the fire crackled and sent sparks into the darkness, the chatter around camp was more subdued. Even though the stampede had been squelched and the cattle turned and rounded up, Grandfather and the other scientists were chastened by their part in what could have been a disaster, especially when they'd learned how close Linnea had come to being trampled.

They lost a number of recently collected specimens, and the presses were damaged. Grandfather and Dr. Greely insisted that they would replace the lost research, and Dr. Johnson claimed he'd fix the presses, while Dr. Parker offered to build new ones if necessary. Everyone reassured her. Except Flynn, who didn't speak to her once.

As the evening wore on, her chest tightened until she couldn't think about anything except loosening it. She knew only one thing would. As she stood, Dr. Greely, her grandfather, and the others rose from their camp chairs, watching her expectantly.

She would have preferred sneaking off quietly, but they were only being gentlemen, and she couldn't fault them for maintaining good manners even in the untamed prairie.

"I think I shall turn in early tonight."

Grandfather's brows had maintained a perpetual crease all evening. "You're certain you are unharmed, young lady?"

"Yes, Grandfather." She gave him what had to have been

at least the hundredth reassuring smile of the evening. "I'm perfectly unharmed." Except perhaps her pride.

With a chorus of good-nights, the men sat back down. She made her way to the wagon, passing Ivy and Dylan playing their usual game of cards. Instead of climbing into the wagon bed, she circled around behind it until she reached Flynn. He was bent over the tongue tightening a bolt.

With his back facing her, she wasn't exactly sure how to get his attention without frightening him.

He paused, cast a slight glance in her direction, and then resumed his efforts.

She should have known he'd hear or see her approach—or perhaps both. "Flynn?"

His hands grew motionless.

"I'm appalled I put you in another situation where you had to save me."

He shifted, and his eyes were blazing mad. "What you did out there was real reckless and plain stupid."

"I was trying to save all our research—"

"Don't matter. You never, ever get in front of a stampeding herd of cattle like that again. D'ya hear me?"

"Yes."

"Not for any reason."

"I won't."

He turned back around, muttering angrily.

"I apologize—"

"I don't want your blasted apology, Linnea." He pivoted so he was now facing her fully. He opened his mouth as if he wanted to yell at her for a little while longer. But as he took in her face—and hopefully her contrition—he clamped his lips closed.

"I haven't known you long, Flynn, but already I can see what a brave man you are for taking on so much responsibility, not just with your family, but now with us too."

His beautiful, expressive green-blue eyes met hers. The spark of anger was gone, but the turmoil remained.

"No matter how good you are at taking care of everyone, you're not God. And you can't blame yourself when bad things happen to people."

"Sometimes you can't keep from blaming yourself"—his voice was low—"especially when you know you could have been there to do more."

Linnea had the feeling they weren't discussing what happened earlier in the day anymore. She stood quietly waiting for him to elaborate, but he shifted, focused on the bolt, and twisted it again, the muscles in his arms rippling with the movement.

She was half tempted to grab his hand and draw his attention back to her. But what good would that do? Except to stir up something between them that didn't need stirring.

"Good night, Flynn."

"'Night."

As much as she wanted to stay, she forced herself to walk away.

Flynn stood in the shadows and watched Dylan creep out from underneath a covered wagon across the caravan circle. With everyone fast asleep except for those on night guard, the low light of several campfires hardly touched on the moving figure. But Flynn had seen his brother disappear under the wagon with one of the young women he'd been flirting with

JODY HEDLUND

all day. Flynn had debated going over and yanking Dylan out, but he felt terrible making a scene with his brother when he was far from perfect himself.

Good thing Dylan was paying attention to the passing of time and knew when they needed to relieve Jericho and Nash.

As the kid came slinking back to their campsite, Flynn stepped away from their wagon. Dylan startled. "Holy tarnation, Flynn. You scared me."

"You ready to head out?"

Dylan began stuffing his shirt into his trousers. "Yep. Ready as ever."

"You didn't get any shut-eye."

"Got a little."

Flynn cocked a brow.

Dylan grinned. "What?"

"You need to watch yourself with the young ladies." Flynn shoved his hands into his pockets. He was past due in having a man-to-man talk with his brother about the consequences that could come of doing things with the ladies he shouldn't be.

"Don't get your feathers in a ruffle." Dylan combed a hand through his mussed hair before he situated his hat back in place. "I'm careful."

"Careful isn't good enough. There's a reason the Good Book instructs us to abstain from—" Flynn paused and searched for a tame way to spell out his concern. "You don't wanna end up having a baby. Not at your age."

"Shucks, Flynn. I didn't sleep with the gal. We just had a little fun kissing is all."

"Reckon kissing is something special that oughta be saved for a special woman."

Dylan's grin kicked up higher. "She was mighty special."

"You know what I mean."

Dylan shrugged.

"Kissing might seem innocent enough, but once you get started down that rushing river, it ain't easy to stop against the flow."

"I take it you're speaking from personal experience?"

Flynn's mind flashed to the times kissing with Helen and getting carried away—something he wasn't proud of. "Yep. Reckon so."

Dylan fastened a shirt button he'd missed earlier. "Reckon if you had to learn your lessons from personal experience, then maybe I will too."

"I didn't have anyone pointing me to a right, wise path. You're lucky I'm here to warn you and keep you from making mistakes."

"Yep. Real lucky." Dylan's voice was laced with sarcasm.

Flynn felt more like an old man every day as he tried to be both pa and ma to his siblings. Linnea's words from earlier in the evening clamored around his mind. *"No matter how good you are at taking care of everyone, you're not God. And you can't blame yourself when bad things happen to people."*

He'd been stewing on her almost getting trampled during the stampede and blaming himself for not watching out for her better. Why had he taken on the job from Dr. Howell? What had he been thinking? He didn't exactly have the best record for protecting people he cared about. He'd failed with Brody. And he'd failed with his ma. Miserably.

The day she died, her tortured screams had filtered out of the old farmhouse to the alfalfa field where he'd been haying.

All the while she labored, he drove himself to exhaustion in order to keep himself busy. After endless hours, the midwife delivered another dead baby—a boy.

When the midwife finally allowed him into Ma's bedroom, he sat by her side, holding her limp hand. The sagging mattress seemed to swallow her up—at least what was left of the shell of the woman she'd become.

"Flynn?" She opened her eyes and sought him out through the darkness settling over a room that smelled of blood and death.

He squeezed her hand. "Right here, Ma."

"I'm sorry." Her words were laden with sorrow and regrets, no doubt a heavy burden she'd carried since marrying Rusty.

"You just get better, d'ya hear?" He tried to keep the sadness out of his own voice. She needed him to be the strong one.

She drew in a shaky breath, then peered up at him intensely. "Take care of the kids."

"I will. I always do."

"I know. You're a good son." Her lashes fell. Her lips closed. And then she was gone.

All he'd been able to think about was how he should have tried harder to convince her to stay while he still could. And now he didn't want to fail with anyone else—not with Ivy, Dylan, or even Linnea. He didn't know how he'd be able to live with himself if he failed again.

Tugging his coat around him more securely, he jerked his head toward the area where the cattle were resting. "Let's go."

Dylan didn't budge. "Maybe Nash is right. Maybe you need a woman to help you loosen up."

Half a dozen feet from the wagon, Flynn halted, his back stiffening at the insult.

"I see the way you've been lookin' at Linnea. Reckon getting under a wagon with her might do you some good."

He had half a mind to turn around and wallop Dylan. There was so much wrong with what the kid said, especially the part about using a woman instead of cherishing her. But Flynn took a deep breath and forced himself to remain calm. "Didn't you listen to a thing I just said?"

"Nope." Dylan began to softly whistle a melody and strode past him without a glance back.

As Flynn stared after Dylan, his gut churned. Somehow he had to do better, try to get his brother to see reason, to keep the kid from straying further. He wasn't sure how. But no matter what Linnea had said about him playing God, he wasn't gonna give up on his family. After all, God had put him in charge, and he aimed to make sure he didn't fall short in doing the job he'd been given.

CHAPTER

7

"The heifer's birthin'!"

Dylan's call jerked at Flynn's attention, but he couldn't pull it away from Linnea and Dr. Greely strolling among the trees that grew along the banks of the Pawnee Fork. Both carried long tin containers that hung by straps from their shoulders as well as a pouch they used in their plant collecting.

Linnea had told him the name of her tin container—a vasculum. And she'd opened it up to demonstrate how it allowed her to carry around plants without crushing them. She'd also given him an inventory of what was inside the pouch, showing him all the items she used in her botany research, including clippers, small shovels, and notebooks, among other items.

Over the past couple of weeks since the stampede, his gruff rebuke hadn't scared her away because she was as friendly as if nothing had happened. She made a point of walking with him every day, chattering on about the plants she was collecting, about the importance of the book her grandfather was compiling, and about the process they went through to dry, draw, and diagram each item.

At first, he hadn't been especially eager for her company, but lately he'd found himself anticipating the time with her and viewing the world around him through her eyes, noticing more details, seeing the beauty, and appreciating the littlest things in nature in a way he never had before. She was easy to talk to, sharing stories of her family back in New York, especially about her mother's and sister's suffragist beliefs. The more he learned about her family, the more he began to understand her.

One thing he'd come to realize was that she wasn't singling him out but was instead just plain friendly. She visited with lots of other travelers, including Dr. Greely. And for a reason Flynn didn't want to analyze, the image of the two of them together was starting to burn like a brand in his hide.

He straightened from the wagon wheel he was repairing and tried to drag his attention from the couple. But his sights stayed planted right on her as Dr. Greely placed a hand upon the small of her back.

"Flynn!" Dylan's call came louder. "The heifer's ready."

The news must have spanned the distance of their camp and reached Linnea because she spun around and sought out Dylan, her body suddenly rigid. She said something to Dr. Greely, then handed him her supplies. As he took the items, his features creased with disappointment, but Linnea had already picked up her skirts and started to run toward them, revealing her unladylike bloomers underneath.

"Is it time?" She let her bonnet blow off her head, and

the afternoon sunshine poured over her hair, turning it a flaming red.

"Yep! She separated out from the herd." Dylan grinned at Linnea, watching her approach with undisguised adoration. "And now she's on the ground."

Flynn reached for the rag draped across the wheel and started to wipe his hands of the dust and grease that coated them. Although cow birthing didn't bother him the same way a human birthing did, he still didn't like them. Not anymore. Especially not today, not this one, not after what he had to do once the calf was born.

His gut twisted just thinking about it. But he had to go through with it, or he'd risk the entire herd. Already they'd resorted to a near crawl because the heifer's swelling abdomen had slowed her down. In the four weeks since they'd left Council Grove, they only managed to make it to Pawnee Fork at Fort Larned.

He couldn't completely blame the pregnant heifer for the delay. While they'd had smooth traveling and decent weather since Cottonwood Creek, a thunderstorm at Plum Buttes had caused the herd to stampede again, and they'd wasted the next day rounding up stray cattle. At least Linnea hadn't been in the way that time. In fact, she'd happily spent the delay clipping samples and drawing illustrations from the plum bushes after which the site was named.

They'd had another delay when they reached Walnut Creek Crossing and faced the river, which had flooded from the thunderstorm. They had to camp with other wagon trains along the bank, waiting for the water level to subside. By the third day, Flynn had been as anxious as the rest when they'd finally pushed across. Even then, a wagon in another group had capsized, and a woman with her two children had drowned. It'd only served to remind him of how close Linnea had come to meeting the same fate back in the Neosho River.

When they'd reached Fort Larned a few days after Walnut Creek, the cracked rim in one of the wheels had forced them to hold over. Thankfully, the military outpost had a blacksmith who'd been able to solder the piece. And though Flynn wasn't a wheelwright, he had enough know-how to make adjustments and salvage the wheel.

But it had cost them another day of travel. Always at the back of his mind was the pressure to get the cattle to Wyatt on time and in good condition. Wyatt had let him down too many times to count, and Flynn had to prove he was different from his brother—more reliable and responsible.

Dr. Howell and his party of scientists hadn't complained once of the slow pace or the delays. In fact, like Linnea, they seemed to relish the extra time to do more research.

"Come on and hurry." Dylan started in the direction of the herd grazing to the north of the Santa Fe Trail. It was already mid-June, and they were having to seek out grassland whenever they stopped because of the overgrazing from other livestock traveling the trail ahead of them. He'd heard that farther along, water could become as scarce as grass, and he only prayed that didn't happen.

Flynn took his time rubbing the rag at the grease on his hands, telling himself he wasn't waiting for Linnea. But when she reached the wagon, he fell into step next to her. "I take it Dr. Greely didn't want to watch a birthing?"

"Oh." Her eager stride faltered. "I didn't think to ask him. Perhaps I should?"

"Reckon he can make up his own mind."

"You're right." She picked up her pace. "And truthfully, I'd like a break from him. But please don't tell him I said so."

Flynn had half a notion to spin around and shout over to Dr. Greely to stop pestering Linnea every spare minute of every livelong day. Although Flynn was in charge of her safety—and had done his best to keep her from any more dangerous incidents—he had no right to interfere with Dr. Greely's efforts to win Linnea's affection.

In fact, he oughta be encouraging the union. Then, when they arrived at the Front Range and split ways, Dr. Greely could marry Linnea and take over her supervision. The almighty truth was that the woman needed someone to watch over her.

Ever since she'd nearly been trampled by the herd, he never felt completely secure unless she was in his line of vision and close enough for him to run to her rescue. Even at night, whether he was taking his turn doing guard duty or catching a few winks under the wagon, he kept half an eye and ear cocked on the back of her wagon. She was every bit as scattered as Dr. Howell had said, and then some.

He was earning his two hundred dollars from Dr. Howell, that was for sure.

"I imagine you're quite the expert on birthing cows," she said.

"Yep. Done my fair share."

"From all the cows you raised on your farm?" Linnea started an easy conversation with him as always, keeping her tone friendly, even sisterly, like she did with Dylan. She'd done her best, just as she'd said, to be a friend and nothing more.

And he'd done his best to keep his thoughts from wandering

where they shouldn't. He wasn't gonna lie. The effort wasn't easy. Especially after watching her so much, he couldn't keep from liking what he saw.

She smiled and waved at people from several other wagons as they passed by. He didn't know how she did it, but she was always making friends wherever she went and with whomever she met.

She was also drawing the attention of the men wherever they went. Like yesterday when they'd gone inside the fort, every single man on God's green earth had stopped what they were doing to gawk at her, almost as if they hadn't ever seen a woman before.

Even now as she hurried alongside him, heads turned and appreciative gazes followed her. "Will you be able to help the cow if she has any birthing problems?"

"I'll do just fine. No need to worry." He had half a mind to tell her to put her bonnet back up so her pretty face wasn't as visible. But doing that would clue her in on the fact he was thinking about how she looked, and he didn't want to let on how hard it was for him to ignore his attraction to her.

As she turned her soft brown eyes upon him, his insides warmed like johnnycakes in a skillet. With all the sunshine, he'd expected a redhead like her to burn and fill up with freckles. But her face had turned a smooth honey tone.

"I'm sure you were a good farmer, Flynn. I'm just sorry again you couldn't keep your family's farm and that Rusty got away with stealing it from you."

Over the course of their conversations, she'd plied him with countless questions, drawing him to talk about more than he had with anyone else. Of course, Ivy was a fount of endless information too, probably telling Linnea every last detail of everything he'd ever done in his entire life.

Ahead, Dylan and Ivy were already kneeling next to the heifer, stroking it. Even if Ivy was free with her tongue, he couldn't deny Linnea's presence had been a godsend. Just seeing the neatly formed braids falling across the girl's shoulders was a case in point. Somehow Linnea had convinced Ivy to wash and brush her hair, all without a scolding— something he hadn't been able to do in months.

"Maybe you'll be able to get your own farm once you reach Colorado." She reached up and brushed at the dried grass on his shirt, likely sticking there when he'd crawled under the wagon to make adjustments to the hound braces.

"Maybe." The touch of her fingers against his chest, though innocent, was something a wife would do to her husband, and it only sent heat spiraling low inside.

She dropped her hand from him. Her expression filled with an innocence that told him she had no idea of the effect she had on him or anyone else. "I'd certainly like to travel up to South Park and discover what kind of plant life exists there. From what I've heard, it's quite arid, so I would guess growing the usual corn, wheat, oats, rye, and barley would pose some difficulties. Although, I wouldn't know for sure unless I tested the chemical composition of the soil."

He knew a little bit about soil and crop rotation from his years of overseeing the major cash crops their farm had produced. And he'd studied up a bit on farming in Colorado, although it hadn't yet been done up in the mountain valleys. "Don't forget, you've got to take into account the higher elevation and its effects on the growing season."

She halted so abruptly that she stumbled and would have

fallen if he hadn't reacted rapidly and taken hold of her arm. She pressed a hand to her forehead and bit at her bottom lip, drawing his attention there. Were those lips as soft and full as they looked?

"You're absolutely right, Flynn."

Her declaration startled him, and for a second he scrambled to remember what they were talking about.

"Of course we'll need to take the elevation into consideration before we decide which crops to plant. I don't know why I didn't think about that myself."

He gave himself a mental shake. If he didn't know better, he'd almost believe she was already aiming to head on up into South Park instead of Denver.

As he reached the heifer, he assessed her in one glance. From the way she was positioned and breathing, the birthing, her first, would be soon. Thankfully, it wouldn't delay their leaving in the morning.

Dylan placed a flat palm against the heifer's abdomen. "Contractions are real strong now."

"Good." Flynn pressed his hand to the warm velvety underside. The Shorthorn herd had a couple dozen cattle that were mostly red with white marks. And this heifer was one of them, her white markings mainly on the forehead, legs, and belly. At two years old, she was sturdy and seemed to have maintained a good body weight over the past weeks of traveling.

He reckoned she'd make a fine mama cow—if he gave her the chance, which he couldn't.

It didn't take long for the front feet to emerge the way they should. Linnea exclaimed every time the feet went back in, even when he reassured her that was normal. Finally, the head appeared, and within an hour, the calf lay in the grass, a perfect Shorthorn specimen. Flynn had to give the heifer a hand in delivering the afterbirth, but she was soon up and licking the calf clean.

He kept himself from feeling anything during the entire process, which was difficult with Linnea looking on the birthing of a calf for the first time with such awe and amazement. But even when tears streaked her cheeks as she watched the newborn resting in the grass, he steeled himself.

These animals weren't pets. They were intended for human consumption. That's all. In the end, they'd be slaughtered and turned into beef. At this point, he had to consider profit above everything else, including the life of the calf.

He stood and removed his revolver from the holster at his belt and popped open the cylinder. He checked the chambers, noting two of the six were empty of bullets. He wouldn't need more than one. Hopefully.

As he pressed the cylinder back into place, the only sound was the wind rustling the long grass. His gaze dropped to find three pairs of eyes staring up at him. Dylan sat back on his haunches, his expression growing somber. Ivy's eyes rounded, but she didn't say anything, likely guessing with Dylan what Flynn intended to do and accepting it as the way of things.

Linnea, on the other hand, sniffled and brushed at the dampness on her cheeks, her gaze registering only confusion at the sight of his revolver.

"Dylan, you go on now and take Linnea back to camp."

Thankfully, for once Dylan didn't argue with him or make light of the situation. Instead he stood and reached out a hand to Linnea.

She took his offer of help and rose. "I'd like to stay with the calf for a while longer, if that's okay with you. The sweet creature is so beautiful, I can't tear myself away just yet."

Ivy stood now too, her bare feet black with the dust and dirt of the trail.

"I sure would like to see the calf nurse for the first time," Linnea said. "Won't he do it soon?"

Flynn didn't answer. Didn't know how.

Ivy just swallowed and ducked her head. Dylan toed a clump of grass but met Linnea's gaze. "Best for the calf and mama not to get attached." He gave a nod toward the revolver.

Linnea glanced at the gun again, went still, then her gaze shot up to Flynn's, her face going as pale as freshly churned butter. "You're not intending to kill the calf, are you?"

Again, he remained silent, hoping she could read his answer without having to spell it out and make things harder.

"No." Her eyes welled with tears.

Ivy sidled next to Linnea.

Linnea blinked rapidly. "Why? I don't understand. The calf is perfectly healthy from what I see."

"It won't survive the drive." Dylan's tone gentled.

"Our pace has been leisurely enough. In fact, we'll slow down even more for a while. I'm sure Grandfather won't mind in the least."

Dylan exchanged a glance with Flynn, one that said he had reached the limits of his ability to reason with Linnea. It was Flynn's turn. Flynn cleared his throat. "Listen, ain't none of us want this. But we can't jeopardize the whole herd on account of the calf."

"No," Linnea said again louder, pulling away from Ivy. "You cannot murder the calf."

Flynn pressed his lips together, wishing he knew what to say to calm her. It had obviously been a mistake bringing her out to watch the birthing and see the calf.

She crossed toward him, each step firm and her eyes no longer holding tears but fire. "Surely we can find another option." She halted a foot away from him.

"Nope. Don't have a choice."

"We always have a choice. And you can make the decision to save this calf instead of being so callous and uncaring."

He braced his feet apart.

As though sensing his resolve—or perhaps seeing it in his expression—she released a cry of frustration, rushed at him, and slapped her palms against his chest. "I won't let you."

He shoved his revolver into his belt and captured both her arms. Even as she twisted against his hold, a sob escaped, first one, then another, until she was openly crying. "You can't kill it. Please, Flynn. Please."

Ivy and Dylan watched the unfolding scene with widening gazes.

He did the only thing he could think to do. He wrapped Linnea in his arms and tugged her against his body. As he pressed her tightly, he wasn't sure what he expected—maybe for more struggling. He wasn't prepared when she slipped her arms around his waist, sagged against him, and buried her face into his chest.

He motioned with a nod for Ivy and Dylan to head on off. He should have sent them away when Linnea first started having the breakdown. She deserved privacy. And he aimed to give it to her while she pulled herself together.

The two scurried off, casting anxious glances at him over their shoulders.

He understood their panic. He wasn't used to hysterical women either. But he guessed the killing of animals came more naturally to him and Ivy and Dylan since they'd grown up on a farm, and the slaughtering of chickens, pigs, and cows was just a way of life, something that had to be done every now and again.

For a moment, he held Linnea stiffly, still not exactly sure what to do. Her body shook with her weeping, and her tears dampened his shirt. Her arms were wrapped about him as tightly as if she were drowning in the Neosho River. And as he shifted, she clung to him even harder.

He blew out a tense breath and tried to loosen the tautness in his muscles. She just needed a little comforting was all. He'd gotten to know her well enough to understand that this outburst wasn't normal. She was always cheerful and positive, rarely complained about anything. She'd been shaken up pretty badly to react so emotionally.

Was holding her like this enough? Or did he need to do more?

He lifted one of his hands from where he'd crossed them over her back. Hesitantly, he held it near her head. Her usual coif was elegant, but after going without her bonnet, the strands were loose and flyaway. Before he talked himself out of it, he brushed her hair.

It was as silky as he'd imagined. And warmth began to stir his blood.

His fingers stalled. Thunderation. This wasn't about him. He shouldn't be thinking about the pleasure he felt in touching her hair. This was about her and trying to soothe her.

Pressing his lips together to keep from cursing at himself for his selfishness, he caressed her hair again, this time gently sweeping back the loose strands and smoothing them down.

After several more strokes, her sobs began to soften. Were his efforts working? Maybe he could do even more? He let his thumb graze her ear. At the contact, she quieted. He skimmed the contours again, letting his fingers glide against her cheek. He wiped at the tears before combing upward into her hair.

Her body stilled against his.

Was he overstepping himself? Should he pull away now that she'd stopped crying?

Even as he hesitated, she expelled a deep, shuddering breath and settled more securely against him, as though she had no intention of going anywhere.

If his simple touch was helping to calm her, then a few more moments wouldn't hurt. He stroked her hair again. Then curiosity drove his fingers to the soft curls at the back of her neck, the shorter strands that didn't pull up into the coif.

As he gently fingered the hair, his other hand rose from the base of her back to between her shoulder blades. He made a path downward and then back up.

She released another breath, and her arms around him loosened. He expected her to pull away and was unprepared when she pressed her face more fully against his chest.

As her fingers unfurled and splayed against his lower back, something unfurled inside him. Something hot and dangerous.

He clenched his jaw and forced back the gut reaction to hold her just because he wanted to. He had to keep this hug about her comfort and not his pleasure.

"I'm sorry about my outburst, Flynn," she murmured. "I don't know what came over me."

"It's alright. I should have made you stay away, knowing what I did about the outcome."

She shifted, giving him a view of her profile, flushed and pink from her crying but never more beautiful than at this moment. "What if I can find a way to save the calf? Someone to take him in? Will you let me attempt that before you—put him down?"

When she lifted her head and peered up at him with her eyes so full of tenderness, her long lashes wet, her cheeks still damp, he knew right then and there he'd carry that calf on his shoulders the rest of the way to Colorado for her if she but asked him.

"Please, Flynn?" Her hand at his back moved higher, making him all too conscious of her nearness and the fact that she was pressed up against him so he could feel every sweet inch of her.

"Alright."

"Alright? Alright, as in you'll let me see if I can find a home for him?"

"Yep."

Her pretty lips curled up into a smile. "Oh, thank you, Flynn."

He allowed himself to relax but couldn't make himself let go of her quite yet.

"And will you forgive me for all the terrible things I said about you?" Her lashes dropped, making his stomach do a strange drop too. "You're not callous or uncaring."

"Maybe I am."

Her gaze opened wide, revealing the innocence and gentleness he'd come to expect there. "No, Flynn. I spoke in anger. I have no excuse for ever saying such things. Please believe me when I tell you, you're one of the kindest people I know."

He started to shake his head, denial on the tip of his tongue. Before he could say anything, she stood up on her toes and touched her lips to his.

The shock of the contact froze him in place, rendering him motionless. What was she doing? Her lips clung to his for a heavenly second before she pulled back. "I'm sorry. I don't know what I was thinking." Her arms slid away. "I was trying to say thank you again."

He didn't release her and instead drew her against him sharply, angling in and doing what he'd secretly dreamed about for the past weeks since meeting her. He meshed his lips to hers. The very touch reached down inside and unlocked everything he'd been working at holding back, and the emotion swelled behind the kiss, giving it a surge of passion that only stirred up his longing for more.

But even as desire pounded hard, the moment her arms slid back around him to welcome him, he broke the kiss as abruptly as he'd begun it. This time he released her entirely and spun away. What in holy horses was he doing?

CHAPTER

8

Had she really just initiated a kiss with Flynn McQuaid?

Linnea could admit she was sometimes impulsive. But really? How had she turned this interaction with him into kissing time?

He swiped off his hat and stuck his fingers in his hair. With his back facing her, his shoulders were tense, his body rigid.

Strange heat puddled at the bottom of her stomach, making her wish he was still holding her. He'd been so tender and his touch so gentle that her angst over his plans for the calf had subsided. The solid strength of his embrace, the steady pulse of his heartbeat, even the caress up and down her back, had soothed her.

She palmed her cheeks. Who was she jesting? His hold had done much more than soothe her. It had roused feelings inside her—feelings her intimacy with Asa had hinted at but had never awakened.

Desire.

Yes. In only seconds, Flynn's innocent, comforting touch

had made every nerve quaver with desire for him. She supposed she'd started off intending just a quick kiss to his cheek. But with his mouth so near, she'd aimed there instead. And, oh my. She lifted her fingertips to her lips, still feeling the pressure of his response.

At first, his reaction had been slow and surprised. But then it had changed. Rapidly. And the kiss he'd given her back had seared her lips, blazing a trail all the way down to her toes. She'd never had a kiss like that before, never knew kissing could be so pleasurable, never had any contact with Asa that had come even close.

She had the urge to approach Flynn from behind, lay her hand on his back, and tell him he could kiss her like that any day.

Her face flushed at the very thought of being so brazen. She'd done well over the past few weeks in honoring Asa's memory, and she couldn't stop now. Surely any good wife would continue to grieve for a while longer instead of throwing aside the memory of her husband for the first handsome man to come along.

"Flynn, I'm sorry—"

"I'm sorry too." His voice was hoarse. He didn't turn around and instead stared off into the distance. "I made a mistake and won't let it happen again."

A mistake? To kiss her? Of course he was right, but his words stung nonetheless.

"We got caught up in the moment. That's all. Didn't mean nothin' at all."

Again his words pricked her. Did she want the kiss to mean something? She shook her head. She'd vowed to be just friends, and she'd been doing fine . . . until she ended up in his arms.

How was it possible one simple embrace had fanned a shower of sparks, and now she wasn't sure she could stamp out all the embers? Yet, no matter how difficult, she had to do it. For both of them.

From the rigidness of his back and shoulders, she guessed he still must love Helen, at least to some degree. If he'd kissed Helen with such passion, no wonder he was missing her.

At the image of Flynn locked in another woman's embrace, a strange disconcertment settled over her. She certainly wasn't jealous. She simply needed to keep her focus on her research, where it belonged.

"This is my fault, Flynn. Let's put the—ah—the incident behind us. And we can pretend it never happened."

He remained unmoving for several moments longer. Then he eased out a breath and put his hat back on. When he turned, he focused on the calf. "I'll get the calf nursing, then head into the fort and see if anyone wants it."

"Do you think someone will?"

With an outstretched hand, he approached the cow. "With all the work involved in keeping it alive without a mama to nurse, it's gonna be a long shot."

"I'll go with you into the fort and help with the inquiries."

"Nope. I'll go alone." His clipped tone told her he wouldn't allow her to argue her way into the fort like she had yesterday.

Fort Larned had been moved and renamed several times over the past few years. But now it sat near the Pawnee Fork and was a hodgepodge of sod and adobe buildings, consisting of the soldiers' barracks, officers' quarters, bakery, meat house, blacksmith, saddler shop, and carpenter.

With so many people—mail carriers, teamsters loaded with freight, and other travelers like them—coming into the plains, the Indians had grown increasingly hostile because of the disruption to their way of life. The presence of the fort and soldiers seemed to be deterring confrontations.

Even so, after visiting the fort yesterday, she realized the soldiers who remained and hadn't gone East to fight were a rough cast. The order of the day consisted largely of drinking, gambling, cursing, and fighting. As she'd passed through the grounds, Flynn had nearly attacked one of the soldiers for speaking suggestively to her. To stave off the attention, he introduced her by her married name without mentioning she was a widow.

She understood why he didn't want her to return to the fort today. And yet, she'd promised to find the calf a new home. "As I'm the one wanting to save the calf, I ought to be the one doing the work to find it a new home."

"You ain't going in there again, Linnea." He didn't look at her, not even the slightest glance. "Put it out of your mind."

He guided the heifer to the calf. After some shifting of the calf's head, the newborn finally made contact with the udder. As it began to suckle, tears once again pricked Linnea's eyes at the beautiful miracle of birthing and motherhood.

An ache formed deep inside, one she didn't understand but that made her want to weep. Her emotions teetered on a shaky ledge the rest of the day. She guessed the exhaustion of the trip was finally catching up with her and making her weepier about the calf and its fate, especially when Flynn arrived back at their camp later and informed her no one within the fort was willing to take on the care of the helpless creature.

After a dinner of bean soup, bacon, hard bread, applesauce, and tea, she was helping Clay wash and put away their dishes when Ivy approached.

"I think I'm dying." Tears glistened in the girl's dark eyes.

Linnea paused in tucking a tin plate back into their supply chest. "Dying? How?"

Ivy swiped at her eyes and then glanced at Clay.

Linnea took hold of the girl's arm and guided her away from her grandfather's manservant, praying Ivy truly wasn't dying. Graves littered the trail, some fresh—like from recent drowning victims—and some from years past. They were constant reminders of the toll the untamed lands of the West exacted from those who dared the journey.

"What ails you?" In the waning daylight, Linnea scanned the girl from her head to her toes, looking for signs of measles, cholera, consumption, small pox, or any other disease that afflicted travelers.

Ivy's tears spilled over onto her cheeks. "I started bleeding today, and it won't stop."

"Bleeding?" Linnea searched the girl again, her anxiety mounting. "How did you hurt yourself?"

"That's just it. I didn't hurt myself. It's just leaking out and getting worse by the hour. . . ."

"Leaking out where?"

Ivy dropped her head, a blush stealing into her cheeks. Linnea had never seen Ivy embarrassed about anything. At times the girl even put Linnea's mother to shame with her boldness.

Linnea gently squeezed Ivy's arm. "You can tell me."

"It's in my underdrawers." The whisper was filled with horror.

Understanding dawned, and Linnea's worry fell away, leaving her drained. Even so, she managed a small smile. "You have no reason for concern. Everything is fine."

"It is?"

"Yes. Perfectly." Apparently Flynn had neglected to talk with Ivy about her first menses. Linnea didn't blame him. It wasn't exactly a topic for an older brother to address with his twelve-year-old sister. It was something for a mother to explain. Linnea's own mother hadn't minced words in telling her about the reproductive cycle. But Ivy hadn't had the benefit of a mother's input.

Linnea peeked at Flynn on a camp stool nearby gutting fish. He'd avoided looking at her since their kiss. Surely, he wouldn't mind if she educated Ivy in the ways of a woman.

She pressed a hand against Ivy's cheek and lowered her voice. "Your bleeding is normal, sweetheart. It's the sign your body is maturing and changing into that of a woman."

Ivy's forehead crinkled into a frown.

Linnea could see she would need to say more. "You will have bleeding every month for several days at a time, and then the bleeding stops once you are with child. . . ."

Bleeding stops. With child. An abnormal quiet, like that before a storm, descended over Linnea. She counted the months backward, attempting to recall the last time she'd had a monthly cycle, the last time she used lamb's wool to line her drawers.

She hadn't needed the supply once since leaving Fort Leavenworth at the beginning of May. In fact, she couldn't remember using any since burying Asa in March. What had happened? Was the strain of the journey interfering with her monthly cycle? It was possible. Even though she'd always been regular and never had any trouble, perhaps her body had yet to adjust to the rigors of trail life.

Yes, that had to be it.

Though she tried not to let it, her mind spun back to early March when she'd first arrived in Fort Leavenworth and the last time she'd been intimate with Asa, only a few days before he'd died. As embarrassed as she'd been by her mother insisting on sending preventative measures with her, Linnea had used them, agreeing with her mother that she needed to wait to have a child until after she was done with the expedition.

After using caution, certainly she couldn't be carrying Asa's child, could she? But what if she was?

At the thought, she grabbed on to Ivy to keep from sinking to the ground.

Ivy clutched her back. "Are you alright?"

Flynn looked up from his fish-gutting work, his eyes narrowing in on her, more alert and attuned to her than she'd expected.

She forced a smile, first at Flynn, then at Ivy. Neither smiled back.

Again, she scrambled to count backward. She'd missed three cycles—in June, May, and April. While she hadn't felt as sick as her sister had when she'd been pregnant with her first child, Linnea had been experiencing some strange tenderness in certain womanly areas of her body. Of course she was more tired and hungry than usual, which she'd attributed to all the walking and fresh air. But what if it had more to do with having a child growing inside her?

And her emotional outbursts of late? Especially the uncharacteristic one earlier today over the calf? Was that related to a pregnancy?

"What's wrong?" Ivy asked.

Flynn was standing, his fish abandoned, his attention riveted to them.

She had to remain composed. She didn't want to bother him today more than she already had. In fact, with how upset he was at her for the kiss, she wanted to minimize her interactions with him.

"I'm just fine. Just a little tired." She pulled herself up. Nothing was wrong. She was surely only borrowing trouble where none was needed. "Let's go into my wagon, and I'll give you a few supplies."

She hurried to the wagon and climbed in, suddenly eager to hide. She only prayed she'd soon find herself needing her supplies as much as Ivy did.

The morning always came too soon. Thankfully, now that they were well into June, Linnea no longer awoke shivering. But at half past four, the night sky was still black, and she readied herself in the darkness of the covered wagon bed.

All of her traveling suits were dusty and soiled. None of her attempts at hand washing her garments seemed to get them clean. She supposed her inability had something to do with the fact that she'd never laundered a single one of her garments before in her life, since servants had always taken care of the chore. Even with the spots and stains remaining in her skirts and bodices, she refused to accept Grandfather's offer to have Clay do her laundering with his. She could only imagine the disparaging look Flynn would give her if she did such a thing.

With a tired sigh, she finished rolling her hair and began sticking the pins in place. Outside the canvas came sleepy voices, yawns, and the jangles and clanking of men saddling horses and yoking oxen.

"Linnea?"

She paused at the sound of Flynn's voice at the opening of the wagon bed. Holding half a dozen pins between her lips, she couldn't answer. The truth was, she didn't want to answer. After having the night to think about her kiss and the foolishness of it, she'd grown more mortified with each passing hour.

He flipped the canvas open and held the lantern up, illuminating her and the scattering of blankets and night clothing she'd yet to fold and put away. He took in the crowded interior before he settled his gaze upon her.

At the sight of the pins in her mouth, his lips stalled around whatever he'd been planning to say, and he released the canvas as though he'd caught her half clad.

The lantern light continued to glow outside the canvas as he waited. She slowed her efforts, wanting to put off facing him as long as possible. At a soft bleat, her heart picked up pace. She spit the remaining pins into her palm, pocketed them, then opened the canvas to find the newborn calf standing beside Flynn. He was gently stroking the curly hair beneath one of its ears.

She climbed down and knelt in front of the creature, smoothing her fingers over his soft wet nose. "Good morning, little one. And how are you this fine day?"

"He's just eaten." Flynn rubbed behind the calf's other ear.

The newborn turned its dark eyes upon Linnea as though searching for its mama. Her heart welled with unexplainable tenderness. This baby was so sweet tears stung her eyes.

She was getting emotional again, and she had to keep herself under control. And it wasn't because she was expecting a baby of her own. She couldn't be, not when she'd been careful.

She simply wasn't at a point in her life where she was ready or willing to become a mother. She had so much yet she wanted to accomplish, especially on this trip. In addition to her grandfather's manual, perhaps she'd make so many discoveries she'd have her work published in the *Botanical Magazine*. Or maybe her contributions would become part of the Botanic Gardens at the Smithsonian Institution.

Whatever the case, she wanted the freedom to explore. That's why she'd married Asa in the first place. Not to have his child but so she could pursue her career to its fullest without any more hindrances than she already had.

She'd lost track of how many women and men alike had scoffed at her aspirations to be a botanist and told her she belonged at home. If she had a child, she'd garner even more admonition to stop her career and stay at home.

She scratched the calf's head for several moments, then leaned in and kissed him.

When she glanced up, she caught Flynn watching her before he shifted his gaze to Clay nearby, who was helping her grandfather with his bow tie.

She wished the silence between Flynn and her didn't have to be so strained. But it was her fault. "The calf seems to be doing well."

"Yep, he's doing everything right on schedule."

"Good." She stroked the length of him.

"If you still want to find a way to save the calf, it'll need to ride in a wagon."

"Oh." So that's why he'd sought her out. Not to see her. Not to make amends. Certainly not to converse.

He nodded toward the open flap of her wagon. "From the looks of things, we have more room in our wagon."

"Yes, with the presses along with the containers of research, it is quite crowded." She'd been working hard to locate and replace the specimens that had been trampled during the stampede.

And she'd doubled her efforts to be more careful. Even with all the caution, she discovered yesterday that more of the specimens were gone than she'd realized. She tried to be meticulous with her organization system in the crates that made up their herbarium, and the men had gladly given her the task. But somehow several key samples hadn't been in their files, and no amount of searching had produced them.

"Then you'll have to keep an eye on him over in our wagon."

"That will be no trouble. I promise." At least she hoped it wouldn't cut in to her work time.

He stared down at the calf.

"Riding in the wagon is a wonderful solution. Thank you for thinking of it, Flynn. Now we won't need to slow the whole herd." She patted the calf's flank. "Will he be able to make it all the way to Colorado?"

"Nope. He can ride in the wagon a week or two at most. Then he'll be too big and weigh down the teams."

Her enthusiasm deflated. But she tried for a smile anyway. "I won't complain. You've given me two weeks to find a new home for him. And for that I'm grateful."

He didn't speak for several heartbeats before he cleared his throat. "Thank you for talking to Ivy last night about— well, about womanly things."

Though the darkness of predawn shadowed his face, she

could almost feel the heat radiating there. She held back a smile as she imagined what Ivy had said to Flynn and how embarrassed he'd been.

"Much obliged," he spoke softly.

"You're welcome, Flynn."

He nodded, then scooped up the calf and walked away.

With his back turned to her, she allowed herself to stare at him, wishing more than anything to be in his arms again.

Chapter 9

The view was stunning.

Flynn breathed in deeply of the hot, dry air. From the top of the outcropping known as Rock Point, he took in the barren prairie. Miles and miles of flat land stretched to the west. To the south he could make out the wooded areas along the Arkansas River.

The trail had grown drier and sandier, slowing the travel, even though the long grasses and flowers Linnea collected had given way to short grass.

Next to him, Ivy released her breath, her sun-browned face filled with contentment. "Told you it was real pretty from up here, and that it would be worth the climb."

"Yep. It's mighty fine." Even better than the view was the truce he'd gained with his little sister. The antagonism between them had lessened with every passing day.

He had Linnea to thank for it. He'd known Ivy needed a woman in her life, but he hadn't realized exactly how much until Linnea came along.

He peered down the outcropping to the worn path where their wagons and cattle had slowed to a crawl. Linnea was easy to spot, ambling and examining every plant she passed. In the late midmorning light, she was as radiant as always—fresh and vibrant even weeks into their travels.

"Do you think those are buffalo?" Dr. Greely perched on the rocks nearby with Dr. Howell, and he dug in his leather satchel before he removed his spyglass. The scientists had gone on several outings in an attempt to hunt the wild creatures but always returned empty-handed.

Flynn wished they'd have luck one of these times. He was hankering for fresh steak something fierce, especially as their food staples dwindled down to the same old bacon, beans, and biscuits.

They were ten days out from Fort Larned on the branch of the Santa Fe Trail known as the Wet Route, which ran along the north side of the Arkansas River.

They'd camped near Dodge stage station the previous evening. There, finally, Linnea had managed to convince the stationmaster and his wife to take the calf and raise it. Although the couple had been reluctant, Linnea's charm was hard to resist. He should know.

When they'd broken camp that morning, she squared her shoulders and marched stiffly onward without looking back, leaving the creature without a word of complaint.

In spite of the dark, he'd seen her swiping at tears on her cheeks, and he'd nearly halted his horse and gone back for the calf. But there was no telling if they'd find anyone else willing to take it farther up the line, so he'd resisted the urge.

"Elk." Dr. Greely's announcement contained a note of disappointment as he passed the spyglass to Dr. Howell. "I suppose we could try our hand at hunting elk. What do you think, Doctor?"

It hadn't taken long for Flynn to learn that not only was Dr. Howell a botanist, but he'd also trained as a medical doctor. Flynn got the feeling the other scientists weren't impressed by the dual degrees, almost as if Dr. Howell wasn't quite as genuine a botanist because of that.

Holding his top hat to keep it from blowing off, the older gentleman squinted into the lens. "Strangely enough, I do believe there is a horse with the herd, and it seems as though it is wearing a saddle. I wonder what has become of its rider?"

With wrinkled brow, Dr. Howell handed the spyglass to Flynn. "Why don't you have a look, young man, and see what you think?"

Flynn hadn't ever looked through such an instrument before, and for a moment the whole plain seemed wobbly and out of focus. As he steadied the lens over his eye and closed the other, the images became sharper. Still, he fumbled to find the herd. When he landed upon it, amazement rippled through him at how close they appeared and the detail that was visible from so far a distance.

Slowly he examined the elk, which were stockier than deer and had cow-like faces. Some of the bulls had horns rising as high as four feet. Sure as sunrise, a bay-colored horse with a long black mane grazed near the herd. Dr. Howell was right. It was wearing a saddle.

Flynn gave the spyglass back to the gentleman. "Probably just a horse that got away from another train. I'll take a closer look and see if I can round it up."

Dr. Greely nodded vigorously, causing his spectacles to slip to the end of his nose. "I'll go with. I'd like to try to shoot one of those elk with the spectacular antlers. A rack like that would be a wonderful souvenir to take home from this expedition."

Flynn didn't want Dr. Greely tagging along. The scientist got under his skin worse than a splinter. But he couldn't forge out by himself and break his own rule about not going anywhere alone.

He began to climb down the rocks, and his sights strayed again to Linnea bending near a clump of blue flowers. His blood froze as he took in a prairie rattlesnake less than an arm's length away from her with its head reared. A sandy color with dark brown-and-black blotches down its back, it blended into the dry, dusty ground.

He wanted to yell out to her to back slowly away. But he also didn't want to startle her and draw further attention from the rattler. Instead, he withdrew his revolver as he leapt down the rocks, needing to get to a closer range before he took a shot.

The rattler's tail shook but, of course, Linnea was too absorbed in examining the plant life to pay attention to anything else surrounding her. As she took a step closer to the snake, Flynn's pulse spiked with new alarm. He halted in midstride, held out his revolver, and took careful aim, praying his hand would stay steady.

As he pulled the trigger, the echoing gunshot drew her attention. She started to straighten and look for the source of the sound. But as the bullet slammed into the snake only a foot away from her, she jumped. Then, as she noticed the rattler, she screamed and stumbled backward.

Thankfully, the reptile lay motionless. But Flynn wasn't about to take any chances and fired a second shot. Keeping his revolver trained on the snake, he finished scrambling down the rocks and hustled toward Linnea.

She'd moved a dozen paces away from the snake and stared back at it, her eyes wide and face pale. Flynn approached the rattler first, verified it was dead, then turned to Linnea.

Her knuckles were white around the handful of flowers and plants she'd collected. She took another step back, then swayed.

He launched toward her, catching her arm. "Whoa now."

"That rattlesnake almost attacked me." Her whisper was threaded with terror.

"But it didn't."

No doubt she was remembering an incident from a few days ago, when a fella from another caravan had crawled under his wagon to rest from the heat of midday and had been bitten by a rattler. His arm had discolored and swelled. And even though Dr. Howell attempted to bleed out the venom, the man suffered a painful death, sweating, salivating, vomiting, and wheezing.

"Were you the one who shot it?" she asked.

"Yep."

She pressed her free hand to her forehead. "You saved my life again, Flynn."

Another few seconds and she might have been dying in the grass, poison slithering through her blood. Trouble had a way of tracking Linnea Newberry, closer than a coon dog catching a critter.

Ivy bounded up next to him, breathless and grinning. "That was some real fancy shootin', Flynn. Look at that thing's fangs."

Linnea peered more closely at the snake, then cupped a hand over her mouth. A second later, she bent over and retched into the grass, although nothing came up.

"Hush up now, Ivy." Flynn placed a steadying hand on Linnea's back. "You're making things worse."

Dr. Greely and Dr. Howell scrambled down the rock formation, exclaiming over the danger Linnea had just escaped. Dr. Greely launched into a tale he'd heard earlier in the day of a teamster getting bit by a rattler and having to chop off his own leg to save himself.

Linnea straightened, but as Dr. Greely's voice rose with his gruesome story, her face turned even paler and she swayed again.

Flynn wanted to shove a handful of grass into the man's mouth and tell him to hush up the same way he had Ivy. Instead, he reached for Linnea, scooped her up, and stalked past the gathering crowd. He was half afraid she'd resist his help, but she rested her head against his shoulder and didn't try to wriggle free.

Ever since that kiss he'd given her the day of the calf's birth, she'd gone out of her way to steer clear of him. As long as he'd been able to keep an eye on her, he let the distance stand between them, figuring it was for the best since he enjoyed that kiss a whole lot more than he should've, and relived it more times than he wanted to admit.

But after this morning's loss of the calf and now the brush with the rattler, he reckoned she needed someone to lean on. If Dr. Greely wouldn't step up and be that person, Flynn was gonna do the job.

He veered toward her wagon. The train—comprised of their two wagons and half a dozen others that had left Dodge

Station with them—had halted, likely in response to the gunshots so near. They needed to keep moving for another hour or so until their midday break, hopefully at the first fork of Middle Crossings where they could rest by the Arkansas River and water the cattle.

But he wasn't gonna complain about the stalling, at least not until he got Linnea situated. When he reached the back of her wagon, he flipped down the tail and stepped up. He ducked under the canvas into the crowded interior.

With the arched bows and canvas brushing his head, he had to crouch, inevitably pressing closer to her. Her exhalations echoed near his ear. Her hair tickled his cheek. And her womanly softness melded against him.

The minute his thoughts turned south, he jerked them north. He couldn't go there again. All he was doing was getting her out of the sun and giving her a chance to calm down away from everyone.

He stepped to her pallet and began to lower her.

Her arms slid around his neck, and she held on as though she didn't want him to let go.

His heartbeat switched from the fast rhythm of dread it'd been tapping since laying eyes on the rattler, to a sluggish pace, one that beckoned him to linger and enjoy the feel of this beautiful woman.

Closing his eyes, he clenched his jaw. If he gave in, one moment would lead to another and then another until he was kissing her again. And he couldn't let that happen. It would only make things more awkward.

The almighty truth was that he wanted to go back to the comfortable way things were between them before the kiss, when they'd been able to talk and pass the time together.

He missed her camaraderie and talkativeness, her laughter and smiles.

As her back touched her bedroll, her arms didn't lessen their hold. For an agonizing second, he pictured her pulling him down and then himself willingly settling on top of her.

His breathing quickened. *Oh, Lord Almighty.* He opened his eyes and held himself away from the temptation.

"You should rest." His voice came out tight.

"Okay."

She loosened her grip enough that he was able to lay her down and sit back on his knees. He wiped a hand across his eyes, not daring to look at her just yet, not until he could rein in his stampeding desire.

"Thank you, Flynn." Her shaking fingers brushed against his other hand.

Was she still frightened by what had happened? He squeezed her fingers and allowed himself to gaze upon her again. Her face was still pale, making her brown eyes darker and bigger and highlighting the fear there.

"You're gonna be just fine."

"What's wrong with me that I'm always running into such mortal danger?"

He situated his hand more securely in hers. "Ain't nothin' wrong with you."

"But why me?"

"Because you love life and are always living it to the fullest." It was the truth. He'd never seen anyone else approach life with so much energy and enthusiasm as Linnea. Trouble was, such enthusiasm distracted her from seeing the danger around her. But she didn't need a lecture from him again. At least not now.

Her lips curved up into a wobbly smile. "Thank you. That's the nicest thing anyone has ever said to me." A tear spilled over and ran down her temple into her hair.

He couldn't stop himself from brushing at it with the pad of his thumb and searching his mind for some other way to reassure her. Why wasn't he more irritated by her crying the way he'd been at Helen when she resorted to weeping nearly every time he'd seen her last autumn?

He thought he'd loved Helen, thought her tears would move him to reconsider their relationship. But the more she cried, the more he wanted to leave for the West.

With Linnea's crying, all he wanted to do was pick her up into his arms and hold her.

He brushed at her temple again. At a clearing throat outside the wagon, he jerked away and rose as best he could under the canvas.

Dr. Greely stood in the wagon opening, squinting inside through his spectacles. He'd removed his hat, and his dark hair speckled with gray was plastered to his head with sweat.

How much of their interaction had he witnessed?

"Mr. McQuaid, thank you for transporting Mrs. Newberry." Dr. Greely studied Linnea, but she'd closed her eyes. "I'm guessing it was not easy for you to carry a full-grown woman in such a manner, especially with your damaged leg."

Flynn bristled. He never liked when people talked about his leg. Didn't like drawing attention to it. Especially because it had disqualified him from fighting in the war, made him feel weaker and less of a man.

"Shall we be on our way to investigate the herd of elk?" Dr. Greely's question came out as a demand.

Flynn's spine stiffened. "Yep."

"Good. I believe Mrs. Newberry needs uninterrupted rest for her recuperation."

Was Dr. Greely telling him to stay away from Linnea?

Before Flynn could stop himself, he stroked Linnea's cheek, slowly and intimately.

Her eyes flew open and locked on his.

"Promise you'll stay in here until I get back?" He brushed back a strand of her hair, making sure Dr. Greely could see every move he made.

"If you want me to." Her breath had a hitch to it, one that told Flynn she wasn't immune to his touch any more than he was to hers.

He nodded. Then, before he did anything else foolish, he made himself leave. As he hopped down from the wagon, Dr. Greely's scowl trailed him. The claim on Linnea hadn't been lost on the man.

With each limping step Flynn took toward his horse, the more he wanted to slap a palm to his forehead. What was he doing? He had no right to fight with another man over Linnea. Even if he'd been in the market for a wife—which he wasn't—she wasn't his to have, wasn't someone who could fit into his world. And he surefire wouldn't fit into hers.

She didn't put on any airs and was one of the sweetest women he'd ever met. But the difference in their stations was about as far as the sky meeting the horizon.

As he rode alongside Dr. Greely toward the elk herd and the lone horse, it didn't take long for the scientist to bring up Linnea. "You seem as though you're growing to care a great deal about Mrs. Newberry."

Flynn was tempted to tell Dr. Greely the truth, that there was nothing to worry about, that he didn't plan to let anything develop between Linnea and him. But with a sideways glance at the gentleman and his proud bearing, Flynn loosened the reins on his tongue. "She's a mighty fine woman. A man'd have to be heartless not to care for her."

"Of course. But she's young and friendly. And in spite of being a widow, she's also yet quite naïve and could be easily influenced into the arms of another man."

Flynn's muscles tightened at Dr. Greely's insinuation that he'd take advantage of Linnea. "Reckon you better not be influencing her then."

"I wasn't speaking of myself."

"Then you don't think she's attracted to you?"

"I wasn't saying that either." Frustration edged Dr. Greely's tone.

Flynn knew exactly what the man was getting at. He didn't want Flynn taking Linnea's attention away from him. And somewhere deep inside, Flynn didn't want to draw Linnea's attention from Dr. Greely either. But he wasn't about to stand back and let the man order him around. "I suspect a woman can't help it if she's attracted to one man more than another."

His words fell as hard and heavy as the thud of their horses' hooves. As soon as they were out, he wished he could tether and drag them back, especially as Dr. Greely lagged behind a pace.

"Listen, Dr. Greely." He slowed his mount as they drew nearer to the herd. "You've got nothin' to worry about. Dr. Howell hired me to guard Linnea from getting into trouble. That's all."

"So you're her bodyguard?"

"Something like that."

Dr. Greely didn't say anything for a moment. "So you don't hold any aspirations toward Mrs. Newberry?"

Did he? Flynn shook his head. "Nope. None at all. Just doing the job Dr. Howell's paying me to do." Even as he said the words, he tried to convince himself they were true.

"Well, well, well." Dr. Greely's lips curved into a smile, one that set Flynn on edge. "I never would have guessed it. But now I understand why Dr. Howell let his granddaughter remain on the expedition, especially with all his concerns for her safety."

Flynn pressed his lips together. Why, for the life of him, had he gone on about his business? He didn't have to explain himself or his interactions with Linnea. "Dr. Howell doesn't want Linnea to know about the arrangement. I'd be obliged if you kept quiet about it."

Dr. Greely was silent for a dozen paces.

Flynn's gut churned with every step.

"I certainly can respect the good doctor's wishes." Dr. Greely's expression was too calculated. "As long as you keep your conduct strictly businesslike with Mrs. Newberry, then you have nothing to worry about, do you?"

Flynn shrugged. Yep, he'd been a blamed fool for yammering and should have known a proud man like Dr. Greely would twist a situation to his advantage.

Flynn reined in his horse, the herd only a hundred feet away. He'd purposefully approached in a roundabout way to keep the creatures from catching their scent.

Dr. Greely halted beside him and tugged his rifle from the scabbard tucked into his saddle. He was focused on the elk, a new gleam in his eyes, that of a hunter closing in on his prey.

"Hold off on taking a shot 'til I've got the horse." Flynn

slid down, eyeing the Morgan at the rear of the herd. Cautiously, he started toward the horse, uncoiling the rope he'd brought and forming a noose. He didn't figure he'd need to use it, especially if he could grab the reins dangling over the horse's head.

He crept nearer, staying downwind. If he frightened the elk, the horse would bolt with them, and he'd lose his chance of catching the creature. Reaching out a hand, he murmured words of assurance.

At the sudden, echoing crack of Dr. Greely's gun, the horse neighed and reared its head. Flynn dove for the reins and snagged them just as the horse kicked its legs and started to charge after the elk, which were racing away and leaving a cloud of dust behind.

The Morgan was powerful and dragged Flynn in its fright. But Flynn dug in his heels and held on tight, sweet-talking the creature and drawing it to a halt. When he finally had the horse under control, his gaze trailed after Dr. Greely who was whooping and hollering as he galloped after the elk.

It was no wonder the scientists hadn't been able to shoot any game. Not if Dr. Greely's shenanigans were the way of things.

Flynn rubbed the horse's forelock to its muzzle. "You're alright. And you'll be even better if we can get you back to your master."

The horse bumped Flynn's hand as if to agree.

Flynn trailed his hand over the crest and withers, searching for any signs of distress. When he reached the flank, his fingers came into contact with a sticky film.

Blood.

He examined the horse more carefully, searching its belly,

even its legs, and finding no obvious wounds. As he shifted his attention to the fine-looking black saddle, he touched the wet spots that had pooled in the crevices. More blood. And it was fresh.

A shiver of apprehension crept up Flynn's backbone. Something had happened to the rider to cause him to lose a lot of blood, maybe even to lose his life.

Flynn scanned the prairie. Was someone watching them?

A cold foreboding wrapped around him. He needed to get back to the wagon train, to his siblings, and to Linnea. If danger was closing in, he wanted to be nearby.

Looping the rope around the Morgan, he mounted his horse and started back. Dr. Greely chased the elk for a short distance before they outpaced him. Flynn made sure the man had turned and started following him before he urged his mount into a gallop with the Morgan trailing him.

Only when he saw the long line of wagons and cattle rambling onward over the flat grassland without any trouble did he slow his pace. Even then his pulse didn't return to normal. Not until he caught sight of Dylan driving their wagon and Linnea sitting at the rear of her wagon with Ivy strolling along behind.

At his approach, Linnea lifted a hand in greeting and jumped down. She'd obviously taken to heart his admonition to stay in the wagon until his return and now was seeking her freedom to explore again.

He released a tight breath. If only he could be in all places at all times. Then maybe he'd be able to keep everyone safe.

"*You're not God.*" Linnea's comment came back to taunt him.

Maybe if God did a better job of protecting those he

loved, then he wouldn't need to try to be God. As soon as the thought came, he ducked his head. Who was he to speak about the Almighty so boldly?

For a half second, he waited for God to reach down and wallop him. Then with a shake of his head, he pushed the accusation back into the far corners of his mind, out of sight where he wouldn't be able to think on it again.

CHAPTER
10

The howls of wolves echoed in the night air. From where Linnea sat in the back of the rolling wagon, she clutched her blanket tighter to ward off the shivers that crawled over her skin with each chorus.

Although the wolves were a danger, especially to the cattle, they weren't the worst of their enemies or the reason why Flynn had decided not to stop but to keep traveling through the night.

After he'd returned with a stray horse, its saddle streaked with blood, he'd ridden at the front of the wagon train, his rifle in one hand and his revolver in the other. They'd gone only another hour before they'd come upon a wagon that was overturned, its belongings strewn over the ground.

As Flynn and several other men tried to right the wagon, their expressions turned grim. Curiosity had drawn Linnea along with the others to the scene of the accident. But Flynn waved them all back and ordered Dylan to take Linnea and Ivy away.

Although Dylan made an effort to do as Flynn instructed, Linnea had remained close enough to see the men dragging mutilated bodies out from beneath the wreckage.

Even now in the blackness, the images of the corpses made her shudder. The men had dug graves, buried the dead, and then salvaged what they could from the wagon's wrecked contents. As they'd started underway and passed by the freshly turned dirt with the crude grave markers, Linnea wanted to weep.

Lately, it seemed her tears came at the slightest provocation. Like when she'd glimpsed the dead rattler near her feet. She hadn't wanted to cry, hadn't wanted Flynn to see her have another breakdown. But her tears trickled out no matter how hard she tried to hold them in.

She laid a hand on her abdomen. While she wanted to keep denying she was with child, she had no other explanation for all the signs: her fragile emotional state, missing another of her monthly courses, and the slight—imperceptible to others—swell of her stomach.

A baby was growing inside her.

She calculated from conception in March to the end of June—which put her gestation at approximately fourteen weeks. Her estimates meant the baby was due sometime in mid-December.

Linnea tried not to let discouragement creep in. She couldn't change the facts, as much as she wanted to. Somehow she needed to accept the idea that she would be a mother much sooner than she'd ever anticipated.

For now, she was still early in the pregnancy, and she didn't want to worry herself or Grandfather, especially when he was already so concerned about her. What could they do about it anyway? They were too far along the Santa Fe Trail for her to return to Missouri. She'd have to finish traveling to Colorado.

No doubt once they reached Denver, Grandfather would insist on taking her back home, utilizing a stagecoach so they could go much faster. Even if she protested his leaving and insisted that she could journey by herself, he'd never allow it. He'd accompany her to ensure her safety and to be there if the birthing came early, before she reached New York City.

The trouble was, she couldn't let him leave the expedition, not when he'd worked so hard to obtain the grant, not when he'd have to give up so much, especially the honor of overseeing a project of this magnitude and having his name attached to the manual.

No, for now, she had to keep her pregnancy hidden. When she got further along, she could wear her skirts looser and cover her bodice with a shawl. Once she could no longer hide her swelling stomach, she'd make a case for staying in Colorado with him so he could finish the expedition.

She wasn't sure how she'd manage a baby in a strange place without the assistance of her mother and sister, but surely she could hire help. Maybe she could even find a way to continue with the research. After all, a woman could still use her intellect and talents while raising a child, couldn't she?

The wagon hit a rut and jostled her. On the floor beside her, Ivy didn't stir, having fallen asleep hours ago as easily as if she were in a featherbed. Tonight, Flynn had insisted the two of them ride together. Although he hadn't said so, she'd surmised that he thought he'd be able to protect them better in the same wagon.

But protect them from *whom*?

Some said Confederate Irregulars were responsible for stirring up fear and trying to draw the Union soldiers out of the forts along the trail. Known for engaging in irregular warfare tactics, the unruly bands had earned the nickname *Irregulars*. The men hid out in Kansas and Colorado, wreaking terror on everyone who came into contact with them.

Others claimed the murders contained the trademark violence of the Comanches who often preyed upon travelers in the Middle Crossings. It was a popular stretch of the trail because the Arkansas River was typically shallower, allowing those heading into New Mexico to cross over safely. As a result, many wagon trains, teamsters, and mail riders camped in the low banks. With so many congregating in one place, the wagons and livestock had become easy targets.

When their wagon train had arrived at the first stopping point of Middle Crossings earlier in the evening, the other travelers had spoken of little else but the fact that the Comanches and Osages were gearing up for a battle.

Because of imminent danger, Flynn had wanted to push forward out of the Middle Crossings as quickly as possible, even if that meant traveling all night. He wasn't alone in his push. Many other wagons had joined them.

At another chorus of howls, Linnea threw off her blanket and crawled to the wagon opening. She peered out. How close was the danger? Only a dozen paces away, the moonlight revealed Flynn following the wagon on foot, leading his horse along with the one he'd found earlier in the day.

With lead lines in one hand and his rifle in the other, he was scanning the northern side of the trail. Was that where the wolves were congregating?

The other men in the caravan had agreed to spread out

along both sides of their wagon train, providing a guard throughout the long night. Some were walking, others riding, all with weapons ready.

"Linnea," he hissed, motioning at her. "Don't come out."

She started through the opening. "With the presence of the wolves, I cannot sleep."

"Stay inside anyway."

She perched on the edge and then hopped down, having perfected her dismount from the moving wagon early on in the journey, which hadn't been difficult since the wagon's speed never increased beyond that of a brisk walking pace.

Flynn was at her side in an instant, grasping her arm and steadying her, though she didn't need it. "Thunderation, Linnea," he growled, his rifle tucked under his arm. "What are you doing?"

"The riding is unbearable. I would much rather walk."

"It's too dangerous."

"I cannot bear the thought of returning inside. Please, may I walk with you for a little while?"

His footsteps faltered, then evened out. He took several more steps before he sighed. "Fine. But only for a few minutes."

"Thank you, Flynn."

He let go of her but stayed beside her, giving her a sidelong glance.

Though she'd decided to sleep in her traveling suit and shoes in the event of an attack, her hair was unbound. She suddenly felt strangely undressed with her hair falling in such abandon, and she began wrapping it into a coil, only to realize she'd left her pins inside the wagon.

She released the knot and let it fall over her shoulders, the loose curls tickling her cheeks and bringing back the feel of Flynn's fingers when he'd laid her in the wagon yesterday and so tenderly wiped away her tears.

Though she didn't witness his gentle side often, it stood in stark contrast to his powerful build and steely determination and made it all the more noticeable.

He slid her another look, one that made her body tingle with an awareness of him, of the way his fingers curled around his rifle, the low-riding brim of his hat, and his shadowed eyes, so dark and so full of a magnetism that pulled her regardless of how much she resisted.

She forced her attention away from him, to the side of the road where she spotted more *Solanum rostratum*, called buffalobur by the other travelers. Even in the moonlight, she could distinguish the five-lobed, one-inch-wide yellow flowers. She'd studied several earlier in the day, fascinated with the five stamens and four anthers, one of which was purplish and longer than the others.

But at the moment, the flower couldn't keep her interest, and it shifted rapidly back to Flynn. "Why aren't you riding?"

"Giving the horses a break." His voice dropped with weariness.

She could only imagine the pressure he was under to safely lead them through so dangerous an area. "Why don't you sleep for a couple of hours in the wagon, and I'll manage the horses."

He released a short, almost scoffing laugh.

"I'm perfectly capable."

He remained silent.

She caught the hint of a smile. It softened his rejection of her offer and sent a delightful tremor through her. "I'm glad I could provide you some amusement. At least I am good for something."

His smile widened.

The sight of it made her insides flutter like the beating wings of the painted lady she'd captured recently. She'd missed being with him during the past days of traveling, missed their easy companionship.

But after their unfortunate kiss, she'd resolved to stay away from Flynn to the best of her ability. And she had until yesterday. Until she'd witnessed the panic in his face as he rushed to rescue her from the snake. Until he carried her to the wagon so protectively. Until he knelt beside her pallet and comforted her.

What did it all mean? Was he getting over Helen and allowing himself to care about someone new? Her?

The very idea was preposterous. But her curiosity got the better of her. "Are you planning to send for Helen once you get settled in Colorado?"

He stumbled a step. "How do you know about Helen?" Before she could answer, he glanced to the canvas opening and scowled. "Let me guess. Ivy told you."

"Yes. She's quite informative."

He snorted but didn't say anything more.

"I can only imagine how difficult it was to leave Helen behind."

"It wasn't difficult."

It was her turn to stumble.

He slowed his pace, lowering his head almost as if his admission embarrassed him.

"Ivy said you were planning on marrying her."

"Yep. But that changed."

"Why?" The moment the question was out, she touched his arm. "I'm sorry. I shouldn't have asked. It really is none of my business—"

"After Ma died, my priorities changed. I don't have room in my life for marriage anymore."

His answer was so straightforward and devoid of emotion, she didn't know what to think. "But that doesn't mean you stopped loving Helen, does it?"

He didn't answer right away. Instead, he looked down at her fingers wrapped around his forearm.

Did he want her to remove her hold?

She smiled and drew nearer, tucking her hand farther into the crook of his arm, almost daring him to pull away.

His muscles hardened beneath her touch, but he didn't extricate himself.

The night air for late June was warm, and the trill of crickets and the chirp of bullfrogs provided a soft serenade most nights. The sky was clear and the expanse of stars vast. If not for the image of those mutilated bodies at the forefront of her mind, she would have believed the night was among the most beautiful yet.

"So, do you? Still love her?" She wasn't sure why she persisted, why she cared about his answer.

"Helen's a sweet girl."

Linnea drew in a breath, unable to keep her steps from slowing. "Then you miss her?"

"No. Honestly. I don't." His answer was soft with a thread of guilt.

She exhaled the pent-up air and patted his arm. "It's okay. I can honestly say I don't miss Asa."

"You don't?" His voice rose with a tinge of surprise.

She was suddenly mortified by her frank admission. "Oh dear. That didn't come out right."

"Do you still love him?"

She couldn't begrudge Flynn for his bluntness after the questions she'd asked him. But she was too embarrassed to answer. She started to slip her hand away, but he pressed it closer to his body, trapping it. "Flynn . . ."

"Do you?"

"It's complicated."

His body tensed beneath her hand. "Then you do."

She swallowed and then forced the words out. "I never loved him. And I'm ashamed to admit it."

Flynn's rigidness eased. "I reckon it ain't nothin' to be ashamed about. Lots of people get married for reasons other than love."

"You don't understand." She hung her head.

"Your grandfather told me you picked Asa because he supported your botany."

She looked up at Flynn to find him watching her curiously. "Isn't that horrible of me?" He started to shake his head, but she continued. "He promised that if we got married, I could come on this trip. I wasn't attracted to him, but I agreed because I thought attraction might grow with time."

"And did it?" He blew out a breath. "Listen, it's none of my blamed business—"

"He was a good man. But, no, I wasn't attracted to him like I am—" She caught herself before making the biggest blunder and comparing Asa to Flynn. She couldn't deny an attraction with Flynn flared whenever they were together. But she'd already scared him away on more than one occasion and didn't want to again.

The best thing to do was switch the subject of the conversation back to him. "So, you're not planning to send for Helen once you get settled?"

"Nope. Like I said, I've decided I ain't getting married."

"For now, maybe. But what about when you settle down? Ivy and Dylan won't be around for many more years. And surely you'll want a family of your own."

He shook his head almost vehemently. "Reckon I know what I want. And a wife and family ain't part of it."

She paused, unable to keep disappointment from pricking her like a stray thorn she hadn't anticipated on a stem. Certainly she hadn't expected Flynn to want to take her as a wife and her baby as his family, had she?

No, of course not. Just because an undeniable chemistry existed between them didn't mean she wanted to marry him. Such a notion was far-fetched, in fact, outrageous, and nothing she'd ever consider.

Of course when her family, including Grandfather, learned she was with child, they would likely urge her to find another husband. But she had no reason to harbor any regret that Flynn wasn't interested in a future with her. Perhaps such knowledge would free them to interact without the underlying pressure or worry that their relationship could ever amount to more than friendship.

"Since we're being honest with each other"—she withdrew her hand from his arm and hugged herself to ward off a sudden chill—"I should admit I have no desire to get married again either. At least not in the near future, not until I have the chance to finish exploring the West and conducting my research."

"If Dr. Greely has his way, you'll be married to him before summer's end."

A laugh escaped before she could contain it. Biting her lip, she glanced around, hoping he wasn't riding anywhere nearby. She didn't want to offend Dr. Greely. He was, after all, on the board of the Department of Botany at the Smithsonian. He had a great deal of influence over whose specimens would become a part of the Botanic Gardens.

"Dr. Greely is a very kind gentleman and quite knowledgeable in classification systems as well as taxonomic analysis. However, I refuse to place myself into another awkward marriage with a too-eager husband."

Flynn cocked his head, his eyes raised at her from beneath the brim of his hat.

"Not that my marriage was awkward or Asa eager." She realized her mistake too late, that she'd revealed more than she intended, and she was relieved for the darkness hiding the flush that was sure to be staining her cheeks. "Very well. If you must know, it was slightly awkward. But I'm sure with time, I would have grown more comfortable with . . . with him."

Flynn cleared his throat but didn't speak.

"Oh dear." She fanned her face with her hand. She had to change the subject again. Right away. "Tell me about your broken leg." She hadn't yet broached the personal subject with Flynn. She was sure the topic wasn't easy for him to talk about, but under the cover of the night, maybe he'd feel safer sharing with her. At least she hoped so.

He was quiet, the creak of wagon wheels and the soft plod of the horses' hooves filling the silence.

"You don't have to tell me if you don't want to. I just thought—"

"Rusty did it a few years back." His voice was low, almost

resigned. "I went after Rusty for the way he kept on hurting my ma. Figured I was bigger and stronger. But Rusty somehow grabbed hold of a broken weather vane and used the pipe to bust me up."

Even though Ivy had relayed the details of the beating, hearing them now from Flynn made Linnea's heart ache.

"He got me real good. Broke my leg, ribs, and an arm. Probably would have killed me if not for Ivy's screams alerting Brody, who threatened to shoot Rusty if he didn't stop."

For a while, Flynn opened up about how hard it had been living with his stepfather, the control he'd exerted over their ma, and the years of having to step in and protect his siblings from Rusty's hard hand, especially after Wyatt left.

When she asked him about Wyatt, he shared his frustration with his brother's absence, the heavy responsibilities he'd shouldered, including trying to figure out how to keep Brody out of the war but failing. They talked about the war, their fears, the frustrations and hopes for the future of their country.

Eventually, the conversation turned to their own personal hopes and dreams, and she discovered Flynn was a good listener as she shared about her aspirations to make a name for herself as a female botanist, not for fame but to help further the cause of women being allowed the same opportunities as men in using their God-given abilities.

She could have gone on talking with him all night. And she sensed he would have allowed her to. But when one of the other men called out to alert Flynn of danger, Linnea crawled back into the wagon next to Ivy. As she stretched out and yawned, her thoughts stayed firmly on Flynn, her heart full but light.

CHAPTER 11

When Flynn had agreed to drive Wyatt's cattle, he'd never expected the journey to be so dangerous.

By dawn the wagon train had moved beyond the Cimarron Route turnoff. The well-traveled, shorter Cimarron path meandered southwest into New Mexico Territory, while the Bent's Fort Route led directly west to Colorado before it, too, veered south into New Mexico. While both eventually ended up in Santa Fe, Bent's Fort Route was touted as the safer road.

Flynn prayed it was true since they still had a ways to go before getting through the Middle Crossings. For hours, he'd been scanning the area for signs of trouble. If there were any Indians, he didn't see them.

From atop his mount as the first rays of sunlight warmed his back, he gestured to Nash to begin moving the herd toward the riverbank for watering. Though he wanted to keep traveling, the cattle were in sore need of a break. One of the stockiest bulls was struggling with tender feet, and Flynn feared he might have to leave the creature behind.

At the sight of Linnea poking her head out the back of the wagon, he rubbed a hand over his mouth to hide the smile that surfaced every time he thought about their conversation a few hours ago. She was bold—bolder than any woman he'd ever met. And something about that quality made his body thrum like strings on a fiddle.

She didn't hold back. She told things just like they were. Even if it embarrassed her to no end.

Awkward. That was the word she'd used to describe her marriage bed.

Strangely enough, he'd taken too much satisfaction in the fact that she hadn't been overly attracted to her late husband. For a reason he couldn't explain, just the thought of her sharing intimacies with another man needled him worse than a rusty nail in a horse hoof.

And he had to admit, he was more than a little satisfied to hear she didn't have the least hankering for Dr. Greely. He shouldn't feel that way, but he couldn't help himself.

He peeked at her as she descended, this time her hair bound into the knot she normally wore at the back of her neck. She'd accepted his pronouncement that he was set against marriage. And she admitted she had no desire to get married herself, wasn't looking for another relationship to replace the one she'd had with Asa.

That meant he had nothing to worry about. They'd spelled things out plain and simple. And afterward, they'd been able to talk for a long while into the night like old friends. In fact, he talked more to her in one night than he ever had with anyone else in his life.

The almighty truth was that he could've gone on jabbering with her for hours on end. Probably because he didn't have to worry she'd take things the wrong way and think he was interested in more. 'Cause he'd been serious. There was no way he was planning to get married. And no way he'd ever risk subjecting a woman to child birthing.

"Good morning, Flynn." She started toward him where he was riding alongside the herd.

"Morning."

She walked with a bounce in her step and wore her usual innocent, wide-eyed expression. Just one more thing he liked about her, that she woke up every morning eager to begin the day, excited for whatever was in store.

"I sincerely pray the danger has passed with the night and that we will be able to rest easier today."

"We're gonna rest a spell. But we'll still need to be on the lookout for trouble."

As she drew up alongside Rimrock, she bent and plucked a flower even as she kept pace with him. "Will we be stopping soon?" She straightened and pressed the flower to her nose. "I'm famished this morning."

Her face was already pretty, but as she closed her eyes and breathed in the fragrance, he wanted to lose himself in staring at her. With things out in the open between them, he could do a little lookin' and appreciatin' every now and again without doing any harm, couldn't he? She was mighty fine, especially with the early morning sunlight glinting off her hair and turning it a golden red.

After a moment, her eyes flew open and sought his. He jerked his attention away from her toward the herd, now veering in the direction of the long, sloping banks that led to the bottoms and the wide clay-colored Arkansas River.

"What's wrong?" she asked.

"Tired." Maybe he was gonna have to be careful not to look and appreciate after all.

"Then I insist we stop so you can sleep for a few hours."

"You insist, do you?"

"Yes, I do."

Her tone was so serious, he couldn't keep his grin from breaking free.

"Am I amusing you once more?"

"Nope. Not in the least."

She pushed at his boot within his stirrup and smiled up at him. "It's good to see you smile, Flynn. You're much less intimidating with a smile."

"Reckon I best stop. Wouldn't want to ruin my image."

"You're also more handsome when you smile."

"More handsome?"

"Of course, you're a fine specimen of manhood already. No one would argue that point." The moment she spoke the words, she cupped a hand over her mouth, and her eyes widened.

He couldn't hold back a laugh. There she was going on again and speaking her mind without thinking.

She lowered her hand and smiled, letting her embarrassment easily fall by the wayside. "It's good to see you laugh too. You should do it more often."

He didn't laugh much. That was true. But something about her made him forget about the troubles of his life and the world around them—even if only for a few minutes. "Not every day I get told I'm a fine specimen of manhood."

This time she laughed. "If it makes you laugh, perhaps I need to start telling you so every morning."

He had the sudden vision of waking up next to her, rolling over, propping up on his elbow above her, and seeing her smile first thing. The image shot heat into his blood as fast and hard as a bullet.

"Flynn McQuaid, you're a fine specimen of manhood." She stated the words matter-of-factly, as if she were cataloging one of the specimens she collected.

"Gonna start drawing and labeling me like you do your plants?"

"Maybe I will." Her eyes were sparkling with humor.

He couldn't keep from sharing a smile with her again. In light of the conversation from the previous night, it struck him that he'd never done much smiling or laughing or talking with Helen. In fact, they'd done a whole lot more necking than anything else.

After stirring up physical longings with Helen, now it was all the harder for him to control his desires. He reckoned that was one of the reasons the Good Book said not to stir up love before the time was right for it.

"Mrs. Newberry." Dr. Greely was riding toward them, his slumped shoulders making his paunch more prominent. His middle-aged face creased with weariness, and dark circles had formed under his eyes.

Flynn had to give the scientist a measure of respect for willingly riding alongside the wagon train all night and keeping a lookout for attackers. But now as his gaze roved over Linnea possessively, Flynn clamped his jaw to keep from saying something he'd regret.

"I told your grandfather I'd check on you."

"Thank you, Dr. Greely." All traces of Linnea's smile and humor evaporated, replaced by the serious expression she wore whenever she was with the scientists. Was it possible she needed someone to make her smile and laugh more often, the same as he did?

Dr. Greely reined in beside them, not bothering to acknowledge Flynn's presence. Flynn supposed that's what he got for admitting Dr. Howell was paying him to protect Linnea. Now Dr. Greely saw him as a hired hand, no better than Clay, maybe even lower in status.

"You may tell Grandfather I'm faring well."

"Then the traveling didn't disturb your sleep?"

"Just a little. But I got up and walked with Flynn for a while."

Dr. Greely's eyes rounded. "In the middle of the night?"

Linnea paused, her forehead wrinkling. "Yes, I thought it would help pass the time more quickly for both of us."

"My dear, you cannot cavort in such a manner." Dr. Greely descended from his horse and pulled Linnea to a stop with him. Flynn slowed his mount, but when Dr. Greely glared at him, Flynn guessed his conversation and time with Linnea had come to an end for the morning.

Just as well. He veered in the direction of the herd. Even if he and Linnea were clear about what they each wanted for their future, that didn't take away the facts that she was mighty pretty and that he was as attracted to her as lightning to a metal rod. The trick now was to keep the sizzle from striking and burning.

Linnea's dirty laundry and the bar of soap lay discarded in a heap along the shore next to her shoes and stockings. She needed to attend to the washing, but instead she waded deeper, letting the river water rush against her feet and ankles.

The coldness took her breath away, but at the same time was soothing in the high heat of the afternoon. She'd rolled up her bloomers and bunched up the hem of her skirt, heedless of the impropriety. She was simply too hot to care.

With perspiration trickling down her back between her shoulder blades, she bent and used her free hand to splash water against her face, letting it dribble down her blouse. The water was muddy from all the livestock as well as other campers making use of the river. But at the moment, it was the coolest place to be.

She'd tried to find a more private area away from the rest of the travelers, but she stayed within sight of Dylan and Ivy sitting along the edge, submerged up to their necks, laughing and talking.

If only she could take the liberty of drenching her entire body the way they were. But she was a grown gentlewoman and subject to rules of decorum, as Dr. Greely had so sternly reminded her earlier in the day when he'd discovered she'd cavorted with Flynn during the night.

Cavorted.

Linnea almost laughed at his word choice to describe her innocent excursion with Flynn.

As it was, she'd accepted Dr. Greely's rebuke as humbly as possible and assured him she would be more careful. She intended to keep her promise. Even if she subscribed to women gaining more privileges equal to those of men, she was a lady, after all, and as such needed to remain above reproach.

"Well, well. What do we have here, fellas?" A voice from the river's edge startled her.

She straightened and spun to find several men loitering on the north bank less than a dozen paces away. They all had overgrown hair and scraggly beards, long hunting shirts with fancy embroidered patterns, and several revolvers holstered at each of their waists.

One wore a hat with its brim curled up tight against his head and stood slightly apart from the others. Without the brim to shield him, his face was browner than toast. He didn't look like he was much older than she was, perhaps younger. But something in his expression spoke of experiences that had aged him far too quickly.

"You're sure a fine filly." His gaze slid over her in a way that left her feeling slightly undressed, and she dropped the hem of her skirt to cover her bloomers and ankles.

She glanced upriver to find that Ivy and Dylan were preoccupied with something below the surface and weren't paying her any attention. Apprehension shivered up her backbone. Something about these men told her she needed to leave, immediately. That she wasn't the least safe with them.

She took a step upriver. Did she dare make a run for it?

The curled-brim-hat man held out a hand, as though sensing her fear and attempting to calm her. "You ain't got nothin' to be afeared of with us, little filly."

Flynn. Her heart thudded with a sudden and overwhelming need for him. However, after taking a turn at guard duty that morning, he was finally getting a well-deserved rest in the shade of the wagon at their camp. Before lying down, he'd warned her not to wander off.

She hadn't believed she was *wandering off* by seeking a little privacy. But she guessed Flynn wouldn't approve of how far she'd gone. And now she desperately wished she'd stayed closer to the camp—or at the very least, closer to Ivy and Dylan.

"Come on over here, sweet thing." The young man reached out a hand and lowered his voice as if he were speaking to a spooked animal. She was spooked, but she had to stay strong and get away.

"My husband is just in the woods there." She nodded behind them. "He won't take kindly to me speaking with strangers."

The two at the rear glanced into the cottonwoods that crowded against the bank.

"He'll be right back." She stumbled against the current, the sand and silt squishing beneath her bare feet as if to hold her in place.

"Now hold on." The curled-brim-hat man waded into the river, the rigid set of his mouth and dullness in his eyes telling her that killing had become all too easy for him.

Though she hadn't seen an Irregular yet, the tales of the guerilla soldiers abounded around the campfires at night. From what others had described, the Confederates were young men who'd fled to the backcountry to escape the Union occupation of the Border States. They camped out in the brush and attacked and harassed Union troops as well as travelers.

Were these men a part of such a group?

"Linnea." Flynn's sharp call barreled into her, nearly knocking her to her knees in relief. He strode along the bank down toward her as fast as his limp would allow, his rifle in one hand and revolver in the other. Behind him, Dylan stood dripping wet, a pace back from the place he'd been swimming only moments ago, his weapons both aimed at the men. Ivy was nowhere in sight.

"That's my husband coming for me right now." She moved another step away from the scraggly trio.

"Don't get any closer to her," Flynn's voice was as unyielding as granite, "or I'll turn you into wolf bait."

The curled-brim-hat man reached for the handle of one of his revolvers, but at the movement, a shot rang out from Dylan's direction. The bullet cut a line through the leather of the holster.

"Next one goes into your heart." Flynn kept his attention and guns riveted to the three even as he splashed through the water and reached Linnea.

She wanted to throw herself into his arms, but she forced herself to stand by his side.

"Cool your pistols." The man released his gun handle and took a step up the bank. "Didn't realize she was your wife, or I'da left her alone."

"Yep, she's mine." Flynn's voice was hard and possessive. "Mine and only mine. Got that?"

"Yessir." The young man gave a mock salute, one that left no doubt he didn't care one way or another if Linnea was any man's wife. He backed slowly away, his gaze darting between Flynn and Dylan.

His companions did likewise. When they reached the tree cover, they turned and slipped away through the brush as silently as they'd come.

Flynn didn't move, kept his gaze trained on the woods for so long that Linnea was afraid the three would bound back through and start shooting. Or what if they returned with reinforcements? More of them might be just beyond the river bottom, eager to join in a fight.

"Head upriver." Flynn finally spoke, his voice low and edged with urgency. Did he sense the same danger still lurking?

She didn't wait to find out. She sloshed toward Dylan, who also still had both of his guns pointed at the woods. The hammers were cocked, his knuckles white, and his eyes narrowed.

When she skirted behind him, she caught a glimpse of Ivy farther away from the bank, her hands twisting together with worry. Had she shouted the warning to Flynn?

"Go on to the camp with Ivy." Dylan's strained whisper prodded Linnea out of the river.

When she reached Ivy, the girl took hold of her hand. "You alright?"

Linnea nodded, a swift lump forming in her throat and preventing her from speaking. She couldn't make her feet work to walk away, could only watch Flynn having to be the protector just as he'd always been for everyone in his life, including her now.

Carefully, slowly, Flynn grabbed her belongings from the riverbank, then backed up the river, all the while keeping his guns out and aimed. Upon reaching Dylan, he stood in front of his brother for another endless moment, then lowered his arms. "They're gone."

Dylan nodded. "For now. But how long before they come back?"

"Don't know." Flynn's shoulders radiated tension.

Linnea had the feeling he would have said more if she and Ivy hadn't been standing nearby.

When he turned and looked at her, his brows rose, revealing murky green-blue eyes. "You okay?"

Linnea nodded.

"They didn't touch you, did they?"

"No, thank the Lord and thanks to you and Dylan."

He handed her the shoes and stockings, then swiped off his hat and jammed his fingers into his brown hair.

"I guess I went too far—"

"Blamed right you did. Especially after I told you not to wander off. What if I wasn't halfway here when Ivy came running? What if I'd still been catching shut-eye back at camp?"

"I'm sorry." Her voice dropped to a whisper, and guilt rushed in swifter than a flooded stream.

"You've got to pay attention to what's going on around you."

"I will. I promise." She had been doing better . . . until the rattlesnake incident, and now this run-in with Irregulars.

Flynn regarded her through narrowed eyes. Ivy and Dylan watched the interaction, their usual levity absent. If not for Dylan's quick shot, she shuddered to think what could have happened.

As if thinking the same, Flynn's forehead creased with concern. "Go tell everyone to be on the alert. Me and Dylan are gonna scout the area."

"Do you really think you should?" The words were out before Linnea could stop them. "I have the feeling those men wouldn't hesitate to kill anyone they come across."

"Good to know." His tone rang with frustration again. "You go on now. Me and Dylan'll find out how many Irregulars there are and what kind of threat they pose."

As Linnea wound through the cottonwoods with Ivy, she trembled at how close to trouble she'd come once again. She'd been playing a game of cat and mouse with danger the whole expedition. What made her believe she could outrun and outwit the danger when her own father hadn't been able to?

When she reached her wagon, she climbed up inside before Grandfather or any of the scientists saw her and learned of her newest escapade. As she plopped onto her clothing trunk, she leaned her head against the canvas and placed her hand on her stomach and the slight swell. She had another life to think about now. She couldn't forget that.

As her sights swept around the cluttered interior, she sat forward with a start. One of the research crates was tipped over and the contents spilled out.

She scrambled forward. What had happened? When she'd left the wagon earlier, everything had been in perfect order. She'd made sure of it, especially since she always seemed to be misplacing specimens from their files, important specimens from early in their trip that they couldn't replace.

Whenever one came up missing and she inquired after it, the other team members only looked at her with exasperation, as if to say of them all, she was most likely to lose or damage the research. Finally a few days ago, Dr. Parker had kindly suggested that he'd be willing to take over the organizing of their work. But Grandfather and Dr. Greely had intervened, giving her the benefit of the doubt.

Gingerly, she began to sort through the stiff, dried papers that contained each carefully catalogued flower, blade, and leaf they'd been able to find. A few were bent and a few others torn. But hopefully she could flatten and fix them.

The weight in her stomach sank lower. She'd wanted so badly to contribute to the trip, to be valuable to the team, and to help her grandfather in every way she could. But somehow she was always making things more difficult for everyone.

It was her carelessness, wasn't it? Or had someone come

inside—maybe someone from another caravan—hoping to find valuables?

She studied the remaining trunks and containers, all closed and untouched.

With a sigh, she resumed her work. They couldn't afford to have any more mistakes or accidents. Too much was at stake.

CHAPTER

12

Flynn lay flat against the sandy hill, peeking his head over the ridge at the herd of buffalo grazing in the flat, grassy valley to the north of their camp. The long-bearded bulls were powerfully built and mostly ignored their youthful companions, who jumped about playfully kicking or attacking one another. A number of reddish-brown calves grazed near their mothers.

Cowbirds hovered all around the herd, alighting on the backs of the shaggy creatures, eating the pesky blackflies that seemed to be everywhere. Flynn swatted one off his neck, his skin already chewed up and getting worse by the day.

After spending the past five days pushing the cattle hard to get out of the Middle and Upper Crossings, they'd finally made it to a safe resting place at Aubry's Spring. Although it wasn't a real fort, the army had created Camp Wyncoop at the site and used it as a resting spot for troops in transit as well as for stationing Union soldiers whenever trouble with Indians flared up.

Made of dugouts and crudely built adobe buildings, the place wasn't even fortified with a stockade. Still, with the presence of the soldiers nearby, Flynn had slept last night for the first time since the run-in with the Irregulars.

After the confrontation at the river, he and Dylan had tracked the three for only a short distance before they came upon the remains of their camp. Piecing together the clues, they guessed there were about fifteen Confederates, and they all rode Indian ponies. In doing so, Flynn guessed they could easily disguise their crimes so the blame fell on the Indians. Was that what had happened with the overturned wagon and the corpses they'd come across after passing Rock Point?

Whatever the case, he was relieved the Irregulars had decided to leave them alone. Maybe Dylan's sharpshooting had scared them off. Flynn could only hope that was the last they'd see of any more of that kind of trouble.

After such long days of traveling, the cattle were suffering. In fact, upon arriving at Aubry's Spring, he'd made the decision to lay over and let the herd rest their sore feet. The buffalo grass was plentiful for grazing, and the freshwater spring, after which the site was named, flowed in abundance.

Every day they lost could cost them grazing land and water farther along the trail. But he had to take his chances, couldn't keep pushing, or the steers would start dropping dead with exhaustion. It was a real problem and possibility since they'd already passed by livestock other travelers had left behind, the carcasses rotting in the sun.

He couldn't let that happen. Especially not to Wyatt's cattle.

Dr. Howell had been in agreement with the few days of resting, especially upon the anniversary of Independence

Day. A number of other wagon trains were camped at the springs. And while there wouldn't be any big displays to celebrate the day, he'd heard rumors of a dance.

As it was, the day had been peaceful and quiet. Ivy and Dylan and Jericho had taken to practicing trick riding and fancy dismounting at every stop. Once Dylan and Jericho had moved on to wrestling, Ivy had persuaded Flynn to take her and Linnea to see the buffalo herd some of the other campers had sighted. They'd ridden farther than he'd wanted in order to track down the herd. But he'd done it because several officers and sergeants had come with them, eager to see the buffalo as well.

On one side of Flynn, Ivy breathed out a sigh of pure bliss. "I ain't never seen nothin' as beautiful in all my live-long days."

Lying on the ground on the other side of him, Linnea released a happy sound too. But her soft sigh did something to his insides he couldn't explain. Her chin rested on her arms, and her brown eyes were bright and sparkled with delight. And her smile. It was prettier than the pearly gates of heaven itself. With the wind teasing loose curls around her delicate features, he reckoned he'd never seen nothin' as beautiful as her in all *his* livelong days.

"There's gotta be hundreds of them. Don't you think so, Flynn?" Ivy slanted him a look and caught him staring at Linnea.

He quickly shifted his attention back to the herd but could feel Ivy's gaze boring into him.

"Don't you think so Flynn?" she asked again.

"Think what?" He kept his focus on the buffalo, but all he saw was the image of Linnea's pretty smile.

During the recent days of traveling, Linnea had stayed close to him and the wagon, clearly shaken by the incident at the river with the Irregulars. His heart still thudded clear out of his chest every time he pictured her standing in the river with the men closing in on her.

He'd been so frightened, he forgot about his sore hip joint when he raced after her, his guns aimed to kill. In fact, he couldn't ever remember wanting to kill as much as he had at that moment.

She was just too pretty for her own good. Even today, as they'd been saddling up to ride out to look at the buffalo, the officers eyed her with too much interest. He'd ambled over and made a point of referring to Linnea as his wife. That took care of the looks—at least mostly.

He prayed the Lord Almighty would forgive him for lying, but he reckoned she was better off with everyone assuming she was his. He wasn't as stocky as Wyatt, but he and all his brothers had inherited their pa's intimidating strength and size. And he didn't mind that one glare could make most men squirm in their boots.

Besides, she was the one who'd pretending to be married at the river, referring to him as her husband.

Ivy blew out a soft whistle. "Howdy-doody, Flynn. You've got it bad."

"Got what bad?"

Ivy's lips curved up into a smile, and she cocked her head toward Linnea.

He gave a curt shake and leveled a glare at her.

She just stared ahead with a smug smile.

Thankfully, Linnea had her full attention upon the buffalo and wasn't the least aware of Ivy's insinuation. Ever since that night they'd walked together behind the wagon and laid out their intentions, things had been nice and easy. They'd had plenty more conversations. Mainly she was sweeter than honey cakes, always listening to him and encouraging him, which made it real hard not to seek her out.

Now with the way things were going, he didn't want to do anything to send her running. He was gonna have to make sure Ivy knew they were just friends before she started meddling. But now wasn't the time or place.

Linnea gave a startled cry.

He stiffened and pulled out his revolver. "What's wrong?"

She rose to her knees. "The soldiers have their rifles out as if they're intending to shoot the buffalo."

He followed the direction of her gaze downwind, where the officers had taken up a position on the next rise. Sure enough, they were belly-crawling forward, sneaking up on a nearby bull that stood apart from the rest of the herd.

She released another murmur of protest and then grabbed Flynn's arm. "You need to stop them, Flynn."

Ivy sat up, her eyes rounding upon Linnea. "They're hunting. Ain't nothin' wrong with that."

"I've heard tales of the needless slaughter of these magnificent creatures." Linnea's fingers tightened around his bicep. "How hunters murder them for the pleasure of making the kill only to leave the dead bodies behind in the dust."

Flynn had heard the same. While he didn't condone needless killing, everyone said that millions of buffalo roamed the West. The soldiers havin' a little bit of sport wouldn't hurt nothin'.

As the officers drew nearer to the bull, they kept low until they were within range. Then they aimed.

"Please do something, Flynn." Linnea tugged his arm. "Surely you can distract them."

Ivy stared at him with riveted, almost amused interest.

Flynn trained his gaze on the buffalo. "If they bring one down, no doubt they'd give us some of the meat, and then we can try buffalo steaks tonight for supper."

"Buffalo steaks?" Linnea's voice rose on a note of horror. "I would never consider eating the poor buffalo. Who would want to?"

He sure as holy horses would. "Heard they taste an awful lot like beef."

Linnea shook her head, the wind tangling the red curls that had come loose from her knot. "I can't bear the thought of such slaughter. Isn't there anything we can do to stop those soldiers?"

As she turned her pleading eyes upon Flynn, he cocked the hammer on his gun and pulled the trigger, sending a shot into nothing. But the echo of the blast was enough to startle the herd and send it galloping at full speed, kicking up enough dust to form a cloud.

With the shaggy creatures stampeding away, the tension evaporated from Linnea's face. The pressure of her fingers upon his arm eased.

It was still enough for him to be entirely too conscious of her nearness, and his muscles rippled with the pleasure of her touch.

"Thank you, Flynn." Her widening smile only made her all the more beautiful.

He nodded and holstered his gun. He was gonna have some explaining to do to the officers, but her relief was worth the censure from men he'd never see again in a few days.

"I can't believe it." Ivy's voice broke through his haze.

"Can't believe what?" he replied.

Ivy was staring at him with another smug smile. "You do have it bad. Can't believe I haven't noticed it before."

"Bad?" Linnea chose that moment to finally listen to Ivy.

"Yep, Flynn's got it real bad for—"

Flynn clamped a hand over Ivy's mouth to cut off her words. Her eyes flashed with pleasure, as if she were laughing at him. "Hush up, Ivy."

She mumbled something more beneath his hand.

"Don't go looking for trouble where there ain't any."

Her eyes continued to sparkle.

"What kind of trouble?" Linnea asked. "Should we be heading back?"

"Yep. Reckon it's time."

"Very well."

He didn't know whether he should release Ivy's mouth yet or not. But he couldn't sit on the hill the rest of the day smothering her. He eased his hand away, slanting her a warning glare.

Linnea stood and brushed at her skirt, her gaze sweeping over the buffalo and the vast prairie. "I'll never forget this sight. It's truly amazing."

Ivy bounded up. "I'm guessing Flynn ain't never gonna forget this sight either." With a giggle, she waggled her eyebrows at him and cocked her head toward Linnea.

He had half a mind to strangle her.

She giggled again and then raced down the hill toward the horses.

Linnea tore her attention from the buffalo and smiled after Ivy. "I love hearing Ivy laugh. She's such a sweet girl."

Flynn loved hearing Ivy laugh too, but not now and not about this.

As she reached the horses, she turned and made kissing motions into the air.

Flames shot into his face. He prayed to the Lord Almighty Linnea wouldn't figure out what Ivy was doing.

Thankfully, she was as distracted as usual and already bending to pick flowers. This was one time he was glad she didn't pay attention to the things around her very well. Mighty glad indeed.

Linnea laughed breathlessly as she finished another turn of a cotillion with Dr. Greely. The fiddle music filled the night air along with the clapping and stomping of onlookers. The light of a dozen lanterns along with several blazing bonfires lit up the center area of Aubry's Spring, illuminating the Independence Day celebrations.

Those with flags had posted their Stars and Stripes, so true patriotism was displayed not only throughout the army camp but also among the wagon trains. Earlier they'd listened to a few short speeches, sung "The Star-Spangled Banner," and observed a moment of silence for the government and brave men struggling to maintain the rights the forefathers had labored so tirelessly to hand down to posterity.

The men were full of talk about the war, especially the death of the Confederate officer Stonewall Jackson. Since news of the battles and happenings trickled to the forts and travelers weeks after the fact, an unsettled undercurrent always existed because no one truly knew the tide of the war and whether it was in favor of the Union or the Confederacy.

But tonight, everyone seemed to have thrown off their uncertainty and misgivings to celebrate—everyone but Flynn. He'd been the first to volunteer to watch the cattle and take guard duty.

Now with the last of the dancing, Linnea had glimpsed Flynn reclining in a camp chair beside her grandfather. After finishing his shift, he'd likely noticed Grandfather sitting by himself and decided to keep him company. Flynn was sensitive. He saw things others didn't.

"Lovely dancing, Mrs. Newberry." Dr. Greely mopped his brow with his handkerchief. The night had brought little relief from the heat, and the sheen on Dr. Greely's face likely mirrored that on hers.

She pressed her hands to her overheated cheeks. It had been too long since she'd danced. The last time had been at a party that family friends had hosted the night she'd agreed to marry Asa. She'd forgotten just how much she enjoyed such occasions. Even if Dr. Greely had become obnoxious in claiming her as partner, she'd savored the evening and wished it didn't have to end.

But the fiddler had already warned them he was winding down. "One last dance," he called, starting a slower song meant for couples.

"Shall we, Mrs. Newberry?" Dr. Greely held out his hand.

Before she could accept it, Ivy swooped in and dragged her away from the dancers. "Come on now, Linnea. It ain't fair that you're only dancing with Dr. Greedy."

"Greely."

"He's Dr. Greedy in my book."

"Ivy, you mustn't say such things." Linnea's smile begged for release, though she shouldn't encourage the girl's disrespect.

"Flynn deserves one dance tonight, don't he?"

Only then did Linnea realize Ivy was towing her toward Flynn, and she attempted to slow her steps. "I don't think he wants to dance, Ivy. He's likely too tired from standing guard these past hours."

"Nope. I know for a fact he's mighty eager to get a dance with you."

"And how can you know that for a fact?"

"'Cause he can't keep his eyes off you."

Linnea glanced at Flynn again. With his long legs extended and crossed at the ankles, he relaxed with his arms folded behind his head, highlighting the broadness of his chest and his rounded biceps. He'd taken off his hat, and his tousled brown hair needed combing. Even so, he was starkly handsome, and a swarm of honeybees fluttered to life in her belly.

He was nodding at something Grandfather was saying, but Ivy was right. He was looking at her. His gaze was direct, unabashedly so. And it didn't swerve as she drew nearer.

"Get up, Flynn!" Ivy called.

He didn't budge.

Linnea wished she could read his expression. Why was he looking at her? Did he want to dance?

"Come on and dance with Linnea." Ivy didn't stop until they were standing in front of Flynn. "I can tell you've been itchin' to punch Dr. Greedy in the face and take a turn with Linnea."

Flynn shot a glare at his sister but didn't deny her statement, making the honeybees in Linnea's stomach swarm faster.

"Get on out there." Ivy nudged Flynn with her bare toes.

"You're a real good dancer, and Linnea could use a better partner for a change."

"Stop it, Ivy," Flynn growled.

Ivy's smile widened. "Dr. Howell, don't you think Flynn should take a turn dancing with Linnea, especially after how hard he's been working?"

"Quite right." Grandfather adored Flynn, and it was easy to see why after the consideration Flynn always showed him. "Flynn deserves the simple pleasures as much—if not more so—than anyone."

Before Linnea knew what was happening, Ivy shoved her forward so hard that she tripped and fell into Flynn.

"Whoa now." Bolting up from his camp chair, he caught and steadied her before she made a fool of herself and sprawled across his lap.

With his hands gripping her upper arms, she found herself face-to-face with him. Why not have one dance with this man tonight? It certainly wouldn't cause any harm. "Grandfather is right, Flynn. You deserve to enjoy yourself once in a while."

"I'm resting a spell—"

She began to tug him toward the other dancers. "You can rest when the dancing is finished. Now, let yourself have some fun and join me." When he didn't resist her pull, she smiled at him over her shoulder. "That is, unless you don't know how to dance."

"I know how."

"I'll be the judge of that." Again she gave him a look, one containing her mirth. She was hoping for a smile in return, and when he grudgingly offered her a slight one, she willingly took it.

As she drew him into the fray of other revelers, she wasted

no time in positioning one hand upon his shoulder, twisting him in the steps of the dance. He remained rigid for a fraction of a second, then took her upraised hand and settled his other one at the small of her back. The moment his fingers connected with the sensitive spot, a charge zipped to her limbs and all the way to her toes.

She couldn't keep from arching into him slightly.

He'd already started stepping to the tune, sweeping her along, his attention on her face. His nostrils flared imperceptibly at the same time the green-blue of his eyes darkened.

Was he feeling the chemistry between them the same as she did from time to time? Though she did her best to ignore it, there were moments—like now—when it was undeniable.

She couldn't allow herself to dwell on it. Couldn't, wouldn't. Such meandering thoughts would only bring trouble and heartache. She'd done well recently in curbing any such feelings for Flynn, and she couldn't allow herself to get carried away with him because of one dance.

"You're right, Flynn."

"Of course I am."

She chuckled. "Don't you even want to know about what?"

"I'm a good dancer?"

"Yes. Surprisingly, you are very good."

"Surprisingly?" His voice turned light and teasing just the way she loved.

He was making her giddy. Why did he have such power over her? "And whom do I have to thank for turning you into such a good dancer? Helen?"

His fingers at her back tightened and tugged her closer. And though their bodies weren't touching, she felt suddenly breathless.

An instant later, he ducked his head, and his breath brushed her ear. "Sounds like you're jealous of Helen."

His whisper ricocheted through her. "I am absolutely not jealous of Helen."

"Good. You shouldn't be." His words were low and sincere.

Thankfully, he pulled back a safe distance before she did something embarrassing like kiss him again. They danced for several more steps, and she felt weightless, as if she were twirling in the air. "You should have joined the festivities earlier."

"And watch you dance with Dr. Greely? No thanks."

"Sounds like you're jealous of Dr. Greely."

"Yep. Ain't gonna deny it."

His admission made her happier than she cared to admit. "You know Dr. Greely isn't my type of man. I told you that already."

The lantern light reflected off Flynn's face, revealing the rugged lines and dark stubble. Without his hat to shield his face, his eyes were bright and as lively as the music. "What is your type?"

"I don't have a type."

"Every woman has a type she prefers."

"They do?"

"Reckon so."

"And what type do you think I like?"

"I ain't an expert on women, but if I had to take a gander, I'd say you'll settle down with a real distinguished, rich fella, with a whole lot of education, who lets you do as you please."

After only a few minutes with Flynn, her pulse was alive

and her body humming. She wished she'd had the whole evening with him and not one last dance.

"I'm right, ain't I?"

"Only on the letting-me-do-as-I-please part."

Flynn's grin made another appearance. "And he's gonna have to be willing to put up with you getting yourself into trouble every other day."

She playfully slapped his arm. "That's not true. I haven't gotten myself into any trouble today, have I?"

"The day's not over yet." His tone was gentle and teasing.

She couldn't keep from laughing.

He glanced sideways. "Don't look now, but Dr. Greely is shooting mad that you're having more fun dancing with me than him. Looks like he's the jealous one now."

Her laughter spilled out even more, and she had to cup a hand over her mouth to prevent herself from making a scene. The merriment in Flynn's eyes did nothing to curb her own amusement, especially when she sneaked a peek at Dr. Greely. Flynn was right. He was scowling fiercely at them.

She tried to rein in her humor. She didn't want to offend the gentleman. But for tonight, at this moment, she couldn't make herself worry about his or any of the other scientists' acceptance. Somehow, Flynn's easy acceptance of her was all that mattered.

The dance ended all too quickly and everyone began to disperse. Dr. Greely was at her side in an instant, insisting on walking her to the wagon.

She was hoping Flynn would offer to do it since she wasn't ready for her time with him to come to a close. But at a glare from Dr. Greely, Flynn gave a curt nod before he made his way back to Grandfather.

As she allowed Dr. Greely to escort her, her gaze strayed to Flynn where he carried the chairs and slowed his steps to match Grandfather's. She didn't have a *type*, as Flynn had insinuated. But if she did, she wouldn't mind having a man as kind and thoughtful as Flynn McQuaid.

CHAPTER
13

Danger lurked nearby.

Flynn skimmed his fingers across the horse prints in the soft, sandy soil. The lantern light wasn't bright, but it was enough to see that the tracks were fresh. From the looks of things, he guessed a whole passel of horses had been through the area.

Had Indians been spying on the camp, aiming to attack? From everything he'd heard, the Indians rarely ambushed at night. They usually waited until the early morning hours or even full daylight. Just the other day, a passing caravan claimed they'd lost half a dozen of their best horses to an Indian ambush.

But what about the Irregulars? Were they roaming around the outskirts of Aubry's Spring even now, itching for a confrontation with the Union soldiers? The backwoods fighters wouldn't think twice about using the cover of night to terrorize unsuspecting wagon parties to draw out the soldiers.

At the crunch of footsteps, Flynn straightened and drew

his revolver. In the next heartbeat, he had it out, pointed, and his finger on the trigger. He shifted the lantern higher to expose the intruder.

Linnea halted, her eyes widening at the sight of his gun.

"Thunderation, Linnea!" He jammed his weapon into the holster, his pulse galloping at breakneck speed. "What in holy horses are you doing sneaking around here? I could've shot you."

A dozen paces away, she didn't move, her face pale and her body frozen as though she, too, was realizing how close she'd come to taking one of his bullets. Her long curls fluttered in the breeze as did her nightdress, which she'd covered with a lacy shawl. Her feet were bare and damp with dew. In all white, her red hair stood out in greater contrast.

She could've been an angel standing there, except he doubted an angel would appear bed-tousled and so blamed tempting.

He rubbed a hand across his eyes to block out the sight of her. Lord Almighty, this woman was gonna be the death of him one way or another. "Get on back to the wagon, Linnea. And go to bed."

"I saw you itching your fly bites when you passed by, and I thought you could use some of the salve I concocted today."

Inwardly, he cursed himself for walking past her wagon on his way to take his shift watching the cattle. He'd only wanted to reassure himself she was where she needed to be. Especially since she'd been sore with him for going with the officers buffalo hunting earlier in the day.

He hadn't been able to resist their invitation, not after Ivy ribbed him nonstop about firing that shot yesterday, insisting he was salivating over Linnea like a pup for a bone. He needed to prove to himself that Ivy wasn't right, that he was still his own man. He wasn't so addled over Linnea that he couldn't make up his own mind about taking down a buffalo.

For a few hours, he'd been able to forget about her during the thrill of the hunt. They'd crawled, flat on their bellies, up to the herd within a hundred paces. Somehow the bull they sighted sensed their presence and put up its short tail in distrust. Before it could bolt away, Flynn had risen and taken the shot, sending his bullet through the ribs between its shoulder blades.

The beast swayed at the impact but stayed on its feet. Flynn rapidly fired again, this time aiming for the heart, which was deeper in a buffalo's chest than the heart of other game. The bull remained on its feet, trotting away—although more clumsily. The officers cheered Flynn's efforts, and he gave them the chance to take the final shots and fell the fierce creature.

The moment they returned to camp with as much of the buffalo carcass as they could carry between them, Linnea blanched and spun away. For supper, he'd tried to enjoy the thick, juicy slab of steak, but with every bite, all he could think about was her distress.

"Thought you were spitting mad at me over killing the buffalo." He lowered the lantern so the darkness shrouded her somewhat.

Her footsteps padded closer. "Of course I wasn't mad at you. Really, it's silly of me to care so much about slaughtering one of the magnificent animals, not when the meat could be used to provide a feast like it did tonight."

As she stepped into the circle of light again, he forced himself to gaze over the cattle, most of them lying down in clusters, necks relaxed and heads resting on their flanks. The beef cattle didn't require much sleep, upward of four hours a night compared with the ten to twelve needed by dairy cows. That made the beeves easier to drive, but it also meant a greater call for keeping an eye on them at night to prevent them from wandering off. And of course he didn't want to chance any thieving.

He'd made it halfway to Wyatt's ranch without losing a single stock, and he aimed to keep it that way. At least until he met up with Wyatt. The instructions the Missouri breeder had given him indicated Wyatt hoped to meet them at Bent's Fort. From Aubrey's Spring, Flynn figured they had two or three days of traveling before they crossed into Colorado Territory. Maybe a week or two at most before they reached Bent's Fort.

"Do you forgive me for making such a fuss?" Linnea's voice was as sweet and innocent as always. He didn't know how a single living being could hold a grudge against her longer than the blink of an eye.

"Ain't nothin' to forgive. You've got a soft heart is all."

"Thank you, Flynn." She was close enough now that she reached out and squeezed his arm.

Her touch burned straight through him. "Best head on back." He took a step away from her, breaking contact.

She lowered herself to the ground and patted the grass. "Sit down and let me doctor your fly bites first."

"It's the middle of the night, and it ain't proper for you to be out here with me alone."

"We're not alone. Dylan is right over there." She nodded across the pasture to where the moonlight revealed his brother's outline.

She was right. The boy could see everything in the lantern light as easily as if the sun were shining right down on them.

"Fine." Flynn released a tight breath. Already he was scratching again at the bites on the back of his neck. The flies had been bad around the spring, worse than anywhere else so far on the trail. And even though he'd taken to wearing a neckerchief, the buggers seemed to favor his neck and shoulders anyway.

He set down the lantern and situated himself, extending his legs and leaning back on his hands. Linnea rose to her knees and fiddled with the knot in his neckerchief. She brushed against him, the sweet waft of her scented soap filling his nostrils. When her fingers grazed the back of his neck, he about jumped up with the need to put distance between them.

Having her so close and touching him was a bad idea. A very bad one.

He didn't start breathing again until she removed the neckerchief, dropped it, and sat back on her heels to open the crock with whatever salve she'd made up.

She was chattering on about the plants she'd found and all that she'd done to mix up the ingredients. But he couldn't focus on her words, was suddenly too conscious of the fact that she was in her nightdress.

"Everyone else has appreciated my salve today." She leaned in. "They're saying it's working wonders on their bites. And I have the feeling it will work wonders on yours too, Flynn." A second later, cold and slimy goop pressed against his neck. Thankfully, it doused his rising temperature and made him forget about her touch . . . for the space of ten seconds, until she finished on his neck and took hold of his hand.

"Do you have bites anywhere else?" She lifted his hand into the light and examined it. Then she ran her fingers up his sleeve.

His temperature spiked as fast as a fever. "I'll be fine now." He tugged his arm free.

She brushed her hand across his back, sending the fever spreading through his body. "How about on your back? Everyone else complained of having bites on their backs."

"Reckon I have a few, but the worst is my neck—"

She started tugging his shirt out of his pants.

"Woman," he growled, "you're killing me." He jumped up and stalked several paces away. He jerked his hat off and stuck his hands in his hair. Heaven help him.

She was so quiet that he guessed his abruptness had offended her. But he couldn't help it.

"I was just trying to help." Her tone was contrite.

"Pulling off my clothes ain't helping."

"I wasn't pulling off your clothes in the way you're insinuating."

He stood stiffly, unable to turn around to face her.

"I was acting in the role of a doctor the same way I did to others earlier."

"Well, I ain't like the others."

She grew quiet, as though finally understanding his reaction to all her touching.

He blew out a breath and dropped his hands from his hair. Had he hurt her? He hated the thought that he might have. But he didn't know what else to say without spelling out the truth that he was attracted to her, and that as hard as he was trying to pretend he wasn't, he was failing.

"Don't we have an understanding that neither of us is interested in pursuing any kind of relationship?"

The confusion in her voice drew him around, and he found himself looking at her again in all her glorious beauty, her curly hair falling nearly to her waist, her shawl hanging loose and revealing more of her nightdress.

"I thought we were friends."

His entire body tightened with the need to cross to her, sweep her into his arms, and forget all about friendship. Why was he so blamed set on not marrying, anyway? Somehow, somewhere, he'd decided having a woman would hurt him. But for the life of him, at this moment with Linnea sitting in the grass only a few steps away, he couldn't figure out why.

"We are friends." He forced the words, but they came out gravelly.

"Are you sure? Sometimes I feel as though you don't like me, Flynn."

"Course I like you." He liked her too much, but he couldn't say that. He couldn't tell her that last night, her dancing with Dr. Greely had tortured him until he'd about gone crazy. He couldn't tell her that when he'd taken a turn with her, he hadn't wanted to let her go when the music ended. He couldn't tell her that he'd practically dreamed about her all night long.

Flynn swallowed hard and stuffed his hat on. Then he patted his pocket, stuck his hand in, and retrieved the paper he'd folded. "Found these for you." He held out the packet.

She stood and approached him cautiously, as if he were one of those temperamental buffalo that would bolt at the least hint of human contact. She stopped a hand's span away and took his offering. "What is it?"

He nodded at the paper. "You'll see."

She opened it up and then stared wide-eyed.

He scratched the back of his head. What had he been thinking to give her those? They probably weren't worth anything.

"Flynn," she whispered.

"Toss 'em if you don't need 'em—"

"Wherever did you discover them?" She fingered the two items as gently as if they were rare jewels.

"Saw 'em when I was out hunting earlier. Didn't think you had them but wasn't sure . . ."

"No, I don't have either. The yellow one is the *Helianthus petiolaris*, the prairie sunflower. And the other—well, I'll need to ask Grandfather, but it looks like it's a milkweed from the dogbane family."

Whenever she started rattling off the names of plants, they sounded foreign to him. Even so, he loved how smart she was and how animated she became. Now the delight in her expression chased away the insecurities he'd felt since picking the flowers.

"Flynn McQuaid." Her eyes filled with adoration. "I think you're the sweetest man I've ever met."

He started to shrug, but she threw her arms around him and hugged him. He willed himself not to hug her in return, to remain immobile, and to let the moment pass as quickly as possible.

But as she pressed against him and squeezed, he lowered his arms around her, hesitantly.

She rested her face against his chest. "Thank you."

"You're welcome." He held himself rigidly a heartbeat longer, then allowed himself to relax. He was doing just fine holding her. No trouble at all. He could corral his reactions, keep them in check when he needed to. Like now.

"Maybe tomorrow we can go out to where you located both specimens, and I can sketch them."

"I reckon we can make the time."

She pulled away slightly and smiled up at him. "You're a good friend, Flynn."

Except friends didn't have an overwhelming urge to bend down and kiss the freckles off upturned noses. He tucked her face gently into the crook of his neck before he gave in to the need to kiss her.

He closed his eyes and dragged in a breath, fighting against his urges. But as she nestled in and released a contented sigh, his fingers glided down, burrowing into her silky curls as if he'd just discovered gold.

A warning whistle blasted in his conscience. But his body betrayed him, and his fingers just kept on mining through the riches, going deeper, until he was hopelessly tangled. He pressed his face to the top of her head, relishing the softness of her curly strands.

He could go all night with her in his arms. He could go his whole life like this. The truth was, he wasn't sure how he'd be able to go his whole life without it . . . without her.

Tense longing zinged through every muscle.

As if sensing the yearning, her arms tightened around him, and she clutched at his vest and shirt. Her body had stiffened, no longer malleable and soft. Her breathing grew more ragged. For all her talk about friendship, there were times—like now—when she sure didn't act like just a friend. When she acted like she wanted him as much as he did her.

What would it hurt to kiss her again? The merest thought of meshing mouths was enough to make him go crazy. Oh Lord Almighty, he needed help, and fast.

Swallowing hard, he extricated first one hand from her hair, then the other. The effort was harder than anything else he'd done on the journey west. Besides, he couldn't forget Dylan was watching. A sixteen-year-old didn't need to see him losing all self-control with a woman who wasn't his and never would be, especially not when he kept having to chastise Dylan for spending too much time with the young ladies.

Flynn had failed to set a good example with Helen. And now he had the chance to show Dylan how to respect a woman. Teach him to use restraint.

As he loosened his hold on Linnea, she clung to him, her fingers digging in harder.

He shut his eyes, clenched his jaw, and tried to draw in a fortifying breath. Then, before he changed his mind, he dropped his hands away. "Go back to the wagon, Linnea. And don't come out here again." His voice was strained, even hard. But he couldn't help it.

She hesitated, then released him, taking a rapid step back.

He spun around, stuffed his hands into his pockets, and waited for her to go.

A few seconds later, her bare feet pattered away. Only when she was out of sight and well on her way to the wagon did he allow his shoulders to sag.

Pueblo was only a month away. One month. Then they'd split ways as the botany expedition headed north to Denver and he drove the cattle up into the mountains.

He'd resisted his feelings for her so far. All he had to do was make it a little longer without giving in to the storm brewing within.

CHAPTER
14

Linnea's tongue stuck to the roof of her mouth, her thirst making her nearly delirious. Even in the shade of the wagon, the mid-July heat suffocated her.

"Keep on diggin'." Flynn's urgent command penetrated her haze.

In the unrelenting sun, each of the men shoveled at the sandy bed—all that remained of the Arkansas River. Their grunts rose into the hot, dry air. The breeze—when one blew—was like the bellows of a flaming forge, doing little to provide any relief. The few green ash and honey locust dotting the banks were shriveled and provided scant shade. Even the hardy sand sagebrush drooped in protest, the silvery green the only color in the plain brown prairie of eastern Colorado.

The hundred-degree temperatures, lack of rain, and many livestock and people traveling ahead of them had depleted the water. And for the past three days, they'd gone without, carefully doling out the last drops in their cups and canteens.

"I'm so thirsty." Ivy leaned her head against Linnea's shoulder, her pretty face flushed and her eyes closed in weariness.

Linnea pressed a kiss to the girl's head. "I know, sweetheart. I know." Linnea had lost count of how many times Ivy had complained of thirst, especially as they'd traveled today. When they'd started out in the morning, they'd hoped to reach Bent's Fort and find water there. But the cattle had given out by midafternoon.

Flynn's forehead had furrowed like the cracks in the dry ground. With the piles of sun-bleached cattle and mule bones littering both sides of the trail, she could only imagine how difficult it was for him not to worry about what would happen to his brother's cattle.

Not only was the water gone, but so was the rich *Bouteloua gracilis*, the blue grama, that was so hardy and able to withstand drought conditions. With their slower pace, many other travelers had passed them, and now Flynn was having to drive the cattle farther away from the trail to find grass, causing more delays.

After the night she'd put salve on his fly bites and hugged him for his thoughtful gift of flowers, she'd expected things to be awkward again between them. Thankfully, Flynn's frustration over her forwardness hadn't lasted, and the next day he'd fallen into step next to her as he usually did.

She enjoyed their daily time together, ambling along and conversing about everything and anything. But over the past week with the deteriorating conditions, she'd seen less of him—since he'd been so focused on the cattle—although yesterday and today, he'd made a point of stopping every few hours to give Ivy and her sips from the tepid water remaining in his canteen. She tried refusing, not wanting to take the sustenance away from him. He needed it more than she did. But he insisted every time.

His shirt was soaked with perspiration, and his hair stuck to his neck. In the process of ramming his shovel into the sandy riverbed, his sights shifted to Ivy and her. Concern radiated from every muscle of his body.

His gaze darted to the trail to the west. But the horizon was as empty as it had been every other time he'd looked. No doubt he was hoping to see Dr. Greely, Dr. Parker, and Dr. Johnson, who'd offered to ride ahead to Bent's Fort and return with water. Too weak to travel, Grandfather had remained behind, lying in the wagon to stay out of the heat. With the sun beating down on the canvas, the interior was like an oven. And Linnea feared he wouldn't last much longer without some relief.

Flynn tossed a heavy load of sand from the hole, then paused. "Let's try lowering the wagon bed now."

With Jericho, Nash, Clay, and Dylan all working in tandem with Flynn, they hefted the wooden box into the sandy dugout. They stood back, shovels idle, and stared down. Flynn had proposed the experiment, since water existed under the sand. The hope was that it would seep up into the wagon box if they dug far enough.

She lifted a prayer heavenward, not for herself but for Ivy, Grandfather, and the baby growing inside her. Though she hadn't expected or even wanted a baby at this point in her life, now that she was pregnant, she was gradually becoming accustomed to the life growing inside her, especially now that she felt flutters from time to time.

Since she was already thin, she was still able to hide the

slight swell in her abdomen and hoped she'd be able to do so for a while longer. As far as she could tell, no one suspected she was carrying a baby, and she wanted to keep it that way and not add to Grandfather's stress.

The expedition was already challenging enough with the setbacks from the few times the research had been lost. Now, over the past week, they'd had little strength and energy to devote to anything but merely surviving. That meant once they reached the Front Range, they would all need to work incredibly hard to make up for the missed research. She wouldn't let her pregnancy be the cause for further problems.

Dylan whooped and threw his hat into the air. "We've got water!"

More cheering and whooping erupted from the other men, and relief poured through Linnea. Flynn had been right. Now he dipped a bucket into the wooden box, and when he removed it, water brimmed to the top.

"Thank the Lord." Linnea tried to push up. She had to start a fire to help boil the water before they could drink it. Grandfather always insisted on the practice with river water, claiming that the heat served the purpose of killing potentially dangerous organisms. While many other travelers didn't adhere to the practice and didn't seem to languish, Linnea had followed her grandfather's instructions, as had Flynn.

Flynn stalked toward her, and she climbed to her feet. "You did it."

He nodded, his sun-bronzed face lined with the dust of the trail. "I'll set the water to boiling for you and Ivy and Dr. Howell."

"I can do it. I'm sure you're eager to drive the cattle down and let them drink."

He moved past her and grabbed several of the buffalo chips Ivy had gathered earlier. "You're more important than the cattle."

Ivy reclined against the wagon wheel, watching them with glassy eyes. "Linnea's a whole heap more important than the cattle, ain't she, Flynn?"

Linnea was too hot to read into either Ivy's or Flynn's statement. Instead, she followed after him, grabbing the biggest kettle and the corked bottle where she stored the matches.

Within minutes, flames licked at the kettle.

"Finish this while we wait for the water to boil." Flynn held out his canteen.

She pushed it back. "You need it more than I do."

The shake of his head was almost angry. "Drink it, Linnea."

"I'll give it to Grandfather and Ivy—"

"Blast it all. You've been giving your ration to them every time. If you don't have something soon, you're gonna pass out."

Unfortunately, her legs chose that moment to buckle, causing her to sway. He was at her side in an instant, slipping his arm around her waist and bracing her. "See what I mean?"

She steadied herself and tried to pull away.

"Whoa now. You're not going anywhere until you drink this." He held up his canteen and tugged the stopper out with his teeth.

She was too tired to fight and gave way to the solidness of his body and the strength of his arms. When he lifted the rim to her lips, she allowed him to tip the remaining contents into her mouth.

All the while, his worried gaze never left her face.

She swallowed, letting the liquid soothe her parched tongue and throat. "Thank you, Flynn. I don't know how you do it."

He tipped the canteen back up, forcing her to take another sip. "Do what?"

She relished the water even though it had a metallic taste after having sat for so long in the container. "How do you take care of everyone else without one thought to yourself?"

He shrugged.

She lifted a hand to his cheek, wanting to soothe his worry. "You're an amazing man. Has anyone told you that?"

He didn't move away from her touch. "I've got plenty of faults."

"Name one." She brushed her fingers over the stubble covering his jaw. She was being too forward but she was unable to stop herself now that she'd begun

"For starters, I couldn't keep Brody from enlisting."

Her roaming fingers stilled. "Flynn McQuaid, you cannot blame yourself for Brody's enlisting. He's a grown man with a mind of his own." She'd already told Flynn that during one of their many talks. But he couldn't let go of the heavy responsibility he'd taken upon his shoulders.

He shook his head and looked off in the distance. "Ma gave me one job on her deathbed. And that was to watch over the kids."

"And you are. Look what you're doing for them. You're braving this journey to give them a better life."

His jaw flexed beneath her fingers. She loved the solidness

of his muscles hardening. She loved the texture of his scruff. And she loved standing this close to him with his arm circling around her.

"You are amazing. And it's about time you knew it." She let her fingers skim down to his chin. After getting to know him over the past two months of traveling together, she could honestly say she'd never met a better man.

He didn't reply this time. And when she chanced a glance up, his attention was riveted to her lips. The green-blue of his eyes was murky with a wanting that made her insides tremble.

She waited for him to bend down and kiss her with a wanting of her own that took her breath away, a wanting she'd felt each of the few occasions he'd held her. At the boldness of her thoughts, she flushed all the way down to her toes. She dropped her hand away from his face and prayed he hadn't been able to read her thoughts.

"I reckon you oughta just get it over with, Flynn," Ivy said from where she still sat listlessly in the shade of the wagon.

He didn't look at Ivy. Instead he released Linnea and added another buffalo chip to the flames, then inspected the water beginning to bubble inside the kettle.

"Just do it," Ivy continued. "It's as clear as sunshine you've got a hankerin' to kiss her in a mighty bad way."

"Hush up, Ivy." Flynn's glare could have withered the clusters of lace hedgehog cactus that grew in the dry soil.

Linnea couldn't contain a smile at the girl's antics. She surely enjoyed riling up her big brother.

"From the way Linnea's been watchin' you, I know she wouldn't mind one bit. Right, Linnea?"

Linnea's smile slipped away, and mortification rushed in to

replace it. She folded her hands and stared at them. Though she couldn't deny Ivy's suggestion, neither could she outright admit she'd just been thinking about kissing Flynn.

"See, since you both want to, you might as well go on and do it."

"Ivy." Flynn's voice was filled with warning.

Linnea forced herself to speak calmly and logically as she did from time to time with the girl. "Now, sweetheart, a woman cannot walk around and kiss handsome men whenever she wants to. It simply isn't proper."

"Then you think Flynn's handsome?" Ivy's retort was quick for someone so lethargic.

"Of course he is." As soon as the words were out, Linnea wished she could take them back, especially when Flynn slanted one of his brooding looks her way.

"So it's settled then?" Ivy persisted. "You're gonna kiss?"

Flynn straightened. "You're gonna get a whupping if you don't hush up."

Ivy grinned and leaned back against the wagon wheel.

Silently, tensely, Flynn finished the boiling and pouring the water into cups.

Linnea stood and watched, uncertain what to say or do. They shouldn't have touched. That was the problem. Whenever they had any contact, it only lit sparks between them.

Did he want to kiss her as much as Ivy claimed? Linnea had the sudden urge to ask him and find out the truth. But, of course, such a question would be as inappropriate as Ivy's had been. And it would serve no purpose since Flynn always made it clear he had no intention of crossing any lines, even if an attraction flared from time to time.

But what about her? Did she want more? Could she see herself having a future with Flynn McQuaid?

The question plagued her throughout the rest of the afternoon. As she helped Grandfather and Ivy sip their water and replenish themselves, her body thrummed with a strange sense of heightened awareness of Flynn. Even as she tried to squelch it and keep herself busy, her attention strayed to him all too frequently.

Thankfully, he didn't notice since he was busy bringing the cattle in groups to the watering hole, making sure they drank slowly and in steady increments so they didn't overindulge, bloat, and get sick.

By the time the men finished with the cattle, the sun was setting into ominously dark clouds. Flynn had paused on several occasions to study the sky, and after conferring with men from another wagon train that had stopped to use Flynn's watering hole, they corralled the wagons around as much of the livestock as possible and tethered the rest. Then they dug holes to secure the wagon wheels just in case the winds grew fierce enough to blow them over.

As the changing weather front drew nearer, there was talk of tornados and hail and terrible lightning that frequently accompanied such storms. With new urgency, she and Grandfather worked to cover all the research to keep it dry and safe.

Darkness had fallen when the wind finally picked up and raged with a ferocity that rivaled a New York nor'easter. With the possibility of the canvas top not being able to withstand the gusts, Flynn had insisted that she, Ivy, and Grandfather wait out the storm underneath the wagon. He tacked down the canvas and made sure they were as secure as possible before he headed out to take his turn at standing guard.

As the hail and rain and wind rattled the wagon and ripped at the canvas, Linnea huddled next to Ivy and Grandfather, clinging to her cloak, praying for Flynn to remain safe, and wishing he didn't have to take the brunt of the storm, especially with the lightning striking so close and vibrating the ground.

Rainwater found a way into their dark tent, dripping in from above the wagon as well as dribbling in from cracks in the canvas. But overall, thanks to Flynn's ingenuity, they stayed mostly dry.

After the blistering heat, the cooler air at first soothed her overheated body. But as the night wore on, Linnea wrapped her waterproof cloak tighter to ward off the chill.

When the worst of the storm had passed, a hard rain continued. Exhaustion finally claimed her. She wasn't sure how long she slept before the lifting of the canvas woke her. Lantern light shone in, revealing Flynn crouched outside, the rain pelting his oiled poncho.

She pushed herself to her elbows.

"Didn't mean to wake you," he said so quietly she almost didn't hear him above the patter.

"How are you? Are you soaked completely?"

"I'm doing alright." He thrust his lantern under the wagon and peered around, taking in Ivy and Grandfather who were rolled up in their cloaks and still asleep. "You staying dry?"

"A little damp, but I certainly cannot complain, not when I've been safe here while you've been out there."

His attention snagged on one corner near her end of the wagon where the rainwater was pouring in like a spigot left open. He belly-crawled under the canvas, placed the lantern next to her, and then flipped over on his back and began to fiddle with the leak.

Within a few seconds, he managed to staunch the flow. "Is it leaking anywhere else?" He shifted and surveyed the rest of the wagon bed above them.

She rolled over to face him. "We're doing fine. I have no doubt we're the driest of all the other campers."

"You sure?" His gaze dropped to her before he resumed his examination of the wagon bed.

"I'm positive."

He homed in on a steady drip at a spot close to her head. He reached above her, the movement causing their shoulders to brush.

She held herself motionless, suddenly conscious of how close he was.

For several moments, he tucked and poked at the canvas until the dripping abated. "There." He dropped his arm and leaned away, breaking the contact. "The worst is over. You should be fine the rest of the night."

"Thank you, Flynn. I simply don't know what we'd do without you."

"Have the feeling with everyone being wet, we'll pull out real early. Best sleep now while you can." He began to inch toward the opening.

Her hand shot out and made contact with his arm.

He froze.

She pulled away, again self-conscious of their proximity. "You should sleep too."

He nodded, then once more moved as though to leave.

"Wait." She scooted closer to Ivy. "I really think you

should just stay under here. You'll be much drier, and I'll make room for you."

At the widening gap, he halted. He eyed the space warily. "Nope—"

"Oh, Flynn, I promise I won't even breathe on you, and I promise I won't make you uncomfortable in any way." Like she had earlier in the day when she'd brushed his cheeks.

He ducked his head as though remembering the same.

She glanced sideways to Ivy and Grandfather who hadn't budged. In fact, Grandfather's snores rose into the air. "If you'd be more comfortable, I'll switch places with Ivy." She lifted a hand to rouse the girl.

"No, don't wake her," he whispered. He hesitated a moment longer, then secured the canvas where he'd entered.

At his intention of staying, she cleared more space beside her, sidling as close to Ivy as she could. When he leaned back and sprawled out, he was still less than a body's width away from her.

Her muscles tensed with a readiness she couldn't explain.

He held himself stiffly for several heartbeats, then he turned and blew out the lantern. Even when the darkness shrouded them, she was all too keenly aware of his presence so near. When she heard him expel a taut breath, she wished she could help relieve some of the stress he was under. He carried so much of the burden of both his own party as well as theirs. She was tempted to reach out and brush a soothing hand across his forehead, the same way she did from time to time with Ivy.

But she'd promised not to touch him, no matter how innocently. And even if something about their relationship was changing, she had to respect his wishes to remain platonic. She tucked her hands into her cloak. "Good night, Flynn."

"Night." His reply was terse. Silence fell between them, broken only by the pelting of rain.

She settled against her damp pallet and hugged her arms to herself. Even if he wasn't thrilled to sleep near her, she was relieved he was there, safe and out of the storm. That was all that mattered. At least that's what she tried to tell herself.

CHAPTER

15

Flynn awoke with a start. For a moment, he fought against the panic that had recently clamped around his chest and hadn't let go. The same panic he'd experienced when he held his ma's hand and watched the life ebb from her face.

But at the steady tap of rain through the darkness, he let the tension ease from his muscles. The rainwater was filling up their barrels and pails and every container they had. He'd made sure of it during his hours on guard duty. The people he cared about wouldn't have to suffer from thirst any longer.

His mind flashed with the image of Linnea's face so pale, her lips so parched, her body so listless. The instant he pictured her, he breathed out a prayer of thanksgiving that the Almighty had protected them. He'd never before done as much praying as he had yesterday during their plodding forward. He'd spent hours begging God for some means of saving the group. At first he included the cattle.

But as the hours had dragged on, he realized he didn't care

one whit about the cattle, that he'd gladly lose every single one and grovel before Wyatt, if only he could save his siblings.

Who was he kidding? Linnea had been at the top of his mind. As much as he wanted to deny it, his feelings for her had pressed in harder and hotter than a branding iron searing cow flesh. The almighty truth was that he'd spent more time worrying about her than he had anyone or anything else.

He blew out a breath only to remember where he was, that he was sleeping underneath the same wagon as her. While he couldn't see her, he sensed her presence.

She was still curled up next to Ivy, but the span between them had diminished. And it was his fault for spreading out rather than keeping himself aloof and rigid as he'd initially determined to do. At least he hadn't done anything stupid in his sleep, like reach for her and wrap his arms around her.

Since the moment he'd crawled underneath the wagon, a low warning at the back of his mind had urged him to get out, had reminded him he was only flirting with temptation. Yet, when she'd pleaded with him to rest there, he hadn't been able to resist, especially when she assured him she'd stay right by Ivy.

He heard what she'd left unspoken, that she realized how her casual touches always seemed to stir up longing between them. She'd all but promised not to initiate anything anymore. If something happened between them, it would be his fault.

He heard her shift and release a soft sigh. The sound hit him smack in the gut and sparked a flame. He stiffened and stared through the darkness at the wagon bed. The rain was lessening, and from the tempering of the night, he guessed dawn was only an hour or two off. Maybe it was time to get up and away from Linnea. He'd slept for a few hours, and that was good enough. He'd catch a few more winks when they stopped midmorning.

He shifted, propping himself up on his elbows.

"Flynn?" Her whisper was sleep laden.

He had only to picture her tousled hair and half-lidded look for another punch to hit him low and hard.

"Are you awake?" she asked.

"Nope."

She released a soft laugh.

In spite of the danger of the fire burning in him, a grin tugged at his lips.

"Is it time to get up?"

"Not yet."

"Good. You need to sleep longer. You never get enough sleep."

At the slight strain of worry in her voice, he eased back so he was lying flat. He liked knowing she was concerned about him, but he didn't want her to fret more than necessary. He'd rest, then once she was asleep again, he'd slip out.

She was quiet for only a few seconds. "I'm really proud of you for saving the cattle. I can't stop thinking about how resourceful and inventive you are."

He had half a mind to admit he hadn't been focused on the cattle when he'd dug through the sand to find the water, that he'd been digging like a mad man for her sake.

"Wyatt will be very proud of you too."

"Not so sure about that." In one of their many talks, Flynn had explained to Linnea how deep his rift with Wyatt was.

"If Wyatt's not proud of you, then I intend to tell him

each and every one of your brave deeds on this trip to protect the cattle."

Flynn pushed aside the bitterness toward his older brother as he'd done earlier when he'd been praying. Maybe it was time to let bygones be bygones. Besides, he didn't want to think on Wyatt tonight, not while he was whispering in the dark with Linnea. "Hate to remind you, but most of those brave deeds have been spent saving you from trouble."

"You hate to remind me, do you?" Her whisper contained a note of teasing. "I think you like it when I keep you busy coming to my rescue."

"One of these days you're gonna scare me clean out of my boots."

She chuckled again. "I'd like to see that happen. But I intend to make the last couple of weeks of our trip together as trouble free as possible."

Last couple of weeks. He'd been biding his time until their parting, but now that the end was in sight, he had the sudden need to slow down.

"It's sure going to be strange not to be with you." Her voice was wistful. "I know you'll probably be relieved to go our separate ways, but I admit, I'll miss you."

"By *you* do you mean everyone or me specifically?" He couldn't keep back the question.

"Why, Flynn McQuaid, are you wanting me to miss you specifically?" A smile laced her tone as if his question had pleased her.

"Maybe." He rolled to his side and laid his head on his bicep. Though the canvas shrouded their tent, he could see her outline. She was lying on her side and facing him too.

"Well then, just maybe I will miss you specifically." Something softened in her declaration, something that sent a magical warmth over his skin.

"Just maybe?" What was he doing? He had to put a stop to this flirting. It couldn't go anywhere, could it?

"If I told you I definitely would," her whisper dropped, "what would you say in response?"

What would he say? That he didn't want her to leave, that he wanted her to stay with him, that he couldn't imagine life without her?

He gave a shake of his head but couldn't stir up the anger at himself he usually did whenever his thoughts got carried away. Instead his mind jumped back to Ivy's suggestion from earlier in the day: *"It's as clear as sunshine you've got a hankerin' to kiss her in a mighty bad way."*

Ivy hadn't read him wrong. Usually she didn't. She was too keen for her own good. The fact was, the more he'd gotten to know Linnea, the more he liked everything about her, and the more he thought about kissing her. Lately, the thought had been burrowing deeper so that even when he forced himself to treat her like a sister or a friend, the hankering never went away.

Maybe if he just did it—like Ivy had suggested—he'd get Linnea out of his system and be able to say good-bye a whole lot easier in a couple of weeks.

"What would you say, Flynn?" she asked again.

He reached for her. Lord Almighty, help him. He shouldn't do this, but he knew he was going to. He skimmed his fingers over the high arched cheekbone even as he leaned toward her.

Her breathing hitched.

The soft intake added fuel to the low-burning fire inside. He couldn't stop himself now—didn't want to stop. He let himself caress her ear and then find the back of her neck. As he used the pressure to tug her nearer, he shifted his weight, bringing himself against her.

She sucked in a sharper breath. Before she could say anything, he swooped in and let his mouth close over hers. The pressure of hers in return was like a gunshot into his veins, exploding him. Her arms snaked around his neck at the same moment he deepened the kiss, just the way he'd dreamed about doing.

When she released a soft whimper of pleasure, he realized too late he wouldn't be able to quit with one kiss. Instead, her noise was a sort of welcome to a whole passel of kissing. And as she opened to him more fully, he dug his hands into her loose hair to keep them from wandering where they shouldn't go.

"I sure do like when I'm right."

Linnea gasped and released him before Ivy's sleepy voice penetrated his stupor. At the girl's giggle, he rolled away from Linnea. Thunderation. What had come over him to make him lose his mind and self-control like that?

He guessed he needed to explain himself to both Linnea and Ivy, but he couldn't get his mind to have one coherent thought. Instead, he scrambled backward and out from underneath the wagon faster than a man fleeing from a burning house.

Once he was standing in the drizzle, he lifted his face and let the rain smack his skin, both cooling and punishing him at once.

What in the holy horses had he just done? He'd known it was a bad idea to lay down in there with her. He'd known it was a bad idea to start the bantering. And he'd known it was a bad—no, terrible—idea to give in to his need to kiss her. He'd convinced himself doing so would sate him. Maybe it would have with Helen or some other woman. But not with Linnea. . . .

He felt as though he'd only gotten the briefest tastes of something he wanted to have again. Maybe even something he wanted to have forever.

Was it possible he was changing? That he'd met a woman who could make him forget what had happened with his ma? Could he really contemplate having a future with Linnea?

He shook his head, unable to allow himself the possibility of watching her swell with a child. It was too dangerous.

But even as his past fears reared up, he couldn't let her go without first exploring ways to make it work. With her botany, maybe she'd be willing to put off having babies. There were ways it could be done even if he didn't know exactly how.

The light rain soaked his hair and face, a refreshment after the past days of being so parched. And somehow her kiss was water to his parched soul, quenching a thirst deep inside. It was a quenching he wanted—no, *needed* again and again.

Linnea couldn't move. She held herself rigidly even as Ivy squirmed on the ground beside her.

"So how was it?" the girl whispered. "You gonna let him kiss you again?"

Another gust of mortification buffeted her. "This isn't what you think."

"It sure is what I think. You and Flynn are falling in love. Plain and simple."

Falling in love? She cared about Flynn, liked him, and was attracted to his good looks and kind ways. But that didn't mean she loved him, did it? "Ivy, sweetheart. Please don't read more into this—"

"You might as well go on and get married." Ivy scooted closer.

Linnea shook her head.

"Then you won't have to leave us when we get to Pueblo." Ivy's plea was low and desperate. "You can ride up to Wyatt's ranch and live there with us."

Linnea was never more relieved than at that moment for Grandfather's ability to sleep so heavily. His snoring hadn't abated once through the kiss or now through Ivy's impassioned declaration.

"Please say you'll live with us, Linnea. I don't think I can go back to living with Flynn without you around."

How had this conversation so quickly escalated into such unfamiliar and rocky territory? Linnea closed her eyes and tried to form a coherent answer. But her heart was pounding too fast and her body still too much alive from Flynn's kiss to concentrate on anything else.

The kiss had been unexpected, struck her like a bolt of lightning, charging through her body and burning her up so all she could think about was kissing him in response. Every nerve ending had sizzled with need for him, and the feelings were overwhelming.

Even now as she touched her lips, sweet heat lingered, making her long to be back in his arms. In fact, she wouldn't mind lying with him all day, whispering and kissing and teasing each other.

She'd never felt that way with Asa. As tender as he'd been,

she'd always been eager to put an end to his attention and had never wanted to linger any longer than necessary. Was Ivy right? Was she falling in love with Flynn? Maybe in a way she hadn't loved Asa or any other man?

"Please, Linnea?" Ivy's whispered appeal broke through her hazy thoughts. "Promise you'll stay with us? Stay with Flynn?"

Linnea tried to relax against her pallet, but the tension remained in every limb. "Oh, sweetheart. I cannot promise you that. I've got work to do as part of this expedition, and I can't walk away and leave it all behind." Not after being allowed to come on the expedition. Not if she wanted Grandfather and the other scientists to take her seriously. She couldn't give up her aspirations because of a growing attraction to a man.

"Dr. Howell can come too, and you can keep on collecting your plants and such up at the ranch."

If only life could be so simple. "I doubt the other scientists would agree to the plan—"

"Don't matter a lick what they think."

It did matter a great deal. In fact, her career as a botanist wouldn't go anywhere if she didn't retain their approval.

"Ivy, you must know I care about you. But even though Flynn and I . . . well, just because Flynn and I shared a kiss, doesn't mean he wants me to come live with your family."

Flynn had made his position very clear. He was adamantly against marriage. She—and Ivy—had to resolve themselves to the fact Flynn didn't have plans for a future with her or any other woman.

"Please, Ivy. I need you to accept that Flynn and I are not meant to be."

"I can tell he wants you. How about I ask him if it's alright for you to come live with us?"

"No, sweetheart, you cannot possibly do so." The suggestion was awful, would make Linnea appear desperate. In addition, Flynn would probably think she put Ivy up to it. "In a delicate situation like this, it simply isn't proper for a lady to make such a request of a man. It would put him on the spot and make him feel coerced."

"What's coerced?"

"Fooled or tricked into doing something that wasn't his idea to begin with."

Ivy was silent, as though digesting the revelation.

She patted the girl's arm. "The best thing is to put the notion far from our minds."

"But if it's his idea to begin with, then he'll give it a go?"

"No, I didn't say that either." The conversation kept taking one bad turn after another. She tugged her cloak back around her, the dampness of her garments and the ground sending a chill over her skin. "I'm sorry, Ivy. But my kiss with Flynn shouldn't have happened. It cannot lead anywhere now and most certainly doesn't hold a future. From here on out, I'll do my best to avoid a reoccurrence."

"Good luck." Ivy snorted.

Linnea guessed she wouldn't need any luck, that Flynn would ensure it didn't happen again. He'd recognize that kissing her had been a mistake. Just like after their first kiss, he would pull away and make a point of keeping his distance.

Maybe it would be harder this time, especially with the depth of the friendship they'd built. But Flynn was a strong man, and he'd find a way to resist. Of that she was certain.

CHAPTER

16

Heaven help him. He wanted to kiss her again.

His attention drifted to where Linnea moseyed next to Dr. Howell, who'd perked right back up after getting plenty of water and rest the previous night. The two had veered to the north of the wagon train, getting off track as they often did during their exploring. The rain dripped from their cloaks and the long cylinder containers slung across their shoulders, but as usual they were oblivious to anything but studying plant life.

She straightened, arched her back, and glanced to the herd, her gaze flitting from one rider to the next until it stalled on him.

His heart kicked against his ribs like a bronco ready to be set loose. And his mind went back and relived their early morning kiss as it had already a hundred times.

As if sensing his thoughts, she spun away and dropped her attention back to the ground. She wasn't avoiding him, was she?

He hadn't thought much of her aloofness earlier when they'd broken camp before dawn. They'd both been occupied with their duties. Over the hours since, she'd continued to keep busy.

But now? She hadn't come near him and hadn't spoken to him in hours. No doubt about it. She was avoiding him.

Was she embarrassed by their kiss? He shook his head. There was no way on God's green earth he'd imagined her response. She'd welcomed him, opened herself to him, even made that soft noise that kept repeating in his head. She had found pleasure in those few moments of kissing every bit as much as he had.

Even so, that didn't mean she wanted to do it again. Could be she was afraid he'd push her for more. Did he want to push her for more? Not just for more kissing, but for more in their relationship?

That question plagued him worse than the fever and ague. He'd considered pretending nothing had happened, as he'd done after other intimate encounters, but for some reason, this time was different.

At a call from ahead, Flynn shifted his attention to Dylan riding farther down the line of cattle. "Riders heading our way from the west!"

Had to be Dr. Greely and the two other scientists who'd gone ahead. They'd sure taken their sweet old time in returning with water. After the storms that had rolled through last night, no one needed the water anymore. In addition to the fresh water filling every possible container, they could wring at least a barrel from their sopping blankets and garments.

No sense in halting the entire wagon train either.

Flynn gestured to Nash to keep moving.

The lanky cowboy replied with a hand signal, verifying the command.

Ahead on the barren plain filled with little else but sagebrush and brown grass, riders were heading their way. The man at the forefront was broad-shouldered, well-built, and muscular with a familiar, jaunty tilt of his hat.

Wyatt.

Flynn tightened his fingers against the reins, and he slowed his mount even as his pulse sped. He'd known this day was coming from the minute he'd accepted the invitation to come west. But even after weeks of resigning himself to the inevitable, he wasn't sure he was ready to see his older brother again.

A few seconds later, Dylan whooped, recognizing Wyatt too. He kicked his horse into a gallop toward their brother, which of course drew Ivy's attention from where she sat driving their wagon.

A second later, the bored look was gone from her face, replaced by excitement. She rose from the bench, almost as if she intended to jump down and run ahead with Dylan. But then, with a glance toward the team of oxen pulling the wagon, she lowered herself, reins still in hand.

Flynn guessed now was as good a time as any to stop for their midday break. He shouted out the instructions to Ivy and Clay. Then he rose in his saddle to survey the surrounding land for decent grass. He didn't need to worry about watering the cattle. With the rainwater drenching the stalks and tufts, they'd get enough through their grazing.

He pivoted in his saddle and again signaled to Nash and then to Jericho. With a nod, the two began the process of steering the line toward the north.

The wagon now at a standstill, Ivy hopped down and ran at top speed toward Wyatt, her long, dark brown braids bouncing against her back and bare feet slapping at the ground and kicking up mud.

At Dylan's approach, Wyatt reined in his horse and hopped down. In the same moment, Dylan slid from his mount. He hesitated in releasing the reins. Wyatt, however, wasted no time. He strode forward and grabbed Dylan into a hug so tight it brought an ache to Flynn's throat.

In the next instant, Ivy was there. Flynn was too distant to hear their greeting, but it was easy to see Wyatt was surprised at how grown up Ivy was. Even so, he reached out, mussed her hair, and then wrapped her in a hug. Not shy in the least, Ivy threw herself into Wyatt's embrace as if that's where she belonged.

The lump in Flynn's throat pushed higher. He was happy for their reunion. Ivy and Dylan had missed Wyatt more than he or Brody had. And he wouldn't begrudge them the special bond. It was a bond he'd never understood. He'd been the one to stick around and take care of them. He'd been there to protect them from Rusty's rages. And he'd been the one to ease their fears, soothe their hurts, and doctor their injuries and illnesses. Not Wyatt.

So why did they like Wyatt more?

As Wyatt finished hugging Ivy and released her, his gaze zeroed in on Flynn. He gave a curt nod. Flynn replied by tipping the brim of his hat. He wasn't about to ride ahead and greet Wyatt the same way as Dylan and Ivy. As much as he'd vowed over the past couple of days to put the past behind him, just seeing Wyatt reminded him of all the frustrations that had been building for years.

He veered his horse with the herd. Nash had moved to the front, turning the lead cattle to the right, causing them to circle around and draw tighter, until they stopped altogether.

Dr. Howell and Linnea strolled back to the wagon toward the other scientists, who were in the process of dismounting. Wyatt and Ivy and Dylan were still standing where they'd met, and from the way Ivy's hands moved, Flynn had no doubt she was giving Wyatt every little last detail of their trip—the good and the bad.

After Flynn made sure the cattle were all accounted for and grazing, he couldn't put off talking with Wyatt any longer. He forced himself to ride to the wagons where Clay had started a campfire and was warming coffee along with potatoes, beans, and the leftover prairie chicken Dylan had shot and roasted yesterday.

Wyatt finished walking his horse the last of the distance, still in conversation with Dylan and Ivy. As Flynn dismounted, Wyatt halted and pushed up the brim of his hat, revealing his dark brown eyes and inky black hair the same as Brody's. The two were the spittin' image of their pa, except that while Pa had a full dark beard, Wyatt only had a thin scruffy layer covering his jaw and chin. His poncho was slick from the drizzle, but underneath his loose-fitting shirt and vest contained the dust of the trail, as did his neckerchief.

"Flynn." Wyatt didn't smile.

Flynn's backbone stiffened. "Wyatt."

Wyatt reached out a hand, holding Flynn's gaze steady. Something in Wyatt's eyes seemed to plead for forgiveness.

Flynn hesitated for only a second before accepting the handshake. His brother's grip was hard and secure and confident.

When Wyatt pulled away, he tugged at his neckerchief. "Appreciate you getting the cattle this far without losing a one."

"About lost them all yesterday."

"Ivy said your idea of digging in the sand for water saved them."

Flynn shrugged. Ivy and Dylan watched them both, their gazes bouncing back and forth. From the wariness on Dylan's face, he guessed the boy hadn't forgotten the angry words the two had exchanged the last time Wyatt was home. It had been three—closer to four—years ago. Wyatt had returned from one of his failed ventures. When he'd seen the big bruise under Ma's swollen eye, he yammered on about it as though somehow Flynn was to blame for not keeping Ma safe.

Flynn had stewed for an entire week until he'd finally given Wyatt a piece of his mind. He let loose when he walked into the barn to see Wyatt tying down his bags to his saddle, getting ready to leave.

Flynn stopped short, shovel in hand, sweat running down his face after a day spent planting corn. "Where you goin'?"

Wyatt didn't turn but continued to focus on the leather strap. "To Colorado."

A deep sense of helplessness crept inside the empty places in Flynn's chest. "Reckon you're gonna find gold and get rich and solve everybody's problems?"

"That's what I'm hoping."

Clearly Wyatt hadn't picked up on the sarcasm in Flynn's question.

"For once, did you ever think about staying?" Flynn didn't want to admit that the heated pressure inside was sometimes too much to bear on his own, but the truth was, he was tired of bearing the brunt of Rusty's cruelty alone. "Did you ever think maybe you could be of more help by being here?"

"By doing what you are? That's real helpful, ain't it?" Wyatt shot him a censuring look.

It was the final needle to set the unraveling into motion. Flynn tossed his shovel against the barn wall. It clattered against the other tools leaned up in a row, causing them to tip over. Knowing he'd have to pick them all up later only added to the swirling rage inside. "At least I have the courage to stick things out instead of tucking tail and running every time the goin' gets rough."

"At least I have the determination to find a solution instead of sitting back year after year doing nothin' but turning into a punching bag for that lowlife."

The words had whacked into Flynn every bit as much as Rusty's fists. A deep black anger pushed him to lash back. "Go on and get out of here. You're nothin' but a coward anyway. We don't need your help, now or ever."

Their words had been cruel, their parting hostile. In hindsight, Flynn realized he could have handled the situation a whole lot better. He'd had a heap of growing up to do.

But that didn't change the fact that Wyatt had left him to take care of everyone. Or that he'd left Ma at Rusty's mercy instead of watching out for her. If Wyatt had stayed, maybe they could have figured out a way together to keep Rusty from getting Ma pregnant every blamed chance he had.

"Upriver, the Arkansas still has some water." Wyatt glanced to the north where the herd was grazing. Though his expression remained neutral, Flynn guessed he was calculating just how thin and worn out the cattle looked. "Once we get past Bent's Fort and away from the Santa Fe Trail, it'll get a mite easier without so many travelers."

"That's what I'm hoping for." Flynn didn't want to admit to Wyatt how rough the past few days had been and just how worried he'd been.

"You've done real good, Flynn. Thank you."

Flynn fumbled for a response to Wyatt's sincerity. Was it possible Wyatt might not find fault with something after all?

"Wyatt's missing his wife already." Ivy smiled up at Wyatt, adoration shining in her eyes. "Says Greta and her little sister, Astrid, are looking forward to having me there."

Wyatt had mentioned his marriage when he'd written to Flynn last autumn in response to the letter about Ma's passing.

"Wyatt says Astrid's real sweet and that we'll be good friends."

Dylan grinned at Wyatt with the same adoration as Ivy. "Wyatt's gonna hire me on as one of his cowhands."

Flynn knew he shouldn't let their comments pester him, but frustration hiked in and prodded him anyway. Here was Wyatt, making promises and offering them all the good things of life until they were practically worshiping the ground he walked on.

"Best not to make too many plans." Flynn couldn't keep steel from edging his tone. He'd hidden away the hundred Dr. Howell had already given him. And he'd have another hundred soon. Plenty enough to get supplies for building a house on a claim of his own. He might not be able to start until spring, but he surefire wasn't living with Wyatt until then. "Once we deliver the cattle, we'll be getting our own place."

"No need." Wyatt ruffled Ivy's hair again. "Me and my partner, Judd, we've been working all winter and spring building a bigger place, fixin' to hold everyone, or nearly so."

Ivy's smile couldn't get any wider. "You hear that, Flynn? It ain't no trouble to stay with Wyatt."

Flynn bit back a comment. He wasn't about to get into a tussle with Ivy in front of Wyatt. Didn't need Wyatt seeing his miserable parenting skills.

Wyatt took in the covered wagons and settled upon the scientists who'd pulled out their camp chairs and gathered around the fire. "Met these rich fellas at Bent's Fort and was surprised to find out you'd hitched up with the likes of them."

"Flynn agreed to it because he's got a big hankerin' for Linnea."

"That's not true." Flynn slanted his brows at Ivy at the same time Wyatt's rose. Of course, Wyatt's attention shifted to Linnea, now standing in front of the fire attempting to dry out her cloak. She was easy to spot since she was the prettiest woman east or west of the Mississippi, and the only other woman present.

"Matter of fact, his hankerin's so big," Ivy continued, "he was under the wagon with her this morning—"

Flynn managed to clamp his hand over Ivy's mouth in time to keep her from embarrassing him to no end, yammering on about that kiss. He leaned in and whispered in her ear, "You wanna cause a scandal for Linnea?"

Her eyes widened, and she shook her head.

"Then hush up."

She mumbled something beneath his hand he took as her agreement to be quiet. He cast her another warning glance before removing his hand.

Wyatt was watching them, amusement flickering in his dark eyes. "The ladies always did like you, Flynn. The way I remember things, Helen Fairchild had her sights set on you. Guess you put an end to that?"

"Yep." He wasn't about to go into the details of his past relationships with Wyatt. Was none of his brother's business.

"He broke poor Helen's heart." Apparently, Ivy thought it was her business. "But you ain't gonna hurt Linnea, are you, Flynn?" The girl flung one of her braids over her shoulder while tossing him a look of censure.

Linnea took that moment to glance his way. Her expression was curious and flitted from him to Wyatt and back.

Ivy was right. He couldn't hurt Linnea, didn't want to lead her on. But what if there was a chance they could make a life together? The question rose again, taunting him with possibilities as it had been since the kiss under the wagon.

"Come on, Wyatt." Ivy motioned toward him. "I'll introduce you to Linnea since I have the feeling Flynn's gonna want her to keep on going with us right on up to your ranch."

"That so?" Wyatt's brow cocked higher. And Flynn had the feeling it wouldn't be long before his brother was teasing him about Linnea the same as Ivy.

"Yep." Ivy started across the flattened grass toward the campfire. "Don't see why she can't do her plant research up there just as well as anywhere else."

Was Ivy right? Could Linnea do her collecting in the mountains? Would she be willing to travel farther with them? It would give them both time to see if their relationship had the potential to work.

Wyatt peered out at the cattle. "I take it Brody's with the herd?"

Flynn froze and exchanged a glance with Dylan, whose smile vanished.

Wyatt's attention jumped back to them.

Of course Wyatt didn't know Brody had run off. Flynn hadn't thought to send him word.

"Brody didn't come?"

"Nope."

"Why not?" Wyatt's jaw hardened along with his tone.

"Reckon you can guess why."

Comprehension darkened Wyatt's eyes. "Blast it all, Flynn."

Flynn had the urge to spin on his heels and avoid the tension that had always existed between him and Wyatt. But he held himself to his spot. "Listen, Wyatt. Brody's a grown man with a mind of his own."

"You could've stopped him—"

"You don't think I tried? I worked at it for months."

Wyatt rubbed a hand over the back of his neck and stared between him and Dylan as if he could somehow figure out what went wrong.

The simple, frustrated gesture was enough to remind Flynn of how badly he'd failed once again to protect Brody. Even so, resentment reared faster than a bucking bull's hind legs. "The night before we were set to leave, Brody snuck off without a word."

"Did you try tracking him down?"

"I did my best and delayed as long as I could."

"Where'd you look?"

"If you think you could've done better keeping Brody from enlisting, then you should've been there to do it yourself."

At the silence coming from the campfire, Flynn realized

the volume of his exchange with Wyatt had escalated, drawing the attention of the scientists, including Dr. Howell and Linnea.

As if noticing the same, Wyatt kneaded at his neck before he dropped his hands and blew out a tense breath.

Flynn didn't wait for Wyatt to offer an excuse or say anything more about Brody. He grabbed the lead line of his horse and stalked toward the herd, his footfalls pounding against the damp soil, weighing as heavily as his heart.

He hadn't wanted to get into an argument with Wyatt. A deep part of him had hoped the passing of time would've changed them both so they could get along. But from what he could see, Wyatt was still the same—acting superior and passing judgment.

Flynn had half a mind to ride off and leave Wyatt to drive his cattle the rest of the way to South Park by himself. Would serve him right.

But his chest tightened against the prospect. He was a man of his word. He'd told Wyatt he'd help get the herd to the ranch, and he'd see it through. Once that was done, he was moving on, and he didn't care what Ivy or Dylan said.

CHAPTER

17

Linnea had avoided Flynn for four days. Four whole days. But with each additional day, hour, even minute, her misery was growing exponentially because he was in misery, and she hated seeing him that way.

With her plant press open in front of her, she sat back on her heels and couldn't keep from watching him stride away from their midday camp and disappear into the thick salt cedar, cottonwood, and willow trees that led to the river bottoms.

Next to her, Ivy was helping her to arrange the delicate *Stephanomeria pauciflora* onto the thin paper of the press. The pale pink flower heads were a part of the aster family and no longer blooming on the subshrubs that grew in the sandy soil. But Linnea had been fortunate to find several in the area.

Thankfully, she'd kept the files organized without losing anything else . . . except for one time a few days ago when she'd returned to the wagon to find several pressed specimens pulled out of the crate and left on the floor beside it, almost as if someone had taken them out and neglected to put them back.

Although she hadn't been able to exonerate herself from the other accidents with the missing specimens, she'd known for sure she wasn't to blame for the recent carelessness. Someone else had clearly been inside the wagon, digging through the files.

"I know you're dying to talk to him." Ivy carefully smoothed the smaller basal leaves so the press would capture every nuance of the plant just the way it needed to be before it was added to the rest of their herbarium.

Linnea forced her attention to the stiff stem with its cylindrical base. "He told us to stay here and not to move an inch while he's gone."

She'd been trying hard to stay out of trouble. Lately she'd been doing well, and she didn't want any further mishaps.

Earlier in the week, they'd passed Bent's Fort and branched off from the Santa Fe Trail at La Junta. Now they were heading in a northwesterly direction toward Pueblo and the Rocky Mountains, still following the Arkansas River closely, which was getting deeper and flowing faster again after several days of rain.

She frequently scanned the horizon, waiting for her first glimpse of the renowned mountains. But so far, the land only spread out flat and brown for as far as they could see.

"You can't steer clear of talking to him forever, even though I know you're working at it real hard."

Linnea sat up again. Clay and Grandfather were both asleep in their camp chairs in the shade of the wagon. Jericho and Nash were slumbering under their wagon, and Wyatt and Dylan were taking a turn with the cattle. Thankfully, Dr. Greely had gone with a group to hunt a herd of mule deer sighted not far from their resting spot. She hated to admit it, but Dr. Greely's hovering had become as suffocating as the hot July sun.

Since his return from Bent's Fort, he seemed to spend nearly every waking minute of the day at her side walking and exploring. In the evenings, he monopolized her time around the campfire, so she was having a harder time remaining civil to him. But she also didn't know how to put an end to his attention without alienating him and in the process losing any chance of getting her work into the Botanic Gardens.

Dr. Greely wasn't the man she needed. And she realized now that Asa hadn't been either. After the friendship she'd developed with Flynn and then after their kiss under the wagon, she understood what loving could be like between a man and a woman—the exquisite beauty of the union, the power and the passion, the mutual pleasure.

She also understood to an even greater capacity that she could never again be satisfied with a marriage of convenience. She wanted a marriage based on love or none at all.

Perhaps as a result, she'd held herself more aloof from Dr. Greely. Or maybe Dr. Greely had finally sensed her attraction to Flynn—which she supposed had been harder to hide since that kiss. Whatever the case, she'd breathed out her relief the moment he left to go hunting.

Ivy cast a sidelong glance at Jericho's feet sticking out from under the wagon. Though Ivy tried not to act interested in the young man, her crush on him had only grown over recent weeks. Jericho, however, didn't appear to see her as anything more than Dylan's little sister.

Ivy sighed and then resumed her work. "You should go talk to Flynn now while you're out of Dr. Greedy's jail."

Though Linnea knew she shouldn't encourage Ivy's behavior, she couldn't contain a chuckle.

Ivy gave her gentle push. "Go on."

"Flynn will be angry with me for leaving when he expressly forbade it."

"He'll be right near heaven's door to see you alone. Maybe he'll even kiss you again."

"Ivy." Linnea tried to make her tone stern. But heat spread into her cheeks, and she fiddled with the leather straps used to tighten and hold the plant press closed. "I've already told you, the kiss was a mistake. And I'm sure Flynn is just as determined as I am to ensure it doesn't happen again."

"Oh shoot. Flynn'll kiss you again in half a second if you give him a chance."

The very prospect made Linnea's heart flutter wildly, but she had to remain calm for Ivy's sake. And her own. "If so, then all the more reason not to seek him out."

Ivy was quiet for several seconds, then responded more seriously. "You know you gotta go to him, Linnea. He's having a hard time now that Wyatt's here, and you're the only one he can talk to about it."

Linnea stared in the direction Flynn had disappeared, the heaviness weighing on her once more. Ivy was right. Flynn needed a friend right now. And she could be there for him.

"Very well." Linnea stood. "I'll go talk to him."

Ivy focused on the plant press and smiled in triumph.

"Talk as friends, Ivy. That's all."

As Linnea made her way through the shrubs toward the riverbank, she let the litany of *"talk as friends"* repeat itself. She was so intent upon chastising herself as she pushed through the brush that she didn't see him until too late.

He stood up to his waist in the river. And though the water shielded his lower half, there was no missing the fact that he was as bare as the day he was born.

A startled gasp flew from her lips.

In the process of splashing his face, his attention jerked to her. With water dribbling down his hair and face, he paused.

"Oh dear." Her hands fluttered up to her chest. "Flynn, whatever are you doing?"

He glanced first at the bar of soap in one hand and then to his clothing strewn out on the shore.

Her question was inane. Of course he was bathing.

She needed to turn around and run back to the camp as fast as her legs would carry her. Stumbling upon him in this predicament was entirely inappropriate. But for the life of her, she couldn't make herself look away.

He remained as immobile as she was, staring right back. Something smoldered in his eyes, something that burned into her and left her feeling light-headed and breathless. When he dunked the bar of soap and began to lather his chest, she suddenly felt the need to swoon.

She had to leave. This was exactly what she'd feared would happen when she came to talk to him, that this attraction would rise between them and become inescapable.

"Thought I told you not to leave camp." He dropped his focus to sudsing his arms.

"I wanted to . . . I thought maybe . . ."

He paused, a grin teasing his lips. "Just spit out the truth, Linnea. You wanted to watch me wash up."

"Oh my. Not at all." She spun so her back was facing him,

and she fanned her flaming face with her hand. "I came down here to talk. That's all."

"You sure about that?"

"Of course I am. I had no idea that you wouldn't be . . . wearing your clothing."

"Most people shed their clothes when they take a bath." His tone was laced with humor.

She wanted to join in the banter, but all she could think about was his beautiful broad chest and the water running down it. She had to leave. Now.

She took a step. "I'll come back later."

"No, don't go." His plea stopped her retreat. A second later his splashing drew near to the river's edge. "I'm done. Won't take me but a second to be decent."

She stiffened. Was he really daring to get out of the water with her there? At the rasping of clothing a moment later, she fanned her face again. "Are you finished yet?"

"Almost."

Ivy had likely known Flynn was taking a bath and had sent her to visit him anyway. Linnea would need to chastise the girl for the trickery. "Ready?"

"Reckon I'm good enough."

She peeked over her shoulder to find he was wearing his trousers but was still buttoning his shirt. His undershirt was all that showed. Even so, there was something strangely intimate about watching a man dress, and she pivoted around to give him more privacy.

She plucked a leaf from the cottonwood overhead and fingered its coarse teeth, studying the flat petiole.

"So what do you want to talk about?" His voice came from directly behind her.

220

She jumped.

His hand braced her waist, likely intending to steady her. But his touch seared through her skirt so that she had to spin out of his reach or burn up.

As she faced him, she took in his dripping hair, the brown made darker from being wet. His shirt clung to his shoulders, the material now damp, likely from not drying himself off properly. It hung untucked along with his suspenders. And his feet were bare.

She pressed a hand against her chest to calm both her breathing and her racing heart. He was much too handsome, especially with his green-blue eyes alight with humor, taking in her every reaction to the situation.

"You've been avoiding me."

"No, Flynn. Of course not."

His brows rose.

She sighed and stared at his feet, too embarrassed to hold his gaze. "Very well. You're right. I have been avoiding you since the—well, after, you know."

"Yep." His voice dropped low, giving her no doubt he knew exactly what she was referring to.

She didn't dare look up. "I didn't mean for it to happen—"

"I know."

"You do?" Her attention snapped up.

He was staring at her mouth.

Heat spilled through her belly. Was he thinking about kissing her again?

Swallowing hard, he stuffed his hands into his pockets and set his sights on a spot in the cottonwood behind her. "I take responsibility for it."

"You didn't want to stay under the wagon with me, and I made you."

"Reckon no one can make me do anything I don't already want to."

It was her turn to swallow hard. She had to change the course of the conversation before they made another mistake. "I've noticed the tension with Wyatt, and I wanted to make sure you're doing okay."

Flynn blew out a taut breath. "I'd be doing a whole passel better without him around."

"Do you think he's blaming you for Brody enlisting?"

"Yep. He's always blaming me when things go bad. Did the same thing when Ma was getting busted up by Rusty. He goes away for months at a time, then jumps in and thinks he could have done better than me."

"No one can do better than you. Just look at how well you're taking care of everyone and everything on this trip." Her tone must have contained a little too much passion because he almost smiled. "Ivy and Dylan—and Brody—are blessed to have a big brother like you who cares so much about them."

"But then Wyatt comes riding in like a blasted knight in shining armor making all kinds of mighty fine promises. And, of course, they end up liking him better."

At the pain in Flynn's voice, she couldn't keep from reaching for his hand and squeezing it. "You've had to be a parent to them. And parents have to go through both the good and the bad, teaching children right from wrong, nursing them when they're hurt and disciplining when necessary."

Flynn gave a curt nod, his fingers tightening around hers.

"But with Wyatt, I would compare him to a grandparent

who comes in for a little while and has the luxury of earning their favor without all the complexities of raising them."

"Yep. That's it."

"You've had to be the one to do the hard stuff. They might not appreciate you right away, but when they grow up, they'll realize just how much you did and how many sacrifices you made for them."

"I don't know about that. Once we get to Colorado, they want to live with Wyatt instead of me."

Flynn was such a devoted brother and loved his siblings more than himself. "If they do, then maybe Wyatt can have a turn at experiencing the parenting for a while. It might do him some good and help him empathize with all you've had to shoulder on your own."

He stared at their intertwined hands. "Sometimes I can't help thinkin' he's right."

"He's not at all. He doesn't know the struggles you've had to go through, so it's easy for him to question you and cast doubt upon your hard work." She loved talking with him so openly like this. All the weeks of sharing had given them a deep and real friendship. And at the thought of losing such a good friend, her heart thudded a beat of protest.

"What if I could have done more to stop Brody?" The question came out a strangled whisper.

This time, she reached up and smoothed a hand over his damp cheek, unable to stop herself. "You were willing to upend your entire life and move west to stop him, Flynn. But he didn't want to be stopped."

He finally met her gaze. His eyes were dark with the blame that had tortured him, likely since the day he'd realized Brody was gone.

"Reckon no one could make him do anything he didn't already want to." She repeated his statement of a few minutes ago, imitating his southern Pennsylvania drawl.

He studied her face, as though reading there the truth of everything she'd said. At least she hoped he was seeing the truth.

"Flynn McQuaid, you're the kindest, sweetest man I've ever met. And if Wyatt doesn't see that, then he's blind."

A grin played at the corners of his lips.

Conscious that she was still touching his face, she let her hand fall away. "I am entirely serious."

"I know you are." He tugged on the hand he still held, drawing her a step closer. "And you're mighty pretty when you're all fired up."

"Pretty? Then maybe I should get *fired up* more often."

"Maybe." He pulled her again, diminishing the distance between.

Her heart began to thud hard as if it wanted to jump out of her chest and finish closing the space.

He loosened his grip on her hand, only to fan his fingers between hers. At the caressing slide and low grip, her breath stuck in her chest. And when his gaze became suddenly languid, her legs turned to liquid.

She grabbed his shirt to hold herself up.

His chest was hard beneath her fingers, and she pictured him the way he'd stood in the river, his broad shoulders and muscular torso, bare and beautiful. She had an unholy urge to flatten her hand and let her fingers glide over him.

Oh dear. If she wasn't careful, she would end up begging him for a kiss. She couldn't. Absolutely couldn't. She released his shirt and his hand and forced herself to back up, putting a safe distance between them.

While he made no move to chase after her, he watched her with heavy-lidded eyes that didn't conceal his desire.

It seemed to reach out for her with an invisible strength. Had he given up resisting the powerful pull that existed between them? Had their kiss torn down the barriers he'd erected?

Worry whispered through her at the thought. If he didn't resist, then was he leaving it all up to her? What if she wasn't strong enough to hold him at arm's length the way she needed to?

"Linnea." He whispered her name, almost as if pleading with her to give in.

He was like a swift current dragging her into the deep with him. But what good could come of their passion when they were parting ways so soon? "We both know what we do and don't want for our futures, and we cannot let a little emotion guide the course of our lives, can we?"

He shoved his hands into his pockets once more. Was he doing it so he wouldn't reach for her? "What if I'm having second thoughts about my future?"

Was he referring to his declaration that he never wanted to get married or have children? Did he want to have a future with her?

Her nerves tightened, and she wasn't sure if she wanted to know the answer. A future with him wouldn't be possible, would it? Not when she had her botany to think about. She guessed Flynn would understand and support her work. After all, he'd only ever been positive about it so far. But he wanted a place of his own in the West. He'd talked about staking a claim and growing crops up in the high country. Where would that leave her botany? The expedition?

"You gonna say something?" His brow crinkled above vulnerable eyes.

"I don't know what to say."

He was quiet for several heartbeats. "Reckon your not knowing says enough."

"I'm sorry, Flynn." Something razor sharp pierced her chest. "I'm not so sure I can ever have second thoughts about my future. I love my botany work. And I've always wanted to prove that as a woman scientist, my contributions to botany are just as valid and important as a man's."

She hadn't been born the son her father wanted. And she supposed in some ways she still wanted to prove she was every bit as valuable as a son would have been.

Flynn's expression remained somber. "You're a good botanist."

"Thank you—"

"You're already as important as any one of the other men, Linnea. And I ain't saying so to get you to change your mind."

She couldn't respond past the lump rising in her throat. Instead, she managed a nod and a wobbly smile.

He stood silently a moment longer. "We best be heading back."

There was so much more she wanted to say. But she didn't know where to start. Besides, saying anything else would make the situation more complicated and their parting more difficult.

She left Flynn behind to don his shoes and socks in private. With each step she took away from him, the pain in her heart wedged deeper. If leaving him now caused her this much heartache, how would she accomplish it when they reached Pueblo?

As she climbed the last of the distance to their midday camp, she could see that Ivy had abandoned the drying presses to talk with Jericho, who'd climbed out from underneath the wagon. As Ivy chattered away, he watched Dr. Greely and the other scientists with narrowed eyes.

The men had apparently returned from their hunt while she'd been gone. She could only heave a breath of relief that none of them had passed by the riverbank and caught her with Flynn attired so indecently.

At the curl of smoke wafting from the back of their wagon, Linnea gasped. She started forward, her thoughts racing ahead of her. What could have happened? Was the research in danger?

Her heart tapped a rhythm of dread. "Did something catch on fire in the wagon?" Her panicked question rang out over the camp, waking her grandfather and Clay. As they and the other scientists tried to make sense of the situation, Jericho was already on his feet, grabbing a pail of water and circling toward the canvas opening.

She crossed toward him. "Be careful of the research!"

He climbed up, flipped open the canvas, and smoke billowed out in heavy waves. Ivy jumped up beside him and peeked inside. "Yep, there's fire, but it ain't big yet."

In the next instant, Jericho threw the water and began beating at the interior with a blanket while Ivy tossed things out of the wagon. Within seconds, the two jumped out with soot-darkened faces.

"The flames are out." Ivy coughed from having ingested

smoke. "Thanks to Jericho's quick work, we kept it from spreading."

Linnea pushed past Ivy and Jericho and peered inside. *Please, God. Not the research.* But even as the prayer formed, it fell away as she took in the blackened remains of one of the crates.

She would have collapsed except Grandfather was at her side and caught her. Together they stood silently side by side, staring at the weeks of work gone in a single instant. The dismay on her grandfather's face brought a lump to Linnea's throat.

She reached for his hand and squeezed it, only to realize he was shaking.

"How did this happen?" His question rose into the quiet, broken by soft, muzzled buzzing of grasshoppers.

Although no one answered Grandfather, Linnea guessed they were all thinking the same that she was—that the fire could have started from a dozen sources, likely a runaway spark from the campfire.

After all the other setbacks with their research, they didn't need this too. Once the Smithsonian board and the sponsors of the expedition learned of the disasters, they would surely call into question Grandfather's leadership. His reputation, the manual, the entire expedition, it was all in jeopardy.

"Oh, Grandfather," she whispered, through a tight throat. "What can we do?"

Beneath the shade of his top hat, his features creased with determination. "We press on, young lady. We press on. We won't let anything stop us, will we?"

She shared her grandfather's penchant for optimism. She wanted to nod, to assure him that they'd collect the lost specimens on their way home. But before she could form the words, the baby inside gave a thump against her abdomen, as if to remind her that yes, indeed, something—a tiny someone—could stop her grandfather. Linnea just had to figure out a way not to let that happen.

She stood on her toes and pressed a kiss to his cheek. "Nothing will stop us, Grandfather. I promise."

CHAPTER
18

The hair on the back of Flynn's neck prickled.

He scanned the desertlike landscape, taking in each dry shrub and craggy rock formation. But he didn't spot anything other than the usual prairie dog mounds and the wind-tousled buffalo grass.

"What is it, Flynn?" Ivy rode next to him on the Morgan he'd captured with the elk herd near Rock Point. Although he'd asked around in an attempt to return the horse to its proper owner, he finally acknowledged what he'd known all along—the Morgan belonged to those unfortunate souls whose wagon train had been ambushed.

Ivy had taken a liking to the Morgan, calling her Poppy after one of Linnea's favorite flowers. And she'd started helping drive the cattle while Linnea handled the wagon. Lately, Linnea had seemed almost relieved to have the chance to sit down, at times rubbing her lower back and even her feet when she thought no one was looking.

He'd worried about her tiring more easily over recent days and lacking the energy she'd had earlier in their expedition.

But as far as he could tell, she was holding up. The sore feet and exhaustion were normal. That's why Ivy wanted to ride more often. And why the cattle moved even slower than usual.

"You see somethin'?" Ivy persisted.

"Reckon I'm seeing trouble where there ain't none to be had."

With Pueblo only a day away, Wyatt had been riding ahead, scouting the route, especially after they'd gotten word from travelers heading east that Irregulars were stirring up trouble. With the Confederate hangout, Mace's Hole, south of Pueblo, the area was crawling with Irregulars, especially since the federal battalion from Fort Lyon had marched against Mace's Hole. The Union troops captured a number of the troublemakers and imprisoned them in Denver, but the rest fled into the hills.

After seeing signs of various bands of Irregulars all along the Santa Fe Trail and Mountain Route, Flynn suspected the Confederates were attempting to rally together again and increase their forces. He wouldn't rest easy until they were camped near Pueblo.

Pueblo.

He let his attention stray to Linnea on the wagon bench holding the reins loosely. Though she tried to maintain a proper ladylike posture, her shoulders sagged lower with each passing hour of the afternoon as the hot, dry sun beat down upon her. With the coming of August, the days blended together with unrelenting heat. Thank the Lord Almighty, they hadn't gone without water again. But the heat still wasn't easy on any of them.

"How in the blazes are you gonna get by once she's gone?"

Ivy had followed his gaze. Even if she hadn't, he would've known exactly who Ivy was talking about.

The thought of parting ways with Linnea as soon as tomorrow ripped his heart from his chest. That's why ever since she'd caught him taking a bath earlier in the week, he'd been putting the leaving from his mind and staying as busy as possible. "I'll get along just fine."

Ivy snorted. "You ain't gonna get along fine. So quit tryin' to act like you are."

He wanted to deny her again. But what good would it do? Ivy had always been able to read him as easily as a New England primer. She sensed his moodiness and had been dropping comments about how much she would miss Linnea. He reckoned the parting was gonna be as hard on Ivy as it was on him.

He tightened his fingers around the reins. Who was he kidding? Linnea's parting would be the death of him. And he wasn't sure he could let her go.

But what choice did he have?

Ivy released a noisy sigh. "You're as stubborn as an old coon dog barking up the wrong tree."

He slanted a look at her. He wanted to tell her to quit yammering like a woman and shoot straight like a man. But with her pretty pert face peering up at him, he stopped himself short. If he wanted her to start acting like a woman, he had to stop treating her like one of the fellas.

"Just ask her, you dummy." Ivy's voice was laced with exasperation.

For the better half of a second he considered pretending he didn't know what she was talking about. Then he shrugged. "Already did."

"You did?"

"Yep."

"You told her you want to marry her?"

"Not in those exact words."

"What words *did* you use?"

"I don't know." All he'd done was hint at a future together, but she'd shot him down faster than he could hit a straight-flying pheasant. Yep. He was sore about the rejection. It'd hurt worse than taking a bullet, knowing she didn't care about him as much or in the same way he did about her. But he couldn't be mad since she'd been clear all along on her position.

"Did you tell her you loved her in the same breath?"

He hadn't peeped a word about love. But if what he was feeling for Linnea wasn't love, he surefire didn't know if anything else ever could be.

Ivy scowled, apparently seeing the answer to her question in his expression. "Any man with half a brain knows you gotta tell a woman you love her when you ask her to marry you. Ain't no wonder she turned you down."

"She's more interested in her work than in having a relationship."

"She likes you a real lot. I can tell. You need to ask her to come up to the ranch. Then leastways you'll buy yourself more time."

He cast another glance in Linnea's direction to find her smothering a yawn. "She doesn't want to stop her botany or the expedition." In fact, she'd made it mighty clear her plants took precedence over him and everything.

"Landsakes, Flynn. You can't make her give up her work to come live with us."

"Don't expect her to." But did he? What other choice would she have if she left her grandfather's expedition? How would she be able to keep doing her botany?

Ivy rolled her eyes. "Never knew a man could be so dense."

Frustration pounded inside his chest, making him want to turn Rimrock loose into a thundering gallop. "Why don't you just spell it out for me"—he ground out the words—"since you seem to know it all?"

"Fine. I'll spell it out line by line. You talk to Linnea and tell her you want the whole expedition to come on up to South Park and do their research there."

"The whole expedition?" He shifted his sights to Dr. Howell, Dr. Greely, and the other scientists walking and collecting their specimens along the dusty trail ahead.

He wasn't keen on the idea of having Dr. Greely in South Park. But if it meant he'd get to stay with Linnea, maybe it'd be worth it.

"Yep. And once she's there, she won't wanna leave."

"Don't know about that." Maybe the whole idea was foolhardy. Maybe he oughta just put her out of his mind and go back to his previous resolution to keep his distance from women. He'd been happy enough living on his own. And after tomorrow, he'd get used to not having Linnea around anymore. Eventually.

Yep. Staying away from all the heartache that came with loving someone was for the best. Especially since he seemed to have a knack for failing to protect the people he loved.

"What do you think, Flynn? You gonna ask her?"

"Reckon we were getting along fine before she came along. Reckon we'll get used to life again without her."

Linnea swayed dangerously on the bench. She was falling asleep. And the next time the wagon hit a rut, she'd be thrown right off.

Flynn dug his heels into his mount and slapped the flank, veering toward her. If she didn't crack her head open or break a bone during the fall, she'd end up being trampled by the livestock following nearby. They'd passed a family last week grieving the loss of their boy who'd fallen and been run over and crushed by the wagon wheels.

Eyes closed, Linnea leaned farther toward the edge.

Fear jolted through him. "Linnea! Watch out!"

Her eyes blinked open, and she lurched awake. The oxen, sensing something amiss, reacted with expected nervousness, picking up their pace. Thankfully, Linnea gained quick control and brought them to a halt.

He reined in beside her. "You alright?"

She nodded, her face pale.

"What happened?" He tried to keep his voice level, but frustration crept in regardless.

"I was so sleepy, Flynn. I was doing everything I could to stay awake, but I just couldn't do it."

Ahead, Clay and the others came to a stop.

"You could have killed yourself."

She swallowed hard and pressed a hand against her stomach.

"If you wanna drive the wagon, you gotta stay alert."

"I'll try harder. I promise."

Her promise wasn't good enough. Suddenly nothing was good enough except that she promise to stay with him. He could deny his need for her all he wanted, but it wouldn't change how much he cared about her—loved her.

Yep. Ivy was right. He'd gone and fallen in love with Linnea. Heaven help him.

Gunshots echoed in the air. Shouts rang out along with more cracks of gunfire.

Down the line, Wyatt galloped toward them low on his horse, his features taut. "Irregulars! Take cover!"

Once again the hair at the back of Flynn's neck prickled. He'd suspected someone, somewhere, was watching them and waiting for the perfect opportunity to strike. Like now, when they'd stopped.

For an instant, all the blood-chilling stories he'd heard from other travelers flashed into his head—tales of the Confederate guerrillas killing and mutilating soldiers and civilians. Their tactics were brutal and inhumane, the work of men who'd sold their souls to the devil.

He slid down from his mount. Ivy had her sights set too eagerly forward. And Dylan already had his guns out, as if he intended to join in a battle. Flynn had to find a safe place for them. And Linnea. "Ivy. Dylan. Get on behind the wagon! Now!"

Flynn lifted Linnea from the wagon bench into his arms. Impatient to get out of harm's way, he didn't bother setting her down and instead cradled her tight and started 'round the wagon.

"What's happening, Flynn?" Linnea craned to see the commotion.

"Looks like we're under attack."

Ahead, Dr. Howell and the other scientists were running to take cover near the wagons, their faces reflecting their fear.

Flynn knelt behind the rear wheel, searching frantically for a better hiding place—boulders, trees, anything. But the shrubs and tallgrass wouldn't provide a barrier against the attackers any better than the wagon.

More shots filled the air, this time nearer.

Linnea clung to him a moment before she released her hold around his neck, allowing him to set her on the ground.

He drew his revolver and sidled back the way he'd come. "Stay down and don't go anywhere."

"Where are you going?"

He had to corral Ivy and Dylan and then get his rifle from his horse. Before he could do so, Ivy barreled toward him, leading both of their horses with Dylan on her trail.

He allowed himself a breath of relief, then grabbed his rifle from the scabbard. "Stay here with Linnea and don't come out for any reason."

He didn't wait to see if they followed his instructions. He eased around the wagon bed to find Wyatt at the back end of the other wagon, where Dr. Howell and his companions were hunkering down and fumbling to load their weapons.

The three wagons they'd been traveling with for the past few days had halted too, their men taking cover, Jericho and Nash among them.

"How many?" Flynn called to Wyatt.

"Half a dozen." Wyatt sighted down his rifle. "At least that I could see."

Half a dozen they could handle. Flynn prayed to the Lord Almighty that was all there was.

"What do they want from us?"

"I reckon anything they can get their grubby hands on." Wyatt fired a shot.

Dylan sidled next to Flynn, his rifle extended. Flynn had half a mind to tell him to get back with the women, but at the determination etched into Dylan's face, Flynn swallowed the words. His brother was bordering on being a man and wanted to prove himself. Besides, Dylan was as close as they had to a sharpshooter.

A bullet came zipping past, too near their wagon for Flynn's comfort.

For long minutes, they exchanged gunfire.

At the growing distress among the cattle, too late Flynn realized the attackers were stirring up the herd. Already the lead steers had moved out of line and were headed toward the river bottoms, and the other cattle were following straight on their heels and picking up speed.

"They're working the beeves into a stampede!" Wyatt shouted over his shoulder.

After traveling for close to four months with the herd and not losing a single one, Flynn's muscles stiffened in protest of having this kind of disaster when they had less than two months left.

"We're not letting them steal the cattle," he called to Wyatt.

"What can we do about it?" Wyatt's voice was riddled with frustration. He leaned away from the wagon and fired another shot.

"Stop the stampede." Flynn gauged the open span to the river and the danger of riding the distance without any cover. Once they were in the river bottoms, they'd have the natural defense of trees and rocks and would have an easier time turning and corralling the cattle. But getting there was the problem.

"You got any ideas?" Wyatt called.

"Dylan and the other men are gonna keep firing. Distract those Irregulars while you and me hightail it after the herd."

It was a dangerous plan, but the only one they had. From the somberness of Wyatt's eyes, he knew it. His life, his family, his future depended on this herd. If he lost them, what would he do? What would they all do?

Flynn set his shoulders with determination. They couldn't let the Irregulars steal them. That's all there was to it.

As Wyatt called out instructions to the other men, Flynn rounded the wagon.

Ivy knelt beside Linnea. At the sight of him, they both started to stand. He motioned at them to stay down. "Me and Wyatt are going after the cattle. We've gotta try to save as much of the herd as we can."

Linnea stared up at him with rounded eyes. "Such a plan is much too perilous. Please don't go."

He grabbed the reins of his horse. "Don't have a choice." He shoved his rifle back into the saddle.

She pushed herself up from the ground. As he started to slip his foot into the stirrup, she wrenched on his arm. "No, please, Flynn. What if you get hit? Or . . . worse?"

"I'll be fine." He let his eyes feast upon her face, lingering over her beautiful features, needing to take the memory of her with him just in case it was his last.

"Be careful," she whispered, her lips trembling.

"Stay behind the wagon."

She nodded.

He wanted to bend down and steal a kiss to take with him, but with Dr. Howell and the scientists looking on, he forced himself to break free of her hold, mount his horse, then search for Wyatt.

His brother was already atop his horse. They locked gazes. And for the first time in a long time—since before their pa

239

had died—they were on the same side, fighting against someone else instead of each other.

Flynn nodded. With a nod in return, Wyatt nudged his horse away from the wagon out into the open. Flynn kicked at Rimrock, leaned in, and then began a ride for his life.

CHAPTER

19

Linnea wanted to scream at Flynn to come back, but all she could do was watch him gallop away.

He kicked his horse faster, kept low, and held his revolver out, pointed in the direction of their attackers.

Even so, Linnea's heartbeat pounded harder than the horses' hooves hitting the dirt. She clutched at the end of the wagon next to Ivy. Dylan stood at the corner in Flynn's place. He aimed his rifle at a target down the trail and released a shot.

"Ivy, you reload for me." Dylan's terse command sounded much like Flynn's.

Ivy wasted no time in obeying her brother, taking the rifle and making quick work of locating the cartridge box in his pocket. She slipped out a cartridge, ripped the top off with her teeth, and then poured the gunpowder into the muzzle followed by the paper and bullet. She jerked the ramrod out and rapidly stuffed it inside the muzzle, pushing the powder and bullet down.

While waiting, Dylan fired his revolver, except his shots didn't go as far. "Hurry, Ivy!" He had half his attention on Wyatt and Flynn and the other on their attackers.

Ivy dug for a cap in his cartridge box, stuck it in the hole next to the hammer, then pulled the cock back all the way before she shoved the rifle into Dylan's waiting hand.

He took careful aim, sighting down the long barrel, before firing. He didn't wait to see what happened and instead handed the rifle back to Ivy, who was ready with another cartridge, pouring the powder inside and thrusting the ramrod right on its heels.

Linnea wished there was something she could do besides watch. Her mind turned over every option, but she settled on sticking to the wagon where Flynn wanted her to remain.

As a bullet narrowly missed Flynn's head, she sucked in a sharp breath. Another hit the dirt in front of him.

He flattened himself against his horse and kicked his heels, urging the beast to go faster. She took comfort from the realization that he and Wyatt were already well within reach of the herd.

Ivy continued to load Dylan's rifle with an expertise far beyond that of a girl her age.

"Come on, Ivy. Go faster." Dylan jerked another box out of his other pocket and counted out six bullets, then slid them into each of the slots in the open chamber of his revolver.

From the other wagons, the men were shooting too. But it was clear Dylan was a better gunman than everyone else combined.

"Please, Father in heaven." Linnea hadn't prayed so hard

in her life, not even for Asa as he'd lain dying. "Please save Flynn."

Just as soon as the prayer left her lips, a bullet hit Flynn in the shoulder, and she couldn't hold back a scream. "Flynn!"

He wavered for only a second before righting himself and gripping the pommel. An instant later, he rode out of sight down the bank and into the river bottoms.

She pushed away from the wagon.

Before she could take more than two steps, Ivy gripped her arm and wrenched her back behind the cover of the wagon. "Where do you think you're goin'?"

"Flynn's been hit."

"Ain't nothin' you can do about it now."

Ivy was right. But desperation prodded Linnea. "I need to go to him. He's injured."

"He's still riding, which means he's fine enough."

"How do you know? What if he's fallen and lying unconscious? The cattle might trample him, or the bandits could very well kidnap him."

Ivy gave her a shake. "Get ahold of yourself."

Linnea paused and tried to take a breath, only to find that she was shaking.

"Load the rifle, Ivy." Dylan's sharp command broke through Linnea's dread. "If we wanna save Flynn and Wyatt, then we've gotta stop these fellas from going after them."

The gun battle seemed to rage for what felt like hours, and all the while, Linnea could only picture Flynn lying somewhere, gasping for his final breath. When at last the shooting ceased, Ivy and Dylan made her wait while some of the other men went out to make sure all was clear and that the Irregulars had indeed left the area.

Linnea paced back and forth by the wagon. The sun pounded against her as if to punish her for attempting to push aside her feelings for Flynn over the past week, ever since he'd hinted at wanting a future with her. At this moment, she couldn't bear the prospect of him dying and never being with him again.

"Please, God. Please let him live," she whispered through dry and cracked lips, not taking her eyes from the direction of the river. If he survived the day, she wouldn't resist the pull to him again. Could she gather the courage to tell him she didn't want to part ways? But where would that leave her career?

With a toss of her head, she shook off her reservations. She bent and plucked several strands of *Bouteloua gracilis*, blue grama. She ran her finger along the comblike spike that was in bloom, with white stigmas protruding from the top and yellow anthers hanging below.

She'd always lived by her favorite verse about grass of the field, the one that said if God cared about grass, how much more He cared about His children.

He cared. She knew He did. Another one of her favorite verses from the Psalms had always reassured her that though their lives were as short and fragile as grass, the Lord's love and mercy was from everlasting to everlasting.

If she truly believed that He cared about her more than an intricate blade of grass, then could she stop having to push forward with all her plans?

She'd finagled her way onto the expedition regardless of all the reservations. And look what had happened? Instead of making a contribution, she'd been more of a liability, losing and ruining their work at times, causing setbacks, making the compilation of the manual more difficult, and earning disregard from the other scientists instead of respect.

Not only that, but once she revealed her pregnancy, she was sure to cause the expedition even more trouble, especially Grandfather. . . .

Was it finally time to stop trying so hard in her own strength and to let God carry her where He would, working things out in His way?

When at last a sorrel horse appeared over the ridge, she held her breath. It was Rimrock carrying Flynn.

"Flynn!" She started across the distance only to have Ivy yank her back.

"Wait, Linnea. We don't know if it's safe yet."

As Flynn drew nearer, she could see he'd tied a piece of linen around his arm near his shoulder, likely to staunch the flow of blood. The rag was saturated in deep crimson.

Her heart quavered. He was alive but surely in a great deal of pain.

Dylan was the first to meet Flynn, running alongside him and filling him in on what had happened. "We kept at it, holding them off until they got fed up and moved on."

Even with the explanation, Flynn scanned the surrounding area with a narrowed gaze, as though expecting another barrage of bullets.

"Where's Wyatt? Did you get the cattle?"

"Wyatt's fine. And we rounded up the cattle, all but two."

Dylan's expression was still serious, his rifle and revolver both loaded and ready. "I better head on down there and help Wyatt."

"Yep, go on ahead. We're aiming to camp in the river bottoms for the night." As Flynn reined in next to the wagon train, his gaze flitted from person to person until it landed on her.

He took her in, as though reassuring himself she was unharmed. As he finished his inspection, he seemed to release a breath. An instant later, he slumped in his saddle and began to slide off his horse.

Linnea released a cry, yanked away from Ivy, and ran toward Flynn. Thankfully, Dylan caught Flynn and helped him dismount. As Flynn's feet touched the ground, she was at his side, bracing him up on the side opposite Dylan.

Through the hole in his shirt, the wound bubbled with blood. "Oh, Flynn." Dismay edged her voice.

"I'm fine." He struggled to push himself up. "Nothin' much to worry about."

Her grandfather and Ivy had raced to Flynn too. And now Grandfather pulled out his monocle and inspected the injury. "The bullet is lodged inside, and we need to remove it as soon as possible."

Flynn shook his head. "First we have to get out of the open and down by the river where we'll be safer."

"Young man, with the pain and blood loss, I don't see how you will make it a dozen more steps much less down to the river."

"I'll drive the wagon."

Ivy snorted. "You just climb up in the back and let me take care of the wagon."

Flynn stumbled and nearly buckled to his knees. When he allowed them to lead him to the wagon bed, Linnea guessed he had to be in a great deal of pain not to offer any further protest. After Dylan and Grandfather situated Flynn on a pallet, no one objected when she insisted on staying with him.

As the wagon rolled forward, he was deathly still, his eyes closed and his face pale. She placed a hand on his chest to hold him as steady as possible during the jolting ride.

A second later, he lifted his hand and placed it over hers. And when she glanced up to his face, she found that his eyes were open and fixed on her. They were hazy—likely from the laudanum Grandfather had given him.

She brushed her other hand across his forehead. Without his hat, his hair still had a hat ring, and she combed her fingers upward and loosened the flat strands.

Was she overstepping the boundaries again? Her hand stalled. Even though he was injured, she had to be careful.

"Don't stop," he said hoarsely.

She hesitated, then brushed his hair again.

His body remained rigid. "When those Irregulars were shooting at me, all I could think about was Brody."

She smoothed his few wayward strands and waited for him to continue.

"How many times has he had to run through a volley of bullets a hundred times worse?" Flynn's tone turned harsh with his emotion. "Where's he been wounded? And what if he didn't make it?"

She slid her hand to his cheek and pressed it there, wanting to soothe him, guessing his inner pain matched his outer. What words—if any—could bring him comfort? He needed more than mere platitudes.

"This skirmish today was difficult enough," she whispered, "especially watching you put yourself into such jeopardy. I cannot imagine what you must feel knowing Brody is living through a nightmare every day, perhaps even multiple times a day."

He swallowed hard, his Adam's apple bobbing.

"No matter what happens," she continued softly, "we have to trust that God is watching over Brody and can take his hardships, injuries, difficulties—whatever he might be facing—and use them to eventually shape him and change him into a better man."

"Maybe. Still, I'm afraid of him dyin'. And nobody being there to hold his hand like you're doing for me."

"You are not dying, Flynn McQuaid. Don't you even think about it."

A ghost of a smile hovered over his lips. "Would you miss me?"

"Of course I would, but that's beside the point. I won't let you die."

"You won't?"

"I do believe you are too stubborn to die."

"Reckon I am. That, and I don't want to miss out on seeing your pretty face, not for a single, livelong minute." From his sleepy slur, she guessed the laudanum was loosening his tongue. She didn't mind. In fact, she rather liked having him pour out his feelings.

"So you think I'm pretty?"

"Darlin', never met another woman who can begin to compare."

The bumping of the wagon through a rut jarred her. They'd learned long ago to secure every moveable item within the wagon to prevent spilling and breaking. But she braced herself against the wagon bed to keep from falling on Flynn and hurting him even more.

When the wagon righted itself, Flynn's eyes were shut and his face creased with pain, too much pain for talking.

As she squeezed his hand, she realized she never wanted to let go.

Grandfather was as particular with his surgical methods as he was about the cleanliness in other areas. He sterilized his tools and washed his hands with the utmost care, requiring Linnea to do the same as she acted as his assistant.

Fortunately, the bullet hadn't gone deep enough to shatter a bone. When the surgery was complete, Grandfather projected that Flynn would have no long-lasting complications—unlike what had happened when he broke his hip.

Grandfather prohibited traveling and insisted Flynn lie abed. Linnea wasn't surprised that Flynn was a terrible patient. He obeyed the doctor's orders for the better part of one day before he got up for supper.

"Too unsafe for us to wait here. Not with those Irregulars waitin' to strike again." Flynn sat on a crate near the fire, leaning back against the wagon, his face pale and strained from the effort of being up. With his shoulder bandaged and his arm in a makeshift sling, he scraped awkwardly with a spoon against his tin plate, finishing the biscuits and beans that had become their daily fare, along with whatever fresh game Dylan could bring in, which had been several pheasants today.

Wyatt sat on a crate next to him. Though Linnea considered offering to switch places with Wyatt, she remained where she was, with her grandfather on one side and Dr. Greely on the other.

"It's much too soon for you to travel." Grandfather had already finished his meal and was reclining in his camp chair.

The smoky waft of the burning brush mixed with the lingering scent of the roasted fowl.

"I agree with Grandfather." Linnea took a sip of the watery coffee, made with the few grounds they'd saved from earlier in the day. Even though Grandfather had purchased more supplies along the way at the stage stations, they continually ran short on staples, since they hadn't planned on their journey spreading out over so many weeks.

Grandfather eyed Flynn through his monocle. "You risk opening your wound and suffering infection."

Flynn scooped a last bite. "Rather risk that than let those Irregulars have another chance to attack. Next time we won't be so lucky."

"Luck had nothing to do with our situation, young man. Our heavenly Father was watching over us. And Dylan's sharpshooting skills played no small role."

The other scientists added a chorus of agreement and began to talk again of the battle.

Flynn shifted his attention to Linnea for an instant before focusing on the fire.

Though she'd been helping Grandfather take care of Flynn's wound, her conversations with him had been short and none too private. Now at the thought of arriving in Pueblo and ending their traveling together, she had to figure out a way to let Flynn know she was rethinking her future too.

How did a lady go about telling a man that she wasn't quite ready to give up on them?

"Reckon Flynn's right," Wyatt said as he polished his revolver. "If those rebels come back through here again, they'll be wanting more than cattle. They'll be lookin' for blood." As he spoke the words, he lowered his voice and glanced in the direction of the river where Ivy, Dylan, and Jericho sat on the bank, their feet dangling in the water that sparkled with rays of the setting sun.

Above their heads and to the west, the sky was brilliant, ruby laced with hints of gold and bronze and even amethyst. They'd seen many beautiful sunsets during the journey, but now that the outline of the Rocky Mountains loomed on the horizon, the beauty had become almost too majestic to describe.

Flynn wiped his mouth across his sleeve, then placed his plate in the grass. "If you don't mind my speaking my piece, Dr. Howell, with all the Irregulars hiding out, the Pueblo area's too dangerous right now for research."

"I agree." Dr. Greely tossed his drumstick into the fire, the bones picked clean. "I think we should go directly to Denver. We'd planned to research there eventually over the winter. Why not now?"

"You could keep on traveling with us and head up to South Park." Flynn spoke the words casually. "Reckon you can do your plant collecting there just as well as anywhere else."

Linnea's breath snagged in her lungs. What was Flynn saying? Was he trying to tell her that he wanted her to come with? Through the smoke curling up, she willed him to look at her so she could read his expression, but he kept staring straight ahead into the fire.

"Well now, that's a fine idea." Grandfather stretched out his legs, the creases down the front of his trousers a testament to Clay's recent ironing. With the faithful servant's help, her grandfather always managed to look put together, more so than Linnea did, especially recently.

Wyatt gave a curt nod. "Fairplay's a real nice little town. You'd have no trouble finding rooms at one of the hotels."

"Pardon my saying so, Dr. Howell." Dr. Greely had stiffened and was watching Flynn with narrowed eyes. "But going to South Park was not part of the plan for this autumn."

"True." Grandfather took a sip from his steaming tea. "But after losing so much of our prairie research, perhaps we need to shift the focus of our manual and make it more specific to the mountainous regions of Colorado."

"That's quite a big change, Doctor. And I'm not sure our sponsors will approve, particularly when they learn the lost specimens were primarily the handiwork of you and Mrs. Newberry."

"We can still include a small chapter on the prairie and Front Range. But I'm sure they'll understand once we explain the hardships we've experienced along with the rationale behind the adjustment."

"We've already made more than enough adjustments." Dr. Greely shared a look with Dr. Johnson and Dr. Parker. After the most recent fire in the wagon, were they calling into question Grandfather's ability to continue leading the expedition?

She needed to lend him her support. It was the least she could do. "I concur with Grandfather. Perhaps the scope of the manual is too wide, too ambitious. Why not focus more specifically on the mountains, an area that is sure to pique the interest of more people anyway. We can start researching the high country yet this year and finish next."

Flynn's attention snapped to her. His brows arched above questioning eyes. Was he trying to read the meaning behind her words the same way she had his?

She wanted to nod, to smile, or even to tell him she wasn't ready to leave him yet. But with everyone looking on, she forced herself to remain composed.

Beside her, Dr. Greely shifted in his chair, his gaze darting from her to Flynn and then back. "Of course Flynn would suggest that Mrs. Newberry travel to the high country. Then he can continue to extort money from Dr. Howell for guarding his granddaughter."

Extort money? Flynn guarding her? What was Dr. Greely talking about? She opened her mouth to voice her questions, but at the glance her grandfather exchanged with Flynn, she could only stare between the two with a sinking feeling.

At the sudden awkward silence, Dr. Johnson and Dr. Parker stood and excused themselves. Wyatt, too, rose, tipped his hat down, and sauntered away toward the cattle.

Dr. Greely cleared his throat. "Flynn informed me early in our trip that Dr. Howell hired him to guard Mrs. Newberry from trouble. And now that he's inviting our party to proceed further with him, I can only assume he's doing so for the money, since he assured me he had no aspirations toward Mrs. Newberry."

Grandfather had hired Flynn? She shifted to face her grandfather, and her pulse stuttered. After her near drowning in the Neosho River, she'd been afraid he would send her back to Fort Leavenworth and had been surprised when he had allowed her to keep going. Now she understood why— because he'd made arrangements with Flynn to watch over her.

The guilt creasing Grandfather's forehead only confirmed the truth of Dr. Greely's accusation.

"You could have told me," she whispered.

"I knew how much you wanted to be a part of the expedition." Grandfather's voice was stricken. "I didn't know what else to do."

She nodded, her own guilt rising to constrict her throat. She had the urge to place her hand on her abdomen and the baby growing inside her. How could she condemn her grandfather for his dishonesty, when she was engaged in an even greater deception?

"I'm sorry. I should have told you, Linnea, but I didn't want to hurt your feelings."

"I understand." What she didn't understand was if anything that had happened between Flynn and her was real. Or if it had all been part of his job in guarding her.

Her mind raced back to all the accidents she'd had over the past few months. In almost every case, Flynn had been close enough to rescue her and keep her from harm. She assumed his proximity, his spending time with her, his searching her out had been because of his attraction. But what if it had all simply been part of his job?

Maybe not *all*.

She swirled the last of the coffee in the bottom of her cup, forcing herself to think rationally. She'd gotten to know Flynn well enough over the summer, and he was the type of man who would have helped even if he hadn't been paid.

Even so . . . the nature of their relationship hadn't been what she'd thought. She'd made much more of it than she should have.

Flynn shifted on his crate, his expression stormy. "Listen, Linnea—"

"Please don't say anything, Flynn. Please." Had he really told Dr. Greely he had no aspirations toward her? Of course as a hired guard, he'd tried to keep her at arm's length, tried to do the honorable thing. But she'd pushed herself upon him time after time, wearing down his resolve, giving him little choice but to socialize with her.

What must he think of her?

She bolted to her feet and pressed a hand over her mouth. She'd made an utter fool of herself. She didn't know how she could bear to look him in the eyes ever again.

Flynn stood, as did Dr. Greely. She could feel both men appraising her, but she stared unseeingly at the riverbank. "If you'll excuse me, please. I think I'll take a short stroll before darkness settles."

"I shall accompany you." Dr. Greely started toward her, situating his hat and adjusting his coat.

"No!" Her tone was sharper than she'd intended. She took a deep breath and forced herself to speak calmly. "While I appreciate your solicitation, Dr. Greely, I respect and admire you as a colleague and nothing more."

He took a slight step back as if her words had slapped him across the face. His mouth hung open for the space of a few seconds before he closed it and sat down abruptly.

After already mishandling the research, now she'd likely just ruined her last chances of his acceptance and validation for the contributions she was making to the expedition. But what had she expected? That he'd accept her as a woman scientist in her own right?

All along, she'd held out hope that she could prove herself, not because she was married to Asa, but because her work in the field was capable, intelligent, and worthwhile. Yet none of other scientists, including Dr. Greely, took her as seriously as they did each other. Was she wife material and nothing more?

She stepped outside the circle of chairs. She could feel Flynn watching her, but she ducked her head and lengthened her stride. She couldn't look at him, not right now. If she'd harbored any thoughts of continuing with him tomorrow, they were gone.

CHAPTER
20

Let her go.

Flynn couldn't tear his focus from her stiff back as she made her way to the river. His muscles flexed with the need to sprint after her. But he had to resist. Now was the opportunity to sever all ties with her. Now that she loathed him.

Her anger, frustration, even embarrassment had been unmistakable.

And, anyway, what could he say to make things better?

Nothing. That's what. She had every right to be sore with him. He shouldn't have agreed to Dr. Howell's plan to keep the guard duty a secret. He'd known from the start that holding back information was only going to cause a heap of trouble.

A breeze blowing off the river teased the loose curls around her neck, and the fading sunlight glinted off the red, turning it afire. From the moment she'd come into his life, she lit up his world the way no one else ever had before.

Let her go.

He shut his eyes. He'd done as Ivy had encouraged and invited the expedition to come to South Park. For the shake of a lamb's tail, he'd believed he and Linnea might be able to find a way to have a future together.

No doubt, Dr. Greely had been itching to drive a wedge between them. And now he'd done it. The only consolation was that the stuffy scientist had whupped himself in the process, finally forcing Linnea to spit out the truth about not being interested in him.

Flynn blew out a tense breath and opened his eyes. He couldn't keep from seeking out Linnea again. She was ambling over the rocky bank away from camp but still within sight. Her head was down, and she lifted a hand to wipe at her cheek.

Was she crying?

He stiffened.

She brushed at her other cheek, and then her shoulders heaved.

Thunderation. She *was* crying.

He started after her, limping along. Even if the effort of moving jarred his wound, he reckoned he'd done his share of bringing those tears to her eyes, and now he had to do his part to take them away.

"You're aspiring above yourself, McQuaid," Dr. Greely called after him, "if you think Mrs. Newberry will ever want a man like you."

Dr. Greely was probably right. Why would Linnea want him? A man with a broken hip, a broken past, and not much of a future to speak of. He oughta head downriver in the opposite direction. But as her shoulders lifted and fell again, he picked up his pace after her.

"Now, Dr. Greely, that's not true of Mr. McQuaid." Dr. Howell's voice carried on the breeze. "He's a fine young man, with many fine qualities."

Flynn appreciated Dr. Howell's praise. But he wasn't planning to take any more money. In fact, he aimed to give the kindly scientist back every dollar he'd already paid him. He didn't want the money anymore.

He was almost upon Linnea when she heard his approaching footsteps and glanced over her shoulder. She quickly turned her face and wiped at the streaks on her cheeks.

"Go away, Flynn." Her voice was loaded with sorrow. "While I appreciate all the work you did to keep me safe for the duration of this trip, I don't need you to guard me right now."

Frustration clamped around his gut like a trap snapping shut. "I didn't come after you to guard you."

She kept going, the rocks making her steps uneven.

His were more unsteady than usual too, each one causing his shoulder to throb. "Linnea, heaven help me. Let me apologize."

Her pace slowed.

"I didn't like the idea of keeping my role from you, and I told Dr. Howell so from the get-go."

She halted and spun so fast, he almost tripped. Her rich brown eyes were almost black with emotion. When she peered past him toward the camp set back from the river among the sandy grass and under the shade of trees, she promptly hastened behind a cluster of brush.

He glanced around too. Every living creature within a dozen miles had to be watching them, including Ivy, Dylan, and Jericho sitting a short distance away.

With a heavy sigh, Flynn followed Linnea. If they were gonna speak their piece, they didn't need to do it with everyone gawking.

As he rounded the brush, she waited, her arms crossed. "I'm mortified, Flynn." Her cheeks were flushed, her chin lifted, and she'd never looked so full of life.

"You are?"

"Terribly mortified." The life fled from her voice, replaced by a soft catch, as though she was going to cry again.

He suddenly felt so helpless. He had half a mind to caress her cheek, but held himself back. "I'm sorry."

"For what?"

"For not telling you the truth about your grandfather asking me to watch over you."

"That's not what I'm upset about."

"It isn't?"

She shook her head. "Oh, Flynn. I'm embarrassed to admit that I thought you were paying attention to me because you were attracted to me. I didn't realize you were spending time with me because you were paid to do so."

Lord Almighty. Was that what she thought? He could think of only one way to prove his attraction to her had nothing to do with her grandfather. He closed the distance between them and dipped in, catching her lips against his.

She gasped, but he captured the sound at the same moment he wound his free hand behind her neck and guided her, taking possession of her mouth totally and completely. When she rose into him eagerly, he delved in with all the desire building within him since their last kiss.

He wanted to take his sweet, old time and get his fill. But he sensed he'd never be satisfied with a stolen kiss or two from this woman. Even as her grip against his shirt tightened, he broke away.

"Your grandfather ain't paying me to do that." As her breathing bathed his lips, he couldn't stop himself from bending in and letting himself get another taste.

Her soft murmur of pleasure set him on fire.

But even as the flames burned through his blood, he forced himself to pause. With a control he hadn't known he possessed, he pulled back. "Your grandfather didn't pay me to do that either."

"Are you sure?" Her cheeks were flushed, lips swollen, and her lashes lowered.

He stuffed his free hand into his pocket to keep from reaching for her again. "When I woke up after the surgery yesterday, you're the only one I wanted to see."

She peeked at him, almost shyly.

"I invited everyone to come to South Park because I don't wanna leave you at Pueblo."

Her lips curved into a smile.

"Have I convinced you yet?"

"Maybe, a little."

For a second he considered convincing her with more kissing, but his attraction to her was near to overflowing, and if he let himself get carried away, he wasn't sure he'd be able to stop—even with his best intentions. And he cared about Linnea too much to go down that path. He aimed to do things proper-like with her, and that meant keeping his desires corralled.

"I already decided, I'm not gonna take a single cent from your grandfather." He set his sights on her beautiful mouth, knowing the looking would have to be enough for now.

As if seeing the direction of his gaze, she nibbled at her bottom lip. "Flynn." Her voice gently chastised him.

He lifted his gaze and soon found himself drowning in the swirling warmth of her eyes.

"If Grandfather is giving you money, then you need to take it—"

"Nope."

She ducked her chin. "It was well earned."

He chuckled. "I ain't arguing with you there."

She smiled.

"Then you'll travel with us to South Park?"

"It doesn't sound like Dr. Greely is agreeable to the idea."

"You and your grandfather can come now. The others can travel up next spring."

"I like that idea." She cast him another shy look.

His heart filled with a warmth that made him feel like he'd swallowed laudanum again. He hadn't told her he loved her and wanted to marry her. But this was a start and would give them more time to figure out how to make a future work between them. She was a sympathetic woman and would understand his fears about having children. With her passion for her botany, maybe she'd be too busy with her work and decide to put off starting a family until he had the chance to make peace with his past.

As he winced at the pain in his shoulder, she reached for his arm. "Time for you to resume resting as Grandfather ordered."

"I think I know when I need to rest and when I don't."

"You know how to take care of everyone but yourself, which is all the more reason you need me to come along with you to South Park." She gently steered him out from the shrubs.

"So you can boss me around?"

"Once in a while, you have to allow someone else to help carry your load."

"Only if that someone has pretty red hair and brown eyes."

Her smile came out once more. "Then you'll let me take care of you without causing trouble?"

"Nope."

"Flynn McQuaid."

"Gotta give you a little trouble once in a while, seeing as you give me a whole heap of trouble nearly every day."

She laughed just as he'd hoped she would. And the warmth inside expanded.

As they walked side by side, he wanted to reach for her hand. But with everyone watching, he reckoned the safest thing was to be on his best behavior. After all, she'd only expressed interest in traveling together a little farther, not in marrying him.

The next morning during the darkness of dawn, as Linnea rolled over on her pallet, a fountain of sweet pleasure flowed through her at the memory of the previous evening's interaction with Flynn.

She touched her lips and was glad for the privacy so no one else could see her reliving Flynn's kisses. He'd kissed her twice along the riverbank. And each time, she wanted to cling to him and keep on kissing him.

Outside, the low hum of voices penetrated the canvas. She started to rise but then paused at the tense, angry conversation.

"The lad said he saw you leaving the wagon," Grand-father said.

"He has no idea what he's talking about," Dr. Greely scoffed.

"What reason would he have to lie about the matter?"

"Maybe he's attempting to undermine our partnership."

A beat of silence fell over the darkness. "I hate to say so, Dr. Greely, but perhaps you're the one undermining our partnership. There's no other fathomable explanation for why you would purposefully set fire to our research."

Set fire to the research? Linnea almost gasped but pressed a hand to her mouth before the sound could give away her eavesdropping. Had someone witnessed Dr. Greely going into the wagon right before the fire? Perhaps Jericho?

He was a keen-eyed, intelligent young man. And he'd been there at the time of the fire.

"If he thinks he saw me—" Dr. Greely's voice turned haughty—"then why didn't he come forward with his ac-cusation sooner?"

"Actually, the young man did inform me that day of his suspicion. I just didn't say anything. I didn't want to level any blame until I had further proof of misconduct."

"Misconduct?" Dr. Greely released an undignified snort.

"After your statement last evening about what research has been lost, I had Clay help me look through the remain-ing crate and discovered that you're correct. A large number of my contributions to the expedition, along with Linnea's, are missing."

"Is that a surprise? Mrs. Newberry has proven to be care-less—"

"No, Dr. Greely. Like my son, Linnea may have a penchant

for getting caught up in her work to the detriment of herself, but she's absolutely meticulous with her research. In fact, she's one of the most thorough researchers I've ever known, which is why the losses have been so puzzling."

Grandfather thought she was meticulous? Thorough? Linnea let his compliment warm her.

"We both know the truth, Dr. Greely." Grandfather's tone became low and sad. "If the problems with the research during the course of our trip were accidental, then we would see an equal distribution of the loss among all the contributors, not just Linnea's and mine. Because that hasn't happened, I can only surmise that you—and perhaps Dr. Johnson and Dr. Parker—have been sabotaging the expedition."

Dr. Greely didn't immediately respond. And Linnea held her breath in the ensuing silence. Was it possible she hadn't misplaced and lost research? That all along Dr. Greely had been tampering with the specimens in an effort to undermine Grandfather? What reason could he possibly have for doing so?

Dr. Greely finally spoke. "Your accusations are entirely preposterous. And unfounded."

"I sincerely wish I was wrong, but because I can no longer trust you, I think we must part ways in Pueblo today. Since you weren't keen on the idea of going up into the high country over the autumn, I imagine this diverging of our paths won't be a hardship."

Again, Linnea pressed her fingers against her lips to hold back her reaction. What would this mean for the entire project? The manual? The Smithsonian sponsorship?

"If you insist, Doctor." Dr. Greely's voice had grown increasingly cold. "But since we're being honest with each other, you should know we're all in agreement that the leadership of this expedition should have been given to me. Not to you."

Of course. Dr. Greely wanted his name to be the most prominent on their field manual. He wanted the recognition and the accolades that came from being associated with this kind of exploratory trip. Was that why he'd tried to hurt Grandfather's efforts? To make Grandfather look bad? So that the board might award him with the recognition instead?

Not only had he harmed Grandfather, but he'd undermined her as well, putting her career in jeopardy and making her doubt herself. If Dr. Greely had any feelings at all for her, how could he have done so?

"When I have the first opportunity," Grandfather continued, "I shall telegram our sponsors of our splitting of ways and that we shall be compiling two smaller manuals. You and Dr. Parker and Dr. Johnson will have the opportunity to complete a book of your own on the flora of the Front Range, while Linnea and myself will work on a manual of the high country. I hope you will find the compromise satisfactory."

Grandfather's compromise was much more than Dr. Greely deserved. He ought to be sent home in shame. But Grandfather couldn't be spiteful even if he tried. And she'd do well to follow his example and attempt to forgive Dr. Greely. After all, now she had the wonderful prospect of partnering solely with her grandfather, knowing he trusted her and valued her input.

She almost allowed herself a smile, but then lowered her hand to her abdomen. The baby.

Without any of the other botanists, Grandfather would need her assistance more than ever. How could she possibly let him down with the news of her pregnancy now? She didn't want him to regret choosing her over the men.

Before helplessness could seep in and fill her with despair, she pulled herself up. She still had autumn to prove herself useful and capable to Grandfather. Once he understood that she could handle everything just as well as the others—that he hadn't made a mistake in aligning himself with her—then she'd share the news of the coming baby.

Surely keeping the pregnancy secret awhile longer wouldn't hurt anyone, would it?

CHAPTER

21

The wail of a newborn rose into the log cabin.

"You did it. A fine little boy." Linnea squeezed the hand of the new mother. Red-cheeked and sweating, the woman nodded and fell back into the sagging mattress of the bed built into the wall.

As Grandfather cut the umbilical cord, the infant kicked his arms and flailed his legs. Linnea could only watch the tiny baby with a sense of awe. To think that in four months she would bring her own child into the world.

She spread her free hand across her stomach. At twenty weeks, the swell was becoming more difficult to hide. Over the past week since branching away from the other scientists at Pueblo, she'd managed to expand the waistline of several skirts. Doing so privately had been her biggest challenge, and several times she worked by lantern light in the back of the wagon when she should have been sleeping.

Lately, she considered telling someone else, maybe Flynn.

With the way their relationship had progressed, he deserved to know that a future with her meant having Asa's baby.

"He looks very healthy, Mrs. Cooper." Grandfather examined the squalling infant.

After laboring through the night and most of the morning, the woman managed a tired smile. Linnea had started to worry the birthing would never happen. But then, over the last hour, everything had gone quickly and smoothly.

Their wagon train had arrived in Cañon City several days ago to find abandoned buildings, empty cabins, and half-finished structures lining the quiet streets. Apparently, over the past year, the once-bustling mining community had deteriorated into nearly a ghost town as a result of divisions in sentiments between Union and Confederate sympathizers.

Though a few businesses were operating for the stalwart citizens who hadn't left, the town was nothing like Linnea had expected. Thankfully, the hotel was open and Grandfather had insisted on staying there in order to enjoy the luxury of rooms, beds, and baths for the first time since Fort Leavenworth in May.

Linnea had convinced Ivy to join Grandfather and her in the hotel, but Flynn and the other men were guarding the wagons and livestock on the outskirts of town. Though they hadn't encountered any more Irregulars since the Pueblo area, the locals claimed the danger still remained. Even so, Wyatt had made the decision to rest the cattle a few days before the arduous trek into higher elevations.

Linnea had relished a bath along with eating meals in the hotel's dining room with Grandfather and Ivy. Word spread rapidly about the visitors, particularly the news that in addition to his botany work, Grandfather was also a physician.

Several people sought him out with their ailments. And when Mrs. Cooper's travail pains started, her husband, who ran the stage station, had pleaded with Grandfather to help with the delivery.

Now as Grandfather began to swaddle the infant, he swayed on his feet, his face pale.

"Grandfather!" Linnea rushed to him and took the newborn.

He pressed a hand against his forehead. "It's nothing to fret about, young lady. I'm just experiencing a mild case of vertigo."

She guided him to a crudely made bench at the table. "You're exhausted and need a rest. I'll ask Flynn to take you back to the hotel." Linnea quickly finished wrapping the baby, placed him with Mrs. Cooper, and then stepped outside the cabin, breathing in the crisp air of the summer morning.

As the door closed behind her, Mr. Cooper stopped his pacing in the dry, rocky clearing in front of the cabin and fixed his worried eyes upon her.

She offered him a reassuring smile. "Your wife and new son are just fine. I'm sure they'd love to see you."

Tears sprang to the man's eyes, and he bustled past her.

Linnea stepped away from the cabin and searched eagerly for Flynn. At the sight of him working in the shadows of the stable, his shirt pulled taut across his broad back, her heart picked up pace as it usually did at the prospect of being near him.

He'd arrived at dawn several hours ago, apparently having learned about the birthing from Ivy. He'd stayed on to lend a hand when the stage arrived. And now he was tending to

270

the mules, likely the several pair that had come in with the last stagecoach.

She paused and admired the mountains that took her breath away every time she looked at them. The craggy foothills with their reddish tint rose a short distance away with the larger dark majestic peaks hovering beyond. While the landscape was arid and devoid of the lush vegetation she'd expected, the grandness of the mountains was unlike anything she'd seen before.

Pinyon, *Pinus edulis*, grew in clusters over the sandy hills along with juniper, *Juniperus scopulorum*. The yuccas, prickly pears, and creeping thistle abounded, so that she'd long since stopped collecting samples.

Just yesterday she'd discovered a new plant even Grandfather couldn't name. After a great deal of discussion and examination, she'd proposed that the towering stalks with bright yellow flowers belonged to the mustard family. The lower leaves had the feathery appearance of the species *pinnata*. And she was excited to locate more of the plants and compare them to each other.

But not today. Today she'd stay with Mrs. Cooper and make sure the mother and baby were doing well. She couldn't leave Mrs. Cooper to fend for herself yet.

The late-August sun poured over Linnea as she started across the yard toward the stable, a mangy dog with only one ear trailing her. The station was situated at the eastern edge of Cañon City. And though the hotel was visible down the wide dirt street, surely Flynn wouldn't mind assisting Grandfather.

As she neared the stable, she took him in, strangely hungry for the sight of him. She hadn't seen him nearly enough in their recent days of travel. With their departure at Pueblo from the other scientists, she and Grandfather had set to research in earnest, their collection and drying taking up hours every day. In addition, their party now had fewer men to take guard duty. Though they'd tried to band together with other groups of travelers, Flynn and Wyatt and Nash had taken on the bulk of the extra work.

She'd only had a few occasions to talk to Flynn and hadn't had one moment of privacy. She'd dreamed about nothing else but the kisses he'd given her by the river. And she was embarrassed at just how much she wanted to kiss him again. The desire had been growing with each passing day, and she'd even begun plotting ways she could get alone with him.

Could she kiss him now?

She peered around. No one else was within view.

Her stomach did a somersault, and she lengthened her stride, suddenly almost breathless with her need. "Oh, Flynn McQuaid. What have you done to me?" she whispered.

When she reached the fence rail of the corral, she halted and watched him work, appreciating not only what a handsome picture he made but what a generous and kindhearted man he was to help Mr. Cooper even though he had no reason to.

His injured arm was still in the sling, but he was using his hand more every day. He vigorously brushed the mule's dusty coat as it drank from a full water trough.

She unlatched the gate, slipped through, and didn't stop until she stood directly behind him. Her pulse quickened at being so close to him. And she waited for him to turn, hoping he'd take her in his arms.

He brushed several more strokes, then paused. For the

first time since seeing him in the stable, she became keenly aware of the tension radiating from his body. His muscles were taut, his body rigid, his breathing hard.

"Flynn?" Something was wrong.

He didn't answer.

She laid a hand on his back, only to have him flinch at her touch. "What's bothering you?"

He hesitated another moment before he slowly pivoted. His expression was grim. "Reckon the child birthin' is bringing back a whole passel of memories I don't wanna think on."

During one of their many conversations on the journey west, he'd opened up and told her about his ma's stillborn babies and her health decreasing with each birthing, culminating in death last year after a particularly long and hard delivery. "That's understandable—"

"No, Linnea. You don't understand. I hate it."

At the stark pain in his eyes, she reached up with the need to somehow comfort him.

He took a rapid step back. "After everything my ma went through with each baby she lost, I can't ever do that . . . to a woman . . . to my wife."

Linnea dropped her hand. Wariness stole through her. "You don't have to worry, Flynn. What happened with your mother doesn't happen to most women." At least not with any women she'd known.

"That's why I told you I wasn't aimin' to ever get married," he continued almost as if she'd never spoken. "Because I can't bear the thought of havin' a babe."

"Mrs. Cooper went through all those hours of labor, and now she's safe and secure with a beautiful baby boy. Everything is perfectly fine with both the mama and baby."

"It could've gone bad in a split second."

"But it didn't." She had to make him see reason, convince him that his fears were irrational. "It'll be different for you, Flynn."

"The almighty truth is that I don't wanna have children."

"But look how it turned out for Mr. and Mrs. Cooper. They have a family now."

"I should have told you sooner." He had told her. He'd been upfront right from the beginning that he didn't want a wife or family. She supposed she'd just held on to the hope that maybe if he was starting to think about having a future with her, he'd also concede to have a family.

She swallowed a swell of desperation and tried to make her tone as positive as possible. "Mrs. Cooper will likely have plenty more children and never have any stillbirths."

"I can't, Linnea. I just can't." His gaze strayed to the cabin, and his eyes again filled with the torture of living through one too many nightmares.

Linnea wanted to drop a hand to her abdomen, had the sudden need to protect her unborn child from this discussion. She didn't want her child to be rejected by anyone, not even Flynn. Especially by Flynn. But she forced herself to keep her hands at her sides.

"I understand that what happened to your mother was traumatic. But please try to see reason—"

"Just hearing Mrs. Cooper's cries near to killed me. I can't go through that again. Not with any woman, especially not with the woman I love."

Love? Was he insinuating he loved her? "Birthing doesn't last long. Just a few hours. And then you have a blessing for a lifetime."

He rubbed a hand across his forehead and eyes. "Thought maybe I could change—maybe I was changing. But after last night, I reckon this is one thing I ain't gonna be able to change. At least not anytime soon."

She certainly couldn't tell him about her pregnancy now. And if she couldn't now, how would she ever? A lump rose into her throat. "Seems to me that if you truly love a woman, then you would try to accept her feelings in the matter and not just think about your own."

He hung his head, his shoulders slumping. "Was hoping real bad you'd be able to understand and be patient with me."

She wished she could be patient. But she couldn't. She physically couldn't, not with the baby coming by the year's end. And she had the sudden terrible premonition this was the end of any future with Flynn before it had a chance to begin.

"I came to ask if you'd accompany Grandfather back to the hotel while I stay with Mrs. Cooper and the baby." She started across the corral, praying he would say something to stop her. Tell her that he'd compromise. That, at the very least, they could discuss the issue more.

But his silence followed in her wake, along with the finality of his decision. As she slipped through the gate, her chest burned, and she couldn't keep the tears from sliding down her cheeks.

Why oh why had they decided to set aside their reservations about building a relationship? They shouldn't have crossed the line they'd initially drawn. She should have known doing so would only lead to trouble and heartache.

For the rest of their journey, she'd have to do her best to

stay away from him. Once he learned of her pregnancy, she didn't want him feeling any sort of obligation to remain with her. As much as it would hurt and as hard as it would be, she had to set him free.

But was it too late? Had she already irrevocably fallen in love with Flynn McQuaid?

CHAPTER

22

He missed Linnea somethin' awful.

Even though she was only a hundred feet away, it could've been a hundred miles with the gulf that had opened between them.

She was strolling arm in arm with her grandfather, the wide-open valley of South Park spreading out before them. And though she made it seem like she was holding on to her grandfather, Flynn guessed she was lending the older man her support since he was still suffering from mountain sickness, although not as bad anymore.

Dr. Howell had fared poorly ever since they'd started the climb into the higher elevations. He'd been short of breath, tired, achy, and had taken to riding in the back of the covered wagon for longer spells. Linnea had spent most of her time with him.

Flynn reckoned she'd done so to stay clear of him, and he didn't blame her. He could've figured out a better way to tell her his insecurities about having children. At the least, he could've waited a spell until he had time to calm down after having to listen to Mrs. Cooper's screaming and crying for hours on end during the birthing.

He still shuddered every time he thought about the sounds he hadn't been able to drown out, even in the stable. When Linnea had come outside, he'd been in no frame of mind to discuss anything.

With a gut-wrenching sigh, he tore his gaze from her and focused on the mountains surrounding the basin. The rising crags were even more majestic up close. Covered in pine, the dark green was broken by jagged ridges and rocks, until giving way to barren peaks.

The treeless prairie filled the basin between a range on the west and one on the east. With rich, sun-cured hay, the land was plentiful enough to feed thousands of cattle. Even with the seemingly endless supply of buffalo grass, wheat grass, and moss sage, Wyatt said he'd taken to growing his own alfalfa to store away for winter just in case they needed it.

South Park was a little piece of heaven hidden away. He could see why Wyatt had decided to settle here. A part of him envied his brother for finally having a home he could call his own.

Wyatt, who'd been at the lead for most of the past week, had stopped his mount and was peering back at him. Beneath the brim of his battered hat, his brother's expression radiated an excitement that hadn't been there before. They must be nearing his ranch.

"We just crossed over my land," Wyatt called as if seeing Flynn's unasked question.

Flynn nodded. "It's mighty fine."

Wyatt waited until Flynn reached him and fell into step beside him. "I'm fixin' to ride on ahead if you don't mind."

"Nope. Don't mind. Reckon you're wantin' to see how things are faring."

"Yep." Wyatt scanned the horizon ahead.

All the long days as they'd traveled north along Currant Creek through Currant Creek Pass, they'd been anxious to make it through before the nights turned cold. But the going had been slow. The cattle were weary and bone thin. Their hooves were worn down to nothing.

When they finally made it through to the level plains, Wyatt had slipped from his horse, fallen to his knees, and bent his head in prayer. No one had driven cattle to the high country before. And now he'd proven it could be done. After everything they'd faced, it was a miracle they hadn't lost more than two.

They'd continued to remain vigilant for the roving bands of Confederates, especially when they'd reached Buckskin Joe and heard reports that a gang was hiding in South Park, causing trouble in the area.

They hadn't experienced any more run-ins, but the wound in Flynn's shoulder was a daily reminder of the danger Irregulars could inflict. And he didn't blame Wyatt for worrying.

Wyatt shifted in his saddle. "The honest truth is, I've been missing my wife something awful, and I've got a hankering to see her in a real bad way."

The low, pained note in Wyatt's declaration tugged at Flynn's compassion. If he'd had to be away from his wife for months at a time, he'd have felt the same way. In fact, he wasn't so sure he could have left.

Even now, the distance from Linnea was too much.

Flynn pushed past the ache inside. "Your wife's gonna be sweet on seeing you again too."

Wyatt stared straight ahead and was silent for a minute. "Not sure it's my place to say anything about Linnea, but I reckon she's real sweet on you."

"Not anymore. Not after I messed things up with her."

"Ain't never too late to try to set things straight."

Flynn wanted to. But whenever he tried to talk to her, she always made a point of turning the conversation to include anyone else standing nearby. She was too polite to treat him with anything more than her usual kindness. But the camaraderie they'd shared over the summer was long gone.

"It ain't hard to see you still got it bad for her." Wyatt's tone contained a measure of sympathy Flynn wanted to lean in to. But he'd never been able to rely on Wyatt for anything but criticism, and Flynn wasn't about to lean on him now and end up falling flat on his backside when Wyatt decided to pull away.

Flynn kept his comment locked up, and for several seconds, the plod of their horses' hooves against the dry earth filled the silence.

Wyatt watched Linnea and her grandfather before speaking again. "Just want you to know that when you figure out how to turn things around, we can make room for her at the ranch."

"Yep, not sure how to figure things out. But I'm aimin' to get a place of my own just as soon as I can manage it. Maybe before winter, but no later than spring."

"No need. This is your home now."

Flynn could almost feel the heat welling up within Wyatt. "Said I'd drive the cattle out here. But never said I'd stay."

"Dash it all, Flynn. Can't you put the past in the boneyard where it belongs? I know we didn't always get along, but we're family. And I sure as a gun was hoping we could stick together."

"Maybe you should've thought of that when you left the farm." Flynn held his breath, waiting for Wyatt to blow up.

But his brother just pressed his lips together.

"Listen." Flynn couldn't let the trip end with bad blood between them. "One ranch ain't ever gonna be big enough for the two of us. Soon enough you'll have a passel of your own and won't need me, Dylan, and Ivy crowding you."

"You're not taking Dylan and Ivy." The hardness of Wyatt's tone stuck into Flynn like an arrow hitting a bull's-eye.

He'd be hanged if Wyatt thought he was leaving Dylan and Ivy behind. "I've done the hard work of raising them while you were gallivanting all over God's green earth. I reckon I oughta be the one to finish what I've started."

"You know blamed well I wasn't gallivanting. Everything I did was because I was looking for a way to get Ma and everyone away from that lowlife."

"Did you ever think that instead of running off, the best thing you could've done was stay and be there for Ma? For me?" Flynn didn't like making a blathering fool of himself, so he clamped his jaw closed to keep himself from saying anything else he'd regret.

"Ivy told me what happened to your leg. That Rusty busted it."

He hadn't mentioned anything to Wyatt about his limp, and Wyatt had never asked. Now he knew why.

The muscles in Wyatt's jaw worked up and down. "And you're right. I wish it would have been me that Rusty beat near half to death instead of you."

The swell of anger inside Flynn stalled.

"I'll never be able to forgive myself for what happened to you or Ma."

Flynn didn't know what to do with Wyatt's admission.

"I can't forgive myself." Wyatt's voice was low and hoarse. "But I hope someday you'll see fit to forgive me for not being there when you needed me most." He didn't wait for an answer but spurred his horse into a trot. He easily moved out ahead of their slow-moving line of cattle. Within seconds he was galloping across the grassland, riding low on his horse and racing toward home.

Flynn could only watch his brother, confusion rolling in to battle the bitterness he'd held on to for so long. The pain of that last beating from Rusty came rushing back, that day he'd found Ma sitting on the floor weeping over the shattered picture of her and Pa from their wedding day. It hadn't been the black and blue marks on Ma's face that had done Flynn in that time. It had been her broken heart.

With Wyatt's accusation about being Rusty's punching bag still ringing in Flynn's head, he'd marched out to the barn and tackled Rusty. Except he hadn't been Wyatt and hadn't gotten away unscathed.

Flynn shuddered. The only good thing that had come from that day was the fact that Rusty hadn't dared touch him or Ma again.

Flynn watched Wyatt's disappearing form. With how much more Rusty had despised Wyatt, things could have been real bad for him if he'd stayed. Maybe Rusty would have killed Wyatt. Or worse, what if Wyatt had ended up killing Rusty?

All this time Flynn had blamed Wyatt for running off. But had it been for the best?

Flynn tightened the reins around his glove and put the thoughts from his head. They were gonna be at Wyatt's ranch before the day's end, likely within an hour's end. And he was still in sore need of figuring out what to do about Linnea.

He patted his coat pocket. The flowers were still there. The few unique ones he knew she hadn't yet seen. He'd been waiting for the perfect opportunity to give them to her. But how could he when she wouldn't allow him a single second of a single minute to talk?

Time was running out. Once they reached the ranch, Dr. Howell and Linnea would continue on into Fairplay and live there while they explored and researched in South Park. After that, he'd likely only see her once in a while.

He nudged his horse in her direction, wishing there was some way to get her alone, even if just for a few minutes. He half wished she'd get into some kind of trouble just so he'd have an excuse to pick her up and rescue her. But since leaving Cañon City, she hadn't so much as stubbed her toe.

As he reined in alongside Dr. Howell and Linnea, the older gentleman smiled up at him. "Young man, I can't thank you enough for all your help this past summer in getting us here."

"It was my pleasure, sir."

Linnea ambled next to her grandfather and didn't acknowledge his presence.

Heaven help him. All he wanted to do was slide off his horse, pull her into his arms, and tell her everything would be fine. But how could he promise her that?

Dr. Howell cast Flynn a look that was full of questions. Likely questions about his intentions for his granddaughter. No doubt he was wondering what had happened to cause them to hardly speak to each other.

At a shout, Flynn glanced up to find Ivy and Dylan kicking their horses into a gallop. Ahead was Wyatt's ranch. The barn constructed of logs was a decent size. The rough-hewn logs surrounding it made a zigzag corral that would have to be expanded now with the additional livestock.

A smokehouse, privy, and log cabin house stood a distance away from the barn. Wyatt had already informed him that he and his overseer, an older man named Judd, had spent the better part of last autumn and winter adding on to his original cabin, building a second floor as well as another room on the first floor. From all appearances, the cabin looked like a regular two-story house, except it was made of logs with thick chinking. Wyatt had even managed to put glass in his windows.

Flynn felt a measure of pride for his brother that surprised him. It wasn't the Pennsylvania farm that had belonged to their father and grandfather. But it was mighty fine all the same.

As they drew nearer, he could see Wyatt standing in the ranch yard with his arm around a woman who was peering up at him with adoration. His wife, Greta. She was pretty in a simple, country-girl way.

Wyatt was holding a thin wisp of a girl in his other arm and listening to her chatter on about something. That had to be Astrid. He ruffled her light brown hair before he set her down. Then he rubbed the head of a black-and-white dog circling them and barking with excitement.

After that he bent in to kiss Greta. She stood on her toes

to kiss him back. The kiss went on for a spell while the dog and Astrid raced around the couple, playing chase.

Holy horses. Wyatt hadn't been kidding when he'd said he had a hankering for his wife. The kiss was mighty steamy and sent a spear of heat through Flynn's gut. He had a hankering for kissing Linnea the exact same way. But he had no right to even think about it.

Flynn stared down at his hands and repositioned his reins, trying not to look at Linnea.

At the excited calls from Ivy, Flynn shifted his attention in time to see Wyatt break away from the kiss, but only reluctantly and only because Ivy and Dylan were dismounting. Even then Wyatt didn't release his wife while he made the introductions.

Ivy lowered herself to her knees in front of Astrid and the dog, yammering away and already making friends. Dylan didn't hold back either and was flirting with Greta in no time. They looked like a family. A real family. Dylan and Ivy were in a place where they could be safe and happy for the first time in a long while.

An ache lodged in Flynn's chest. Maybe Wyatt was right. He couldn't take Dylan and Ivy away from here. He'd just arrived and already he sensed this would be the best place for them. A place where they'd have Greta's mothering, Astrid's companionship, and Wyatt's provision. Especially because right now, Flynn had none of that to offer. All he had was himself. And somehow that had never been enough.

CHAPTER

23

Linnea stood to the side of the homecoming. She didn't want to impose and wished she and Grandfather had branched off earlier and made their own way to Fairplay. She didn't want Flynn feeling obligated to ride with them, but she suspected he'd insist on traveling to town, which she'd learned was another five miles to the northwest.

"I'm pleased to meet you, Flynn." Greta smiled at him. She and her little sister resembled one another with their light brown hair, blue-gray eyes, and pretty features. Ivy had talked excitedly about the pair, Greta and Astrid, for the past couple of days, telling Linnea everything Wyatt had shared. Now, Linnea felt as though she already knew Greta and Astrid, particularly the story about how Greta had come west as a mail-order bride to help save Astrid from consumption.

From what she could see of Astrid, the girl wasn't suffering anymore. If Ivy's tales were true, then Astrid had found relief from her ailment and was healthy—at least for now.

Greta wore a simple blue calico skirt and blouse, and as

she leaned in to shake hands with Flynn, the skirt hugged her waist, showing off a rounded abdomen. Was Greta expecting a child too? Ivy hadn't mentioned it.

"Pleased to meet you too, ma'am." Flynn shook Greta's hand before he took a step back.

Wyatt bent in and stole another kiss from Greta in front of everyone, and she pulled away laughing, slapping lightly at his chest as if to reprimand him, but her expression was filled with both delight and love.

What did Flynn think of all this? Linnea chanced a peek his way at the same time he sent her a sidelong look. His green-blue eyes were dark and haunted. And yet as his gaze flicked to her mouth, something else flamed in his eyes. Over the course of their days on the trail, she'd finally learned what that look meant. Desire.

Her stomach did a flip that sent warmth cascading through her belly. Even if they were at odds with what they wanted out of life, the attraction that sizzled between them hadn't diminished.

She glanced away, not wanting to encourage what could never be. But apparently she hadn't broken the connection soon enough, because both Greta and Astrid were now staring at her.

"I didn't realize you'd gotten married, Flynn," Greta said with a smile. "But that's so wonderful. I'll surely welcome the company here on the ranch."

"Me too!" Astrid hopped up and down.

Ivy laughed and peered up at Flynn from where she was petting a dog. Her eyes sparkled with mischief.

Wyatt's brows shot up, but he made no move to correct Greta either.

Flynn rubbed a hand across the back of his neck. "This here is Linnea and her grandfather, Dr. Howell. But we—"

"Pleased to meet you." Greta stretched a hand toward Linnea. As she leaned in to clasp it, Greta's attention dropped to Linnea's midsection. "I see you and Flynn are expecting a baby. When are you due?"

Linnea fell back a step, her smile fading.

All eyes locked on her. The humor dissipated from every face and was replaced with surprise.

"Expecting a baby?" Grandfather patted Linnea's arm. "No, I'm afraid you're mistaken on both fronts, Mrs. McQuaid. Linnea is not married to Flynn, and she most certainly isn't carrying his child."

Flynn was staring at her abdomen. And only then did she realize she'd placed both of her hands across her stomach, flattening her skirt and revealing the extended shape she'd so carefully hidden all this time . . . from the men.

But, of course, all it had taken was one woman who was with child herself to recognize the truth.

"You're having a baby?" Flynn's voice was low.

Greta frowned at Flynn. "I don't understand. If you're not married to Linnea, then who is the father of her baby?"

Grandfather laughed. "My granddaughter isn't having a baby, Mrs. McQuaid."

Linnea swallowed hard and forced herself to speak even though all she wanted to do was run away and hide. "I am with child."

Grandfather's smile disappeared, and confusion wrinkled his brow. His attention dropped to her stomach. "I don't understand."

"I am pregnant." Though she was speaking to her grandfather, she met Flynn's gaze. His misery was unmistakable. If she'd held out any hope he'd change his mind and accept her child, she let it die.

"Is Flynn the father?" Her grandfather's voice contained curiosity and not the anger she would have expected.

"No!" She and Flynn both uttered words of protest at the same moment.

Her face flamed. "Grandfather! No, absolutely not. Flynn and I are only friends."

Flynn's countenance was taut. "I assure you, sir. I've never . . . Linnea and I haven't . . ." He muttered for several seconds. "The baby's not mine. Plain and simple as that."

"The child is Asa's." She squeezed her grandfather's arm, hoping to find a way to soothe him.

"Asa?" Astrid popped into the conversation. "Who's Asa?"

"He was my husband, and he died in March from pneumonia while we were at Fort Leavenworth."

"I'm so sorry for your loss." Greta shot a narrowed look at Astrid as though rebuking her to remain quiet.

Linnea started to respond, but Grandfather spoke first. "If the child is Asa's, why didn't you tell me? Surely you've known for some time."

"Yes, Grandfather. I've known for weeks." She hung her head, shame settling upon her. "I didn't want to tell you because I didn't want to jeopardize all your work and the expedition. I was afraid once you knew, you'd insist on leaving it all behind to take care of me and make sure I got home to New York safely."

"Of course I would have. This is no place for a child to be born." Grandfather waved his hand at the ranch and the surrounding mountains.

Wyatt's wife stiffened and placed a hand upon her abdomen, revealing a large swell under her skirt and cloak. "I think the West is a fine place for a baby to be born."

Immediately, Wyatt's attention dropped to her protruding belly, his eyes rounding. Surprise, confusion, and questions filled his expression.

"I was planning to tell you later when we were alone." Greta rubbed a hand across her stomach, and Linnea guessed Greta was at least as far along as she was, if not further.

Astrid joined in putting both of her delicate hands against Greta's stomach, her expression somber and much too innocent. "Greta promised I could get another puppy if I didn't say anything to you about the baby until later."

Wyatt stared between the two a moment longer before a grin worked its way up his lips. "Greta bribed you with a puppy?"

"No. Of course not," Greta replied hastily.

"W-e-l-l, yes—" Astrid smiled up at Wyatt—"as a matter of fact, she did."

Greta's cheeks turned a becoming shade of pink. "I only said so because we could use another cow dog. That's what Judd's been saying all summer."

Wyatt's grin inched higher until he was beaming. He placed his hands over the top of Greta's and Astrid's upon the swell of the baby. "Well, what do you know. I'm gonna have a son."

"Now, Wyatt." Astrid cocked her head in a grown-up way. "Prepare yourself for having a daughter. Because this is a little girl."

"That so?" His sights dropped to Greta's face, and the love shining from his eyes made Linnea want to weep. Weep for joy because of the beauty of their family, but also weep for sorrow because of the despair of her situation. She had no husband to share this experience with and no excitement over the baby's coming.

In fact, her grandfather was upset about the baby. And Flynn . . .

He was kneading the back of his neck and staring down at his boots. From his tense shoulders to his tortured expression, she guessed this was all the more reason for him to reject her.

A pang reverberated through her chest with the hurt that had been festering since that morning in Cañon City.

"Linnea, my dear," her grandfather spoke quietly beside her. "While I rejoice over the prospect of the new life, I must admit, I am rather taken aback."

She tore her attention from Flynn. She had to stop holding out hope, even secretly, that they could reconcile their differences. "I'm sorry, Grandfather. I should have told you sooner."

"How far along are you? Are you able to calculate your due date?"

"I believe sometime in mid-December."

He studied Linnea's face as though searching for the truth. Did he truly think her a loose woman capable of sleeping with Flynn and conceiving his child? She hadn't realized their attraction was so obvious, so palpable.

She lowered her head, shame coursing through her. "Grandfather, please believe me. The child is Asa's."

He patted her arm. "I do believe you. I'm simply attempting to decide how to proceed. It's too late in the year to return to New York City, so I think the best course of action is that the two of us go to Denver for the winter. There we will be able to rent lodging and hire a nursemaid to help take care of the baby."

"I won't be the cause of you having to give up the expedition." Especially after all that had already happened to divide their party. "If we don't stay and work on the manual, your reputation and your work will suffer irreparably."

She wasn't sure how much of her conversation with Grandfather Flynn could hear, but he spun on his heels and stalked toward his horse. He hefted himself into the saddle and started on his way toward the herd straggling behind.

"Not to worry, my dear." Grandfather placed her hand into the crook of his arm, gently, as if she could break with the least pressure. "Surely we can stay through October and leave before snow falls in the mountains. That ought to provide us with plenty of time to start researching."

"But I don't want you to give up the expedition—"

"You and the baby are more important, young lady. Once you are secured, I shall come back next spring and continue."

Of course, he was making no mention of her returning to the high country with him, not after having a baby. With the hesitancy he'd displayed thus far regarding her participation in the trip, his reservations would only increase now.

She was tempted to tell him they could leave right away for Denver. A part of her wanted to run as far from Flynn as possible. But another part wished he would gallop back, wrap her in an embrace, and assure her he wanted both her and the baby.

She straightened her shoulders and pushed down the hurt. This parting of ways between them was for the best. She had to think about her grandfather first and focus on salvaging as much of the expedition as they could.

Chapter

24

Would she ever stop missing Flynn?

Linnea straightened from the *Cirsium scariosum*, the meadow thistle, she'd been examining, rubbed at the aching spot in her lower back. Her heart ached more, and the pain wasn't going away, even though she'd attempted to put Flynn out of her mind.

Even reminding herself that he'd been the one to walk away didn't help. She couldn't stay angry at him. Not when she knew how badly he'd been scarred by what he experienced with his mother's stillbirths and her death.

She placed a hand upon her abdomen. With less than three months left, the baby had grown too large for her to hide her pregnancy. Not that she needed to anymore.

During the past few weeks, every man in Fairplay and the surrounding area had learned she was a widow expecting a child. She'd had at least a dozen proposals of marriage, with more men seeking her out every day, all of them letting her know they'd be happy to become a father to her unborn child.

Apparently plenty of men didn't mind raising another man's child. Why did every single man on this side of the Continental Divide want to marry her and take care of her unborn child, except the one man she wanted?

She tilted her face up to the noonday sun, which was warm for October. As usual, she'd tossed aside her hat and allowed the rays to bathe and brown her face. The high-altitude sun was intense, but she'd discovered just how much she relished the fresh air and the abundance of sunshine.

Grandfather squatted nearby with his monocle in his eye, studying another species of thistle he'd yet to identify. His leather satchel lay open on the rocky hillside with his vasculum beside it. He held a notebook in one hand and a pencil in the other and stopped periodically to jot down observations and draw diagrams.

Yes, she loved doing all this with Grandfather, but she'd loved doing it even more when she'd been able to share everything with Flynn, talk to him about her discoveries, and show him what she was working on. He always listened and always cared, even about the littlest things.

Since arriving, she'd seen him occasionally, once when Greta invited Grandfather and her to the ranch for supper. He'd been on his way out to check on the cattle and had stopped to greet them and ask after their research. She'd also spoken with him after church as everyone gathered outside and mingled, but the interaction had been brief, and he hadn't lingered.

Another early morning she'd viewed him from her hotel window when he'd ridden into town with Greta, helping her bring in a load of her popular jams and fruit pies to sell. Linnea had waited breathlessly for him to seek her out, but the knock never came, at least not before she and Grandfather left for the day.

With the cooler nights and threat of snow in the high passes drawing ever nearer, Grandfather had purchased their tickets for the stagecoach leaving for Denver in two weeks. Two weeks to finish their research. Two weeks until she left South Park and Flynn behind.

"Wherefore, if God so clothe the grass of the field, which to day is, and to morrow is cast into the oven, shall he not much more clothe you, O ye of little faith?"

She'd been repeating the verse during the past few days, trying to remind herself that no matter what happened, God would provide everything she needed for life, even if that meant she'd never see Flynn again. However, knowing the truth didn't ease her bereavement.

Should she be troubled she was grieving more over losing him than she'd grieved for Asa? In fact, she'd wept more tears over Flynn in one night than she had in months for Asa.

As much as she wanted to ignore the truth, she couldn't. She loved Flynn like she had no one else. And she doubted she'd love anyone except him ever again.

She leaned back onto a boulder, perching on the edge, letting her gaze sweep over the valley below, searching to the south and hoping to spot Wyatt's ranch. But she couldn't make out anything distinctly since she and Grandfather had ridden farther up into the foothills today than on their previous excursions. Their hired driver, Mr. Pearson, was familiar with the area from his mining endeavors and had done an excellent job shuttling them around to new locations, each one with slightly differing terrains.

As on other days, she and Grandfather had hiked up into the hills, leaving behind Mr. Pearson and the wagon with the rest of their supplies. Of course, they never ventured far from Mr. Pearson, never beyond shouting distance, since he was armed and they weren't.

She'd heard tales of the wild animals that roamed the foothills—bears, coyotes, and even mountain lions. But other than chipmunks, squirrels, and lizards, they hadn't come across any creatures. Of course, she'd spotted an occasional moose or pronghorn in the distance, but nothing to warrant fear.

Grandfather glanced at her over his shoulder. "Are you tired, my dear? Maybe we should call it day?"

"No. I'm perfectly fine, although I wouldn't mind taking a break and having our lunch if you're agreeable."

At times, her appetite was ravenous, not only from the baby growing bigger and requiring more nourishment, but from all the hiking and fresh air.

Grandfather sat back on his heels and made another note in his book. Attired in one of the suits Clay kept immaculately clean and ironed, Grandfather had recently taken to wearing a smaller, more rounded black hat Clay had purchased for him at one of the stores in Fairplay. Although as distinguished as always, he also looked the part of an explorer. "Well then, let us walk back down and have our picnic. Perhaps Mr. Pearson will surprise us with trout again today."

Linnea stood and stretched once more, but then jumped at the echo of a gunshot in the direction of their wagon. Was Mr. Pearson hunting? Or was he scaring away a dangerous predator?

Another shot discharged, followed by raucous laughter.

"Who is it?" Linnea wished she could see the wagon and Mr. Pearson, but junipers and boulders blocked their view.

Grandfather frowned. "I do hope Mr. Pearson isn't in any sort of trouble."

"Shall I go and check on him?" She gingerly climbed past Grandfather, but he captured her arm.

"No, Linnea. Let me go first."

She hesitated, but he'd only agreed to her accompanying him on the daylong excursions if she promised to stay near him and refrain from anything that would put her in peril.

Flynn would have been proud of her. She'd only gotten lost twice, and Mr. Pearson had easily found her. The time she'd uncovered a snake, thankfully it hadn't been a rattler and it had slithered away. Although she'd tripped and fallen more times than she cared to admit, at least she only had a few cuts and bruises to show for it.

"Why don't you stay right here." Grandfather had already started hiking down the gravelly hillside. "I'll call to you if everything is fine."

"Are you certain?"

"I am most certain."

She rested her backside against the boulder again, taking in the view of the valley. To the north, the aspens had begun to lose their chlorophyll, leaving the bright golden pigment behind. Blended with the silvery ponderosa pine and the darker green of the lodgepole pine, the landscape was as majestic as always. She doubted she'd ever get tired of seeing so many plants and trees all in one place.

A dozen paces down, Grandfather stopped abruptly and flattened himself behind a large boulder. A few seconds later, he peeked around, only to hide again.

She straightened. "What's wrong—?"

Grandfather cut her off with a swift shake of his head and press of a finger to his lips. He began scrambling back up.

As he reached her, his eyes were wide and filled with fear that set her stomach roiling. "We need to hide. Now."

"Why? What's wrong?"

He grabbed her arm and began towing her farther up the hill. "A group of Confederates has captured Mr. Pearson."

Linnea climbed after him. "Shouldn't we go to his aid?"

"There are a dozen of them, and they're all armed."

Linnea stumbled. Of course, everyone in town was talking about Irregulars hiding out in South Park, trying to find gold and raise money for the Confederate cause. Some were even claiming that one band of Confederates had been robbing stages and wagon trains, amassing a fortune. But Mr. Pearson had assured them he'd only take them to areas that were completely safe.

Grandfather raced up the hill and she struggled to stay behind him. At a large boulder surrounded by junipers, he guided her into hiding. Breathing hard, he pulled her down with him as more shots echoed in the air.

Linnea crouched low, her mind flooded with images of the skirmish with the Irregulars they'd had near Pueblo, and Flynn getting shot in the arm. The wound had been healing well by the time they reached Wyatt's ranch. She had no doubt it was fully mended by now. The irrefutable truth was that the Irregulars were dangerous, even deadly. If they discovered Grandfather and her, she shuddered to think what they'd do to them.

It was all too easy in the West to forget that a war was raging and devastating the East. With Denver newspapers finding their way up to Fairplay—albeit two, sometimes three weeks later—they were hearing more about the war now than they had while traveling during the summer.

The biggest news had been the Union's victory in July at Gettysburg, Pennsylvania, although the staggering numbers of casualties being reported for both sides cast doubt upon whether it was really a victory for anyone.

Since the battle had been in Pennsylvania, had Brody been there? In reading the casualty lists, she hadn't come across his name, but she thought about him nonetheless, knowing Flynn was likely beside himself with worry.

Grandfather pulled his handkerchief from his vest pocket, removed his hat, and dabbed his forehead and wiped at his thin reddish-gray hair. "I'm afraid the Irregulars will see our equipment, realize Mr. Pearson wasn't alone, and come searching for us."

Linnea studied the landscape again. "Where shall we hide? Can you think of a better place?"

He peeked out from the rock, peering back down the hill. "I suggest we continue to climb up and hope we get too far so that they give up before locating us."

Grandfather led the way up until the hillside turned into cliffs they couldn't scale. As they took shelter behind a cluster of rocks and trees, more gunshots echoed in the gulch below.

"I should never have let you come on this expedition with me," Grandfather whispered, his fingers clutched around his handkerchief so tightly his knuckles turned white. "All I've done is expose you to one perilous situation after another."

She released a sigh of defeat. She'd hoped Grandfather would learn to view her as a benefit to the expedition and to his research, especially over the past few weeks of working tirelessly by his side. But apparently she hadn't been able to win him over with her skills any more than she'd been able to win the other scientists. "I apologize, Grandfather. I know having me along has been difficult for you."

"Not difficult for me, my dear. I just worry about something happening to you."

"I wish I'd been born a son. Then perhaps everyone would take my contributions to botany more seriously." As soon as she gave voice to the thought, she wished she could take it back. Her grandfather's silence and the stricken slant of his brows only made her feel worse.

"I didn't mean to complain. You've been good to allow me to do all that I already have, and you've given me more opportunities than many other scientists would have—"

"No, Linnea. You're right." He enfolded his hand tenderly over hers. "I haven't taken your contributions as seriously as those of the men. And I don't know why. Your observations are astute, your research thorough, and your organization impeccable."

"Please don't worry about it, Grandfather."

He squeezed her hand. "In fact, you're a brilliant botanist, better than most of the men who joined my expedition."

"You need not flatter me—"

"I'm not flattering you. I mean every word. If I had to choose just one person to assist me, I could think of no one better than you."

He was offering her the highest of accolades. Yet there was an unfinished element to his statement. "But . . . ?"

He sighed. "But you are my granddaughter, a young woman, and soon-to-be mother. And I am too set in my ways to put aside my protective nature and treat you as I would a man."

Did a man need to cast aside all chivalry in order to respect a woman's worth? Or was it possible for men to regard women with high esteem while also valuing their intelligence? She'd experienced some of that with Asa. And even more with Flynn. Both had not only valued her as a woman but accepted her as a scientist.

"You needn't treat me as you would a man. But perhaps you also needn't treat me as helpless. What if a woman is capable of being strong and smart alongside men?"

Grandfather patted her hand. "You have certainly proven that."

"And I can continue to prove it, even after my baby is born and throughout my whole life."

Grandfather was silent a moment, as though contemplating her statement. He'd had a difficult enough time accepting her working as a single young woman. She doubted he'd ever be able to accept her working as a mother with a child.

Before he could respond, voices rang out on the hillside below them, drawing closer, which meant only one thing. The Irregulars were searching for them.

Grandfather sat forward. "You're right, Linnea. I've had my whole life to do everything I've ever wanted and to make a contribution to the science of botany. Now it's your turn." He started to stand.

She grabbed his arm and held him back. "What are you doing? We must stay down."

He stilled for a moment and stared straight ahead at the barren, rocky cliffs.

The voices were growing louder. It wouldn't be long before the Irregulars discovered them.

Grandfather met her gaze, his eyes more serious than they'd ever been. "They know someone else is here, but they might not know there are two of us. I intend to give myself up. Then I want you to remian here until they're gone before going for help."

"No!" Her whisper was loaded with horror. "Absolutely not."

"I need to, for you and the baby. Now, promise you'll stay hidden?"

A terrible ache formed in her throat. She couldn't let him do this, but what other choice did they have?

He bent down and kissed her cheek. "I love you, Linnea. And I'm so proud of you."

Before she could respond, he stood and stepped out from behind the rock, holding his hands in the air. "If you're looking for me, I surrender." Her grandfather climbed down the way they'd come, disappearing from sight.

Linnea waited behind the boulder for what seemed like hours. She heard no more gunshots and could only pray that meant the Irregulars hadn't harmed Grandfather. When the voices faded farther up the gulch, she crept out and started down the hillside, stumbling and falling several times.

Upon reaching level ground, she peeked through the thick junipers. Sunlight streamed over the open area, revealing the wagon sitting where Mr. Pearson had left it. The mules were unhitched and grazing contentedly in the shade as though nothing had happened.

She saw no sight of the Irregulars or of Grandfather and Mr. Pearson. After waiting several moments longer to make sure no one was around, she tiptoed out into the open. Everything in the back of the wagon had been overturned and dumped out. Precious research was scattered on the ground, their drying press smashed, and the extra vasculum broken.

But those items were the least of her concern now. Grandfather and Mr. Pearson's lives were at stake.

She shielded her eyes from the bright sunlight and studied the gulch that cut through the mountain. She needed to ride back to Fairplay and get help. But first she had to find out where the Irregulars were taking Grandfather and Mr. Pearson. Otherwise, how would she be able to direct a rescue effort?

Cautiously, she started up the trail. As she hiked, the path narrowed and the foliage thickened, which would explain why the Irregulars had left the wagon behind.

At the waft of campfire smoke and the sound of laughter, she guessed she was drawing near. Was this some kind of secret hideout? Could she find a way to sneak up without anyone seeing her?

She stared ahead, waging an internal battle. After Grandfather had given himself up to keep her safe, she couldn't put herself in further jeopardy. She had to go.

As she turned and began to make her way back down the trail, voices rang out nearby. She pushed through the pinyon and juniper and scrambled to find something big enough to hide behind. Lowering herself to the ground behind the brush, she prayed no one would spot her.

CHAPTER

25

He couldn't let Linnea leave for Denver. Flynn shoved his hands into his hair as he limped the length of the barn.

He halted in front of Rimrock's stall and grabbed the latch, ready to saddle up and ride into Fairplay even though the day was spent and darkness had fallen. His grip tightened against the cold metal, and he bowed his head onto the top beam.

He needed to go after her and ask her to stay. But what right did he have to do so? They hadn't made any commitments to each other. Yet how could he stand back and let her ride out on the stagecoach?

After coming back from town, Wyatt had been the one to tell him at the supper table that Dr. Howell had purchased stage tickets. Wyatt's piercing glare said he had choice words for Flynn, but he'd controlled his tongue, only because Greta had rendered him speechless as usual with her pretty smile.

Part of Flynn wished his brother would have said his piece. No doubt he deserved a whole heap of chewing out and more.

He tapped his head against the stall beam. Lord Almighty, what should he do?

His insides were twisted into so many knots he wasn't sure he could ever unravel them. He was barely eating, wasn't sleeping, and could hardly work. He'd hoped he'd get over Linnea and be able to go on with his life. But with each passing day, the tangles inside had only gotten worse. He almost wondered if he should hike out to Leadville and join Jericho and Nash in mining. But he had the feeling he'd think about her no matter where he ended up.

He could feel Judd watching him from the loft above where he sat in the hay, his Bible on his lap and lantern lit beside him. Wyatt's older cowhand was a decent fellow. He was quiet and kept to himself just the way Flynn liked. Flynn had been sharing the barn with Judd, and they hadn't spoken more than a dozen sentences to each other.

With a head full of fluffy white hair along with a white beard, handlebar mustache, and bushy eyebrows, Judd couldn't have been much older than their father, had he lived. Although Judd didn't speak of his past, apparently his hair had turned white on the day he'd had to listen to his wife and children's screams as they'd been roasted alive inside their flaming home while he'd been beaten and left for dead by a band of Comanches. After he'd recovered, he left Texas and never returned.

Flynn had half a mind to glare up at Judd and tell him to say whatever it was he was itching to. But Flynn wasn't sure he wanted to hear a reprimand to quit carrying on like a weaning calf and to grow up.

He pushed away from the horse stall and strode back to

the door, now closed against the chill of the October night. He paused before spinning on his heels and stalking back, doing nothing to ease the throb in his hip. He deserved every bit of pain and more. The constant ache reminded him of how he'd failed to protect the people he loved. And he could very well fail again with Linnea. And her babe.

He'd been able to watch over her and keep her safe from all the dangers on the long journey to the West. But the birthing. . . he had no control over that, had no way to make sure she'd survive.

He was helpless when it came to the child growing inside her. And he hated feeling that way.

Flynn paced to the door.

Judd cleared his throat.

Inwardly, Flynn sighed. "Might as well spit it out."

Judd remained silent.

Flynn glanced over his shoulder at Judd, who was staring down at the open Bible on his lap. "Well? We both know you've got something to say."

"Yep." He smoothed a hand over the well-worn pages.

Flynn turned around and leaned against the door, crossing his arms as if that could somehow protect him from whatever rebuke Judd might lob his way.

Judd was silent for another long moment, giving way to the noises of the barn at night—the soft snort from one of the horses, the rhythmic chewing of cud, the swish of a tail. Even though Wyatt had insisted Flynn take one of the upstairs rooms with Dylan, Flynn hadn't wanted to be in the house any more than he had to. He needed his space from Wyatt, especially having to watch him kiss and carry on with Greta every blamed chance he had.

Deep down he knew he was annoyed with the displays because they made him think on Linnea. He was jealous. Plain and simple.

Jealous of Wyatt's ability to love Greta so freely. Jealous of how quickly he'd accepted her pregnancy. Jealous of his joy in having a child.

Was it possible he'd always been jealous of Wyatt? Jealous that Wyatt had been able to leave home and the problems so easily? That Wyatt had gone off and had adventures while he'd stayed behind? That Wyatt could charm people and wasn't always so serious like him?

Judd cleared his throat again, drawing Flynn's attention. "Well?"

"If you find a gold nugget in your pan, you can keep on pannin' or you can go on and locate the mother lode."

Flynn could only stare at Judd. What did mining for gold have to do with anything?

"And best go get the mother lode before someone else takes the treasure right out from underneath you."

Flynn took off his hat and scratched his head. He'd considered staking a claim for the better half of a second, especially after he'd walked away from the two hundred dollars Dr. Howell had wanted to give him. But he'd heard enough tales from Wyatt to know that finding gold was about as easy as shooting at the moon and hitting it.

"Listen. I ain't got plans to do any gold mining—"

"Yep. I know." Judd closed his Bible and ran a ragged fingernail along the worn spine. "This girl of yours that you love . . ." He paused as though giving Flynn the chance to deny that he loved Linnea.

Flynn was tempted to contradict the old cowhand, but

his hankering for Linnea was most likely written into the misery on his face.

"You can hoard that nugget of love you got with her, or you can go on and do the hard work of mining for the mother lode so you can have it all."

Judd's words settled within him. Flynn wanted more than a nugget. But so far he hadn't been willing to do the hard work of making their relationship work.

"Don't wait until it's too late." Judd's deep voice dropped a decibel.

Was the cowhand speaking from experience? Had he somehow missed out on his family, only realizing their worth after they were gone?

"The almighty truth is . . ." Flynn situated his hat on his head and peered in the direction of the horse stalls, too embarrassed to look Judd in the eyes. "I'm scared near to death to have a baby."

"If we tuck tail and run every time we're scared, we'll end up running in circles, never getting anywhere."

"True enough." Even so, Flynn didn't know how he could go through with standing by while Linnea gave birth. But what was his choice? If he tucked tail and ran, he'd never reach the treasure. The only way he would ever be truly rich was by embracing the pain and effort that came with mining.

"If I'm trying so hard to keep the people I love safe, reckon the Almighty could lend me a hand."

"Way I see it, He's busy keepin' 'em safe more times than we know."

If Flynn counted all the close calls Linnea'd had, maybe Judd was right. Maybe God was watching out for them more often than he realized.

"For a real long while, I couldn't swallow any reason why the Almighty let my family suffer but spared me. Figured I shoulda been able to do more to save 'em."

At the low anguish in Judd's voice, a trail of pain burned up Flynn's throat.

Judd stared down at his hands, as though just the mention of his family was enough to unearth every skeleton. "Ain't any way around the pain. Only thing a man can do is say like Job did when he hit rock bottom: The Lord gave, and the Lord hath taken away; blessed be the name of the Lord."

Was that kind of faith even possible?

Flynn was tempted to shake his head. But if it had worked for Judd, who'd experienced the worst of losses, it had to be possible for anyone. Including him.

Behind him, the door slid open. He moved aside as the cold night air wafted into the barn, stirring up the scent of alfalfa and horseflesh.

Wyatt stepped inside, his expression grim. He closed the door behind him. Then, without a warming, he threw a punch into Flynn's gut, hitting him hard and doubling him over.

Flynn gasped out a breath. "Thunderation, Wyatt! What'd you do that for?"

"Because someone has to tell you you're an idiot."

Flynn bent over and bunched his fists, trying hard to resist the urge to plow into Wyatt like an angry bull.

"You're an idiot!" Wyatt practically shouted.

"Heard you the first time. And you're right."

Wyatt, in the middle of flexing his hand, froze. "About realizing that Linnea is perfect for you? And that you can't let her get away?"

"Yep."

Wyatt's shoulders relaxed. "Alright."

"Alright." Flynn straightened and started across the barn toward the horse stall, pressing a hand against his aching ribs. This time when he reached the latch, he jerked it up and swung open the stall door.

"Where you going?" Wyatt trailed him.

"Where else?" Flynn grabbed his saddle from the center divider and tossed it onto Rimrock.

A minute later, Wyatt stood in the stall two down, saddling his horse.

Flynn paused. "Where you going?"

"Where else?" Wyatt imitated Flynn's tone just as easily.

Flynn ducked his head and smiled. Was it possible to build more than ranches and farms here in the West? Could he and Wyatt start over and build a friendship?

Minutes later, they were bundled in their heavy coats and gloves, and their horses were pounding across the prairie, headed toward Fairplay. Flynn's heart was pounding just as hard. What if he was too late? He'd heard that every blasted man on God's green earth had called on Linnea and asked for her hand in marriage.

When he heard about it, he'd given the ax a good sharpening and split enough wood to last every household in South Park through the winter. It would serve him right if she refused to have him after the fool he'd been. But that wouldn't stop him from getting on his knees and begging her to give him a second chance.

By the time the flickering lights of Fairplay came into view, Flynn's nerves were wound up like old twine about to snap.

"She strikes me as a real forgiving sort of woman," Wyatt

said, as though seeing his mounting worry as surely as a thunderhead forming over the western range.

"Hope so." Flynn had never met a woman as sweet and understanding as Linnea. She might forgive him. But that didn't mean she'd want to stay with him. And marry him. Yep. If he could persuade her to have him, he planned on proposing tonight and proving to her he was done running from fear and pain.

"Greta said Linnea and Dr. Howell are staying at Hotel Windsor." Wyatt veered his horse toward Main Street and cantered ahead.

"And what else does Greta say?" Flynn tried to lace his tone with irritation.

Wyatt tossed an amused glance over his shoulder, clearly sensing Flynn was fishing for more information about Linnea. "She hasn't taken up any offers of marriage yet, if that's what you're asking."

"Didn't think she would."

"That right? Then you think she's pining away for you?"

"Hopin' so."

"Reckon you're right. Never did understand why the women all liked you so much."

"Guess they like my real cheerful personality."

Wyatt laughed.

As they slowed in front of the hotel, Flynn studied the up-stairs windows. All dark. Since it was only a few hours past the supper hour, she was probably still in the dining room with her grandfather, hopefully not visiting with other men.

He barely made an effort to secure his horse to the hitching post before he was pushing open the door and entering the establishment. Wyatt was close on his heels.

Flynn couldn't concentrate on the greetings, was too busy scanning the room for Linnea's beautiful red hair.

She wasn't there.

He spun toward the proprietor, Mr. Fehling, who was shaking hands with Wyatt and asking after Greta and their coming baby. "I'm looking for Dr. Howell and Mrs. Newberry." Impatience bubbled up inside, and he didn't care that he was interrupting.

"Dr. Howell and Mrs. Newberry?" Mr. Fehling's face registered surprise. "Why, they haven't returned from their excursion today, and I assumed they were visiting at your ranch. Dr. Howell mentioned doing so as they left this morning."

Flynn's pulse tapped an uneasy pace. "Haven't seen 'em. You sure Dr. Howell said they were planning a visit?"

"Sure enough."

Flynn glanced out the large front window that overlooked the dark street. He'd heard they were doing their research in the surrounding area and hadn't been going too far. He reckoned as long as they stayed close to Fairplay they'd be safe enough.

"They could just be running a little behind," Mr. Fehling offered.

Flynn shook his head. "Ain't nothing for them to see and do after dark."

"You thinking something happened to them?" Wyatt asked.

Flynn's entire body protested the prospect. But what other explanation was there? "Do you know where they were headed?" He directed his question to Mr. Fehling.

The hotel proprietor shrugged. "They've been all over these parts, so it could've been anywhere."

After all of Linnea's near disasters on the trail, maybe she'd gotten herself into some kind of trouble. "What about Clay?" He tried to control the panic creeping into his voice. "Maybe he knows where Dr. Howell and Linnea were working."

They searched for Dr. Howell's manservant and finally located him in one of the taverns several doors down. Clay spelled out as much as he could, that Dr. Howell and Linnea had spent the past week across the river in some of the gulches west of Fairplay. But he couldn't name which one they'd decided to explore today.

Within an hour, Wyatt had amassed a search party including half the men in town, some on foot and others with mounts. Several dozen lanterns reflected the concern in every face. With the dropping temperatures and wild animals coming down from the higher elevations, the wilderness was no place for an elderly man and pregnant woman.

Flynn had half a mind to take off and ride as hard and fast as he could into gulches to the west and start the search by himself. But Wyatt had cautioned him several times to wait. Flynn knew well enough that running off alone would only cause more trouble. But with each passing minute, his muscles were stretching as tight as a hide over a tanning rack.

He'd been a coward to let Linnea go. And if—when—he found her, he wasn't planning to let her go again.

After breaking up into four groups, Wyatt shouted instructions. And as they started out, a commotion from the men on the road to Alma brought Flynn to a halt.

"A wagon's coming!" one of the fellas called.

"It's them!" came another shout.

Flynn directed his horse into a gallop toward the northernmost group. As he reached them, his pulse slammed hard at the sight of Linnea on the wagon bench, clutching the reins with gloved hands. Her hair had come loose and fell in disarray over her cloak, and her face was pale and weary.

From his first quick assessment, he saw nothing wrong with her. Even so, he vaulted from his horse and elbowed aside the men congregating around her and peppering her with questions.

"Give her some space," he groused.

Her gaze alighted on him and her face crumpled. "Oh, Flynn. They Irregulars have seized Grandfather and Mr. Pearson."

CHAPTER
26

He was here.

Linnea sagged with relief. Flynn's steady, strong presence before her was like a miracle. She didn't care that he'd hurt her with his rejection. All that mattered was he was here now and was peering up at her with his beautiful green-blue eyes.

"You okay, darlin'?" His voice was hoarse and his ruggedly handsome features etched with worry.

She held out her arms to him, needing him and wanting him with a fierceness that went beyond rationality.

He lifted her down. The moment her feet touched the ground, she let herself fall against him. He wrapped his arms around her, and she pressed her face into his chest, allowing herself to take the first full breath since she'd started out of the canyon.

"Where's Dr. Howell?" Clay finished fighting his way through the growing crowd.

"What happened to Mr. Pearson?" another man called.

"Hush up and give her a minute." Flynn's reply rumbled with irritation.

She closed her eyes, wishing she could block out the nightmare from earlier.

"It's alright." Flynn pressed a kiss against the top of her head. "Everything's gonna be alright."

She'd already wasted hours and couldn't waste another second, no matter how much she wanted to stay in Flynn's arms. She pulled back, and he released her, although he kept an arm around her waist. "The Irregulars took Grandfather and Mr. Pearson to their camp, and we need to go back and rescue them."

"What camp?" "Where at?" "How many are there?" The questions bombarded her, and she didn't know which one to answer first.

"Whoa now!" Flynn shouted above the clamor. "Everyone needs to slow down and let her say her piece."

As the voices quieted and all eyes focused on her, Linnea leaned into Flynn, needing his strength more than ever. His arm behind her tightened, as though he was reassuring her that he'd be by her side until the end.

She knew it wasn't true. She'd be leaving Fairplay soon. But she wanted to pretend things were right between them, that he would be there for her like this forever. As much as she wanted to be independent and strong enough on her own, somehow with him she was better.

"Take your time telling us what happened." Flynn squeezed her even as he scowled a warning at everyone else. "Then we'll come up with a plan for getting 'em back."

She relayed all that had happened including how she'd been trapped near the camp until dark when she'd finally been able to sneak back to the wagon and hitch up the mules. By that time, the Irregulars had stopped their coming and going and settled in for the night. The darkness had made her journey slow and tedious, and she'd nearly gotten lost on several occasions—but she didn't mention that.

"The federal militia's been looking for where those Irregulars have holed up," said one of the young men who'd proposed to her only last night. "I say we alert the feds, and then together we can make a surprise attack. We'll flush 'em out and pick 'em off one at a time."

"Won't be enough time to rally the troops we need tonight," someone else said.

As more men chimed in to the discussion, Wyatt stepped forward. His presence was commanding, and even before he started talking, the men grew silent. "First thing is to make sure Linnea is safe. Once those Irregulars realize the wagon is gone, they're gonna figure out real quick someone else was there, and that it was Linnea. Then they'll be aiming to silence her from telling anyone the location of their camp."

The men erupted into loud conversation again. When Flynn pressed another kiss against the top of her head, she closed her eyes, weariness and hunger making her tremble. The baby fluttered too, as though sensing her anxiety.

In the next instant, Flynn was placing her back on the wagon bench. He hopped up next to her, pulled her into the crook of his body, and gave a curt nod to Wyatt. "I'm taking Linnea back to the ranch. She'll be safest there."

"You and Dylan and Judd take turns standing guard."

"No," Linnea protested. "Take me to the hotel. I can't stay at the ranch and put everyone there in danger."

"You're coming with me." Flynn grabbed the reins and

gave them a shake, starting the team on its way. "That's all there is to it."

She struggled to sit up. "Please, Flynn. Besides, I want to be in town just in case I'm needed."

"You did your part by getting away. Now you gotta steer clear and let the feds take care of the rest." His arm held her firmly in place by his side, and she was too tired to fight him.

As Flynn drove the wagon away from the men, the darkness of the oncoming night enveloped them. The only sound was the clopping hooves of the mules and the rumbling of the wagon wheels over the hard, dry land. The half-moon above gave the same guiding light as previously when she'd been navigating her way out of the gulch.

After her dangerous ride, she'd been more grateful than ever she'd learned how to hitch a team to a wagon during the journey west, and that she was capable of driving them. She could only pray she hadn't arrived for help too late for Grandfather and Mr. Pearson.

She shivered, more from fear than from cold. But Flynn was already shrugging out of his coat.

"I cannot take your coat, Flynn. I don't want you to get cold."

"Don't worry none about me." He draped it around her shoulders, enfolding her in the warmth that lingered from his body heat. She drew in a breath of his woodsy scent, one that never failed to tantalize her.

She started to thank him, but a noisy yawn escaped instead. She clamped a hand over her mouth.

He drew her to his side once more. She wouldn't have been able to resist even if she'd wanted to, though a warning rang in the back of her mind that she shouldn't allow herself to get close to Flynn McQuaid only to face heartbreak again.

Just for tonight, she'd forget about their painful separation and the fact that he didn't want to have her now that he knew she was having a baby.

Another yawn escaped. She rested her head against his chest and was asleep within seconds.

As Flynn brought the wagon to a halt near the barn, he brushed a curl off Linnea's cheek and whispered another silent prayer of thanks she was there.

He was under no illusion she was safe yet. But the outcome could've been so much different. If she'd been captured by the Irregulars along with Dr. Howell, there was no telling what the men would've done to her, pregnant or not.

Judd hobbled across the ranch yard toward them. "Where's Wyatt?"

"Linnea and her grandfather landed in a heap of trouble with some Irregulars. Wyatt's back with the townfolk trying to figure out how to stage a rescue of Dr. Howell and a fella by the name of Pearson."

Judd's bushy white brows puckered together. "Maybe I oughta go on and give Wyatt a hand."

"They'll have plenty of help once they get the feds involved."

Judd reached the first mule and gave it a friendly pat.

Flynn didn't like to ask for help, but he'd do just about anything to keep Linnea safe. "Reckon the Irregulars might try to track Linnea down, so I brought her here for safekeeping."

Judd began to unbuckle the bridle. "I'll take first lookout, so you can get her settled in the house."

For the first time since Pa died, Flynn felt as though someone else was watching over him, that he didn't have to be the one always doing the protecting. "Thank you, Judd."

The older man gave a nod but continued to work on unhitching the mules.

As Flynn extracted his arm from around Linnea, she roused enough to sit up. After he helped her down, he lifted her into his arms. Even with the growing swell of her stomach, she weighed hardly more than she had the first time he'd carried her out of the Neosho River.

Although he'd done his best to ignore the baby, the rounded belly was front and center and staring him right in the face. He quickly averted his attention, but not before he realized she was watching his reaction.

Greta stood in the open door of the house with Astrid and Ivy on either side. Thankfully, he was spared having to say anything to Linnea because the two girls were already calling out questions, wanting to know why he was carrying Linnea.

Fully awake, Linnea was eager to eat after having gone most of the day without food. And she was obliging and much more pleasant than he was about answering a whole passel of questions the girls were throwing out.

While serving Linnea, Greta was quieter than usual, not too keen on the news that Wyatt was staying with the others and intending to join in the attack against the Confederates. Finally, Greta lowered herself into the rocker Judd had made for her, leaned back, and closed her eyes. Weariness creased her face, reminding Flynn of how Ma had looked at the end of each of her pregnancies—haggard and uncomfortable. Except from what he'd overheard, Greta and Wyatt's babe wasn't due for another month at least.

After finishing her meal, Linnea yawned. Flynn left his post by the window, picked her up, and started up the narrow stairs. He guessed she was able to walk, but he wanted to carry her. And since she snuggled against him, he took that as her consent.

"Don't do too much kissing." From the bench, Ivy made kissing motions in the air just like she had the day of the buffalo hunt. Astrid, who had become Ivy's number-one fan, burst into giggles.

Heat rose into his neck. "Ivy, hush up."

Greta attempted to push herself up from the chair. "Flynn, maybe I should attend to Linnea."

"Thunderation," he growled. What was wrong with these women? "I'm just carrying her to bed. That's all."

Dylan had willingly agreed to give up his room for Linnea and had hauled his stuff out to the barn while she'd been eating. As Flynn reached the second floor, the slanting roof prevented him from standing to his full height so he had to crouch closer to Linnea and could feel her warm breath against his neck.

A short hallway branched off to two rooms of equal size. Astrid and Ivy shared one. In the other, a small window allowed in enough moonlight that he could see the double bed.

As he crossed toward it, every muscle tightened with need—the need to set her down, pull her flush, and kiss her until they were both delirious. Maybe Greta had been right. Maybe she should've come up with Linnea instead of him.

At the edge of the bed, he paused. With his head bent, his lips nearly brushed her cheek. He loved her more than his own life. And he desired her more than he had any right to.

He was just gonna set her down and walk away. That's what he had to do. And not let the emotion of all that had transpired cloud his judgment.

He lowered her until she was resting on the mattress.

She released a soft, shaky breath.

"You'll be fine now," he whispered, starting to back away. "Get some rest."

"Thank you, Flynn." She glided her hands up his chest to his shoulders. The touch was like striking a match, searing him. Her caress moved to his collar, to the back of his head. And then she wrapped her arms around his neck, as though wanting him to stay, the pressure drawing him back.

He couldn't. He wouldn't.

But as she arched and her mouth brushed his, he groaned, bent in, and took hold of her. Oh, Lord Almighty. This was where he wanted to be. With her. Forever.

She responded eagerly, knocking off his hat and winding her fingers into his hair. Her passionate response only fueled his, adding dry kindling to a forest fire.

"Flynn!" Ivy's call broke into the smoky haze.

He was tempted to ignore his sister, didn't want to break this beautiful reunion with Linnea. Now that he was kissing her, he didn't want to stop.

"Something's wrong with Greta!" Ivy's shout from the bottom of the steps finally penetrated. Linnea was the first to pause, her breathing quick and heavy against his lips. As Ivy's words made sense, Linnea sat up, forcing him back.

"Hurry!" Ivy called. "She's moanin' somethin' awful."

An icy splash hit Flynn, and he jumped up so rapidly he bumped his head on the slanted log ceiling. The moaning, crying, thrashing. They all meant one thing. Child birthing. Greta was ready to have her baby.

CHAPTER

27

Linnea stood and crossed toward the door, pressing her hands against her heated cheeks. What had she been thinking to throw herself at Flynn that way? It was almost as if a wanton woman took up residence in her body whenever she was alone with him.

"Flynn!" Ivy called again, her voice ringing with panic.

"We're coming." Linnea's voice wavered in spite of her effort to sound calm.

Flynn remained unmoving except to thrust his hands into his hair. Was he thinking of their kissing? Was he regretting it already? Or worse, was he angry at her for initiating contact when he'd made it clear he didn't want her or her baby?

As he shifted, moonlight revealed the terror in his expression, one that said he'd rather be anywhere else than in this log cabin while Greta travailed to bring new life into the world.

All he'd ever gained from childbirth was heartache and pain. And she didn't want to subject him to that again. "I'll go and attend to her." After watching her grandfather with Mrs. Cooper's birthing in Cañon City, she could help Greta for a short while. "Why don't you ride to town and fetch the doctor or midwife?" She didn't know if Fairplay had either, but the errand would keep Flynn occupied.

He hesitated. Then he picked up his hat and put it back on. "Nope. I'm gonna stay and help you. I'll send Dylan to town."

"I'll be fine—"

"I want to." His tone was low and raw and his body rigid.

Was this some kind of test he was putting himself through? Was he finally ready to face his fears and conquer them? The very thought sent a shimmer of hope through her.

"I'll understand if you change your mind."

"I won't." Flynn's gaze held fierce determination. And something else. Was it love? For her?

"Hurry!" Astrid called out this time.

Linnea wanted to understand what was happening between Flynn and her. But they didn't have the time right now. She could only hope Greta's birthing wouldn't scare him worse and make him run away again.

As they hurried downstairs, they found Ivy already helping lead Greta to the bedroom off the living area. Flynn stepped outside to talk to Judd and to send Dylan after the doctor. In the meantime, Linnea gave instructions to Ivy and Astrid for boiling water, gathering clean linens, and making a decoction that would take the edge off Greta's pain.

"I've been having birthing pains all day," Greta admitted, once she was situated in bed. "But I assumed they were like all the other pains I've had over the past weeks."

Linnea scrubbed her hands and arms up to her elbows in preparation for examining Greta.

When Flynn stepped into the doorway a moment later, Linnea wanted to assign him some other task elsewhere. He shouldn't be present for a birthing. Not only wasn't it decent, but what if something went wrong? After all, the baby was coming earlier than Greta had expected. Linnea didn't want to expose Flynn to any problems, didn't want anything to sever the tenuous reconnection with him. Not after how hard the past month had been. She couldn't lose him again.

She stood and faced him. "Flynn . . ."

"I need to do this, Linnea." Fear still darkened his eyes.

"You don't have to do it for me." She hoped he read what she left unsaid, that she would care about him regardless of what he did or didn't do.

"I know. I have to do it for me." He stuffed his hands into his pockets.

She hesitated, her thoughts returning to that day on the Santa Fe Trail when he'd helped one of the cattle give birth. He'd done so with unmatched proficiency and skill. While birthing a baby was different from birthing a cow, he would be no amateur to the process. If anything went wrong before the doctor arrived, he'd be able to help.

Before she could say more, Greta cried out. Linnea lowered herself to the bed frame next to Greta and gripped the young woman's hand until the contraction passed.

When finished, Flynn approached the bed. "Reckon I can hold Greta's hand while you take care of the rest."

Linnea started to rise to her feet, and in the next instant, Flynn was assisting her. As he steadied her, he tugged her, giving her no choice but to stumble against him. Her belly and the baby pressed into him.

What did he think? Was he repelled by the touch?

326

As though hearing her unasked questions, he settled his hands on her hips. Cautiously, he lifted a hand until it rested on her protruding stomach. Then he bent in and captured her lips in a kiss, one that contained quiet desperation.

He didn't have to say anything. She knew his touch to her belly and lips was his answer. And as she rose up to meet him and kiss him back, she tried to communicate her response. That she loved him. Because she had no doubts whatsoever that she did.

"I knew it!" Ivy's exclamation broke through the kiss.

Flynn backed away from Linnea and tossed Ivy a glare where she stood in the doorway with Astrid behind her. "Go on and take Astrid out to the barn."

Ivy's face lit with a smile. "So that you can kiss Linnea whenever you want?"

"Hush up and get."

The girl's smile only widened as did Astrid's.

Linnea ducked her head, not sure whether to feel pleased or embarrassed.

As Greta cried out with another contraction, Linnea knew she had to put all other thoughts from her mind and focus on the young woman. Now wasn't the time to dwell on her feelings for Flynn and the uncertainty of her future. With Grandfather's capture and Greta's travail, she needed to get through the night first.

Hours passed with agonizing slowness. Each birthing pain grew longer and harder, but Greta made no progress in dilating. As dawn light seeped into the room, Linnea wanted to weep with frustration. From her continuous assessments, everything was as it should be—the baby was in the correct position without any obstructions.

Unfortunately, Dylan had returned without a doctor or midwife. The doctor was traveling, and no one knew where he was. And there was no midwife in the area.

"Oh, Grandfather," Linnea whispered. "You should be here." Exhaustion threatened her—not only from staying up all night but from the emotional toil of worrying about him.

With the opening of the front door, she tried to dry the tears that had escaped. A moment later, Flynn entered the bedroom, his brows furrowed. He'd stepped out to speak with Judd, and he'd only been gone for five minutes. But somehow, even that seemed too long. He'd discarded his hat long ago, and after the hours of digging his hands into his hair, the strands were disheveled. The stubble on his face was darker. And his expression grim.

"I want you to go up and sleep for an hour or two," he whispered. She shook her head, but he cut her off with a growl. "I'll call Judd in here and carry you up myself if you don't go."

Greta's eyes were closed, her face flushed, and her expression free of pain for just a few moments.

"I'll be fine, Flynn—"

"And I'll be fine watching over her while you rest." His tone was steely, giving her no choice in the matter.

The truth was, Linnea was afraid to leave him. He'd stayed strong throughout all of Greta's distress. But his eyes still radiated with a dark fear that told her he hadn't chased away old demons yet.

She smoothed a hand over his cheek, wishing she could soothe his turmoil somehow.

Greta released a gasping cry and thrashed.

"Go." His voice and eyes pleaded with her.

She had to rest for the baby's sake. Even so, she hesitated. "Please, Linnea?"

She wanted to blurt out that she loved him. She loved the sacrifices he was willing to make and the hardships he was willing to face because of how much he cared about others. From the first day he'd plunged into the river after her until now, he'd proven again and again what a selfless man he was.

Even though the words begged for release, she bit them back. Just because he was here and helping her with Greta didn't mean he wanted to forge a life together. And if she spoke of her love, would he feel coerced into something he wasn't ready for?

With a sigh, she nodded. "Okay. I'll rest for a little bit."

As Greta cried out again, Flynn knelt and grasped her hand.

Linnea watched him a moment longer, then dragged herself from the room and up the stairs. As Greta's screams echoed through the house, Linnea fought the urge to go back down and instead forced herself to the bed. She didn't think she'd be able to slumber through the noise, but she was asleep as soon as she closed her eyes.

Linnea awoke with a start. Sunlight streamed through the lone window, revealing an upstairs dormer room, barren of furniture except for the bed she was sleeping in.

For several seconds she blinked and tried to make sense of where she was. Not at Hotel Windsor in Fairplay. Not with Grandfather . . . because he'd been captured by Irregulars.

"Grandfather!" Panic pulsed in her chest, and she sat up. At the sight of the slanted roof and the chill of a draft, the memories of the previous night rushed back. Greta had gone into labor. Flynn had been there. And the labor had been slow.

She stood unsteadily to her feet. How long had she slept? How was Greta doing? And what about Flynn?

Linnea listened, waiting to hear Greta's screams and cries. But a strange, deathly silence greeted her. Along with the scents of bacon and coffee.

"Oh, dear Lord, help." She hurried out of the room and down the stairs. As she reached the bottom step, she halted in surprise to see Ivy in front of a pan sizzling on the stove. Astrid sat at the table, an empty plate in front of her. She was whispering with Ivy and stopped at the sight of Linnea.

Ivy spun, spatula in hand, and smiled at Linnea. "You're awake. Guess Flynn won't tear our heads off if we make noise now."

What had happened to Greta and the baby? "Greta?" Linnea could hardly squeeze the word out past her tight throat.

Before Astrid or Ivy could answer, Flynn appeared in the bedroom doorway. And he was staring down at a bundle of blankets in his arms, his eyes wide with awe. When he glanced up at her, he offered her a tired but happy smile.

"I'd like to introduce you to my nephew," he spoke softly, dropping his gaze back to the blankets and the tiny baby wrapped within.

Linnea cupped a hand over her mouth to hold back the emotion that swiftly rose. Tears stung her eyes. How? When? Greta?

As if sensing her questions, Flynn cocked his head toward the bed. "An hour or so ago. And Greta's fine. Sleeping now."

From the way sunlight slanted in the window, Linnea

guessed it was still early morning, that maybe she'd slept for a couple of hours at most. "You should have woken me."

"It all happened too fast. By the time I figured out she was pushing, I was nearly too late to catch this little runt."

The picture Flynn made standing in the doorway holding his nephew made Linnea's heart ache with such tenderness she wanted to weep at the beauty of the moment. "How is he?"

"He's tiny and perfect."

Linnea's feet started working again, and she crossed the room, excited and eager and relieved all at once. As she reached Flynn, she couldn't tear her gaze from his face to look at the baby. After the difficult night, it was a miracle the baby and Greta hadn't suffered any ill effects. And it was also a miracle Flynn had faced the birthing so courageously.

Her heart filled to overflowing at the realization he'd fought the battle and prevailed. When he caught her staring, she dropped her attention to the baby. The red wrinkled face was scrunched and splotchy. Even so, there was no denying he had the sturdy and handsome McQuaid features.

"He's a fine little McQuaid." She brushed a finger across his soft, smooth cheek.

The baby's lips puckered as though he were kissing the air and agreeing with her pronouncement. She smiled and glanced up to see that Flynn was smiling too.

For a brief instant, she pictured Flynn and her sharing smiles over the baby growing inside her. But was such a picture just wishful thinking?

"Linnea?" Greta's groggy voice cut into the tender moment.

Linnea slipped past Flynn and rushed to Greta's side. "You

did it. Congratulations. I'm just sorry I missed being here with you for the big moment."

Greta peered past Linnea and Flynn to the other room. "Is Wyatt back yet?"

Flynn shook his head. "It's still early." The guarded look in Flynn's eyes told Linnea he didn't expect Wyatt to return anytime soon.

"Maybe if Judd goes after him and tells him about his son, he'll come home." Greta's face held the strain of the long night, but also the worry of a woman who didn't want to lose the man she loved.

As though sensing the same, Flynn gentled his tone. "Listen, Greta. You gotta let Wyatt do his part in this war. If you hang on to him too tightly, he'll get restless and question his dignity, until he can't stand himself and then does something stupid."

From the pensive wrinkle in Flynn's brow, Linnea suspected he was thinking more about Brody than Wyatt.

"You're right." Greta pushed herself up, situating the pillows behind her. "I'm just worried about him and can't wait for him to meet his son."

"When he gets home, he's sure gonna be surprised to see this little fella." Flynn regarded the baby with such love that Linnea's throat clogged.

Greta lifted her arms. "I'll take him. You both need a break. Why don't you go to bed for a little while?"

Flynn's brows shot up. "Bed?"

Greta leveled him a stern look. "Not together, Flynn McQuaid. Not until I see a ring on Linnea's finger."

Linnea didn't dare look at Flynn, didn't want to assume that just because he'd chased down one fear, he was ready to marry her.

Flynn passed the baby to Greta, and she situated him in her arms. "Go on now. If I need anything, I can always call Astrid or Ivy."

If not for the hunger gnawing Linnea's stomach, she would have resisted Greta's dismissal. As it was, the scents of Ivy's cooking drew her out of the room, and Flynn followed on her heels.

Before she stepped through the doorway, his fingers captured hers. His touch, as always, made her entirely conscious of his presence and her desire for him. And when his fingers slid into place between hers and tugged her to a stop, her pulse sped not only with the pleasure of being intertwined with him but of the possibility he might kiss her.

As he tugged her slightly backward and his attention dropped to her mouth, her anticipation mounted, making her breath catch.

"W-e-l-l, it's mighty nice to see Flynn happy for once." Astrid paused with a forkful of potatoes and eggs halfway to her mouth. Perched on her knees on the bench at the table, she cocked her head and wore an impish smile. "He's been so grumpy since he got here. And now I sure do know why."

The couple of times Linnea had visited with the family, she'd easily fallen in love with Astrid.

"And why has Flynn been so grumpy?" Linnea could guess what Astrid was referring to, but she couldn't resist teasing Flynn just a little.

"I ain't been grumpy." He glared first at Astrid, then Ivy, as though ordering them to silence.

"Howdy-doody." Ivy whistled. "You've been worse than a grizzly bear. Best thing for all of us is if you marry Linnea today."

Linnea waited for Flynn to say something—maybe even agree with Ivy. But he released her hand and rubbed the back of his neck. "Reckon I better relieve Judd from guard duty and let him catch a few winks."

Linnea didn't want to be anywhere else except with Flynn. She almost offered to do guard duty with him. But as he left the house and closed the door behind him, she knew if she had any hope he'd eventually find his way back to her, she had to let him go. She just prayed when that happened, it wouldn't be too late.

CHAPTER
28

"Riders coming!" Judd's urgent call from the corral slapped Flynn and woke him in an instant.

He jumped up from where he'd thrown himself in the hay-mow and jogged across the barn, trying not to let his limp slow him down. He didn't know how long he'd slept, but from the lengthening shadows, he reckoned a few hours had passed.

For the better part of the day, he'd taken guard duty to allow Judd to sleep. All the while he kept a vigilant eye on the horizon, he puttered around making repairs, dressing game, and making sure his guns were loaded and his cartridge box full.

Late in the afternoon, Judd had finally ordered him to bed, assuring him he'd keep watch on Linnea. Flynn hadn't wanted to take a break, but he needed some shut-eye if he was gonna be able to stand guard all night.

Now his blood pumped hard and ready. He carried his rifle in one hand and revolver in the other and made his way to the house. Judd was already positioned next to the door with revolvers in both hands. And Dylan stood by the barn out of view but with his rifle ready.

At the thin, almost kitten-like wail coming from inside, Flynn paused to listen, his heart thrilling in wonder, as it had every time he thought about holding the baby just after the birth. The boy's cries had filled the air, loud and strong. He kicked his arms and legs like he never planned to stop. And Flynn had been the one to witness the whole beautiful miracle.

He straightened his shoulders at the realization he'd accomplished something he'd never thought possible since losing his ma and her babies. While he wasn't hankering to go through a birthing anytime again soon, he'd do it in heartbeat for Linnea. In fact, he had to be by her side while she suffered through the birthing. He couldn't imagine being anywhere else.

But for now, he had one goal—to keep her safe from any Irregulars who might be itching for a fight. As the riders drew nearer, he could make out one hardened build among a dozen others.

"Wyatt." He lowered his guns and stepped away from the house.

Judd did likewise, holstering his six-shooters.

Flynn watched his brother, surprised by the strange tightening in his chest. He was actually glad to see Wyatt. In fact, he was near to weeping at the sight of him. Not that he'd ever admit it to him.

As the group rode in, Flynn ambled into the yard, taking in their haggardness but relieved to see that no one was hurt. Including Dr. Howell. The gentleman was tired, unshaven, and dirty, but he was otherwise unharmed.

The house door swung open and Linnea was out and running toward her grandfather before the horses came to a halt. "Grandfather!" She picked up her skirts, revealing her fancy bloomers underneath.

At some point in the day, she'd taken time with her appearance, fashioning her hair into a pretty knot that showed off her lovely form and her elegant neck and cheeks.

Dr. Howell was slow to dismount, relying heavily upon Clay who'd ridden in next to him. As soon as the older gentleman's feet touched the ground, Linnea threw her arms about him.

While Flynn recognized the faces of some of the other riders, including Landry Steele, the mayor of Fairplay and investor in Wyatt's herd, many he didn't know.

"The women are safe?" Wyatt's eyes were wild with worry, his gaze raking over the ranch and taking in every detail.

"Yep. Ain't seen a soul."

"Good." Wyatt's hands shook as he holstered his revolver. "After the militia arrived, we trapped and caught most of the Irregulars. But two of them got away, and we heard they headed this way."

"We ain't seen hide nor hair of any Irregulars." Compassion stirred within Flynn. He supposed in some small way, he could finally relate with Wyatt. They both wanted to keep the women they loved safe and would do anything to make that happen.

Mr. Steele urged his horse out in front. He tipped his hat at Flynn. "Some of us will ride out a ways and scout the area to make sure they aren't hiding anywhere nearby."

Half the men quickly volunteered to go with Mr. Steele, and they galloped away as the rest dismounted.

"Where's Greta?" Wyatt looked to the open door, his brow furrowing at the absence of his wife who always stood in the doorway to greet him whenever he rode into the yard.

Flynn followed his gaze. "There's something you oughta know."

The worry etched into Wyatt's face only deepened, and he started striding toward the house.

Stepping into his path, Flynn put a hand against Wyatt's shoulder to stop him. "Hold up."

Wyatt grabbed Flynn's shirt and shoved him aside. "Get out of my way before I knock you out of it." He jogged the last few steps and disappeared inside.

Flynn shrugged and straightened his shirt. As he exchanged a glance with Judd, the older man tried to hold back a smile beneath his long mustache. Flynn felt a smile working its way up inside him too. He didn't know where all his anger toward Wyatt had gone, but somewhere along the way, Flynn had been able to let it go. And he felt lighter, freer, because of it.

For a short while, the remaining men spilled the details of what had happened over the past hours, how the Union soldiers had joined up with them and they managed to sneak into the gulley, thanks to Linnea's directions. They'd surrounded the Irregulars, closed in, and exchanged gunfire. It had taken a few hours before the Irregulars had realized they were sorely outnumbered and surrendered. The militia was now taking the captives to a prison in Denver.

Mr. Pearson had been shot in his foot when he'd been captured, but the Confederates had allowed Dr. Howell to tend the injury. When they'd witnessed how well he'd taken care of it, they lined up to see him for all their ailments. He spent the better part of the day and night pulling rotten teeth, doctoring old wounds, and helping with rashes, until fighting had broken out and he had to take cover.

As Linnea hugged her grandfather again, Flynn breathed out his relief.

"Flynn!" Wyatt's stern call came from the doorway.

Flynn pivoted. What had he done now? Was Wyatt angry he hadn't sent word to him about the birth?

Wyatt stalked toward him.

Sucking in a breath, Flynn braced his shoulders for whatever wrath Wyatt decided to unleash. As he drew near, Flynn could see tears glistening in his brother's eyes. Then, before he knew it, Wyatt pulled him into an embrace.

Flynn stood stiffly for an instant within the strong arms.

"Thank you," Wyatt whispered in a strangled voice.

As understanding filtered through Flynn, he hugged his brother in return. "You're welcome."

Wyatt slapped his back affectionately and then pulled away, blinking hard and swiping at the moisture in his eyes. "Delivering a babe was the last thing you ever wanted to do. So it means even more you stuck around until the end."

"I needed to do it." Flynn glanced sideways at Linnea still talking with several other men and her grandfather. The sight of the swell of her abdomen still made him want to tuck tail and run. But now that he'd started the battle against his fears, he aimed to gain more ground every day.

Wyatt followed his gaze. "Think it's past time for you to close the deal with Linnea, don't you?"

"Reckon so." His nerves tightened.

Dr. Howell was yammering away with Father Zieber. The Methodist minister had a hint of gray in his brown hair but was ruggedly built and didn't look like any minister Flynn had ever seen. Linnea whispered something to her grandfather, who patted her arm absentmindedly while continuing his conversation. She broke away and started toward the house.

Wyatt socked Flynn in the arm. "Go work your magic."

This was his chance. With Linnea and Dr. Howell's departure coming up, he couldn't delay saying something any longer.

His mouth went dry, but he bolted after her, then caught her hand from behind.

She halted and turned warm, inviting eyes upon him. "Looks like everything ended well, wouldn't you agree?"

"Nope. Not yet."

She tilted her head. "Then you think the Irregulars who escaped will be a problem?"

"Reckon they're hightailing it out of the area as fast as they can go." He tossed a glance toward the path that led down to the river. Part of him wanted to tug her away from the group and have a moment of privacy. But another part of him guessed that here and now was as good a place as any to say what he needed to. He'd already squandered too much time, and he couldn't waste any more.

"The thing is." He rubbed the back of his neck. "I've been a blamed fool—was worse than a stubborn old mule."

"I forgive you."

"You don't even know for what."

"It doesn't matter."

He loved that she could so easily let go of hurts and disappointments. He had much to learn from her about that. "Listen, Linnea. I shouldn't have walked away from you when

I learned about the baby. I was a coward. And I wouldn't blame you if you don't want me—"

"I do."

The conversations around them tapered to silence. Every man in the yard gawked at the two of them, except for Wyatt, who'd headed back inside the house.

Linnea didn't seem to be paying them any heed. Her eyes were filled with expectation, her face tilted up. "I do want you, Flynn. But I can't abide the thought of pressuring you into anything you're not ready for." She laid a hand on her belly.

He swallowed and then placed his hand over hers. "Don't go." He splayed his hand wider to encompass the baby. Then he lowered himself to one knee before her while keeping hold of her abdomen. "I want to take care of you and this baby. I want to be your husband and this baby's father. If you'll let me."

Bright tears welled into her eyes. "Are you sure?"

"I reckon I know what I want."

"Then, yes." She laughed through her tears.

He smiled, warm relief pooling inside.

Cheering and clapping came from the doorway where Ivy and Astrid stood watching them.

"You go on and do as I told you," Ivy called. "Go on and get married today so we don't have to put up with any more of your growling."

Flynn pushed himself to his feet. "Hush up, Ivy. Linnea won't wanna get married today—"

"And why wouldn't I?" Linnea's voice contained a note of eagerness that heated his blood a few degrees. Her cheeks were flushed a pretty pink, and her face was almost glowing. She'd never looked more beautiful than at that moment.

He wanted to draw her into his arms but settled for tightening his fingers within hers. "I don't want to keep you from having a proper wedding and all."

"A proper wedding isn't what makes a good marriage. Besides, you should know by now that I'm not exactly the model of a proper lady."

Dr. Howell approached, his clothes dusty and wrinkled, his face smudged with dirt. Flynn pulled himself up, preparing to convince the older gentleman to let Linnea marry him. "Well, young man. I was sure hoping you'd finally get around to proposing to my granddaughter. I wasn't relishing having to take her back to Denver with a broken heart."

"Then you don't mind my marrying her?"

"You're exactly what Linnea needs. In fact, I couldn't have planned a better match unless I was the good Lord himself."

Flynn let his shoulders relax. "I know you and Linnea were aiming to leave for Denver. And I'll go with—"

"I think Linnea's ready to make a mark of her own in the Rockies as the first botanist to live and work here. We'll finish the current manual together, but then you'll be on your own for the next one."

"Really?" Linnea's eyes glistened.

"Of course, young lady. I need my best botanist here."

She released Flynn's hand and threw her arms around her grandfather.

"I've never seen anyone work as hard as you," her grandfather continued through the hug. "And I didn't realize how much credit the others were taking for your research and findings."

Linnea backed up and swiped at her cheeks. "It's alright, we were a team—"

"No. I had a great deal of time to think about everything you said yesterday. And I believe you were right. You will continue to be smart and capable after your baby is born and throughout your life. I just need to allow you to have the opportunity."

"I don't know how to thank you for giving me this chance."

"You deserve it. I'm just sorry I didn't recognize it sooner."

Linnea was beaming. "Now, Flynn, you just need to find your homestead."

Flynn nodded. "Wyatt mentioned the land north of his might be available for homesteading." The man who'd originally staked a claim had been hanged, but Linnea didn't need to know that.

"Is it good for farming?"

"Not like the farm in Pennsylvania. But I reckon I'll be able to make a go of it."

Wyatt had brought up the possibility of going into the cattle-raising business together, combining their herds and land for a greater profit. While Flynn hadn't ever pictured himself as a rancher, he'd begun to take a hankering to it. And the truth was, he wasn't ready to run away from Wyatt anymore. In fact, he could get used to the idea of being neighbors.

Linnea slipped her arm into the crook of his. "I want you to have the potential to make your dreams come true too."

She was all he dreamed about. But he kept that thought to himself. "Being with my family and taking care of them. That's about as big as my dreams get."

Ivy and Astrid had gone back into the house and now returned with Wyatt, who was carrying the new baby and grinning like a fool.

"How's the runt?" Flynn smothered a grin of his own.

"The runt's just heard his uncle's about to get hitched."

"That right?" Flynn narrowed his eyes on Ivy.

"That's right." Ivy glared back.

Father Zieber glanced between Wyatt and Flynn. "Seems the McQuaid brothers are good at quick weddings."

Wyatt shrugged sheepishly. "Can't help it if the good Lord's takin' to blessing us with mighty fine women."

Father Zieber patted his coat pocket before he removed his prayer book. "We can do the ceremony right here, right now, if you'd like."

"Yes," Linnea spoke breathlessly as more color flooded her cheeks.

At her eagerness to be with him, the love in Flynn's heart surged to overflowing. He bent in and touched his mouth to her ear. "I love you."

She met his gaze. "I love you too, Flynn McQuaid."

The declaration was pure sweetness. Father Zieber took his place in front of them while everyone gathered around—including Dylan and Judd. Flynn slipped his arm around Linnea, and inwardly he lifted a prayer of gratefulness to the Almighty for bringing this woman into his life.

The wedding was over in a matter of minutes. Father Zieber closed his prayer book with a knowing gleam in his eyes. "There's just one thing left to do. Kiss your bride."

"Kiss her, kiss her." Astrid jumped up and down.

Linnea nibbled at her lip with a shy smile.

Flynn drew her around and bent in at the same time, fusing his lips to hers, making her finally his.

Wyatt whistled. "Seems the McQuaid brothers are also real good at kissing their brides."

Flynn couldn't contain a grin and felt Linnea's lips curve up into a smile at the same time.

"I think you might need to show me just how good," she whispered.

"My pleasure, Mrs. McQuaid." And he did just as she requested.

CHAPTER

29

Linnea fell back against the bed. As a tiny cry filled the air, she released a sob.

Flynn leaned in and kissed her forehead. "You did real good, darlin'. Real good." His hand within hers trembled, testifying to the hardship he'd endured over the past hours sitting by her side.

"This ain't like it was with Greta," he'd said when the contractions had awoken her in the middle of the night. "This is you. And heaven help me if I lose you."

With the frigid December temperatures enveloping their upstairs room, she'd snuggled deeper under the warm blankets and then rolled over and kissed him until another contraction forced her to lay back and close her eyes. The contractions had continued, growing more frequent and increasing in strength until she'd finally sent Flynn to wake her grandfather, sleeping on a cot in the main living area with Clay.

Linnea hadn't protested when the two had moved to the ranch to be nearby for the birthing. She also hadn't protested when Grandfather insisted on giving Flynn the two hundred dollars, this time as a wedding present. She convinced Flynn to take the money, and they planned to use it toward a home of their own on the homestead Flynn had claimed to the north of Wyatt's.

"You have a daughter." Grandfather smiled tenderly at the squalling infant. "And I have a feeling she'll be just as pretty and smart as her mother."

Flynn kissed Linnea again, this time on her mouth, hard and containing all the emotion he'd battled during the past hours of labor.

For Flynn's sake, she was grateful it hadn't taken as long as Greta's, only a few hours from when she'd awoken.

He broke the kiss. "I love you, and I'm proud of you."

"I love you and am proud of you too." She was so proud of him for staying even though she knew how desperately frightened he'd been.

The past two months of their marriage had been exquisitely beautiful, so much so that she'd grown fearful that the coming of the baby would change what they had together. When she'd voiced her fear to Flynn late one night as they'd lain in each other's arms, he said something about how he wasn't planning to be satisfied with just having a nugget. He was planning to do the hard work of mining for the mother lode so they could have a rich marriage.

His words of wisdom had come from Judd. A Judd proverb. That's what she'd started calling Judd's advice, which was priceless but only given sparingly. He had a soft spot for Astrid, playing checkers with her almost every night in front of the stove. He also had a soft spot for Tyler, Wyatt and Greta's new baby, cradling the infant every chance he got.

Of course, they'd all taken turns holding the baby and helping Greta finish all her jam making. Her products had become so popular that people from all around South Park came to Fairplay to buy from her.

Greta was a savvy businesswoman and was proving how women could make something of themselves in the West every bit as well as a man. In fact, she'd begun making plans with Wyatt to purchase more land to the south, particularly the land with the hot spring, with the intention of promoting and capitalizing on the healing qualities of the water. They'd already started calling their ranch by the name Healing Springs.

Over the past year, Wyatt had continued his practice of buying oxen from new settlers—primarily miners—coming up into the area. Having a number of calves born over the spring and summer, he'd grown his herd. After adding the Shorthorns they'd driven west, his ranch was thriving, especially now that the new herd had fattened up after several months of eating the bountiful mountain grasses.

The only lingering worry was that neither Wyatt nor Flynn had heard anything from Brody. They'd both sent letters, pleading with him to come home. But they still didn't know if he'd lived or died at Gettysburg. They could only pray that as 1863 drew to a close, the war would draw to a close as well.

"Time to meet our daughter." Flynn stood as Grandfather finished with the umbilical cord.

"Our daughter." She liked the sound of that.

"My daughter," Flynn whispered.

She liked the sound of that even better. The child might not have Flynn's blood, but she would have his heart. Linnea had no doubt about that.

He approached Grandfather. "I'll swaddle her."

348

Grandfather smiled at the wrinkly pink baby. "She's all yours."

"Yep. She sure is."

As Flynn wrapped a blanket around the newborn, Linnea's chest ached with the fulness of her love for the man she'd married. He would make the best father. She'd seen him in action plenty with Ivy and Dylan. And while he wasn't perfect—no parent ever was—his love and sacrifice more than made up for his mistakes.

Once finished, he bent down and placed a tender kiss upon the baby's cheek. "I want you to know," he whispered, "I'll always love you. Maybe not as much as I'll love your mother, but pretty close."

At Flynn's touch, the baby stopped crying, opened her eyes, and stared up at him.

"Oh, Flynn. She loves you back."

He rounded the bed toward Linnea. "Hopefully you won't cause me quite as much trouble as your mother, but I'm guessing I'll need to take care of you too."

Linnea laughed softly. "We'll try not to keep you too busy."

"You can keep me as busy as you want. Especially with this." He bent and kissed her again. And when he broke away, his eyes smoldered with passion and love.

She waited for him to kiss her again, loved kissing him. But he knelt beside the bed and placed the baby in her waiting arms. She brushed a hand over the fuzzy red hair and delicate cheeks and lips. "She's beautiful."

Flynn rubbed a hand over her head too. "Think of a name yet?"

"How about Flora? After all the flora that graces this beautiful wild land?"

The baby was still gazing up at Flynn, clearly fascinated by his handsome face. "Mighty fitting."

"Do you think so?" Linnea had tentatively picked both boy and girl names from among her favorite flowers and trees. Flora had been one of her top choices.

"Yep. Flora McQuaid. Sounds perfect."

Linnea touched her daughter's tiny fingers. What did God have in store for those hands someday? Whatever that might be, Linnea prayed her daughter would understand just how valuable she was to God, more so than even the flora after which she'd been named.

Linnea lifted a heart of gratefulness for all that God had been teaching her during the difficulties of the past months. He'd been there all along through the hardships bringing about His plan, in His way, and in His timing.

She intertwined her fingers through Flynn's and smiled at him. Yes, this place, this man, her new life, was so much better than anything she could have come up with for herself. The God who took care of the grass and the flowers and the trees had taken care of her just as He'd promised.

CHAPTER
30

BRODY McQUAID
PHILADELPHIA
JULY 1865, EIGHTEEN MONTHS LATER

Pain ricocheted through Brody's shoulder and down his arm.

"Down! Get down!" Newt's shout rose above the pounding of the artillery.

Brody's breathing came out in labored gasps, drowning the blasting of rifles and clashing of bayonets. But nothing could block out the agonized cries of the wounded and dying all around him.

Gun smoke clouded the air, hazy in the hot summer sun. Sweat trickled down his cheeks and over his lips, salty against his parched tongue. The acridness of sulfur mingled with the stench of decaying flesh, tingling his nostrils.

Where were Newt and the rest of his regiment?

Brody attempted to shift, but the fire in his shoulder and

arm tore through him, stealing his breath. He could only move his head and found himself staring at Newt's face. His buddy's eyes stared sightlessly ahead, his Union kepi askew, his face pale.

Newt? Brody tried to lift an arm to shake his friend and wake him up, but he couldn't make his muscles work.

The ground rumbled beneath followed by the explosion of a cannonball and the accompanying screams—this time with the distinct frightened squeals of a horse.

Let's go, Newt. We gotta fall back. The words stuck in Brody's throat. But somehow he managed to push himself up to one elbow. As he reached for his friend, he found himself groping at the air and finding only a bloody mass of flesh where Newt's arm and chest should have been.

A cry swelled within Brody's chest. . . .

Someone shook him. "Brody?"

He couldn't breathe, couldn't move, couldn't do anything but stare at Newt's corpse.

"Brody? You're alright. Come on now." The voice was calm, soothing.

Brody's eyes flew open to the high-arched, whitewashed ceiling above him.

Where was he? What was happening?

His chest rose and fell quickly, and his heartbeat raced.

A hand squeezed his arm. "You're just dreaming."

He shifted to find Newt lying in the folding wooden cot next to his. Newt's face was skeletal, his beard and mustache thickly overgrown, and his eyes sunken. Even so, his friend's gaze was warm and steady, just as it had been all along over the past two and a half years of living hell.

They weren't on the battlefield. Brody released a pent-up

breath. And they weren't at Andersonville. His heart rate slowed.

His mind replayed the events of the last couple of weeks, the liberation of the Confederate prison and the jarring train ride north to a federal hospital.

The war was over.

Brody let his body relax back into the cot even if his insides were tighter than a tick on a cow's hide.

Newt squeezed a final time before he let his hand fall away. It dangled listlessly over the edge of his cot, as if his friend didn't have the energy to pull it up. The fella in the bed beyond Newt's was motionless, his bony knees outlined through the thin sheet.

Most of the fellas in the ward were still and silent, their bodies as emaciated and their souls all but gone. Brody guessed they were from Andersonville or some other Reb prison just like him and Newt, having managed to hang on even though they were all nearly starved to death and thin enough to take a bath in a gun barrel.

Voices came from the end of the long corridor, and Newt pushed himself up to his elbows and stared at the entrance. The windows were wide open, but the air remained stagnant, hardly stirring the hair plastered to their heads. Perspiration dribbled down Newt's forehead.

"Aiming to get a look at that young nurse again?" Brody tried to infuse some playfulness into his voice but failed miserably.

Newt held himself in place for the passing of several seconds before he flopped back down. His lashes fell, and his breathing grew erratic and almost irregular. "Naw, all the pretty ones got a hankering for you just like usual."

None of the nurses were all that young or pretty. And certainly none had a hankering for him. But he didn't correct his friend.

"Gotta be honest with you, Brody." Newt's words came out rushed and with a note of desperation that set Brody on edge.

"Never mind right now. Just get some shut-eye."

Newt shook his head, the motion adamant. "I did something you ain't gonna like."

"Course you did. What's new?"

"No, really, Brody." Each of Newt's breaths grew more labored than the previous.

Brody's muscles—or what was left of them—tensed. "You ain't giving up now. You promised if I stuck it out that you would too—"

"*Listen to me*, Brody."

Brody held himself still.

Newt met his gaze head-on. "Back when we were first released . . ."

They'd both been lying in their own filth, flies crawling over them, unable to move. Brody swallowed hard at the memory of six weeks ago.

"First thing I did when those orderlies came in and started carting us out on stretchers . . ." Newt's voice turned low and raw. "I had them send a telegram."

Newt had been writing to his ma the whole time since they'd enlisted. And she'd written faithfully to him in return until they ended up in prison six months ago. Each letter from her had been filled with news of home. Or what had once been home for them both.

Trouble was, Brody had nothing and no one there anymore. His ma was dead and wasn't waiting on him. The farm belonged to Rusty. And Flynn and Dylan and Ivy had moved away.

"I know you and Flynn didn't part ways real friendly like." Newt's chest heaved, and he struggled to draw in a breath.

"Don't matter no more—"

"It matters a whole heap." Newt glanced toward the doorway again.

This time Brody followed his gaze. A nurse was hurrying down the center aisle that ran the length of the ward between the dozens of cots on both sides. Following on her heels was a tall, broad-shouldered man with a limping gait—a purposeful, determined stride Brody would recognize a mile away.

His heart thudded hard against his chest, and he tossed a glare at Newt. "What'd you do?"

"I had to, Brody. I knew he'd come and save you."

"I'll save myself just fine." But even as the low, harsh words spilled out, Brody's chest seized hard, like a fist was closing about it. He couldn't keep his gaze from straying to his brother again, to the long but muscular build and the lean but handsome face concealed in the shadow of his hat. He was gussied up in a black coat, vest, and matching trousers, and he looked more like a fancy gentleman than a farmer.

The nurse stopped at the end of his cot, checked the ticket hanging from the foot of it, and then waved a hand at Brody. "This is Sergeant Brody McQuaid, sir."

His brother tipped up his hat, revealing green-blue eyes that widened with shock and dismay.

Brody hadn't looked at himself in a mirror since before running off from home. He guessed he was a heap of skin and bones just like Newt and everyone else who'd arrived from

Andersonville. Though the nurses had been spoon-feeding most of them, they still suffered from scurvy and other diseases they'd contracted in prison, and the sustenance was hard to keep inside.

Brody didn't say anything, couldn't find the words to greet his brother. Newt was right. They hadn't parted on good terms. In fact, they'd done nothing but argue during the last month together—arguing Brody regretted. He'd had plenty of time over the past two and a half years to think about all that had transpired in those days leading up to his enlistment. And he knew now—too late—his brother had just wanted to spare him all the pain and trauma of war.

But, of course, at the time, Brody thought he knew better, thought he was being noble and brave, assumed he'd make a difference.

What a stubborn fool he'd been. If he could go back in time and change everything, he'd have gone west in a heartbeat and escaped the war. . . . But there was no changing what had happened, no changing the horrors he'd lived through, no changing the shell of a man he'd become.

At least by being there, he'd kept Newt alive. No doubt his friend would have died a hundred deaths without him watching his back.

Newt gave him a slight nod, one that asked for forgiveness for interfering, but one that also encouraged him to reconcile with his family.

Brody nodded back. Newt had never once made him feel bad for his decision to leave his family, but a time or two after getting a letter from his ma, Newt had encouraged Brody to write to his brothers. Brody had picked up a pen once but hadn't known what to say.

Now, faced with his older brother, he still didn't know what to say.

He tried pushing himself up so he could at least extend a hand for a handshake.

But before he could manage, Flynn dropped to his knees between the cots, grabbed Brody, and hugged him so tight, the air near to burst from his lungs. For a long, blessed minute, Flynn just held him like he'd never let him go.

Thick, heavy emotion wedged into Brody's throat. He wasn't gonna be able to talk worth a lick.

"Thank the Lord Almighty you're alive," Flynn whispered, finally pulling back, his eyes glossy with unshed tears. He gripped Brody's upper arms, his expression radiating with so much relief and love that Brody knew Flynn didn't hold anything against him, that their bitter parting was buried in the past. "Left the day I got Newt's telegram but wasn't sure if I'd reach you in time."

Brody cleared his throat. He could only imagine the journey Flynn had taken to cross the country so quickly. "You didn't have to come."

"I wanted to." Again, Flynn's eyes radiated with love and concern Brody didn't deserve.

A pretty young woman holding a squirming infant with red curls stopped a short distance away.

As if realizing where Brody's attention had strayed, Flynn pivoted and held out a hand to the woman. "Brody, this is my wife, Linnea, and this here's my little girl, Flora."

Linnea came forward with a smile. The infant, a petite version of her mother, reached out her arms toward Flynn. He, in turn, brought her down and settled her upon his bent knee.

Leaning her head back shyly against Flynn's shoulder and

sticking two fingers into her mouth, she peered at Brody with her big brown eyes.

Brody guessed he must be a fright to the child—a sickly, hairy skeleton. But to his surprise, she reached out her other hand to him as though to greet him.

Brody's fingers trembled. His fingernails were cracked and dirty, his skin jaundiced, his hands bony. He didn't dare touch her, did he?

Flora reached out farther, as though beckoning him.

He tentatively grazed her tiny, unblemished fingers. "How old is she?"

"A year and a half." Flynn pressed a kiss against the infant's curls. Then he met Brody's gaze again. "It's real good to see you, Brody. Real good."

Brody nodded, his throat constricting and heat burning at the back of his eyes.

"Linnea's grandfather came with." Flynn blinked rapidly and nodded at a distinguished gentleman in a top hat who stood talking with one of the doctors. "We're making arrangements to transport you to New York City, and we'll stay with Linnea's family until you're recovered."

"I can't impose—"

"They want you to recuperate in their home. You'll have better, personalized care, with the best physicians in New York City."

Brody took in the fine quality of Linnea's garments as well as the air of authority with which her grandfather spoke to the doctor. Somehow, Flynn had married into money. Even so, there was no way, no how Brody was leaving Newt behind. Not after they'd made it together this far.

"I won't leave Newt."

Flynn exchanged a knowing glance with Linnea, as if they'd already anticipated Brody's insistence. "We'll bring Newt along too."

Brody's protest died, and for the first time in a long time, he allowed a flicker of hope to fan to life inside. Newt needed better care. Maybe going to New York City would help.

"Did you hear that, Newt?" Brody shifted to get a look at his friend. "We're finally getting out of here."

Newt didn't respond. He lay with his eyes closed, motionless, his chest no longer rising and falling in his constant struggle for each breath. His expression was peaceful, almost as if he were wearing a pleased smile, like he'd done what he set out to do, hung on until Flynn had arrived.

Inwardly, Brody cussed. But outwardly he had no reaction, other than to fall back on his cot and stare at the ceiling.

Bending over Newt, Linnea called out to the nurse and doctor, her voice urgent. Footsteps came running, but Brody had seen death enough to know it was too late.

Newt had given up. And now, what reason did Brody have to keep going? What reason did he have to continue living? Not when his every sleeping and waking moments were haunted with nightmares.

Suddenly a tiny hand pressed against him. And then innocent fingers curled around his. He glanced down to see his infant niece clutching him, holding him tight.

He allowed his fingers to close about hers, and prayed that somehow, some way she could keep him from sinking into the abyss.

Jody Hedlund is the bestselling author of over thirty historical novels for both adults and teens and is the winner of numerous awards, including the Christy, Carol, and Christian Book Awards. Jody lives in Michigan with her husband, busy family, and five spoiled cats. Visit her online at jodyhedlund.com.

Sign Up for Jody's Newsletter

Keep up to date with Jody's news on book releases and events by signing up for her email list at jodyhedlund.com.

More from Jody Hedlund

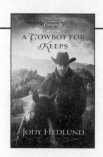

On a trip west to save her ailing sister, Greta Nilsson is robbed, leaving her homeless and penniless. Wyatt McQuaid is struggling to get his new ranch running, so the mayor offers him a bargain: He will invest in a herd of cattle if Wyatt agrees to help the town become more respectable by marrying . . . and the mayor has the perfect woman in mind.

A Cowboy for Keeps
COLORADO COWBOYS #1

THE BRIDE SHIPS Series
by Jody Hedlund

After facing desperate heartache and loss, Mercy agrees to escape a bleak future in London and joins a bride ship. Wealthy and titled, Joseph leaves home and takes to the sea as the ship's surgeon to escape the pain of losing his family. He has no intention of settling down, but when Mercy becomes his assistant, they must fight against a forbidden love.

A Reluctant Bride

Arabella Lawrence fled on a bride ship wearing the scars of past mistakes. Now in British Columbia, two men vying for her hand disagree on how the natives should be treated during a smallpox outbreak. Intent on helping a girl abandoned by her tribe, will Arabella have the wisdom to make the right decision, or will seeking what's right cost her everything?

The Runaway Bride

Upon discovering an abandoned baby, Pastor Abe Merivale joins efforts with Zoe Hart, one of the newly arrived bride-ship women, to care for the infant. With mounting pressure to find the baby a home, Abe offers his hand as Zoe's groom. But after a hasty wedding, they soon realize their marriage of convenience is not so convenient after all.

A Bride of Convenience

⬦BETHANYHOUSE

More from Bethany House

On assignment to help America win the War of 1812, Evan MacManus is taken prisoner by Brielle Durand—the key defender of her people's secret French settlement in the Canadian Rocky Mountains. But when his mission becomes at odds with his growing appreciation of Brielle and the villagers, does he dare take a risk on the path his heart tells him is right?

A Warrior's Heart by Misty M. Beller
BRIDES OF LAURENT #1
mistymbeller.com

Left to rue her mistake of falling in love with the wrong man, Maisie Kentworth keeps busy by exploring the idle mine nearby. While managing his mining company, Boone Bragg stumbles across Maisie and the crystal cavern she's discovered. He makes her a proposal that he hopes will solve all their problems, but instead it throws them into chaos.

Proposing Mischief by Regina Jennings
THE JOPLIN CHRONICLES #2
reginajennings.com

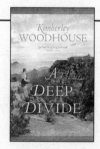

When her father's greedy corruption goes too far, heiress Emma Grace McMurray sneaks away to be a Harvey Girl at the El Tovar Grand Canyon Hotel, planning to stay hidden forever. There she uncovers mysteries, secrets, and a love beyond anything she could imagine—leaving her to question all she thought to be true.

A Deep Divide by Kimberley Woodhouse
SECRETS OF THE CANYON #1
kimberleywoodhouse.com

⬧BETHANYHOUSE